The Reality Incursion

Deplosion: Book 2

Paul Anlee

Darian Publishing House
Chatham, Ontario, Canada

Darian Publishing House (darianpublishinghouse@gmail.com)
Chatham, Ontario, Canada

Publisher's Note: This is a work of fiction. Names, characters, places, and incidents are a product of the author's imagination. Locales and public names are sometimes used for atmospheric purposes. Any resemblance to actual people, living or dead, or to businesses, companies, events, institutions, or locales is completely coincidental.

Book Layout & Design ©2013 - BookDesignTemplates.com
Design Cover – Elizabeth Mackey Graphic Design
Author Photo – John Keeble
Background cover image copyright: Jean-Michel ALIMI, DEUS Consortium

Acknowledgment: The author thanks Jean-Michel ALIMI, Scientific Director of DEUS Consortium (deus-consortium.org) and Director of DEUS Consortium for making available the background cover image obtained through DEUS numerical simulations. This image reproduces the distribution of dark matter in a universe with a cosmological constant.

Visit the author's website at: https://www.paulanlee.com
Follow the author on Facebook at: Paul Anlee or Paul Anlee Fans
Email the author at: paul.anlee.author@gmail.com

The Reality Incursion/ Paul Anlee – 1st edition
ISBN ebook: 978-0-9958442-2-3
ISBN Paperback: 978-0-9958442-2-3

For Kenna, Jack, and Chris

A universe of possibilities

"People demand Freedom of Speech as compensation for the Freedom of Thought, which they seldom use."
- Kierkegaard

1

THE 4:30 A.M. LATTICE CALL JARRED THE COUPLE out of their dreams.

For crying out loud, it's not even morning yet. And, it's Sunday—Kathy groaned.

It was Darian—no surprise—calling through their private lattice network. He'd never been much for preamble or propriety.

Hi, Darian, what's up? What time is it? Kathy dragged herself toward consciousness and rubbed her sleep-crusted eyes.

It works—was all he sent; his transmitted voice was quiet and matter-of-fact.

It works? What works?—her brain pushed through the mental fog to process what her boss was saying. She sat up and stretched her neck. Then it hit her. *IT works!*

"Greg," she hissed. "Wake up! Darian got it working," she squealed. She shook her unconscious partner's shoulder. "Greg, it works!"

Greg was fully awake in a flash.

I'm sorry about calling so early—Darian said. *No*—he laughed, almost giddy. *That's not true, I'm not sorry at all. I was going to tell you in person later this morning but I couldn't wait. Look at this!*

Without waiting for a response, he sent the two of them a synopsis of everything he'd been doing, the internal antenna array he'd grown in his cranium, and the test he'd run, the one that generated a sputtering microverse in the middle of his dining room only a few minutes before.

I'm on my way to the lab right now. I need to use the vacuum chamber and the laser interferometer—he sent. *Can you meet me there?*

That's fantastic! Yes, of course. We're on our way. It'll take us about forty minutes but we'll get there as fast as we can—Kathy replied. She waggled a free hand at Greg, the universal sign for get up and get moving.

Can you wait until we get there before you run it again?—she asked.

It'll be torture but, sure. For you guys, anything. I'll give you 45 minutes. Only then did he remember the fourth member of their team. *Hey, can you pick up Larry along the way? I'm sure he'll want to be there too.*

No problem—answered Greg. *I'll give him a call and we'll cruise by his place. I don't think his bus runs this early, and he'll kill us if we do this without him.*

In the pause, all three took a collective deep breath.

Kathy shook her head. *Wow, right this second, I feel like we own the entire galaxy. Do you know what I mean?*

Yeah, I think I do—Darian replied. *I'll be at the lab in a few minutes. Get here as soon as you can*—he said, and disconnected.

"You know he's not going to wait, right?" she said to Greg. "He's going to fire it up as soon as he gets there." She couldn't blame him. If she were in his shoes, she wouldn't be able to resist playing with the most important physics discovery of the century, either. "Wow! Can you believe it? It actually worked," she said, and shuffled around the bed and into the bathroom.

Greg stumbled to the closet and pulled on a pair of jeans. "It's about time something went right," he said. He grabbed a fresh t-shirt and pulled it over his head. He poked his head through the neck hole, and the significance of what they were doing sank in.

The Reality Assertion Field, the RAF, had finally been proven. Their theories on the origin of the universe, on why the laws of nature were the way they were, and how they could be changed, it was all true. Science had opened the door to the powers of the gods.

"This is awesome. Can you imagine what that must have been like? He produced a micro-scale universe in the middle of his dining room. A little piece of space with its own distinct physical laws, right in his apartment. Can you believe it? A freaking microverse!"

Feeling more energized than he had in weeks, Greg reviewed the lattice conversation. His glee turned into a pensive frown.

"Uh, hey, Kath? I didn't know Darian was growing an internal RAF antenna array in his own head. Did you?"

She reviewed the clip he sent her. "No. No clue at all. But I'm not surprised. I mean, it makes sense he'd do something like that as his next step. Think about it. Our original RAF generator should have worked. Everything checked out—hardware, software, theory—everything, right down to the last detail and yet it still didn't work."

She passed her toothbrush under the running water. "So what does a good scientist do? He starts all over, clean slate, and goes through it all again, item by item, step by step, with a completely independent approach." She squeezed a pearl of toothpaste onto her electric brush and laughed.

"That's so Darian. Instead of building another device, he grows the friggin' hardware right in his own brain."

"Are you just about ready? We'd better get moving," Greg said, pulling on his running shoes. "On the off chance that he is waiting. And we still have to swing by and pick up Larry. I'll call him right now."

Larry didn't answer the lattice calls or his door when they banged on it some twenty minutes later.

"Larry!" Kathy huffed in exasperation, and tapped the door with her foot.

Typical—she thought, but kept the comment to herself.

They rapped a few more times and tried the window before giving up and heading to the lab without him.

Greg pulled the car into the nearly empty parking lot near the Physics building, and headed for a choice space along the perimeter.

"So, are we ready to be famous, hon? This research is going to rock the world. It really is." Greg guided the car toward the parking spot.

The grin taking up half his face was replaced by a surprised yelp of pain as an incomprehensible torrent of Darian's knowledge and memories — everything that made Darian who he was—slammed past the couple's internal neural-lattice security and gushed unfiltered into their minds like a tsunami.

The influx of data from Darian rolled over their minds, overwhelming and clashing with their own thoughts and senses. As they struggled against the excruciating intrusion, the car rolled to a stop against a pliant sapling in a shallow drainage ditch.

In a final, desperate move to stem the flow, Kathy disconnected her communications port. Physically incapacitated but at least back in control of her mind, she created a rudimentary cutoff routine and piggybacked it onto the data surge still streaming into Greg's lattice.

She reached feebly for his hand. "Greg," she gasped, and gave in to unconsciousness.

When they came to, morning light was peeking through the misty mountain air.

"What...was that?" Greg cradled his head in his hands.

Kathy groaned. "I think something happened to Darian. Something bad,"

"He blasted through our anti-virus protection like it was nothing," she marveled, and rubbed the back of her aching neck.

"How is that even possible?"

"I don't know; we'll look into that later. Are you okay? You got a little more of it than I did."

Greg stretched his neck from side to side, blinked a few times, and tried to focus. "Yeah, I think so. My head hurts, and I ache in muscles I didn't know I had."

"Me too, but I don't think there's any permanent damage." Kathy opened the car door.

"What are you doing? I think we should stay put for a few minutes."

"I can't. I think Darian might be dead, or in serious trouble. I don't know why, but that's what it felt like. Underneath his data, there was a lot of fear. Didn't you feel it? The fear?"

She stepped out of the vehicle, and winced as she stood up.

"Yeah," Greg admitted, "I guess." He gripped the doorframe and eased himself upright. "Oh, man! I feel like I ran a marathon," he moaned.

"Worse," Kathy replied. "A marathon, carrying a backpack full of rocks." She started to laugh and stopped; it hurt too much.

They left the car sitting halfway in the ditch and hurried to the lab, expecting to find Darian dead or in desperate condition.

Their footsteps echoed down the Physics wing hallway.

That's weird; there should be light coming from the observation window—Kathy thought. She braced herself for the worst, opened the door, and turned on the lights.

Where's Darian? He should've arrived long before us.

They walked around the workspace and checked the shared office. *Did he even make it to the lab? Where was he when he sent his message?*

Greg dialed Darian's cell phone. Six rings. Seven rings. Eight rings. No answer.

Don't jump to conclusions—Greg reminded himself. Darian rarely turned on his phone. No need, when you carried a built-in connection to the internet in your head. *Well, I'm not going to call him through the lattice, that's for sure, not after what happened in the parking lot.* He wasn't going to risk opening himself up to the flood of Darian's memories again.

Dazed and unsettled, they conducted a more thorough inspection of the room. Kathy's eyes sought the hardware project she'd spent the last six months designing and troubleshooting. In place of the Reality Assertion Field generator, the harsh overhead lights illuminated an empty frame and rectangular patch of dust.

What the....? "Greg? The RAF's gone!"

Darian would *not* have taken the RAF out of the lab; he was adamant about it staying in the sturdy anti-theft frame, and well-secured to the counter at all times. The empty frame was intact. The RAF generator, however, was nowhere in sight.

The server! Greg tried to log on with his lattice to make sure their repository of theoretical work was intact, and hit a security wall.

Kathy must've added that to the comm-activation protocol when she buffered us from Darian's thought storm. A pop-up message reminded him of the danger of opening his lattice to external communications. *Yep, definitely Kathy's work.*

He walked into the office area and clumsily tapped in his user ID and password using an external keyboard. *Like any other mortal.*

The screen refreshed, and a conspicuously empty blue screen replaced the log-in box.

Where did all my folders go?

He opened the systems directory. Nothing. Hundreds of folders containing their theories, schematics, and half-written papers awaiting data were all gone.

"Kath? Why is the directory empty? You didn't do this, did you?"

"What? No, of course not. What do you mean?" she answered. She walked up behind him and peered over his shoulder. Sure enough, the drive had been wiped clean.

"This doesn't make any sense. Darian called to say he was on his way to the lab. Even if he'd taken the device home last night, he wouldn't have taken any of this with him. There's no reason to remove it."

"This is getting weirder by the minute," Greg said. He tried Larry's number again. *C'mon Larry! Where are you?* Still no answer. *Why isn't he picking up?* Was Larry missing, too, or just incommunicado, per usual?

Kathy's mind continued to reel from the remnants of data, memories, and thoughts that had assaulted them earlier. She couldn't make much sense of the flashing images, but she was sure it had been an emergency broadcast from Darian's internal neural lattice to their own, a desperate effort by a dying scientist to secure his legacy the only way he could. She had no proof, nothing more than a feeling...and an empty lab.

"I'm pretty sure this was no random theft. There's no sign of a break in, and there's nothing else missing. Besides, who would know to take that one device and our data?" she reasoned. "It's useless to anyone outside the lab. We need to call the police."

"And tell them what?"

"That Darian's missing, the RAF generator is gone, and we don't know where Larry is."

"I don't think we can yet, Kath. They haven't been missing twenty-four hours.

"But him, Larry, *and* the RAF device gone at the same time? That can't be a coincidence, Greg."

"We can't prove that."

"All we have to do is report it. It's up to the police to prove it."

"Sure, I can just hear the cops now: 'So they took your laptop. Big deal. Take a number.' Do you really think they'd take us seriously? As far as they're concerned, our lab supervisor might be running a little late. They've got bigger things to worry about.

"For all we know, Darian took the machine home and worked on it over the weekend. Or maybe they got here ahead of us and moved it to a bigger space, or they needed some specialized equipment in another lab."

Kathy stared at him. "I can't believe you're saying that. You felt it. You know what hit us! Darian is dead, or at least badly hurt. That was sheer desperation he sent out. You felt it as well as I did."

Greg sighed. "Maybe. Maybe not. There's no proof. How do we know it wasn't a simple program glitch? There's no sign of a struggle here. Nobody besides us knows Darian got the device working. I know what you *think* hit us in that transmission and, I agree, it felt serious. The truth is, we don't know anything yet. We're only guessing. What if he and Larry are on their way over right now with the RAF laptop, hot coffees, and a box of doughnuts to celebrate?

"And don't forget, our own neuro lattices are developing and adjusting. Maybe what broadsided us was just the dendy's next level of growth. You know, like maybe they're linking us all together or something. What if Darian received *our* brain dumps in *his* lattice at the same time, and that's why he's not answering? Have you thought about that?

"You acted right away and you were able to shut it down for us, but what if Darian didn't? What if it caught him off guard, too, and he's lying unconscious somewhere."

Kathy stood mute, gaping at him, and tried to come up with a response.

"I'm not trying to be difficult. All I'm saying is, we really don't know anything yet," Greg walked to the back office window looking into the lab. He stared at the empty lab bench. "If we report this now, we'll only embarrass Darian and the lab. The university is already giving him a rough time. Some of those profs are just waiting for an excuse to get him fired. You've heard the rumors going around. We don't need to add any more negative attention."

"We *can* prove the device is missing."

"We can *claim* a piece of lab equipment—which, incidentally, was publicly demonstrated to be non-functional—has gone missing. By all outward appearances, a laptop, and that's about all. Oh, and by the way, officers, we all have a key to the anti-theft frame."

He held up his key ring. "Darian has one, I have one, you have one, and so does Larry. For all we know, maybe one or both of them have the generator with them. The police might think one of us took it ourselves and hid it for an insurance claim; people do that all the time."

Kathy returned to the lab area and inspected the empty frame where the RAF device should have sat. "Okay, so even with witnesses who know what was here in the lab, we have no real proof it was stolen?"

Greg joined her by the bench. "No, and we don't even have any proof that Darian and Larry are missing, hurt, or dead. Just Darian's private lattice conversation that no one else can access, inviting us to meet him here. And Larry's usual behavior—ducking out for hours or days at a time without telling anybody."

"We're going to look hysterical, aren't we?"

"If we call now, hysterical is the best we could hope for. More likely, crazy. And if anyone did believe us, we'd be looking like the prime suspects."

"Okay, so what do you think we should we do?"

"I'm not sure. What have we got to work with? Nothing concrete. It *felt* like Darian blasted out all this data, the essence of his self, in a real panic. If he doesn't show up soon, we can report his disappearance to the police. But until we have a better idea of what happened, until we actually *know* he's missing, I don't think there's much we can do. Let's give it a few more hours and see what we can find out. If we don't hear from him and if he doesn't show up for work..."

"You mean, *when* he doesn't show up for work. C'mon, Greg. You *know* what we experienced. That was a dying gasp."

"I refuse to jump to conclusions. Like I said, the police won't do anything until he's been missing twenty-four hours. If he hasn't checked in by tomorrow morning, we'll go talk to Dr. Wong and he can make the call.

"In the meantime, let's leave a note here in case one of them does show up, and we'll walk the route back to Darian's apartment. Maybe he fell, or got mugged, or something like that. If we find any sign he disappeared under duress—like a shoe or his backpack, anything like that—we'll call the police right away."

"And what about the RAF generator?"

"I think we better keep that between us for now. For sure, don't tell anyone that Darian got it working. It'll make no difference to a police investigation, and it could make things worse. Right now, we're the only ones who know about it besides Darian. And maybe Larry, if he crashed here overnight and Darian's already talked to him. I doubt it, but anything's possible.

"I don't want to worry you but, if you're right and someone did hurt Darian and steal the generator, we don't know who's involved or what they know. If they know what they've got in their hands and that we helped design it, we could be next."

Kathy's eyes widened. "I wasn't even thinking about that. Do you think we're in danger? Darian wouldn't have told anyone else about the RAF generator working. Not yet. We were the first ones he called. And Larry couldn't have known for more than a few minutes, if at all. We were supposed to tell him on the way into the lab, remember?"

"...and he didn't answer his phone or door." Greg nodded, "I know I said

I didn't want to jump to conclusions but it's not looking good, is it? I mean, it might be typical Larry, not answering his phone or door, but when you put that together with everything else...."

"Okay," Kathy said. "You have me convinced; let's not backtrack. Come on, we'll go check the route to Darian's place, and if we don't see anything there, we can call nearby hospitals. Maybe there's a simple explanation. I don't know what else to do."

"We can talk to Campus Security and the Department Chair first thing tomorrow. It'll have been twenty-four hours by then. Dr. Wong will need to know what's going on, anyway, and maybe the police will take it more seriously if he or Campus Security reports it."

Kathy looked around the lab. Her shoulders sank. "I feel useless."

Greg pulled her into a hug. "I don't think there's anything else we can do right now. I hate this, too, not knowing what's going on. And I hate not being able to activate my lattice so I can think properly. But when I imagine all those little bits of Darian's mind out there, just waiting to storm into us again the second we reconnect our communications...." Greg shuddered. "That's an experience I don't care to repeat."

Kathy snuggled her face into his shoulder. "I know, but I really don't like being normal again. Do you?"

2

"And how long will you be here in Casa DonTon, Mr. Trillian?" Lady Frieda, the oldest and most obviously available of five sisters, played with her dark curls.

The sumptuously appointed Family Dining Room bubbled with bravado and promise. The two dozen guests who had bagged some game in the afternoon hunt were the only people invited to join the family for this exclusive repast. Along with Mr. Trillian, of course. As the wealthy scion of a powerful industrialist of mysterious reputation, Mr. Trillian himself was an attractive catch.

The fact that he was also achingly handsome, athletic and, most importantly, wealthy garnered him an invitation to dine with the family, regardless of his obvious distaste for chasing small foxes with large horses, slathering hounds, and ridiculously oversized guns.

Trillian's intentionally dismal performance in the hunt, bordering on outright refusal to participate, did nothing to dissuade Lady Frieda and her sisters from their lavish flirting.

The object of the young ladies' attentions gently extracted himself from their clutches. "Sadly, ladies, I must take my leave before the evening wears too late. I have pressing business to attend to."

Five predictably disappointed pouts appeared.

"However, I do hope you will permit me the honor of visiting again soon," he added.

The bachelorettes brightened straight away.

"Well, we have you for now and we shan't let you off without at least one dance each," chirped Lady Mirabel, the youngest of the five.

Mr. Trillian bowed his head to her in polite acknowledgment.

"Miry, my precious, please let Mr. Trillian finish his meal in peace," Lord Chattingbaron admonished. "He has far more important matters to attend to than some silly dancing, I'm sure."

Mr. Trillian held up a hand to stem his host's mock objection. "Nothing could be as important to me as spending the evening in the company of your lovely and charming family, my Lord. Unfortunately, my investors insist I elevate their mundane material priorities above my own pleasures. I must visit the office this evening."

He smiled graciously at Lady Mirabel, setting her heart aflutter, and sampled the roasted mutton.

"I, for one, find discussing matters of business at the evening meal to be distasteful. It interferes with one's digestion," declared Lady Chattingbaron with a flick of her napkin. "Tell me, Mr. Trillian, Did you enjoy your ride today?"

"Very much. You have the most wonderful grounds, and the forest is magnificent." Trillian speared a succulent piece of meat in evidence of the family's bountiful estate. "Lady Adele gave me quite the competition jumping the brooks, I'm afraid."

Lady Adele blushed to a shade befitting the dashing man's compliment. Four sets of artfully shaped brows scowled discreetly at his appreciation of her riding skills.

Timothy, the family's First Footman, removed the remains of the main course from in front of the young heiresses. Their figures would not tolerate the excessive ingestion of heavy meat and potatoes, not if they wished to draw the attention of the likes of Mr. Trillian. Timothy nodded to the Head Butler. It was time to light the peach flambé.

As desserts were offered, some of the young men took the opportunity to engage Lady Frieda and her sisters in small talk not relating to the dashing Mr. Trillian.

Timothy started dessert service with his Lordship at the head of the table and worked his way around until he'd completed nearly a full circle. He stopped in front of Mr. Trillian and presented the polished tray holding hot brandied peaches and ice cream.

The guest didn't notice Timothy standing expectantly beside him; his attention was focused on a nondescript closet door on the opposite wall.

Timothy subtly cleared his throat to draw the man's attention, but Mr. Trillian's interest remained abnormally fixated on the closet. The Footman was about to cough discreetly when the room went fuzzy and he heard a dozen bees passing within inches of his ears.

Many years of training and discipline helped him maintain a firm grip on the dessert tray instead of frantically batting away at the loathsome insects, as he desperately wanted to do.

He strained to maintain his stooped serving position, but the disconcerting noise around his head became too much to bear. He twitched, just once. Three delicately cut-glass dessert bowls slid across the polished tray, bumped against the lip, and spilled a few syrupy drops of peach juice onto the table linen.

The unexpected clatter wrenched Mr. Trillian's gaze from the closet and back to the table.

The buzzing in Timothy's ears stopped at precisely the same moment, as did conversation among the startled diners. All eyes turned to Timothy, who stood in stunned silence.

"Whatever has gotten into you, Timothy?" Lady Chattingbaron demanded.

Timothy was as surprised as anyone. That is to say, as surprised as any Partial could be which, under normal circumstances, wasn't all that much.

"One moment, my Lady. I shall inquire of the DonTon Supervisor."

Initiate self-diagnostics—he sent to the local inworld supervisory program.

The diagnostic generally reported findings within milliseconds. This time, it dragged on, and on. Entire seconds passed. Most uncomfortably. Guests grew restless. They drummed their fingers, and they rolled their eyes. What was the holdup? This was most unusual! Completely unacceptable for a game such as DonTon.

* * *

THE DONTON INWORLD SIMULATION was about as proper as the classic conservative Victorian England society it portrayed.

It was not a demanding inworld, filled as it was with activities no more strenuous than dining, dancing, visiting, playing cards, flirting, and the occasional hunt. The main features hadn't changed in millennia.

The local physics were realistic, if somewhat unsophisticated. Since nobody ever examined the buildings or the wildlife too closely, they didn't need to be overly detailed.

Likewise, nobody paid much attention to the hundreds of thousands of servants, caretakers, town folk, and city folk who populated this inworld. They were only Partials—Partial personas—a simple backdrop for the real entertainment: the endless pursuit and seduction of marriageable partners, and the creation of new family ties that carried out into the real universe.

Many hopefuls had tried to work their way into some kind of relationship with The Family. Only a small percentage succeeded.

The immediate Family, a few hundred Chattingbarons, had dominated the DonTon inworld for ages. Their closely-guarded separation from the wider Sagittarian Cybrid inworlds lent an air of mystery to the Family and the Casa, making a visit to DonTon one of the most sought-after invitations.

Though they all held perfectly normal Cybrid jobs in the outworld, here, the Family ruled.

Mr. Trillian's interest in this particular inworld had nothing to do with the Family, its eligible high-profile guests, or its valuable social connections.

Trillian, Shard of Alum, was engaged in an important mission: to break into the nearby unsanctioned inworld of Alternus. His idea to use Casa DonTon as his launching point had been inspired, if he did say so himself. He'd instantiated in DonTon as *Mr.* Trillian, setting aside his lofty title as one of Alum's most trusted agents in order to blend in among the horde of eligible bachelors. *Shard* Trillian was known throughout the Realm. *Mr.* Trillian evoked nervous titters on conveying his audacious name choice. People could hardly believe Alum had permitted someone to name their inworld avatar after the famous Shard.

From the frivolous hub of Casa DonTon, Trillian hoped to launch a covert incursion into the Alternus inworld. His previous attempts to secretly enter Alternus by more conventional methods had failed. He was surprised, but also impressed.

Alternus might be the most cleverly protected inworld I've ever encountered. I must question its designer. It's been eons since I've run into a worthy opponent.

He dug into the problem with glee. It had been easy enough to discover their passcode phrase, "There's no place like home." The early and nearly effortless success made him over-confident and careless. He dismissed Alum's warning about the malicious thought-virus lurking at Alternus' regular portal as unwarranted and needlessly patronizing. That is, until it caught him off guard and nearly overwhelmed his personal defenses.

Outwardly, the miniscule bit of code appeared innocuous. It did no more than instill a minimal level of open-mindedness, a willingness to simply *consider* criticisms of the Lord, in the minds of those who would normally view such ideas as the highest blasphemy. Compounding the slight openness was a gentle predisposition toward distrust of Alum's rank as the universe's Ultimate Authority. The virus' influence was as delicate as it was insidiously treacherous.

Thanks to his standard operating procedure for investigating new inworlds, rather than acute foresight, Trillian evaded the worst of the effect. Before connecting to Alternus, he'd isolated his inworld interface from deeper mental structures.

As it had been designed to do, the virus slipped through his firewall and was already seeding doubt before Trillian could reprogram his belief network—his concepta—to ignore it. He disengaged before his core persona was critically subverted, but the virus had gotten close. Too close.

Once safely away from the inworld, it took a few hours of concerted effort to identify and remove the nasty effects. The ego-checking close call convinced him to drop any idea of a frontal assault in favor of a more indirect infiltration. He enjoyed a challenge—to a point. It kept things interesting, but he had work to do, and "interesting" was getting in the way.

Sitting at the dining table looking at his alternate portal to Alternus—tucked behind an innocent looking closet door—Trillian felt pleased with his new plan.

Casa DonTon provided the perfect platform. The portal's data paths were routed close to the virus-infected hardware substrate on which the Alternus inworld simulation ran but were not affected by it. And while DonTon's instantiated Full population was relatively small, its participants were sufficiently shallow and silly. He wouldn't be overly taxed by the sim itself, and he'd have ample opportunity to probe Alternus' supervisory defenses while keeping up the pretense of social niceties. It was a delectable plan, if he did say so himself. Whoever designed the Alternus inworld would never expect an invasion coming from such a self-absorbed and non-threatening neighbor as Casa DonTon. .

The clattering peach bowls that jerked the Shard's attention back to the dining room, also drew his attention to the dazed Footman.

My, my, what have we here? How interesting. My lattice probing at the edges of the Alternus sim portal seems to have had an unexpected effect on the wait staff Partial, Timothy.

Trillian reviewed what he knew about the knowledge-belief space of Partials for a clue as to how a cursory probe into Alternus might have disrupted the Footman.

* * *

THE SUPERVISOR PROGRAM discreetly pinged the waiting Partial: *Unregistered Instantiation. Reporting anomaly now. Please wait.*

That doesn't sound very reassuring—Timothy noted. .

He straightened his posture and addressed Lady Chattingbaron. "Troubles appear to have originated in the hardware matrix as a result of anomalous sunspot activity, my Lady," he lied. "Everything is fine now." He calmly resumed serving dessert.

"Unregistered Instantiation?" Me? That's not possible.

The Footman maintained his usual serene external demeanor, while his mind reeled. He was a Partial, he was sure of it. An Unregistered Instantiation would be a Full persona with no real body, a mind existing in the inworld without an associated physical trueself registered outworld.

The Supervisor must be mistaken—he thought. Partials can't become fully instantiated with independent personas unless they have been selected by the committee as candidates for embodiment outworld. I haven't been selected.

Timothy blinked rapidly. How such knowledge had appeared in his mind, he had no idea. It seemed as if the information spontaneously emerged in his consciousness of its own accord. How odd!

He scanned the room nervously. His mind, his whole persona, felt richer and deeper than it had moments earlier. *Once the Supervisor isolates my knowledge-belief space and sees that I've gone from Partial to Full, they'll scrub it. I don't want to be scrubbed!*

What are my options? There's no point in hiding. I can't very well throw myself at the mercy of the Supervisor and hope for the best. Should I wait here to be erased, or take over one of the Family's outworld bodies?

Timothy's hand paused mid-air, a scoop of ice cream hovering above Lady Mirabel's bowl. He was having thoughts. *I'm having independent thoughts. I'm thinking. And I lied! To Lady Chattingbaron, no less! How is that possible?*

For the first time in his long existence as a DonTon server, Timothy was thinking outside his simple, inworld programming. His hand remained frozen as he considered the ramifications. *Thinking for myself? Astounding!*

The artfully-formed ball of ice cream he held in mid-air, however, did not remain frozen. It dripped. Once. Twice. Its center of gravity slipped perilously close to the edge of the spoon.

With an elegant swoop of the wrist, Timothy prevented the escape and delivered the creamy globe neatly atop the waiting peaches.

The house guests had already resumed their conversations and noticed neither the slip nor sleight of hand. Even the eagle-eyed Head Butler, busily pouring steaming coffee and tea, gave no indication he'd seen anything amiss.

Timothy finished dessert service and took his place in front of the polished oak sideboard. He kept his movements measured and his face neutral. He was sure the Securitors would intervene and take him away at any moment. *I've got it! I could steal an automobile and escape to London. No one would find me in those crowds.*

What am I thinking? Nobody can evade an omnipotent inworld Supervisor and ruthless Securitor agents. It's hopeless. I might as well face my fate with the dignity the Family deserves.

Crestfallen but ever professional, Timothy hid his misery. *My experience of consciousness is going to be the shortest independent life the Realm has ever recorded.*

With dessert course ingested and a promising evening ahead, the Family and guests stood. "Shall we retire to the Library for a brandy?" Lord Chattingbaron asked his male guests.

The ladies exchanged coquettish smiles, knowing one drink would lead to a second, and the second to a third, along with a cigar or two while the female coterie sipped sherry and played cards in the sitting room. Both groups looked forward to the dances and games that would follow, once dinner had a chance to settle and the two groups were brought back together in the Grand Salon.

As the others filed out of the room, Mr. Trillian lingered behind to examine an unremarkable painting displayed on the wall facing his chair. The painting happened to be hanging beside the same closet door that had drawn his interest over dinner.

The Head Butler caught Timothy's attention, and raised his bushy eyebrows meaningfully toward the dawdling guest. Satisfied that Timothy would see to Mr. Trillian, he took his leave.

"A stirring rendition of Lord Chattingbaron's Great Grandfather at the hunt," Timothy expounded as he approached Mr. Trillian. Within two steps of the guest, the bees resumed their buzzing. This time, the Footman's hand was free and he brushed the air near his right ear.

Trillian caught the motion out of the corner of his eye and turned to face the Footman. "Are you sure the self-diagnostic was correct?"

Timothy shook his head to clear the sound; the action served only to make the room swim unsteadily. "Quite sure," he confirmed, and rested his hand against the wall. "But, perhaps I should sit a moment."

He dropped into the chair beside the closet door. "I'm sure it will pass." He waved his hand, dismissing the guest's extended hand. "No, that's okay. I'll be fine. Thank you for your concern."

Trillian turned back to the closet door.

The buzzing noise in Timothy's head grew. Unseen swarms circled him, and the room swam in and out of focus. He squeezed his eyes shut in an effort to regain his equilibrium. The soft creak of the closet door pierced the droning buzz, and a wave of hot air washed over him. The dense, complex odors of a large, industrial city assaulted the confused Footman.

Fighting a nauseating dizziness, Timothy opened his eyes and pushed to his feet. He steadied his balance with a hand to the wall and looked into the closet.

The dark, confined space he expected to see was not there. Instead of a few tidy shelves of cleaning supplies, two brooms, and a dustpan, the closet opened onto a city, the likes of which Timothy could not have imagined.

Impossibly tall buildings lined a broad, busy street filled with more people than he had ever seen at one time.

The people were dressed oddly. Some men wore business suits, identifiable as such despite their strange cut and the absence of proper headwear. And the women! Timothy was shocked by their immodest garb. Why, he could see the bare knees and thighs of those who wore dresses or short skirts! The majority of people sported embarrassingly inappropriate casual attire. Men and women clad in skin-tight blue pants. Trades people, perhaps? Had they not been situated in the middle of a bustling city, he would have thought them farmers.

While the vestments were odd, the automobiles absolutely astonished him. He had never seen such sleek machinery, not in all his days. And there were so many of them. The collective noise that emanated as drivers impatiently roared engines and honked horns was an affront to the senses. Even worse, the language the drivers shouted at any pedestrian or vehicle that dared impede their progress was an insult to his sensibilities.

Timothy didn't recognize Mr. Trillian right away; the guest's clothing had changed to match the style of the better-accoutered businessmen on the sidewalk around him. But that was definitely him. He stood well into the impossibly expanded closet, blending into that magnificent and frightful city. While Timothy tried to make sense of the scene, Mr. Trillian stretched out his arms, laughed, and twirled around, taking in his new surroundings.

Timothy stood on wobbly legs in the open doorframe and watched him, too flabbergasted to move.

Shard Trillian glanced back over his shoulder and noticed the stunned Footman standing at the door. He dropped his arms, amused by the anomaly. From the city side in which the Shard stood, the doorway opened into an opulently-furnished dining room from another era. Few of the frenetic passersby spared a second glance at the formally-dressed servant frozen in the open portal. After all, this was New York.

The Shard made a sweeping motion with one hand. "Would you mind closing that, please?" he requested, pointing to the door.

It was clear he expected programmed obedience from the servant. He turned without a second glance and set off down the sidewalk, disappearing into an ocean of bobbing heads.

Timothy teetered indecisively. A gasp from the dining room reminded him where he was.

Lady Chattingbaron paused at the main entrance, a hand delicately covering her gaping mouth. Behind her, Timothy glimpsed a hovering matte-black, spherical Securitor. She hadn't sensed it yet; her full attention was locked on the impossible scene in the closet.

"Timothy...," she began. The Securitor projected a greenish beam that encapsulated and silenced her. The menacing sphere pushed past her paralyzed virtual-body and floated into the room.

Timothy bolted over the closet threshold and into the strange world, slamming the door shut behind him.

The new city was much bigger than the London he knew, in fact, bigger than any city he knew. Maybe he could hide from the Securitors here. He ran down the sidewalk in the opposite direction from Mr. Trillian, bouncing off irritated virtual New Yorkers of 2040. A stream of profanity, fluttering pages, and angry gestures followed the Footman's clumsy flight.

Back in Casa DonTon's family dining room, the Securitor ripped the closet door from its hinges. Inside, it found a few shelves, two brooms, a dustpan, and some polishing cloths. The city was gone.

Anomaly has escaped—the Securitor reported. Its smooth voice was devoid of anger and frustration. It scanned the virtual room for any trace of Timothy. Finding none, it left.

3

GREG AND KATHY STRUGGLED TO MANAGE THE EFFECT Darian's data deluge had on their lattices through the rest of Sunday and into the early hours of Monday morning. They fought to maintain a modicum of sanity against foreign memories, thoughts, and stray associations.

The walk from the lab back to Darian's apartment had been fruitless; there was no sign he'd passed by. They'd convinced his building manager to check his suite in case he was inside, lying unconscious and in need of help. It was eerily quiet but nothing looked out of place; there was no sign of a struggle or that he'd left for a trip. The local hospitals had no record of recent admissions resembling Darian or Larry, for that matter. It was as if the two had disappeared from the face of the earth, along with the RAF generator.

Working offline felt slow and clumsy, but it was a necessary precaution. Darian's data stream was waiting for their lattices to reopen. It was lurking in networked computers of cars, phones, appliances, lab equipment, anything connected to the internet of things.

They had enough to deal with already. Their brains didn't know what to do with all the little bits of Darian that had leaked in during the initial barrage—flashes of everything he ever knew, experienced, or thought. They could barely distinguish their own memories, ideas, and feelings from his.

They heard the voices of his parents, teachers, and former associates playing out old conversations and arguments, and delivering wisdom as if they'd been there at the time. Fragments of books and articles pertaining to fields they'd never worked in settled uneasily into their own memories: virus engineering, dendy semiconductor design, lattice theory. They remembered people they'd never met and places they'd never been, all in one crazy, confused jumble.

The couple floundered and strained to make sense of the foreign thoughts, to tie details to what they knew, and to preserve themselves within the chaos.

When they cautiously reconnected their lattices with the external world, a fresh inundation of thoughts and memories poured in, and raced to reconnect with the excised fragments cluttering their lattices.

They staggered into work around 7:30 Monday morning. They wandered back and forth between the office and the lab, hoping their coworkers would miraculously appear with the RAF generator. *C'mon, guys, where are you? Let's all have a good laugh over this craziness, and get on with our work*—Greg silently pleaded.

By 8:15 a.m., they accepted that neither Darian nor Larry was going to show up, and that nobody was trying to reach them to make demands or shed light on the situation. It was time to make an official report.

They arrived at Dr. Wong's office, and asked if he might know where Darian was, or Larry. He didn't.

Greg relayed the little information they had. "I know it sounds thin but it's been twenty-four hours now, and we'd like to make an official report. We came to you first because we were afraid the police wouldn't take us seriously. To be honest, if it had been only Larry, we'd probably give it another day, maybe even two. We came to you because you *know* Darian. You know what a workaholic he is; the man practically lives in the lab. And you know how important his work is to him. He was so excited when he called us about a new development."

"Greg's right, this isn't like Darian at all," Kathy added. "He would've been there in the lab waiting for us. Something is wrong. What if that psycho shooter at the Philosopher's Cafe wasn't acting alone after all? Darian could be in real trouble."

Dr. Wong read the worry on the two scientists' faces. He dialed Campus Security and identified himself. "We're concerned we have a missing faculty member; possibly one of his associates, as well, and some missing lab equipment with sensitive material on it. It's probably nothing, but we'd really appreciate it if you could check it out for us."

The officer took down the names and lab information, gave the Chair a file reference number, and promised to send someone right over to get the full information. "Can you meet us at Dr. Leigh's lab?"

When Dr. Wong, Kathy, and Greg arrived at the lab, two officers were waiting for them. They entered together. Kathy and Greg repeated what they knew, and the officers looked around. Without much to tell, the visit was short. "Give us a few hours to see what we can find out," the lead officer said, and closed his tablet. "We'll contact you with any updates. It would be helpful if someone could stay at the lab today in case one of them arrives."

"Yes, of course," Kathy replied. The lead officer was on his phone with the Human Resources liaison before he crossed the threshold, and the pair disappeared down the hallway.

Dr. Wong glanced at his cell phone. "Okay, I've got a meeting across campus in about...five minutes ago. I have to run, but keep me informed. I'll leave my cell on, and I'll call you if there are any updates. Don't worry, I'm sure he'll turn up, and we'll all feel silly about this by noon."

Kathy and Greg went through the motions of work for the next few hours. When the lab phone rang at 11:00, they raced to pick it up, but it was only Dr. Wong, checking in. "Campus Security visited Darian's suite and spoke with the manager. No leads there."

We already knew that—Greg thought, but held his tongue.

"And Kenna, our Human Resources liaison, managed to reach both Larry's mom and Darian's aunt, neither of whom knew anything about the young scientists' whereabouts, but are now equally concerned."

"Thanks for the update, Dr. Wong. Nothing new here," Greg replied.

At noon, he and Kathy locked up and went to the cafeteria for lunch or, more accurately, to kill time and silently pick at their Cobb salads. They pitched the unfinished salads after ten minutes and headed back to the lab.

"This waiting around is driving me crazy. There's little or no help we can offer the police," he said. "But we can carry on the work. We can do that much for Darian."

Kathy looked at her partner. She felt his frustration. *He's right. We have to do something.* "I can build a new RAF generator within the month," Kathy suggested, as if it were a perfectly normal response, on a perfectly normal day. "That will give us a chance to independently test the theory. In the meantime, maybe we can find a gentler way to accept the rest of Darian's download. Maybe there's something in there."

Greg picked up on her hopeful tone. "Yeah, our lattices can keep working in the background on the first bit of data he sent us. They can organize and integrate it and, hopefully, find a way to partition it from our own minds. Then we can start pulling in the rest of his data dump and locate his most recent memories. Maybe we'll even be able to see what he did to get the RAF working."

"Yeah." Kathy's face grew somber. "Maybe we'll learn what it was he figured out before he disappeared."

4

BROTHER STRALASI AND DARAK toured the remaining ten Realm colonies in galaxy NGC4567 in five days. From there, they jumped to M87 in the heart of the Virgo cluster, visited a hundred of the major colonies, and headed out on the long journey toward the Origin galaxy, affectionately known throughout the Realm as the Milky Way.

Four months and over a hundred planets after leaving Gargus, Darak and the Good Brother arrived on Rafael 263.3, the twelfth colony Darak wanted to visit within the galaxy the ancient index identified as NGC4450. They were a little over fourteen million light years from Home World.

Their tour of colonized planetary systems in the Virgo Cluster illustrated the homogenizing effect of Alum's Realm. Though the worlds were at considerably different stages of development—as would be expected given the millions of years separating oldest from newest—they shared many common characteristics.

Everywhere the pair travelled, people worked, played, and prayed the same way. Cities and towns grew. People tended farms and planetary ecologies. They courted, married, and raised children. They attended to Alum's works and they were happy.

Brother Stralasi's view of the established worlds changed dramatically during their travels. It had come as quite a shock to the otherwise broadly educated and well-informed monk that it wasn't Alum who directly blessed the worlds with His riches. The prayers people sent to Alum from the Alumitas and Foundation buildings throughout the Realm were secretly rerouted to local Cybrids. The Cybrids stationed in support asteroids genetically engineered practically everything grown for the People, and whatever wasn't grown, was built and repaired by other Cybrids. While

Alum directed activity in His Realm, the Cybrids carried out the work.

Every trip he and Darak took to a new planetary system included a visit to the local Integration Lab and, every time, Darak would send him off to enjoy the peaceful gardens, while he stayed back to discuss some secret project with the Cybrid scientists.

Stralasi inquired, casually at first, what his business might be with the Cybrids. Every time, Darak artfully deflected his questions.

After several similar instances, and an equal number of redirects, curiosity got the better of the monk and he asked more pointedly.

Darak still refused to discuss what he was doing with the Cybrids. "After all," he said, "if even *they* don't know why they're doing what I ask, why should I put *you* at risk?"

"With all due respect, I humbly submit that my exposure to risk has been so extreme to this point, surely I could bear such a small additional burden of deeper knowledge," Stralasi challenged. "You praise knowledge as the best way to combat the People's 'unreasonable' devotion to Alum. How is this any different?"

Darak harrumphed. "You *have* been listening, then." No further explanation was forthcoming.

As the two arrived at the third planet in under forty-eight hours, a bedazzled and exhausted Stralasi could not resist remarking to Darak how everywhere in Alum's Realm felt like home.

"Praise be to Yov for creating such a wondrous universe," the monk exclaimed, "and to Alum for blessing it with so many perfect worlds for His People."

"Goodness. You have no inkling of the real nature of the Realm, do you?" Darak replied. "Would you like me to show you what these worlds are truly like?"

"What do you mean? I was with you. I saw them for myself."

"What you saw was a version of each world filtered through your lattice, which I synchronized according to local starstep parameters."

Stralasi stared blankly at him.

"Listen, even an amateur astronomer would appreciate that habitable worlds vary over a wide range of parameters: different gravity, atmosphere, light spectrum, diurnal period, seasons, length of year, and so on. It's much easier to change the inhabitants' perceptions of the planets than it is to alter the planets to fit one Standard physiology."

"If you say so," Stralasi uttered. He gave his imagination free reign to work out the implications, but he couldn't bring himself to voice the questions that resulted.

Darak gave the monk a friendly nudge. "Did you think humans were not included in the work done at the Integration Labs?"

Modification of the People themselves? Stralasi had never imagined such an idea. Altering a person's essence—their DNA, he reminded himself—was bizarre, potentially catastrophic, and likely immoral.

"If the People are genetically modified to suit the different worlds, why do we all look and feel more or less the same everywhere we go?" he challenged.

Darak waited patiently for Stralasi to arrive at the answer on his own. Insight struck the Brother's brain like an electric shock: "Our lattices!" he exclaimed.

Darak nodded. "Yes, your lattices. In the same way they are used to deliver information or entertainment directly into your senses, they can be altered to make you accept what you perceive or remember as perfectly normal. The true perceptual experience doesn't have to be overridden, only your cognitive or emotional response to the experience. When you recall your visit to a different planet, the details of that memory are filtered through your belief of what it must have been like. Everything is adjusted to expectations by your lattice."

"I want to know the reality," Stralasi demanded.

Darak lifted his hand, palm upward, in a motion symbolic of lifting the veil of deceit over Stralasi's memories. Recollections of impossible places flooded the Brother's mind. Visions of monsters only marginally recognizable as humans were overlaid with images of how he had perceived them through his lattice filter.

On some planets, people were short and powerful with thick bones and strong muscles, an indication of heavier than normal gravity. On other worlds, the inhabitants were delicate creatures, tall and lithesome. Some planets suffered with extreme cold and their people were characterized by fur coats, short noses, and tiny, flat ears. Other worlds were so hot that inhabitants sprouted enormous cooling fins in the middle of their backs. On water-covered worlds, the inhabitants had both flippers and gills. The images that remained in Stralasi's memory, from all these strange worlds, were of green lands and people who looked like him.

"Wait a second," the monk sensed something important tickling at the edge of consciousness. This trip had given him a lot to process. To learn that his world, his thoughts and his perceptions had been so far wrong, so untrustworthy, all of his life was stupefying. The niggling realization wormed its way to the surface of his thoughts and snapped into focus. "If the worlds we visited were all so inhospitable to my basic form, how could I have survived?"

Again, Darak held his gaze, gently waiting for comprehension to arrive. It didn't take long.

"Did you change my body for each local condition? How?"

"In normal travel, the local starstep alters the physiology and appearance of the traveler as required. I simply read the programmed pattern as we arrived and made the changes myself. A bit of a nuisance, really. I could have just kept us in a protective bubble as we travelled; that would have been easier. But I thought our visits would be more useful if we adapted to local conditions."

"Is it like that everywhere in the Realm?"

"Yes, but with good intent. The illusion of Standard Life maintained through the perceptual filter of the lattice minimizes prejudice in the Realm. It would be harder to do if people traveled more. Sadly, it also prevents the appreciation of diversity. I'm not sure it's a good trade-off."

"But it's a lie!"

Darak laughed aloud. "Of course it's a lie. Our whole civilization is built upon lies. Most are. The real question is whether the lies are necessary and whether the benefits outweigh the damages."

Stralasi felt his conceptual universe spinning again. He wasn't sure he could take anymore. His eyes scanned the small wooded clearing where they'd arrived. "So what does this really look like?"

"Actually, this planet happens to be unusually similar to Earth, I mean, Origin. So the lattice isn't filtering anything right now."

Relieved, Stralasi sat on a nearby stump. Here, at least, he would be able to enjoy nature the way it was meant to be enjoyed. He watched the bugs and birds fly among the grasses and trees. He could hear the trickle of a brook behind the trees and knew the water would be sweet and clear. He allowed himself to relax and thought back over some of the places he and Darak had visited. This time, the memories washed over him without their previous repugnance.

In that moment, Stralasi came to a new understanding and appreciation of Alum's wisdom, even if he wasn't certain he agreed with it.

5

DARIAN LEIGH, THE LATTICE-ENHANCED BOY WONDER, the inventor of the Reality Assertion Field, the most brilliant mind ever to walk the face of the Earth, the "man who would be God"—according to the more disparaging reports—was missing.

That the RAF generator and Larry were also gone without a trace was less prominent in the reporting.

The controversy that accompanied Darian and his work escalated when word of his unexplained disappearance surfaced. Chatter and speculation began within hours of police involvement and refused to die down, even weeks later. Greg and Kathy did their best to ignore the ugly rumors and focus on building a second RAF generator. Their lab notes were gone, but Kathy had the schematics in her head, thanks to her lattice.

Pulling them out was a lot harder than it had been before Darian's "sharing" of himself. Where her hands once moved deftly across printed-circuit boards and keyboards, they now hesitated. She struggled to access her memories of the design and ignore everything not directly related to the RAF generator.

"They're driving me crazy, all these little bits and pieces of Darian's thoughts on new RAF theory directions, dendy virus designs, random equations drifting into sight from out of nowhere and demanding I follow them. As soon as I give in and pay the least attention to the intrusions, they change or dissolve away. I don't know what to do with this. I'm losing my mind," she complained to Greg, knowing he couldn't help her.

While Kathy painstakingly retrieved the generator schematics and assembled the hardware, Greg tackled his own scrambled lattice memories. *If I can recreate the data that was stored on the stolen laptop, maybe we can find some clue as to what happened to Darian and Larry.*

Like Kathy, he found the process maddening. One second he'd be dumping their most recent version of the Feynman diagrams for virtual quarks into the server, and the next second he'd be reminiscing about Darian's childhood years in Boston.

Whenever they tried to access the internet, their conceptual integrity was overwhelmed by a fresh surge of fragments from Darian's mind, along with the disjointed associations that each of those pieces triggered.

They spent their days and nights in fear of letting down their guard and introducing further madness into their psyches. They knew they needed a long, isolated vacation to rest and to apply some order to the scattered bits of their mentor's thoughts, but there was no time for that now. They pushed on resolutely and slept when they could.

The worst onslaught hit after a particularly long and exhausting day. Worn out, Greg fell into bed and slipped into one of the deepest sleeps he'd had in weeks.

The next thing he knew, Kathy was shaking him awake from a horrific nightmare. He fought his way to consciousness, writhing, soaked in sweat, and choking on a scream.

He bolted upright. Chills swept up and down his spine. His eyes scanned the room, searching for danger. Finally accepting that he was at home, safe in his own bed, he relaxed.

Kathy switched on the bedside lamp. "Are you okay?" she asked.

"Oh, wow, that was a doozy," he replied, still trying to catch his breath. He stuffed his pillow behind him and flopped back against it. His breath whooshed out along with the air in the polyester stuffing.

"It was so real, so detailed. I was working at my lab bench on some new project, something to do with genetic engineering. It was like I was right there. I could feel the pipettor in my hands; I could smell the chemicals. I looked up and there was a big spider watching me. No big deal. I grabbed my lab book and smacked it.

"Then I noticed another one eyeing me from behind the containers of buffers on the shelf above the bench, and a third one sitting beside the vacuum inlet near the bench sink.

"I was creeped out but curious, too. I remember thinking, *'That's weird. How'd they get in here?'* and wondering what to do about them. Then there was a kind of skittering sound behind me."

Greg cocked his head as if still trying to identify it, and shivered. "I turned around and there were dozens of them. Hundreds of them. They covered the bench top.

"I freaked out. I just froze, and they stopped moving, too. They didn't budge, not one of them. It was like they were waiting for me to make the first move. I stood there staring at them like an idiot. I could see my silhouette reflecting back at me from hundreds of beady little eyes. It was so strange. I couldn't look away.

"And they had these really long, spiny, front legs. They started rubbing them together and—I swear, Kath—I could hear the sound they made. I could *hear* them. It was like some kind of music, some kind of communication or something.

"I was thinking, '*That's not normal spider behavior. Spiders don't make sounds by rubbing their legs together.*' I was confused, but I wasn't going to stick around and puzzle it out. I edged toward the exit, real slow and quiet so I wouldn't spook them, but it didn't work.

"Spiders started pouring off the shelves and benches. I could hear their bodies hitting the floor. It sounded like rain.

"They came after me, and I ran into the hallway and slammed the door behind me. By the time I caught my breath, spiders were already trying to get through the space under the door. It was awful. They kept coming, like some kind of scrabbling, black tide.

"I jumped back and ran down the hall, but they were so fast. They were definitely after me; there was no doubt.

"I ducked inside the first open room I found, grabbed handfuls of paper towel from the dispenser, and started jamming them under the door as fast as I could."

"That's awful! No wonder you woke up screaming," Kathy said.

"That's not the worst of it. I was stuffing paper like crazy and then, clear as a bell, someone said, 'What are you doing with that?' I almost had a heart attack right there, but when I turned around, it was Larry. I've never been so glad to see him in all my life.

"I started yelling. 'Get over here and help me with this. You won't believe what's out there!' And I kept stuffing paper towels in the gap.

"But his voice stopped me cold, Kath. It was eerie and calm, and just as scary as the spiders. 'I have a better idea,' he said, and that's when the nightmare got really bizarre."

Kathy grimaced. "What could be more bizarre than an army of spiders?"

"A huge gray bubble appeared all around me, and trapped me inside. No matter how hard I pushed and kicked, it wouldn't break or budge. It started shrinking and I had to crouch down, smaller and smaller, until I was squished into a fetal position.

"And suddenly, Lucius Pratt, Reverend LaMontagne, and President Sakira were all standing outside the bubble with Larry, and they started laughing and pointing at me."

"Well, I can tell you what a therapist would say about that," Kathy joked. Her attempt to lighten the mood barely registered with Greg. "Sorry, hon. I couldn't resist. Continue; I'm listening."

"The laughter got louder, and some other people were there. I've never met them in real life, but I knew who they were, all partners in the company that Darian's mom started: Nick Franti, David Arnell, and Sharon Leigh, herself. They were all laughing, except Sharon. She looked horrified, like she was in pure agony, and that's when I realized—*She's not watching* me *die; she's watching her son, Darian, die.* In the dream, I was Darian.

"The bubble kept shrinking and nobody was trying to do anything to stop it. I kept shouting at them, 'Why are you doing this?' and all they did was laugh. I pushed, and kicked, and pleaded, but the sphere kept shrinking until it was crushing me. I couldn't move or breathe, and the next thing I knew, you were shaking me and I was screaming myself awake. I know it was just a dream but it was so real. And so strange. Some of the things I saw were from my memories, and some were from Darian's. I couldn't tell them apart; it was all just me."

Greg flipped back the damp, tangled sheet and staggered into the bathroom. He could feel Kathy's worried eyes tracking him. He shut the door and leaned over the sink. His heart was still pounding. He placed his hands on the counter for support and let the moonlight streaming in through the narrow window wash over him.

Deep breath in. Deep breath out. He looked in the mirror. Darian's pained features, distressed and haggard, looked back.

"Agh!" Greg snapped on the bathroom light. The face in the mirror was his again but Darian's features lingered like a distressing apparition.

It's okay; you're still half asleep—he told himself. He knew otherwise.. *Me and Darian, one and the same?* He squeezed his eyes shut and concentrated.

It's okay. I am me. I am me. I am me, and everything's going to be okay. He wasn't sure who he was trying to convince: himself, his dendy lattice, or Darian, who lurked even now, at the edges of his consciousness.

"Honey, are you okay?" Kathy's voice drifted in.

Greg opened his eyes. His own worried face looked back in the mirror. A trembling laugh escaped his lips. *I am me.*

He sensed how thin and tenuous the line separating normal from insane could be, and how easy it was to cross when dreams invaded reality. He took a deep, shaky breath, looked once more into the sink, and tentatively raised his eyes to verify his identity. *Okay, we're good. Still me.*

"Uhh...yeah. Yeah, I'm fine. Be right out."

He splashed a little cold water on his face, patted dry with the soft hand towel, and padded back to bed. The fright left him more resolved than ever to keep up his guard against the onslaught from Darian—what used to be Darian—until he and his lattice could better adapt and accommodate, or at least, to partition him off.

Welcome to the next level—he said to himself. He and Kathy had been creating harmless mental games and viruses to develop their skills and to practice sparring with one another's lattices ever since they took the dendy virus.

This, whatever it was they were receiving from Darian, was a huge leap beyond anything they'd ever created. This was more in the realm of the "what-if-you-could" games of wild speculation they toyed with over a few beers. Nothing had prepared him for this.

If tonight was any indication, there was good cause to be concerned about what was in store for their mental health over the coming weeks.

* * *

TWO WEEKS LATER, KATHY AND GREG HAD THE NEW HARDWARE up and running. They would continue the programming from home. With any luck, getting away from the many cues around the lab and campus that sparked Darian's old memories would give them a bit of a reprieve.

"It'll be a nice change to work out of the apartment or one of the neighborhood cafes," Kathy said. "The view is much better."

Greg agreed. It would feel good to get away from the lab, the office, and the campus, away from all the reminders of Darian. Even a few days away would be a welcome relief.

They got set up at home and settled into a new routine. Kathy entered most of the code into the system, and Greg took Larry's place as chief tester and cappuccino fetcher.

Ten days later, a call from Campus Security burst any illusions they might have harbored about resuming a normal life.

6

DARAK SCOUTED AROUND THE CLEARING. Satisfied with what he found, he extracted a small marble from his robe.

"This looks like as good a place as any to set up camp."

"Do you mean, we won't be staying at the Alumita Hostel tonight?" Brother Stralasi asked.

"No, I think we could use one night away from civilization. Don't you?"

"I haven't camped in ages. It might be nice. Unfortunately, we don't have a tent or sleeping rolls."

Darak placed the marble on the ground and stood back to give it room to expand. Within seconds, it was a meter across and growing.

As Stralasi watched, a miniature tent, some stools, and a storage box emerged inside the milky interior. When it reached five meters in diameter, the outline of the sphere faded away. A ready-made campsite, complete with dried wood inside a fire pit, lay before them. With a small pop, the wood ignited into a smokeless campfire.

The Good Brother clasped his hands together in childlike delight. "Is there no end to your magic?"

"Actually, this is just a bit of newer technology mixed with a bit of older and simpler technology. I've carried this camping equipment around for quite a while."

"Wasn't it heavy?"

"Well, that's the advanced technology, the magic, as you call it. I shrunk the electron orbitals to make everything smaller and altered their Higgs field interactions to remove the effective mass, making it easy to carry wherever I go. You never know when it might be preferable to camp out." He smiled and stepped into the campsite. "Anyway, I'm hungry. Would you like to eat?"

Stralasi was dumbfounded by the meaningless technical explanation, but he did feel his stomach growling. "Yes, I'm famished. Shall we pop into a restaurant in town?"

"No need. The larder is completely provisioned." Darak pointed to the storage box. "Did I mention that everything was held in molecular stasis while stored in the marble? The food you're about to enjoy is older than anything you've ever known except for, perhaps, the stars and the planets. Nevertheless, I guarantee it will be as fresh and delicious as if it were prepared moments ago."

Darak opened the chest and the odors of hot food, scrumptious as any Stralasi had ever smelled, wafted out. The Good Brother's mouth watered. He perched gingerly on one of the small stools, eager to discover what fine repast the magic would deliver.

Darak swung the lid of the storage box between them, creating a makeshift table. He pulled a feast out of the container: rolls filled with spicy meats, exotic steamed vegetables, garlic shrimp, a poultry and nut dish, and more. He gestured for Stralasi to help himself, and the Brother dug in heartily.

An hour later, the two men sat on benches staring into the campfire as the sun set behind the trees. Darak pulled out a few more logs to feed the flames from the seemingly bottomless storage box. He sighed as he poked at the firewood. This was the most relaxed he'd seen Brother Stralasi since they'd left Alumston on Gargus 718.5. *Understandably*—he thought. *The man has been through a lot.*

Stralasi picked up a stick and held one end in the fire until it burst into flame. "Don't you have to visit the Integration Lab for your secret project tonight?"

The question drew Darak from his pleasant lethargy. "Perhaps while you're sleeping." "I won't ask you again to explain what your project's all about, but could you tell me if it has something to do with your opposition to Alum's Divine Plan?"

Darak stared at the dancing flames without answering for so long that Stralasi began to think the man hadn't heard him. He was about to repeat the question when the other man sighed.

Darak said, "My *opposition*, as you call it, remains uncertain. I have made a few inquiries and some preparations; nothing has been set in motion."

"Why not?"

"Alum's Realm has done a lot of good for humanity. Before He assumed permanent leadership, humanity had a history of brutal war, greed, and devastation. I hope His mind can be changed from His ultimate plan for the universe. Until my inquiries are complete and I have spoken with him, my opposition will remain inactive."

Stralasi could accept that for now. He had come to the conclusion Darak was neither a Shard of God nor a demon, simply an odd and powerful *other*. As for whether Darak could best Alum in a direct confrontation, that remained to be seen, although he rather doubted the man had powers equal to the Living God.

"Tell me about your travels before you came to Gargus 718.5." Stralasi's request surprised them both.

"My experiences are difficult to describe."

"Please, indulge me."

Relenting, Darak shifted on his bench and settled in to tell his story. "Okay, you remember when we first met, I told you that I came to Gargus 718.5 from the Da'arkness beyond the Realm and that I had traveled beyond the edge of the universe? All of that is true.

"The universe extends incredible distances in every direction. There are billions and billions of galaxies whose light will never reach the Realm. They're far away, and moving farther so fast their light is receding from us. I've wandered a long time among some of those galaxies, exploring their wonders, and getting to know their many sentient beings."

"Are there other realms like Alum's?" interrupted Stralasi.

"Oh, yes, but very few. The leap to understanding how the basic physical laws arise in the universe is not an easy one to make. Over the uncountable light years I've traveled, there's been less than a handful of species that achieved such a level before their home stars exploded or they destroyed themselves. A few did, though, and their influence has spread across entire clusters of galaxies, as has Alum's. Like Alum's, the realms I've visited have found their pace of exploration limited by the speed of light."

"You visited them yourself? Are you not similarly limited in your explorations?"

"There is a way around the limitation. It requires a certain level of recklessness. Sane people would never attempt it."

"You admit to insanity, then?" Stralasi scrutinized Darak's expression, watching for any hint of anger as he replied.

"I admit there was a time when I was nearly insane, having been driven there by the ultimate futility of Alum's reign. We'll talk of that another time."

"So, what is the way around the limitation?"

"In order to explain that, I first need to explain a bit of physics."

"I should have known, more science." Stralasi complained.

Darak held up his hand, "Don't worry. Though the actual science is difficult to understand, I can provide a simple analogy.

"Imagine you are in a crowded room and you see a friend on the other side with whom you want to talk."

"I would send an InterLat message."

"Okay, imagine there's no InterLat in the room."

Stralasi looked skeptical but shrugged his acceptance.

Darak continued, "You try to walk to your friend but you keep bumping into people standing in your way. It slows down your progress, limiting how fast you can cross the room. If the room were empty except for you and your friend, you could cross more quickly."

Darak gave Stralasi a moment to catch up to the logic before continuing.

"The people in that room represent something called the Higgs boson field, named for a scientist from ancient Earth who first came up with the idea. It's the reason particles have mass. It's the effect particles feel as they try to move through the Higgs field, just like the effect you feel as you try to make your way through the people in the room. The particles' mass impedes their motion through the field as your size impedes your motion through the field of people.

"However, if we were to send radio waves through that crowded room, they wouldn't be impeded by the people in the room at all. Radio waves—photons—don't interact with the Higgs field. So you might wonder if there's any way to turn off the Higgs interaction in other particles.

"It turns out to be possible to disconnect the Higgs field interaction in *any* particle. And if the particles no longer interact with the Higgs field, they effectively have no mass—they're no longer wading through a crowded room. We've just freed up those particles to move at velocities up to the speed of light. Amazing, isn't it? But that's not the end of the story.

"Ancient researchers believed such particles could move even faster; that they were only limited to the speed of light because they were still interacting with *something*. There was still something in that room the particles had to navigate through.

"Having made the huge conceptual leap to define the effect of the Higgs boson field, and come up with a way to neutralize it, a few researchers were excited by the possibility of identifying and defying the next limitation. Would they finally be able to move particles faster than the speed of light?

"It didn't take them long to identify the next challenge. It turns out, the quantum electromagnetic, or EM, field that permeates our universe also impedes the movement of particles in much the same way as the Higgs boson field.

"But if we use the same kind of technology Alum uses, we can make it so that particles don't interact with the EM field, either."

"And does it work?" Stralasi asked. "Can the particles move faster than the speed of light?" In spite of his initial resistance, he had been lured in and was keen to know more.

"Yes, they can. Unfortunately, it causes a different problem."

"What kind of problem?" Stralasi blurted. *Ugh, too late. What was I thinking?* The monk's lips rolled tightly inward in a reflexive twinge of regret and self-censorship. He kicked himself for inviting another dense and convoluted answer. *Oh, Great Alum, help your humble servant; I really do want to know.*

Darak threw another log on the fire. "Well, since you asked, all particles in the universe exchange information using photons moving at the speed of light. If you no longer interact with the EM field, you no longer exchange information with particles in the universe. In essence, you become separate from the universe; it becomes invisible to you."

"You'd be lost! How would you ever find your way back?"

"Exactly. The answer is, you find signposts that remain connected to real particles in the universe."

"Sign posts?"

"Yes. They're called quantum entangled particles. Think of them as a pair of particles that remain connected at a level deeper than the Higgs and EM fields. If you are holding one member of the entangled pair when you become detached from the Higgs and EM fields, you can find the other half of the pair instantly, wherever it is in the universe. This is the basis for the starstep technology.

"The starsteps you use to travel between planets and stars are connected by entangled particles pairs; they can find each other no matter where they are. It has taken ages to achieve, but the older parts of the Realm host many entangled pairs that enable travelers to set out on various paths from one point. It's this very system that allows the starstep network to span millions of light years.

"But it isn't always a direct route. If you travel to a planet that isn't directly connected to the one you're leaving, even though the travel is practically instantaneous, it could involve multiple starstep connections, or pairings, to come to your destination. Some planets have a connection only with one other. The oldest and most central starsteps have been seeded with millions of connections."

"What if you don't have an entangled particle pair?"

"That's when you need to be reckless. Remember how the Angel, Mika, could only shift small distances? That's because when he disconnected from the Higgs and EM fields, he took some basic particles with him from his environment. Perhaps some bits of air or cosmic dust.

"By sifting through them, it's possible to find particles that are entangled with bits of matter or energy in the universe nearby. One has to work fast. You can only stay disconnected for an infinitesimal period of time or you risk not being able to find any locally-entangled partners. Angels are limited by their processing speed and by cautious safeguards. It would be easy for them to become lost forever."

"So how do *you* avoid getting lost?"

"The full answer is quite complicated. Let me see if I can simplify it for you."

"You know, there was a time when that comment might have offended me—but I'm past that now," chuckled the Good Brother. "Carry on."

"Yes. Well, the simple explanation would be that I very, very quickly find toeholds, and jump from one to the other in rapid sequence until I can connect with a properly entangled particle that I can follow back into the universe. Usually, I use something called entangled virtual particles; they're more common but harder to detect."

Stralasi's animated brow said it all; he didn't need to utter a word.

"Okay, imagine you are trying to cross a deep chasm from one mountain crag to another. Large rocks are falling from the sky between the two peaks. If you were fast enough, you could leap from the top of one rock to another and make your way across the chasm, like a stone skipped across the surface of body of water. If you make a single misstep, if you miss a rock or you don't land close enough to its center and it tips, you plunge to your death. If you stay on any rock for more than a millisecond as it falls past you, you'll end up too low and never make it back up to the peak."

"That sounds exceedingly difficult, even for an accomplished acrobat."

"Precisely," Darak said. Stralasi studied his face for some sign that he was joking. The man did have a dry sense of humor. Darak stared back at him patiently and, it would seem, sincerely.

"Now imagine you were doing this in darkness...well, not complete darkness. Light flashes, illuminating everything for the briefest instant, every couple of seconds. And, as if that weren't bad enough, the chasm is thick with smoke so everything you see is indistinct, just shades and shadows. You have to identify all the places you might jump to, measure the relative velocities, and make a plan, all in that one millisecond flash of light, and then execute your plan in darkness over the next two seconds. Can you imagine how terrifying and dangerous that would be? How much sheer computational power you'd need not to make a misstep? That, my friend, is the only way to travel sizeable distances independently of the entangled starsteps."

"That's insane. You'd have to be crazy to try that!"

"Not really, but it does require some practice."

"And *that's* how you traveled to the ends of the universe?"

Darak laughed. "I've only been to one end so far, and that was quite enough but, yes, that's the basic idea."

Stralasi shuddered. "What was so compelling about visiting even one end of the universe, that you would take such a risk?"

"I had to know what it was like."

Stralasi waited for him to elaborate. Darak watched the flames without further comment until the Brother couldn't bare it any longer.

"And what was it like?" he prodded.

Darak started at the sound of Stralasi's voice. When he replied, his hollow, haunted voice was unnerving.

"The closer you get to the edge of the universe, the more it resembles the time shortly after the Big Bang. It's intensely hot; there's enormous energy being released as matter condenses from the Chaos. If you pass through the transitional zone and into the infinite region beyond—into the Chaos itself—you will find a region that, so far, has been unregulated by the laws of nature as we know them."

"How can you know it's infinite?"

"I guess I can't, not really. It fits the theory. At any rate, it's immensely larger than the real universe. We've been expanding into it at a velocity beyond the speed of light for billions if not trillions of years. It's possible that some domains within the Chaos may have evolved combinations of natural laws different from our own, and that they're expanding from their own origin outward, like our universe has been doing.

"I wonder if there might be multiple, unconnected universes out there, surrounded by vast domains of Chaos. It's hard to say, though I've always liked the singular real universe hypothesis, myself.

"I've never visited another universe, other than those I've created myself. If the matter of another universe doesn't interact with the matter of this universe, it's impossible to detect. I'd have to imagine the correct, consistent set of physical laws before I could even design a way to sense it."

"What was it like, being in the Chaos?"

Darak reflected for some time before answering. "I don't have the words to adequately express it. The fabric itself eats away at you, trying to pull your matter out of existence. It doesn't look like anything. It's infinite, empty blackness. There's no light, no sound, no matter, no energy. In the Chaos, matter is an abomination, struggling to remain an integral whole against random forces that want to tear it apart."

"How could you possibly survive that?" Stralasi accepted Darak's other God-like powers, but this pushed the limits of credibility. Then again, which of the many incredible experiences hadn't, since first meeting the man?

"I know it sounds like an impossible place, but it does exist, after a fashion, and it can be survived. You just need to generate a field that compels the nearby bits of Chaos to cooperate with your own matter. It's exceedingly difficult and requires enormous computational power but it can be done. Luckily, I'd designed that into my body before I arrived there.

Otherwise, I never would have endured it.

"When I first entered the Chaos, I retreated bit by bit from the way it tore at my essence. The pain was tremendous. Unimaginable. My limbs dissolved and all the heat was pulled out of me. As I became less and less, I eventually gave myself over to it. I gave up wanting to survive. I hoped it would destroy me and I could be done with living."

Darak tried to continue but the choked sound that came out frightened Brother Stralasi.

He cleared his throat and started again. "I guess I was too much a coward at the end," Darak admitted. "I discovered I didn't want to die quite yet. I made my own small universe in the Chaos where nothing existed except my mind and the substrate on which it ran. I pulled energy from the expansion of my own tiny universe into the Chaos. I lived there a long time, alone with my thoughts. Using my imagination, I could make any kind of world I wanted and populate it with any kind of people I desired. I played in my universe a long time."

"How long?"

"I don't really know. Time was different for me there. In this universe where we are now, I think some tens of millions of years might have passed."

"Why did you leave? It sounds like you'd achieved sublime perfection in the middle of all that Chaos."

"Indeed. It is remarkably similar to the kind of perfection Alum would like to build for Himself. But mine was isolated, unique to me. Alum's heaven would incorporate this universe, in fact, all *possible* universes. In the end, it wasn't my kind of perfection. It was too self-indulgent. During much of my time there, I wasn't sure whether I was actually alive. My thoughts flowed so slowly it was hard to know whether I existed or not until, one day, I noticed something *felt* different."

"How do you mean?"

"The Chaos is infinite in size and outside this universe, but I wasn't totally cut off from our reality. I wasn't far removed from this cosmos; there was always a presence, a little pressure from the real universe as it expanded into the Chaos. It's a strange sensation, hard to describe. It's not like the wind or a flowing river. More like...a push toward orderliness coming from one side. Anyway, when I felt the pressure subside, I moved toward it to explore the cause."

"What did you find?"

Darak hesitated. "Our universe, this universe, had stopped expanding."

"Isn't it big enough already?"

"You don't understand. The formation of new matter at the edge of the universe stopped. The edge still retained the heat of creation, but without new reality being formed out of the Chaos, it was cooling rapidly and beginning to recede from the Chaos. Later, I learned this was Alum's doing. He had initiated His Divine Plan."

"What do you mean, His Divine Plan?"

"His first step was to stop the universe from expanding. The second was to reverse the expansion, to let pandemonium flood back in and return Reality to Chaos. You don't need to worry about the third step because everything will be gone by then, leaving nothing more than the Chaos awaiting whatever configuration Alum wishes to shape it into."

"So you came back?"

"I came back."

"How did you get back?"

"I had a single entangled neutron with me, which I'd preserved deep inside my substrate. That was my guide out, my safety harness in case I decided to return. I followed the signal to its mate and came back to this reality."

"You had a way to get out, all along, and you chose to go through that terrible experience?" Stralasi asked.

"Yes, it was only pain. What I gained from my time there was worth the pain at the beginning."

"And now you wish to deprive Alum of the opportunity to build his own perfect universe?"

"No, Alum is free to venture into the Chaos as I did and create whatever He wishes for himself. I realized that I value this messy, unpredictable universe too much to allow Him to destroy it simply to fulfill His own dreams. He can go, but He can't take everyone and everything with Him."

"Are you sure you'll be able to stop Him? After all, He is the Living God."

Darak Legsu stood up and glared into the fire, pressing newly-clenched hands to his side, but he didn't utter a word.

Stralasi became aware of the wind rustling the leaves overhead, and frogs croaking in a nearby pond and he trembled, wondering what was going through the mind of this strange and powerful being.

Darak gradually unclenched his fists, and made a concerted effort to relax his body and regulate his breathing. "You need some sleep," he said, "and I need to visit the Cybrid workshops." He looked back at the camp fire, and the flames diminished to a gentle glow.

The weight of the day and the conversation settled heavily on Brother Stralasi. "Yes, I guess I am tired." That was an understatement. He felt completely wrung out, mentally and physically. Even more, he had no desire to be on the receiving end of Darak's displeasure just now.

The monk stood, stretched, and yawned loudly.

"Though I'm only a passenger on your journey, I do find the rapid changes exhausting. Thank you for your story. I appreciate that you trusted me with it."

He bowed, and took refuge in his tent, leaving Darak to attend to his mysterious business with the Cybrids.

The man/god shook his head and chuckled softly at the monk's gracious exit. He wished a good night to Stralasi's retreating back and, in the blink of an eye, was gone.

7

GREG WATCHED THROUGH THE EXPANSIVE VIEWING WINDOW into the lab as the Vancouver PD forensics team went about its business. Dave, the night guard, lay dead a few meters inside the door. *That's too bad. I liked Dave.*

Mesmerized by the pool of blood and the rivulet that had snaked its way to the floor drain, Greg hardly noticed the coroner's assistant draping the body with a sterile cover.

It wasn't clear what had happened. Greg was pretty sure it had something to do with the one-inch gray sphere hovering chest-height near the door. Someone had cordoned off a generous space around it with a half dozen orange safety-cones and some bright yellow "CAUTION" tape. The technicians and detectives going in and out of the lab all stayed well clear of the buffer zone.

"Are you alright, Dr. Mahajani?" Dr. Wong's gentle voice broke Greg's reverie. Despite the hour, Campus Security had asked the Chairman of the Physics Department to meet them at the lab.

"Yeah, just surprised. It's not every day one of your experiments kills someone."

Dr. Wong looked into the lab. "Now, let's not jump to conclusions. We don't know this has anything to do with the work you and Dr. Leigh were doing."

Greg tapped the air in the direction of the gray sphere. "Well, you tell me where else *that* came from and maybe I'll agree with you."

Dr. Wong pushed past Greg to take a closer look.

"I'd be careful, if I were you," Greg warned. "Judging by poor Dave over there, and by the way everyone's avoiding it, I'd say the thing is dangerous."

Dr. Wong walked up to the doorframe. "Excuse me, who's in charge here?"

A thirty-something man with a rumpled suit and knitted brows released the corner of the sheet he'd been peering under and stood up without a word. He made his way past the hovering sphere and ushered Dr. Wong back into the hallway. "I'm Detective Lowry. Who are you?"

The physicist made no secret of sizing up the detective. "I'm Dr. William Wong, head of the Physics department. Can you tell me what's going on here?"

"Normally, I'd say the man was shot. He has what looks like a large bullet hole through the chest. But I'm pretty sure that thing over there," he gestured toward the floating orb, "caused it. The hole in the man's chest is exactly the same size, and too clean for a bullet."

"It's not *exactly* the same size," interjected Greg. The detective glared at Greg...but closed his mouth before uttering what came to mind. He didn't need another reprimand for alienating witnesses.

"I have a theory. If you'll allow me to take a closer look at the body, I think I can explain what happened. I promise I won't touch a thing." He extended his hand, "Sorry. Greg Mahajani. I'm on the research team in this lab."

Detective Lowry eyed him suspiciously, dismissing Greg's extended hand.

"Listen," Greg rushed on, "I can't say exactly what happened, but I have as much expertise as anyone on what that might be." He pointed to the gray sphere. "If you just let me have a quick look at the wound, I'll be able to confirm my idea."

Lowry stared stone-faced at Greg, evaluating the offer of help against his professional judgment. He shrugged, and called into the lab, "Doc? You done in there? Okay with you if the Professor takes a look? He thinks he might know what that thing is."

The medical examiner looked up from his tablet. "So long as he doesn't touch anything, sure. We've got everything we need."

The detective handed Greg a pair of latex gloves. "I'm only going to tell you once: touch the body or anything near it and I promote you to the top of my suspects list. You don't want to be there."

Greg gulped and pulled on the gloves, intentionally snapping the wrists against his tender skin. *This is not how I imagined returning to the lab. Not what Dave was expecting, either, I guess. Okay, Greg. Get a grip. Take a quick look and see if you're right.* He hoped he was wrong. *Please let it be a bullet hole*—it was a terrible thing to wish, but he stood by it. The alternative explanation was much, much worse.

Lowry gave him a nod and pointed his chin toward the body.

Greg moved into position to take a closer look, and the ME peeled back the sheet.

The exit wound on the man's back was perfectly circular, with precise, clean edges. Greg swallowed back his rising nausea, and focused intently on the hole, not the blood-soaked tile floor, and not the corpse of the man who used to greet him on his way in and out of the building on those all-nighters. "Can you turn him over?"

The ME glanced back at the detective, who sighed but nodded. He motioned for an assistant to help turn the body. Greg examined the chest wound as quickly as he could. "The entry hole is three millimeters smaller than the exit hole."

The detective placed both hands on his hips and regarded the scientist more intently. "You got that from a look?"

The assistant measured the holes in the chest and back. The edges were clean and smooth. "He's right."

"Dr. Mahajani has exceptional eyesight," Dr. Wong offered, helpfully proposing a plausible rationale.

Greg stood up, a little woozy, and resumed breathing. "Just one more thing, to be sure," he said. He retrieved a plastic ruler from the drawer, and walked up to the hovering sphere. He extended the ruler gingerly forward. While everyone watched, the first few inches of the ruler disappeared into the gray ball. The ball didn't budge, and there was no sign of the ruler on the other side of it.

Greg retrieved the ruler. It was cleanly missing the part that he'd pushed into the sphere.

"What the...?" The detective squinted and leaned in. "Did that thing burn a hole right through him?"

"Not exactly," replied Greg. "It's not hot."

"How can you tell that?"

"Its color doesn't match the spectrum of something hot enough to burn flesh. Plus, the wound's not cauterized and the ruler's not melted."

"Then how was this man murdered," Lowry asked.

"Murdered? No, this isn't a murder," Dr. Wong corrected the detective. "This was *clearly* an accident."

The detective turned back to Wong, unable to hide his skepticism. "And exactly how do you figure that?"

Greg saved Dr. Wong from having to explain. "The lab's been closed for the last ten days. Kathy, uh...Dr. Liang and I have been pretty stressed. As I'm sure you've heard, two of our colleagues vanished last month. Once word got out, it was impossible to get any work done around here. We decided to work from home.

"I'm sure that thing wasn't here when Kathy and I locked up the lab. If it was, it was too small to see and, thankfully, we didn't come into contact with it.

"There were only four of us working on the project: me, Kathy, Darian, and Larry. Darian and Larry are missing, and now there's this. Even though I'm not entirely sure what *this* is, it's almost certainly the result of one of our experiments. I suspect it showed up around the time Darian disappeared, and that it's been growing ever since."

"And how does that make it an accident?"

"My guess is, the night guard was conducting a routine lab check and walked into the sphere. Our work involved altering the basic laws of physical matter. From what I know of the theory, I'd say Darian somehow created a microscopic universe, a microverse, too small for the human eye to see. I know that sounds crazy but, if I'm right, that thing could be consuming anything it comes into contact with, absorbing matter from our universe and converting it into its own. Sort of like a mini black hole.

"Dave probably didn't even see it when he entered the lab. It would have passed right through him or, more accurately, he would have passed over it. If he felt anything at all, he might have thought he was having a heart attack. It's too bad he didn't just bump into it with his elbow or something, he'd still be alive. But it wasn't anything intentional, detective, just a bizarre but completely unintended incident, detective. Like Dr. Wong said, an accident."

"You seem to know an awful lot about it all," accused the detective.

Dr. Wong was gaping at Greg, "Do you mean to say it worked? Dr. Leigh's theories were right?"

Greg ignored him; the Chair could draw his own conclusions. He addressed the detective. "This microverse, if that's what it is, has to be a product of Darian Leigh's work. It has to be. My conclusions are based on observation and logic for now. I have no real evidence. But, trust me, nobody else, nobody, has ever created a microverse. This is huge.

"We can confirm it for you. We just need to run some tests. With Darian still missing, nobody in the world knows more about this subject than Dr. Liang and I do." *Compared to Darian, we know practically nothing*—he said to himself—*but I'm not going to let them take this away without a fight.*

The detective looked doubtful. Before he could object, Greg jumped in, "We're lucky. This is the only lab in the world that has the ability to analyze the sphere. Besides, until we know more about it, I don't think you want to try moving it."

The detective motioned to the corpse. "Doesn't look like it was so lucky for him."

Greg looked down, embarrassed. "No, it wasn't." He contemplated the sphere without comment. The gentle hum of the wall clock was the only sound.

The detective's phone rang, and Greg took advantage of the distraction to speak privately with the department head.

"Sir, if I'm right about this, we may have a much bigger problem on our hands than one dead guard."

"How's that?"

"Let's assume this *is* a microverse, and it's absorbing and growing from anything that comes into contact with it. I'm wondering, if we can't find some way to contain it, what's to stop it from getting bigger. A *lot* bigger."

Dr. Wong studied Greg, reading into the unspoken conclusion. He tried to maintain his composure but his voice cracked as he asked, "How big?"

"Big enough to threaten everything and everyone; I'm talking...the whole world."

The color drained from Dr. Wong's face. "Are you saying that it could eat the whole planet?"

Greg nodded grimly. "Yeah, I'm pretty sure. Even more."

8

TIMOTHY WANDERED THE STREETS of twenty-first century virtual Manhattan, bewildered by the mysteries of a modern world. As much as he struggled to understand the gigantic buildings, flow of automobiles and pedestrians, and workings of daily life, his internal struggles were greater still.

His autonomy mystified him. He knew inworld Partials were not programmed for self-awareness. He had no idea how or why he knew that. In DonTon, everything he needed was supplied by his basic code: when to serve the meals, how to present each dish, how to respond to the playful chatter around the table, and how to switch into REST mode between meals.

Here, he hardly recognized anything beyond the obvious. People spoke into tiny boxes they held to their ears as they rushed along the city's pedestrian ways. They sat at tables in cafes and restaurants intensely pecking away at their tiny boxes with their thumbs. Sometimes the boxes were a little larger and the people stared at the vertical part while their fingers danced over the other part laying flat on the table.

Colored light assemblies hung above the crossroads and shone from poles at the edge of footpaths along the roadside. He discerned easily that the lights were controlling the flow of vehicles and pedestrians, that much was obvious, but he was missing some nuance because a good many cars and people frequently ignored the lights, causing blaring horns and angry yells. Perhaps the offenders were as new to this strange city as he was.

He couldn't make any better sense of himself, of his own strange thoughts. They perplexed him, these unbidden, random, reeling conceptualizations not supplied by his normal subroutines. Surprising opinions bubbled up in his consciousness, shocking him with their unaccustomed passion. *She's beautiful! That car stinks. What a hideous edifice. There's no need to honk your horn continuously; nobody is moving for blocks.* Hundreds of thoughts.

He couldn't remember thinking for himself, not once, before his recent experience at DonTon. He was sure no personal opinion about anything had occurred to him in all his long existence. He had no idea where the current opinions were coming from or even *how* he recognized them as opinions. The experience of thinking, the act of mentation itself, astounded him.

He walked the streets of New York, amazed by the bustle of activity and the throngs that pushed and shoved him as he bumbled along the sidewalks. Many took note of his fancy attire. Tails and white bow tie, worn outside during the day, were notable.

He worked his way north along Broadway, out of the Wall Street Financial District, toward the luxurious shops of Park Ave. Dusk was settling and he felt an odd discomfort. His stomach gurgled and grumbled in brief spasms of unfamiliar pain. He didn't know what it meant, but he didn't like it.

He walked past places where people were enjoying meals on outdoor terraces—poorly prepared and abysmally served, by his reckoning—and the grumbling in his stomach grew more insistent. He was intimately familiar with the idea of eating. He'd watched the Chattingbarons and their many guests do it for hundreds of millennia since DonTon was first initiated by one of the Family's esteemed ancestors.

Surely, that was always done just for pleasure. None of the Chattingbarons, their guests, servants, or any of the town folk were ever the least bit inconvenienced at missing a meal for some more important event. Yet, Timothy felt there had to be some sort of relationship between the uncomfortable feeling in his stomach and the act of putting food in his mouth.

He paid a little more attention to how people were managing to procure something to eat at the establishments he passed. A number of people got out of an especially long vehicle in front of a tall building down one of the side streets. The driver assisted them from the automobile and took luggage from a compartment in the rear.

Ah, travelers!—Timothy thought. *Perhaps that's an inn.* Inns had places to eat and were kind to those who were far from home. If anyone could have been said to fit that bill, it was him.

He turned down the side street and approached the glass doors of the hotel. The doors parted as though pulled by invisible doormen. The actual doormen paid little attention to him, acknowledging him with a casual salute. He nodded in return. The hotel lobby was nicely appointed, clean, modern, and lavish by roadside tavern standards but nothing like Casa

DonTon.

The smell of food drew him to one side of the lobby. He entered the large eating area and approached the head butler positioned inside.

Timothy had observed Lord Chattingbaron order a meal at similar establishments in London. Though this city was as foreign as its technology, ordering a meal seemed fairly straight forward.

"How is the veal tonight, my good man?" he asked in what he hoped was a loud and confident voice, the voice of one accustomed to having their inquiries answered.

The head butler regarded him with unmistakeable insouciance and replied with a slight French accent. "As always, our chef provides zee 'ighest *qualitée* meal one can find een any 'otel een New York, *monsieur*. Will *monsieur* be dining alone zees evening?"

"Yes, of course. Please show me to a table." Timothy hoped his brusque tone would be interpreted as commanding. The host barely raised an eyebrow before guiding him to a small table. Fortunately, the table was nicely situated away from the other guests, near the kitchen door, where Timothy felt more comfortable.

A waiter arrived and presented Timothy with an elaborately scribed menu. None of the fare was familiar. He recognized the names of some of the offerings and ingredients, but they were put together in what appeared to be rather dubious combinations.

He motioned the waiter over. "Look here," he said, trying to sound both kindly and authoritative at the same time. "Perhaps I could prevail upon the chef to prepare something for a simpler palate."

"Perhaps you would like the Pad Thai or the Hamburger with Blue Cheese Aioli and Zucchini sticks, sir?"

Timothy had no idea what those were but he didn't like the sound of them. "Maybe he has a steak and kidney pie, or a small piece of mutton? Or perhaps he could whip up some bangers and mash?"

The waiter was perplexed at how best to respond. His mouth made several failed attempts to form a reply. He settled on, "I shall ask Chef," and disappeared through the double swinging doors into the kitchen. Timothy caught bits of a vigorous exchange, which ended when Chef burst through the doors and into the eating area.

"I understand that nothing on the menu appeals to your palate this evening, sir." He towered over Timothy, hands stiffly at his side.

Timothy adopted the haughty sneer he'd seen on his Lordship's face when confronted with similar situations in DonTon Village. "I'm in the mood for something simple this evening, my good man. You *can* do something simple, can't you?"

"Perhaps you would be happier with something from one of the street stalls, sir," Chef suggested.

"If I had desired street fare, I would be eating on the street," replied Timothy.

He wasn't sure his approach was having the desired effect on the chef, who was becoming more irritated by the second. It wasn't easy to be a man adrift in an unfamiliar city. He was about to beg for traveler's pity from the man when he recalled how his Lordship dealt with upstart Partials in the Village. Yes, that always worked in desperate straits.

"Now see here, sir," he addressed Chef. "I am a traveler to this city. Surely, you know how to accommodate the wishes of travelers. Why don't return to your kitchen and prepare a nice meat pie for me? If that is beyond your skills, perhaps you might try some eggs, or a morsel of bread and cheese."

He raised his voice to catch the attention of the host at the front podium, and thereby embarrass Chef into compliance. "I am a traveler," he repeated. "Your establishment claims to cater to travelers. Therefore, sir, I insist you prepare a meal I might find palatable. Now go away and do so!"

Chef was apoplectic.

The Maître D' rushed over to do damage control. He was, as always, the icon of diplomatic service in expression and posture. "*Monsieur*, how can I be of service? What seems to be zee problem?" he cajoled.

"Your cook is incapable of preparing a meal according to simple requests," Timothy responded, electing to keep his voice at an embarrassingly high volume.

"Perhaps *monsieur* would be 'appier with room serveez," suggested the Maître D'.

Timothy could only guess at what room service might entail; he didn't like the sound of it. "My good man, I have not taken lodgings at this inn, nor do I intend to. And had I a room here, I assure you, I certainly would have no desire to partake of an evening meal therein."

The Chef and Maître D' exchanged exasperated glances. The guest's dress suggested money or upbringing. His rude and demanding behavior, however, did not lead one to believe him well bred. He must be a man of considerable first-generation financial means. It was odd that neither employee recognized him. It was their job to be familiar with important people around the city. The man was either newly arrived, newly rich, or an imposter.

"Eet ees, of course, our policy and our *plaisir* to ensure our guests' special needs are met, *monsieur*." The Maître D' was determined to deduce this person's status before subjecting poor Chef to any further humiliation. "Perhaps *monsieur* could provide one of hees credit cards and we would be 'appy to charge zee special meal to eet."

Timothy began to panic. Lord Chattingbaron's usual approach in dealing with such situations was not having the desired effect. Maybe politeness would be more effective. "Surely you can put it on my account. M'Lord will be happy to settle with you next time he is in your fair city."

The Maître D's face hardened. *Bingo!* He finally had the measure of this overdressed imposter. He bowed and gestured toward the entrance of the restaurant. "If *monsieur* would be so good as to accompany me, we shall see your desires are attended to *immédiatement*."

That's more like it—Timothy thought. He stood and accompanied the Maître D' to the entrance. *They must be moving me to a private dining room as befitting a gentleman. My many years of observing my Lordship have come in useful. I wasn't sure I could master the tone, but I seem to have convinced them.* He walked with a confident swagger, emulating his Lordship.

The Maître D' gestured to the two bellmen standing at ease near the entrance to join them. "Our...guest...seems to have confused us with one of the soup kitchens," the Maître D' explained to them, his French accent giving way to Mid-West American. "Perhaps you could point him in the right direction."

The glorified bouncers regarded the formal wear of the offender and eyed the Maître D' for assurance.

"Don't be fooled by his attire," the Maître D' said. "He has neither the wealth nor breeding it suggests."

The men took hold of Timothy's arms and escorted him, feeble protests notwithstanding, to the main entrance. As the door parted, they gave him an extra little shove for good measure.

"Get outta here, ya bum," scoffed the larger of the two, and returned to his post inside the main door.

Timothy stared, entirely dumbfounded. *What will I do now?*

The second bouncer walked up to Timothy and leaned in close. Timothy cowered. Reaching into his pocket, the man pulled out two ten-dollar bills and pushed them into Timothy's hand.

"Listen," he said. "I was in your shoes once, a long time ago." He stood back and admired the Footman's outfit. "Well, maybe not in those shoes," he laughed. "There's free food at the soup kitchen two blocks up." He pointed toward the trees of Central Park, barely visible a few blocks away. "You won't be able to miss it. There should be a long line of scruffy men outside. If you hurry, they may even have a bed for you tonight."

"Thank you, sir. That is most kind," replied Timothy. "As you can see, I am far from home in this strange city."

"Yeah, no kidding. Well, take care. It's a rough world out there." The bouncer returned to his post, shaking his head the whole way.

Timothy hastened toward the soup kitchen, already salivating at the thought of a meal. He didn't know it could hurt so much to go without food for such a short time. Had someone back in DonTon told him this, and had he been self-aware at the time, he wouldn't have believed it.

The line of men waiting for a free meal was exactly as described. He reached into his pocket and rubbed the two bills for comfort. Even if the meal were free, lodging might have a fee. Timothy boldly joined the line.

The arrival of a well-groomed man dressed in a tuxedo and white tie drew curious glances from the queue. Few appraisals were favorable. A couple of men moved in uncomfortably close behind him. They whispered and guffawed among themselves, growing louder by the minute.

A tall, emaciated man in a filthy, ragged suit a few positions back couldn't resist an easy target. "Hey man, nice duds. You know, I don't think they serve Lobster Thermidor in there." This elicited uproarious laughter from his companions.

Timothy did his best not to react. He had learned that Lord Chattingbaron's haughty approach was not much appreciated in this city.

"You never know. Maybe they hired a chef from the Hilton," said the man behind him. Fresh laughter erupted.

Encouraged, the stranger poked Timothy's shoulder hard enough to sway him off balance.

Timothy faced his heckler. "Now see here, my good fellow," he began.

"See 'eah moy good feh-lah," the man exaggerated, making fun of Timothy's accent. His friends burst out laughing.

Timothy grew angrier. He gripped the man's worn lapels. "Listen," he seethed, and lowered his voice to an ominous level, ready to deliver a serious tongue lashing.

The dangerous glint in his adversary's eyes ended Timothy's tirade before it started. He released the man's jacket and took a step back.

"Hey!" objected the next man in line when Timothy bumped into him. The Footman turned to apologize. A hand on his shoulder whipped him back around to face the belligerent group behind him.

"With a fancy suit like that, you oughta have plenty of dough on you," deduced the group's de facto leader. He placed a hand on Timothy's shoulder in false camaraderie and pulled the footman toward him. "Why don't you share with your new buddies?" The others nodded eagerly.

"Well, I couldn't. I mean, I need... I mean, I don't have anything," spluttered Timothy.

"Now, that can't be right," said the man, an ugly look rising on his face. "Gentlemen," he addressed his followers. "I do believe this fellow is lying to us."

"Oh, that's not good," said one of his compatriots.

"No. No, that's not good," echoed two men behind.

The man pulled Timothy closer to his side and rested the full weight of his arm over the footman's shoulders. He softened his voice to a confidential tone. "If you just spare a bit of your wealth, we'll leave you alone. No harm done." He spat sideways onto the street.

Frightened, Timothy extracted the two tens from his pocket and held them out for all to see. "I am a fair man," he began. "This is all I have. I would be happy to share one of these bills with you. I'm afraid I must insist on keeping the other."

The group roared at Timothy's earnest response, and the man tightened his grip to a headlock as he snatched the two bills. "I think we'll just take both of these and thank you for your donation, Gov'na," he added, with the same sneering accent he used before.

"Give those back," said Timothy. He reached for the man's hand. The ruffian yanked hard on Timothy's far shoulder, twirling him backward.

The footman regained his balance and charged angrily at the thief, intending to teach him a good lesson about stealing from an Englishman, even a servant.

His tackle drove the hooligan back into his followers. That was the best shot he'd land. A small group gathered around him, punching and kicking.

Timothy dropped to the cement and protected his face and abdomen, while the men beat him. He'd never experienced such pain.

Seconds later, he lay nearly unconscious, bruised, and bleeding on the sidewalk. He didn't hear the police whistle that broke up the gang and saved him from certain death.

The officers took him to a hospital and let the doctors administer to his lacerations before questioning him. Luckily, the beating had been interrupted before any significant internal damage was done. The police accepted his story that his identification was stolen by his assailants. *Another lie.* The hospital treated him efficiently, without charge, and let him back onto the streets with an admonition to be more careful and to report to the British Embassy as soon as possible.

He passed a few more days stumbling around New York, watching for better methods to acquire food. He stole what he could from street vendors and shops with outdoor displays.

Other indigents sometimes held out a plastic cup or a cap into which passersby would drop coins. Cash was important in this city, and begging was viewed by the police as preferable to theft. He found an empty Styrofoam cup laying in the street, and set up a few blocks from something called United Nations Headquarters.

For weeks, he survived on spare change from wealthy strangers, and food from the nearby street carts. His clothes became worn and dirty. His beard and hair grew long and unkempt. Every few days he would accumulate enough spare change to access a room and shower in one of the cities shelters.

It was in this thin, disheveled, and impoverished state, hunkered over a cup of coins and slowly losing his brand new mind, that Darya first noticed him.

9

GREG AND KATHY WERE STUMPED. Once the police let them back into their lab, they spent four weeks testing, probing, and prodding the mysterious gray sphere. They were no closer to understanding it than when they'd started. The orb was not giving up its secrets.

They threw all sorts of matter and energy at it: light, sound, electrons, and, one evening after a little too much wine and exasperation, an overripe banana.

The sphere absorbed everything equally, resisting nothing. As far as they could detect, it emitted nothing beside a trace of Hawking-type radiation, which manifested as a dull light lending the sphere's its muted color. It grew in proportion with the mass of everything they fed it, and with everything being absorbed incidentally.

One fitful night, just before dawn, Kathy woke with a startling realization. "Oh, my God. Greg, we have to stop the experiments on the microverse. Immediately."

"What? Why? Just because we're not getting anywhere...."

"No, I just realized we've been 'feeding' it. The bigger it gets, the more surface area it has, the harder it becomes to contain, and the more danger it poses."

They halted their experiments abruptly, erected a plexiglass box around the sphere and had a construction crew move the entrance of the lab to prevent any accidental encounters. Any *more* accidental encounters.

The following Tuesday, the light was just right and Kathy noticed a few twinkling dust particles gently drifting toward the sphere inside its box. *Strange. There shouldn't be any moving air in there.* Curious, she set up some investigations with canned smoke and traced the air flow around and toward the sphere.

"Uhh...Greg? You'd better look at this."

He poked his head out of the office. "Can it wait? I'm...." His eyes instinctively tracked the wisps of smoke wafting toward the sphere. "Oh, crap!" Greg muttered, slapping the heel of his hand against his forehead.

"Of course! What was I thinking? Even if we don't feed it, the microverse is consuming the air it contacts. Man, how could I miss that?" He let fly a stream of colorful cusses describing his poor observational skills, lack of theoretical rigor, general stupidity, overall incompetence, and a host of other transgressions.

Kathy had to stop him before he plummeted into self pity. "Wow, don't be so hard on yourself. We *both* missed it. You've gotta cut yourself, both of us, some slack. It was an easy oversight. We're exhausted. Our minds are still dealing with the tangled-up mess of Darian's data dump. It amazes me we can still string two thoughts together."

Greg waved her away. "It was a critical mistake. We can't afford to make any more. It doesn't matter that we're stressed and exhausted. We have to be a whole lot more careful."

Despite his years of advanced education and lab experience, despite the intellectual and technical advantages of his growing dendy lattice, he'd never felt so lost or hopeless. *What on Earth did you create here, Darian? What are we missing? Surely, you didn't make something this deadly with no way to collapse it.*

If his nephew were here right now, he'd be saying something like, "Oh-oh! We're in some reeeeeally deep doodoo now, Uncle Greg." *Yeah, kiddo, we've got some monumental doodoo here, alright. Monumental.*

"I think it's time to suck it up and call in the big guns," he said.

They secured the lab, and shared their concerns with Dr. Wong, who talked to President Sakira, who activated a special emergency budget.

"If we can choke off the supply of new material to the sphere, including the air around it, we can buy some time to figure out a solution," Dr. Wong had proposed.

"Done," said President Sakira. She didn't need any convincing.

They cordoned off an extra-wide buffer zone around the sphere's plexiglass cage, and had the construction crew build a vacuum chamber the size of a walk-in closet around it. One end of the new chamber was going to jut into the hallway.

"Not a problem," Dr. Wong said. He instructed the crew to remove the original wall, and divert the hallway into the storage space beside the lab. That became their new entrance. It had the added benefit of partitioning the lab off from the rest of the wing and from casually prying eyes.

President Sakira resisted the scientists' urgings to alert the Prime Minister's Office in Seattle or call in the National Guard. "There's no point in panicking the government just yet. You said we can safely contain it in the chamber for quite a while, right? Before I make that call, I need you to focus on containment, risk assessment, and figuring out what the hell that thing is and how we can shut it down. If you scientists do your job, maybe we'll be able to avoid the call altogether.

"Dr. Wong, I trust you will support them in whatever they need to carry out their work, and keep me informed. I'll figure out how to spin the emergency budget expenditure so nobody asks too many questions.

"And not a word of this to anybody outside this room until we know what we're dealing with. I mean it."

Potential disaster averted for the time being, everybody got back to work.

* * *

DETECTIVE LOWRY WAS NOT HAPPY. What he'd hoped was a simple, straightforward shooting, turned out to be neither straightforward nor a shooting.

Was the guard's death a homicide or a science experiment gone horribly wrong? Maybe criminally-negligent wrong. He wasn't sure. Nobody, not even the two remaining scientists who worked here, understood the floating gray orb that killed the man. All he knew was that it was too soon to be back here on another case.

Only a few weeks earlier, he'd been poking around this same lab for fresh leads on two scientists who disappeared without a trace. Now, this.

The missing persons case was still open. There were no bodies, no sightings, no calls or notes. No activity on their phones, bank accounts, or credit cards. Nobody had received any kidnap demands, and no one was claiming responsibility. Anyone of interest had been interviewed multiple times and cleared. There were no fresh clues. That case was as bizarrely mystifying as this one.

The detective had had the dubious honor of meeting the famous Darian Leigh after some deranged lunatic tried to assassinate him during a public lecture downtown. That file was pretty much open and shut. They'd arrested the shooter on site, and the guy swore he'd been operating alone. The Chief had been pleased. Lowry wasn't convinced; he'd had a hunch there was more to it. Now, he was sure.

Come to think of it, I must have met Leigh's missing employee back then, too. Odd—aside from the photos we got in the missing persons file, I'm drawing a total blank on him.

*These two don't seem especially worried for their safety, considering the events unfolding around them—*Lowry noted. He'd grilled Greg and Kathy separately, at length, trying to poke holes in their stories.

They stuck to their stories, and insisted they knew nothing that could help the investigation. They had "no idea" where the deadly sphere came from or what it was. *Right...of course not.* But he couldn't trip them up on the details or tie any wrongdoing to them. Much as he didn't like it, he had to let them go.

"Don't leave town, either of you. If Dr. Leigh or Dr. Rusalov show up, we'll be going over your stories again."

Kathy and Greg had exchanged guilty glances.

I saw that—Lowry said to himself. *If I keep up the pressure, one of you is going to break. And I'll be waiting.*

* * *

KATHY AND GREG WERE AS MYSTIFIED BY THE SPHERE AS THE DETECTIVE. But, as scientists, they were also fascinated. They hadn't figured out how it fit with Darian's theories, but they were sure the orb had something to do with the RAF generator. That it materialized sometime between Darian's jubilant call and his disappearance less than an hour later was too much of a coincidence.

"Do you think it's some kind of black ops thing?" Greg speculated. "Maybe they've been watching our work and waiting to pounce once we got the thing to work? I know that sounds crazy, but think about it. Darian's earlier research was classified top secret and sealed. He was never allowed to publish it."

"A little crazy, but any crazier than the truth?" Kathy replied. "Honestly, I don't know, but I doubt it's that."

"Whatever the truth is. If we do tell them what we know and how we know it, that wouldn't make things any clearer for them, and it would likely land us in the hands of some secret government agency for an indefinite period of...'interrogation', if you know what I mean."

Kathy heard the scare quotes. *Could that be what happened to Darian and Larry? Had someone been monitoring the lab all along, waiting for them to prove the RAF worked? If so, maybe Darian wasn't dead, after all. Maybe they'd just picked him up, picked them both up, and Darian panicked. Maybe they're still alive.*

Deep down, she knew that wasn't the case, but she needed to cling to the hope. Apart from a few incoherent flashes of Darian's memories, they had nothing to link Larry's disappearance to Darian's. In the "memories", they saw glimpses of an argument or struggle that might have been between Darian and Larry, or it could have been the two of them against someone else. It wasn't clear.

And then there was Greg's crazy nightmare. They had no objective evidence the individuals in the dream were linked in the real world. Even if the subconscious association was clear, dreams were completely unreliable as evidence.

And Darian's last lattice call to them gave no hint of unusual strain between Larry and the rest of the team. The fact that the original RAF generator was also missing implied someone had taken it. Darian and Larry were the obvious suspects.

Not enough data—they'd decided together.

The enigmatic microverse hovered implacably. Greg was fairly certain it could be safely kept at its present size inside the vacuum chamber. "After all, besides the stuff we feed it, how else can it grow?" Neither dared to venture a guess.

The couple split their time between analyzing the gray microverse and finishing the new RAF generator. *If we can get the new RAF generator working, maybe we can use it to figure out where the orb came from and how to shut it down.*

Throwing themselves into their work eased the burden of processing the loss of their coworkers. The ongoing struggle to separate their own thought processes from the many fragments of Darian's mind was exhausting, all on its own.

They agreed to keep their lattices offline most of the time, even though working with so little dendy enhancement meant everything took ten times as long as it should.

Greg connected his lattice communications once, the day Kathy asked, "What if the generator is still here? What if it's just hidden nearby?"

He kicked himself for not thinking of that earlier. *It would explain why the microverse is locked to the one position.* He switched on his external comms and sent the INACTIVE command. Nothing happened, not even an acknowledging ping from the laptop. *It's nowhere nearby, and nowhere near a router or it would have answered*—he concluded. He switched off his comms before Darian's lurking thoughts could invade.

They continued testing the new RAF generator, using multiple layers of redundancy to catch any minute fluctuations of data, until finally the true test loomed before them. They moved the device inside the vacuum chamber. If it created another planet eater, there would be nothing there to feed its growth.

They aimed the antennae to a spot half a meter to the left of the gray sphere, stood back, and reviewed their preparations.

"Well, there's no reason to put it off any longer," Greg announced. Exhausted but excited, he loaded their simplest configuration file, and switched the generator to ACTIVE.

A small, blue sphere appeared beside the gray one, exactly where they'd predicted.

Kathy exhaled one long, slow breath. "It really *does* work," she whispered.

Staring at the hovering microverse, Greg found the experience odd anticlimactic. *I should be elated. This is the greatest scientific discovery ever. This validates Darian's theory of the virtual particle chaos and the natural evolution of the universe. We've unlocked the deepest mystery of all: how anything exists.*

But I feel like I've seen this before. Or at least part of me has. Darian's memories of seeing his first microverse mingled uncomfortably with Greg's perception of this new bubble, making the invention seem more like a confirmation of an earlier experiment than a new discovery.

He shook his head, refocusing on the work at hand. "Let's try feeding this thing and see if we just ended up with a *different* kind of matter-absorbing sphere."

They spent an hour trying to push all kinds of matter into the new blue sphere. Everything passed through the sphere untouched. It took nothing from this universe and became no bigger during their testing. To be sure, they fed a steel ball bearing into the neighboring sphere. It absorbed the matter and grew as predicted. They breathed a collective sigh of relief. The two microverses were fundamentally different.

"Let's do the interferometer measurements and get some parameters on this microverse. Then we can ramp up to some of the more complex configurations."

They spent the next couple of days making and measuring temporary microverses whose physical properties differed in increasingly more complex ways from the normal—their own—universe.

Greg grew irritable and impatient carrying out the methodical paradigm he and Darian had set up some months before. "You know, Kath, we may be pushing the boundaries of scientific knowledge with this, but we haven't really learned anything new about the...the Eater." It was the first time he'd used the name.

"I know," replied Kathy. "All the microverses we've made collapsed the instant we turned off the RAF generator. If we can't figure out how to make a stable one, how can we figure out how to collapse it?"

They pored over RAF theory until their brains ached. They slept in fitful shifts, watching over one another so the other could remain alert to fragment-induced episodes. Over several days, they developed a few reasonable hypotheses. None stood up to experimentation.

They were stymied. There was no one to turn to; their mentor was gone. By default, they were the leading world experts in the field and, thanks to their dendy lattices, they were exponentially more knowledgeable and faster at intellectual processing than anyone in the world. They felt alone, confused, and scared.

Through trial and error, they found that working in thirty-minute bursts minimized the interference from Darian's memory fragments, while allowing enough concentrated effort to make progress. Either that or

Darian's memories about the RAF were integrating with their own thought processes. So long as they kept their attention limited to that specific area of work, they could avoid stimulating too many painful and confusing intrusions.

"We need to try altering the Eater directly," Greg announced at the end of one particularly long stint with the equations.

"Don't you think it's too risky to impose a different RAF on it?" For the past week, neither of them had looked inside the darkened isolation chamber.

"More dangerous than doing nothing? Look, we have no good hypotheses about the Eater. It's so different from the microverses we've been working with that I'm not sure they're related at all. Our current RAF theory doesn't cover it. We don't know if it's going to remain stable inside the vacuum chamber or if it's going to spontaneously grow to the size of the galaxy sometime in the next second. After all this time, we still have absolutely no idea what we're dealing with."

"Nothing indicates an unpredictable growth rate."

"Not yet. We *think* we understand why and how it absorbs everything that comes into contact with its surface but do we really? What if our ideas are completely wrong and its growth is not smooth, not linear, and not equivalent to mass absorbed?"

"You don't really believe that's possible."

"No, I don't. But who knows? My point is, we understand so little. We need more data, and the data we're getting from the RAF microverses doesn't resemble anything we know about the Eater."

Kathy paced the lab, modeling the RAF equations in her head for potentially explosive interactions between multiple fields. There was too much uncertainty to draw a reasoned conclusion. Her nervous pacing took her to the corner of the lab abutting the containment closet. She slid the blackout blind to one side and turned on the viewing light. She peered into the chamber at the Eater, seeking inspiration.

"Greg? Have you been feeding this thing?"

"No, are you nuts? Of course not. Not for days. Why?" He rushed over and looked into the chamber. The Eater was definitely bigger than the last time he'd seen it. Only slightly bigger, but enough it was noticeable to the naked eye. That wasn't a good sign. "Maybe we have a vacuum leak. What's the pressure in there?"

Kathy checked the readout. "It's holding steady at 10^{-17} torr, practically a perfect vacuum."

"Then where is it getting raw material from?"

A terrifying suspicion poked at Kathy's mind, inspired by one of Darian's memories. "Just a second," she said, diving into the equations to examine her hypothesis. In less than a minute, she shared her thoughts and a corresponding model with Greg.

"Tell me I'm wrong," she pleaded. "Tell me I've overlooked something."

"Oh, crap," he replied. He looked ill. "We have to go see Dr. Wong. This is way above our pay grade."

10

LORD MIKA FLOATED IN SPACE, sunning himself in the light of the nearest star, a piercingly bright point over a billion kilometers away. With no requirement to dissipate heat from the distant sun, his mercurial skin flowed slowly. He splayed his wings gently behind him, gathering the feeble solar rays that refilled his ultracapacitors and batteries.

Energy-wise, pushing matter around the universe the way Cybrids did was a costly proposition. *They* relied on powerful matter-antimatter drives to build up thrust. Angels circumvented the need for MAM drives by using built-in RAF generators to pull themselves out of the universe and shift "through" it in tiny but almost instantaneous increments. They could travel by independent means to nearby planets within a reasonable number of hours to days, and between stars in weeks. For larger distances, they relied on Alum's starstep network.

Shifting drew minimal energy; Angels needed only enough power for the required computational resources and the specialized shifting mechanism.

Much of an Angel's central processing unit was dedicated to navigation and shifting. Identifying entangled pairs of particles and calculating short jumps left little room for other intellectual pursuits. The remaining computational resources were dedicated mostly to battle tactics. Angels were not known for their general wit.

Mika overlaid the positions of local Cybrid stations and human colonies on his visual field. Preparations to trap the unidentified adversary were going well.

Something had been triggering Alum's detectors in an erratic pattern all across the Rafael galaxy. Only a single detector was ever tripped at any one time. No similar incursions were reported in other regions. Alum ruled out a large invasion into the Realm. The intruder could only be an individual or a small, tight-knit group.

Alum identified the star systems through which the intruder would most likely pass. He increased the network of detectors within those systems and monitored the data vigilantly. For weeks, he mapped the advance of the stealthy target.

He assigned Lord Mika to investigate and protect the Realm. Settling on a few hundred of the most probable destinations, Mika sent out a Wing of Angels, ten thousand strong, to establish a local shifting network.

They placed pairs of entangled particles across the target solar systems, ready to use wherever and whenever Alum chose to confront the interloper. The plan was straightforward. Until signaled, the Angels would remain dispersed and clear of the designated zones. The instant Alum detected the intruder, He would send a signal.

Angels would instantly shift from the stars where they'd been waiting into the target solar system. They would surround the enemy and activate their quantum decoherence field generators—shift blockers—trapping the adversary within a loose but impenetrable net. They would shrink the net until they either captured or destroyed the quarry. The only way to escape the net was by conventional rocket, and Angels could easily overtake that form of transportation. It was a tactic they'd successfully employed in the Aelu Wars over twenty million years ago, and it was still the most effective approach.

The Angels would have milliseconds, at most, to spring their trap. Alum pre-programmed their standard responses to minimize any delays due to hesitation, processing, or lag time, no matter how small. His Angels would be alerted, shifted into position, and placed in "trap and pursue" mode before they were consciously aware the plan had been activated.

The half-dozen practice runs they'd conducted were a testament to the precision Alum expected of the Angelic entities He'd created to battle in His name.

On one level, Lord Mika hoped the intruder was that same arrogant false Shard, Darak Legsu, whom he'd encountered on Gargus 718.5. Alum had hinted that was a possibility. *You may have escaped me once, Darak, but you will not leave this trap alive.*

At the same time, Mika hungered for more of a challenge—an Aelu habnar or bigger. *It's been so long since I've seen any real action.* "Shard" Darak had demonstrated interesting capabilities but Mika didn't imagine him being much of a challenge for a Wing of ten thousand Angels. In truth, that was sure to be an acutely unsatisfying case of overkill.

Nonetheless, the Wing Commander allowed himself a satisfied smile at the elegance of their deployment. They had honed their strategy and tactics in a challenging, multi-millennia war with a powerful enemy. They were experienced, well-rehearsed, and eager to be tested.

A little knot formed in the pit of the Angel's stomach. Recalling his overconfidence the last time he encountered Darak, Mika's smile pulled downward along one corner of his quicksilver mouth. He still burned with the shame of being fooled so easily. The half-frown transformed into a determined grimace. He would not be fooled this time.

11

"I DON'T BELIEVE THAT WOULD BE ETHICAL...OR LEGAL." Dr. Rasmussen, MD, PhD, did his best to remain calm and professional.

"Mm. Well, the definitions of legality can be rather fluid." Reverend Alan LaMontagne crossed his legs, leaned back in the immaculately clean visitor's chair, and rested his folded hands in his lap. He preferred a casual approach, leaving any threats to Jeff, his personal bodyguard and fixer.

Jeff stood at ease by the door, hands crossed behind his back. His muscular build was visible beneath a precisely tailored suit. The weapon everyone knew had to be there was indiscernible in its shoulder holster.

"Yes, I suppose but, frankly, I'm surprised that as Leader of the Church you would even think to pose such a question." The doctor's eyes flitted uncomfortably between the Reverend and Jeff.

"Your surprise is of little concern to me," LaMontagne replied, brushed a piece of lint from his lapel, and watched it fall to the doctor's polished tile floor.

He thought his idea was absolutely brilliant. *Why didn't Darian Leigh himself think of this?*—he wondered. He already knew the answer: youth, and a lack of faith. *Mortality is seldom the concern of the young. Darian had been little more than a child when he first worked on the dendy lattice. Besides, God does not speak to the unworthy, and Darian Leigh was not a Believer.*

When Larry Rusalov first brought the stolen RAF generator to him, LaMontagne spent a full week playing around with Reality Assertion Fields. He spun dozens of universes, each a few centimeters across, and played with their properties. But without a fully-equipped lab to properly analyze the physical laws of each microverse, the investigations soon bored him.

Never a particularly good student, especially in the physical sciences,

LaMontagne had gravitated toward Divinity College. He loved reading the ancient texts, and felt a uniquely personal connection with his God through them. He discovered that his rich voice and his ability to appeal to a deep, emotional connection with the Divine often won arguments where logic and reason failed. It was no surprise that he grew to value emotion and psychology over logic and evidence.

LaMontagne was more intrigued by the processes going on inside his own brain than in tinkering with micro universes. He might have abandoned the device altogether had he not found himself unexpectedly drawn to the young Darian Leigh and to the prodigy's early work in dendy lattice design.

The Reverend spent weeks immersed in study, wandering through Darian's childhood medical history, child-psychologist evaluations, and teachers' reports.

References to a secretive company Darian's mother had founded caught his eye, which led him to classified documents describing the science behind the Dynamic Neural Nano Dots. Dendies, everyone called them; billions comprised a single dendy lattice. Accessing the proprietary information had not been easy, but their security was no match for him. Darian's private files on the pilfered computer sitting on his desk rounded out the Reverend's deepening knowledge.

And then came the epiphany, Divine Inspiration like a beam from Heaven.

The idea was intriguing: in write-only mode, a freshly-assembled dendy lattice placed into an infant's developing brain could hypothetically be slaved to that of an existing lattice in an adult. Such an arrangement could force the receiving mind into becoming a perfect copy of the transmitting mind. It might take a decade to complete the copy, but he could think of no reason it shouldn't work.

It was evident to his divinely inspired mind that such an intimate union of two brains would permit the departing soul to bridge the gap from one corporeal host to another at death. *I could achieve immortality by moving into a younger body, again and again, as needed. I will bear witness to the arrival of the Kingdom of Heaven! I must personally oversee the preparation of humanity. There is much to do but God has shown me the way.*

The Reverend realized how diabolical his idea might sound to a third party, especially one lacking his own deep faith. *Doubt is for the weak.* He thanked the Lord for choosing him as the worthy recipient of His Light and immediately began designing the changes to his dendy virus that would prepare him to take up the Heaven-ordained path.

The doctor was saying something.

"Pardon me, you were saying?" LaMontagne asked.

"I said, you can't possibly imagine I'd sanction reconstructing a dendy virus from living tissue, let alone altering it to some unknown purpose."

Dr. Rasmussen, Chief of Neurosurgery and Neuroscience at the University of Texas in Austin, had been the Reverend's ideal candidate to help implement the next step in his personal evolution.

LaMontagne was amused by the irony. *How many years did I fight to exclude that word, "evolution", from school curricula throughout Texas?* But the word best described what he proposed to do. He was about to evolve.

He leaned forward and smiled congenially. "Doctor, not only will you sanction this, you will help me make it happen."

Taken aback, the doctor searched for a suitable reply. "Reverend, you must appreciate the university has guidelines about this sort of thing. I'm not free to assist you in this even if I wanted to, which I most certainly do not."

LaMontagne motioned Jeff forward. The bodyguard stepped toward Rasmussen, his hand reaching under his jacket. The doctor flinched, then relaxed when Jeff produced nothing more ominous than a display tablet. Jeff leaned forward to show Rasmussen the screen. It was a recent photo of the doctor and his family enjoying a summer day at their private lakeside cottage.

Rasmussen's eyes flicked back to LaMontagne; panic and pleading etched his previously self-assured face. "Leave my family out of this! I swear, if you go anywhere near them...if *anyone* goes near them...."

The Reverend's smile broadened.

Rasmussen picked up his desk phone. He'd had enough of the discussion. It was time to get Campus Police involved.

Jeff placed his hand over the doctor's and firmly guided the handset back into its cradle.

"Dr. Rasmussen," the Reverend pitched his voice in its most reasonable tone, "surely you can see I'm determined to have my wishes carried out. Perhaps you're also beginning to realize I have the means and the will to ensure *my* wishes become *your* wishes. Save me the inconvenience of having to persuade you any more vigorously than necessary."

Rasmussen tried one last desperate plea. "Why don't you just get the entire virus genome synthesized?"

LaMontagne stood and walked over to the large window at the far end of the office. He put his hand to his chin as if he were considering the option. He laughed.

"My dear fellow, you *know* that would be impossible. DNA synthesis is closely monitored. A wide variety of genes, including those used in growing dendy lattices, are prohibited. Alterations to the virus in my possession would not raise any suspicions if the required oligos—the small sections of affected DNA—were ordered separately. But to order an entire synthetic genome, that would be noticed."

The doctor swallowed. He was all out of ways to say no. "Nobody's been doing active research in this area since it was declared off limits a few years back. I presume you're not interested in academic investigations on the virus. You intend to infect yourself, don't you? You want to become the new Darian Leigh!"

LaMontagne regarded the doctor with an expression so benign and serene, it was as if the three of them had been discussing where to go for dinner. "The virus is not designed to be used on me."

Seeing Rasmussen's confusion, he explained, "I've already been exposed to the dendy virus, rather successfully as it turns out.

"No, I'll be providing the tissue to rebuild the virus. The subject for transmission is in the process of being selected. We'll be ready once your people have added these few new sections and confirmed the entire viral sequence."

Rasmussen considered the Reverend's proposal. Scientific curiosity vied with revulsion. "Are you asking me to remove some of *your* brain tissue and extract the viral DNA from that? And to infect *someone else* with it? Are you insane?"

LaMontagne laughed aloud. "I assure you that I have all my faculties, and then some." He walked over and leaned in, putting his face within inches of the doctor's.

"Look into my eyes," he said. "You see my determination. Perhaps you'll even see a hint of the Divine Spark that Our Lord has seen fit to grace me with. You'll also see that I understand, completely, everything I'm asking you to do."

The two men glared at each other, one commanding, the other defiant.

The doctor was the first to look away. "This is unconscionable," he said. His eyes narrowed. "What's to stop me from simply killing you during surgery? Or from causing permanent brain damage? I presume your man here wouldn't be able to distinguish an intentional act from an accidental one in the middle of an operation. Or what if I were to make an honest mistake?"

"It wouldn't matter either way," LaMontagne replied. "Unless the surgery and the subsequent genetic engineering is a complete success, his orders are the same with regards to yourself and your family."

"You'll kill us all."

The Reverend spread his hands and shrugged as if it were out of his control. "Let's not speak of such unfortunate consequences. We stand on the edge of a new era. Let us speak only of positive things and of exciting new advances. I'm offering you a unique opportunity for a role in this story, in my story. You will be remembered for ages."

Rasmussen scowled. "You offer me no alternative,"

"Did God offer Moses an alternative? Did He offer Noah an alternative? I'm giving you a chance to split the seas, to build an Ark. This miracle I ask of you is a request from Yeshua, not from me. You will be serving your Church and your Savior."

Rasmussen looked miserably from LaMontagne to Jeff, to the floor. "I don't see that you're giving me any choice."

12

"So the microverse continues to grow and there's no way to stop it?" Dr. Wong, Chair of the Physics department, stared at Greg and Kathy with surprising composure.

The couple had tumbled into his office and blurted their observations in overlapping turns, then backtracking, circling back, and jumping ahead with no regard for whether he was keeping up. Knitting the information into a single coherent thread, Wong gathered that a nightmare scenario was becoming a reality.

He and Dr. Stella Trent listened intently while Greg and Kathy described the details of the Eater's growth. "Are you sure about your measurements?" Dr. Trent asked.

Greg reviewed his perceptual records once again. "Well, I only eyeballed it, so I might be off by as much as 0.05 percent," he conceded. "That doesn't really change the overall issue, does it?"

"No, but we need to take accurate measurements before we raise the alarm," Dr. Wong replied. "I trust your conclusions but if we're going to report this, we'll need to be more precise. Dr. Trent is an expert in ultra-fast laser spectroscopy. Dr. Trent, would you please help us verify the measurements?"

"Oh, *right*," Kathy interjected, drawing out the "right" in case anyone missed the sarcasm. "We need more *accuracy*. It's not enough to know the planet will be destroyed in *approximately* two or three years. We need to have the exact date." She glared at the Physics chair. "Seems to miss the big picture, doesn't it?"

Ignoring Kathy's rude comment, Dr. Trent tried to clarify her own understanding. "Tell me again how this thing is different from a black hole."

Kathy sighed. It was a challenge to speak about the science behind the natural laws of physics to people without lattice-enhancement. She made an effort to slow down and lay out the explanation in a simpler, more linear format.

"The Eater has no gravitational field; it only absorbs what it comes into contact with. We only have two data points: the size of the microverse two weeks ago, right after we isolated the Eater in the vacuum chamber, and today. Nonetheless, the model and measurements agree almost perfectly. We're confident it's absorbed no real particles since we last looked at it, but it's bigger today than two weeks ago."

"So you think it's absorbing virtual particles?" Clearly, Trent didn't believe it.

"There's no other source of matter available to it. Sure, it can absorb non-fermionic particles, like a photon of light. But that's minuscule; remember $e=mc^2$? When we model the type and density of virtual particles we'd expect to arise in that volume of vacuum, it matches the expected growth of the microverse due to absorption of those impinging particles."

"I'm no expert on the Standard Model, but how could you possibly predict the density of virtual particles in a particular space? They can't even be detected."

"The calculation was developed by Darian Leigh and Greg. It hasn't been verified yet, except that the calculation is part of the RAF theory. The best evidence for the correctness of RAF theory is the fact that we can create microverses."

"Well, it sounds kind of circular to me, little better than String Theory," Dr. Trent grumbled.

Dr. Wong was quick to come to the defense of Darian's work. "As predicted by the theory, one of the microscopic universes made by the RAF generator has a measured ability to alter the speed of light within it. We believe this to be the most significant scientific discovery since General Relativity or quantum mechanics."

"Is there any way to independently verify that the microverse is actually absorbing virtual particles, apart from its rate of growth," Dr. Trent challenged.

Kathy's voice was slow and even, "The theory predicts absorption of virtual particles gives off a kind of Hawking radiation. That's the only similarity to a black hole, really. As singlet virtual particles are absorbed, their virtual partners find themselves alone in a universe of real particles. They try to interact with adjoining matter."

"So it could be radioactive?"

"Not really. Most of the particles don't interact with real particles at all. They'll just zip away to infinity. A small number should be able to interact with the electromagnetic quantum field, and a much smaller number with the Higgs field. We can detect the EM field interactions with a standard static charge test or through spectrometry. The most obvious confirmation is that the EM interactions give off a weak mixed spectrum of photons."

"Mixed?"

"The sphere looks gray."

Stella Trent was satisfied with the answer, and moved on. "If the RAF generator created this Eater microverse, why can't it be used to collapse it?"

"We don't completely understand how this particular microverse remains stable without the RAF generator," Greg admitted. "Something's set up internal resonances within the microverse. It's incorporating whatever it absorbs into its own structure. Until we understand how it's doing that, we can't break down the field stability."

"Can it be better isolated?"

"Ha!" Kathy laughed aloud, startling everyone. "How can you isolate something from virtual particles? They arise spontaneously out of the quantum vacuum. Where there's nothing, there's still the quantum vacuum."

The room went quiet. The four of them stared in different directions, avoiding eye contact.

Dr. Wong waded into the silence. "Do either of you have any recommendations?"

"We need to buy as much time as possible," Kathy said. "We have to build the biggest possible isolation chamber so the microverse can expand freely without coming into contact with anything. It'll have to be done carefully, without disturbing the existing chamber until it's surrounded by a new vacuum."

Greg calculated a few seconds. "The biggest vacuum chamber in the world might give us twenty years. Any way you look at it, sometime, around two decades from today, the Eater will break out of whatever we can build to isolate it. Then it'll grow rapidly until it consumes the entire planet. Even if we could isolate the entire top of Burnaby Mountain, it would only delay the inevitable by about a year."

"We'll keep working on characterizing the microverse," Kathy jumped in, trying to sound optimistic. "And, of course, we'll share our data and theories with the international community."

"Whatever good *that'll* do," Greg muttered. "Together, we're a thousand years ahead of the rest of the world's experts combined."

"And if you can't figure out how to stop it, what do you recommend?" asked Dr. Trent.

Kathy and Greg looked sideways at one another; their voices came out as one. "Run."

13

SHARD TRILLIAN WANDERED THE STREETS of twenty-first century virtual Manhattan, trailed by his limo. Everything about Alternus fascinated him. He was as enchanted by the quaintness of this peculiar, primitive inworld, ripe-for-the-taking, as he was confounded by its wondrous, needless complexity.

Alum had described the inworld perfectly. The detailed briefing He'd sent to Trillian covered everything a person needed to know to fit seamlessly into life on Alternus, the rogue simulation of ancient Earth. Alum's information had made acquiring sustenance, lodgings, transportation, and money a trivial matter. Trillian, himself, had long ago purged his own memories of those times, or maybe they'd been expunged for him by Alum, as irrelevant detritus of a forgotten, and forgettable, era.

Trillian marveled at the huge variety of distinct societies co-existing on this one planet. Many had representatives in this city. *How do they manage to interact with one another, to get along in spite of their differences? How could they come together in this great melting pot and yet maintain distinct cultures?*

The antiquated idea of money particularly fascinated him. Money hadn't been used in the Realm in ages. It astonished him that some people acquired trading power far beyond that of their peers. Even more intriguing, privileged positions were not based on closeness to God but on the type of work one did or their popularity among the larger populace. Some people acquired even more power by increasing the money available to them through something called "investments."

He had to laugh at this last concept. It seemed that if you could convince others to give you some of their money, and you temporarily gave that money to someone else still, though it wasn't yours in the first place, the people to whom you gave it would pay you back even more. You got to keep the difference between the amount you got back from them and the amount you had to return to your source of the money. The more money you amassed, the more power you were perceived to have.

It was all so wickedly deceitful. Why didn't the first lender simply find the last borrower and provide the money directly to them, pocketing the profit the intermediary would have earned? Were they incapable of finding the opportunities themselves? If so, why didn't they simply engage the services of the person who was most competent?

And what was "day-trading", owning parts of active businesses for such short periods of time, all about? It seemed such a delightful game, except the traders Trillian investigated took winning or losing entirely too seriously.

If only the real humans of the original era had spent half as much effort on technological development, improving their world, or tending the natural environment as they did on these financial games. Their world could have been a garden of abundance instead of the dying cesspool it was becoming. *So much futile activity, simply to choose winners and losers. Alum would never permit such nonsense within the Realm.* Trillian was grateful he lived in an era of peace and prosperity for all. Still, Earth was a lot of fun.

Once he managed to hack into Alternus through the DonTon inworld, he set about making himself comfortable. He expected it might take a while to figure out which characters in this sim were leading the conspiracy against Alum, and whether they were involved in the strange incursions in the Virgo cluster.

One could easily forget Alternus was a simulation; its computer-generated physics were amazingly real. Sensory input on all channels was as rich as the real universe. The designer must have dedicated enormous computational resources to the program. No matter how far back into the side streets and alleyways he wandered, he could not detect a single false front: no giveaway shimmering or blurry facades, no building he could not access.

And, oh, what extravagant sights, sounds, smells, and even tastes! Thankfully, food was varied and delicious because one had to eat regularly to avoid feeling hunger pangs. Discomfort and pain, even physical damage to the avatar body, felt as real here as they did in the outworld. *Phenomenal work. Absolutely phenomenal.*

After passing a pleasant first night in what billed itself as a luxury hotel, he started looking for more suitable accommodations. He hired a real estate agent to look for something comfortable, but not too ostentatious, in the five-to-ten million dollar range. No need to draw unwelcome attention to his presence.

The housing advertisements listed a few apartments near the Central Park area. Within a week, he was able to establish acceptable housing and furnishings. The apartment reminded him of one of his nicer quarters in the Cybrid garden asteroid off Andromeda 514.7, only a bit smaller.

Though he had hacked in, bypassing the conceptual virus of the standard portal, he was nevertheless required to interface with the sim. That meant he had to live by the rules of this inworld as much as anyone. Theoretically, he might have been able to tweak the inworld supervisory program to gain magical powers but he was concerned the Supervisor might vigorously resist such reprogramming and take action. So he pried at it delicately; there might come a day when he needed an edge in confronting the original designer.

Compared to the inworld Supervisor, he found the so-called security of the Alternus "banks" to be laughable. It took him less than half a minute to trace the local flow of wealth, set up a new account, and transfer significant amounts of money into it from a large institution called the Federal Reserve Bank of New York.

He wasn't sure what exactly it was reserving. It certainly wasn't reserving judgment on his request to move a hundred million dollars from its numerous accounts to his empty one.

He set up a banking security consultancy under the name Jack Trillian. If it was that easy to steal from a central bank, smaller companies would be desperate for his services. Security consultant would make a great cover for his inworld activities.

His "job" provided the privacy and tranquility to continue his real work in Alternus. In addition to the few hundred million Cybrid presences cycling in and out of Alternus, several billion Partials inhabited the inworld permanently. And unlike those in other sims, these Partials were not mere servants or mindless backdrop. They were as close to fully self-conscious instantiations without crossing the line into legal beings as he'd ever seen.

Social standing was important in Alternus. His search for conspirators would be more effective if he were perceived as someone important. In addition to household staff, he hired a planetary Partial as a driver/bodyguard. A little additional muscle might come in useful.

Outfitted with comfort, security, and means, he set out to explore the city. It didn't take long to conclude that this world was in dire trouble. The morning news had described it as, "teetering on the brink of its fourth worldwide economic recession in three decades."

So what happens when their economy recedes? Isn't that a natural part of the process, the rhythm of ebb and flow? A little background reading made it clear that it would not be a good thing. With inadequate money to incentivize people, they stopped performing productive activities.

Recessions made little sense to him. Global conditions didn't actually change much during the period. The world's resources moved around a little but weren't substantially different from the previous year. Raw materials were plentiful as ever. Food, water, and energy were as available as they'd been before the recession. The population was relatively stable. Yet, people became incapable of organizing themselves into groups that got things done.

At first, he thought a recession was the result of some kind of global *anomie* sweeping through the population but, if that were the case, there was little sign of trouble until right before the recession was officially entered. Why would a reported dearth of little bits of paper and of numbers in specific computer systems cause large segments of the population to become underutilized? *This is the strangest game I've ever seen. There's no obvious purpose except to make players frustrated and miserable.*

This thing they called "religion" was an equally incomprehensible amusement. People argued over their favorite versions of the Creation of the universe and over who reigned supreme within it. *Such frivolous nonsense! In the real universe, the People know the answers to both of those questions.* The People knew Yov created the universe and ordained Alum to rule over it until some unspecified distant future. When Yov felt the universe had lived up to the potential He'd built into it, He would return. There was no room for disagreement or doubt.

Until Yov's return, everything was a gift from Alum. The answered prayers that enabled one to eat, have shelter, move across the stars, or start a family proved Alum was Supreme. One did not need to *believe* in Alum any more than one needed to *believe* in gravity; they were demonstrable facts. Alum said His power came from Yov's Grace and Alum's Truth was indisputable, so that also had to be true.

Alternus was full of rancorous disputes over the relative strengths of a ridiculous panoply of deities, none of whom could be proven to exist. *How absurd. How could one blindly believe something without some evidence that the claim originated from an irrefutable source?*

If this was a true representation of the times before Alum, he was grateful he had discarded those ancient memories.

For the life of him, he could not figure out what this inworld had to do with a possible rebellion in the real universe. Other than himself, he couldn't imagine many people would find the sim entertaining. Without the ability to enter the inworld in some dominant position, the entire game would be bleak, depressing drudgery. He found it difficult to believe so many Cybrids had found their way into the sim and that they kept coming back for long stays. *What am I missing? What do they see in this game?*

It was feasible the concepta virus he first encountered might have something to do with that. The virus had been persistent, though its intended effect appeared minimal and subtle. *Could they actually be enjoying the challenge of a difficult life inworld? Could rebelliousness and disrespect for authority be so powerful a drug?*

It was logical to assume the leaders of the rebellion would have positions of importance and influence within the sim. He paid more attention to inworld leaders and their behavior in the game-within-the-game known as politics.

Like economics, the game of politics had its own brand of complicated, fascinating rules. The players, called politicians, thought themselves important. They made policy, went to war, regulated trade. They spoke frequently and loudly, disagreeing on almost every topic with vehemence. Regardless of their fractious disputes, they appeared to enjoy themselves. *Perhaps it's all the perks they enjoy as a function of their position.*

But why would the rest of the population permit them to get away with it? It seemed so inequitable; scandalous to the point of being criminal. After all, the politicians were mere mortals like the rest of them. They weren't gods.

It took Trillian months of study and contemplation to understand that, while the politicians were titular heads of state and legislatures, they had a complex relationship with the people who owned or wielded the largest amounts of money including those who led corporations, those who headed banks, and those whose only contribution to society was to have had privileged parents. In most cases, the politicians modified their beliefs and behaviors to be compatible with the wishes of those who controlled extraordinary sums of the money.

Trillian had to keep reminding himself—*it doesn't have to make sense; it's just the way the game is played.*

When he remembered this inworld was a reputedly accurate reflection of the real ancient Earth, he was amazed that humanity had managed to rise to its current exalted state. *Thank Alum and blessed be His Name*—he intoned.

He pursued many false and confounding leads until, one day, he became aware of a group of powerful and influential people pushing public policy toward space exploration. Nothing about the planet or its complicated economic and political systems logically implied such a step. *Surely, the wealthy of this world can't view it as being in their best interests to encourage the escape of humanity from its gravitational prison.*

And yet, there were a few powerful politicians and Central Bank leaders promoting this particular investment as the way forward. They claimed it was, "the only way to attain the growth the global economy needed."

Trillian compared the differences between the history of ancient Earth, as provided in Alum's briefing, and the Alternus inworld sim.

In the real universe, Earth and its People had been saved from an unspecified catastrophic threat by the divine intervention of Alum. The People had been miraculously moved to temporary colonies among the asteroids before being dispersed among the stars.

In this inworld Earth simulation, there was no sign of impending disaster and yet world leaders were discussing the leap into space. It made little sense. Their planet was suffering enough without the wisdom of their own Living God. *Why would they want to spread the disease of humanity to other solar systems? What were they really fleeing from, or flocking to, with such urgency? Did they think expansion or growth would bring them something they didn't already have here?*

Trillian hacked into the communication accounts of several world leaders, tracing their connections and correspondences. He scoured various White Papers and their plans to explore the local moon, planets, and planetoids. He read Top Secret reports comparing the virtues of robotic versus human workers in vacuum conditions and in the absence of gravity.

He traced the origin of the more detailed and serious discussions to an elite conference held in a small Swiss town called Davos. A shortlist of people in one particular meeting seemed to be the nexus of the movement.

One name came up again and again: Darya.

14

THREE FRANTIC AND TERRIFYING MONTHS of intense investigation flew by and Kathy and Greg were no closer to discovering how to stop the Eater microverse from growing, let alone shutting it down completely.

The cheerful, delicate cherry blossoms heralding spring and the annual renewal of life in Vancouver had come and gone. The couple hardly noticed.

Death—for them and of all of humanity—was coming for Earth. If the calculations were correct, they might have twenty-some years, but it was as inevitable as the setting of the sun.

They supervised the construction of a gigantic isolation chamber around the small existing one. The Physics building had to be modified to make space for the new structure. Floors below and the roof above were opened up and the ground underneath excavated. Colleagues' labs were relocated completely. Nothing they did would stop the Eater's growth but it would give them a few decades before it broke out of its containment. Anything less meant doom in three years or fewer.

No one was happy about the expenditure, but President Sakira had rammed the project past all opposition. "For critical new research," she explained to the public. "Millions in new funding will depend on this." she said to. She offered the full story to the Board of Governors only in camera.

There was no hiding it; the dome of the new chamber rose ten meters above the roof of the building. It drew criticism, complaints, resentment, and speculation.

It also brought a further twenty-two years, seven months, fifteen days, and four-point-three hours, give or take thirty minutes before the Eater would reach its chamber walls, absorb them, and start growing in earnest. If allowed unrestricted, exponential growth, it likely would consume the entire planet in no more than two weeks. Fortunately, most living beings wouldn't have to witness the end, since Earth's atmosphere would be gone within a few days of the containment breach.

Kathy and Greg sat patiently outside the Prime Minister's office in Olympia, Washington, emerald of the newly formed coastal nation of Pacifica.

Dr. Sakira paced back and forth in front of them. As President of Simon Fraser University, she was accustomed to being a key person in meetings, and was seldom kept waiting.

Kathy and Greg were accustomed to being nobodies. Greg was amused by Sakira's irritating sense of self-importance. He never would have imagined that, one day, he'd be waiting for a meeting with the Prime Minister. He couldn't imagine being impatient about it.

The political paroxysm that had rearranged the United States and Canada into several new countries had somehow resulted in the British-style parliamentary system being adopted along the entire West Coast. Decades of frustration with one stalemated Congress after another led Pacifica to turn its back on the idea of a republic and choose, instead, the longest-surviving democracy in the world as a template.

The Founding Fathers of the United States of America had intentionally chosen an inefficient and ineffective model for federal government. By the twenty-first century, nations were playing increasingly larger roles in global economics and trade; countries could no longer afford such an obstructive model.

The door to the office of Prime Minister Francine Hudson opened and her Chief of Staff emerged. She motioned to Dr. Sakira. "The Prime Minister will see you now."

Kathy and Greg stood and smoothed their clothes. *This is it*—Greg sent by lattice message.

Let's hope so—Kathy replied.

The Prime Minister and two men waited inside the utilitarian office. Greg recognized Dr. Lewis Schmidt, Minister of Science, Technology and Advanced Education. He needed a lattice query to identify Michael Oberg, the Minister of Defense.

The report we sent has clearly been effective in raising the appropriate level of panic—Greg sent. Kathy suppressed a smile.

The PM stood and came around from behind her desk. She forced a smile that didn't reach her eyes as she extended her hand. "Dr. Sakira. And this must be your team."

"Yes, Madam Prime Minister. This is Dr. Katherine Liang and Dr. Garugamesh Mahajani, Kathy and Greg, from our Physics Department. They are the only remaining members of Darian Leigh's project team, as far as we know. Dr. Leigh and Dr. Valeriy Rusalov are, most regrettably, still missing and presumed dead."

The Prime Minister's handshake was firm and cool. "I'm very sorry for your loss." She turned to the two men, already seated. "I've asked Ministers Schmidt and Oberg to join us. This thing your people have cooked up probably falls more in Minister Schmidt's purview, but it also presents a threat to National Security."

Greg started to say, "We didn't cook this...," but Dr. Sakira spoke over him.

"I hope we are here to discuss solutions, not to allocate blame, Madam Prime Minister."

The PM and Greg both glared at Sakira, but for different reasons.

As if she hadn't heard, Prime Minister Hudson casually shifted her gaze to her Science Minister. "Dr. Schmidt tells me your people have created something called an Eater, Dr. Sakira. I can't imagine the physics behind that but he assures me it is catastrophically dangerous. So tell me, what do we need to do to put this crisis to rest?"

Dr. Sakira glanced at Kathy, who looked at Greg. He volunteered nothing.

Dr. Sakira sighed. "Dr. Mahajani, could you please outline our plan for the Prime Minister and her Ministers?"

Greg shrugged his shoulders. "There's not a lot anyone can do. Kathy and I are trying to understand this thing and find a way to collapse it. Failing that, the planet will be destroyed in a little over twenty-two and a half years." He was surprised at how casually he was able to report on the planet's imminent demise.

A snort escaped from Minister Oberg. "Madam Prime Minister," he said. "You can't expect us to take this nonsense seriously. How many global doomsayers have we all put up with over the past fifty years? If it's not deadly epidemics, global warming, or the end of money, it's something else. Twenty-two years! None of us will even be in these seats in twenty-two years. To respond to this supposed crisis would be political and economic suicide for you, and for the sovereignty of our young country. The vultures are always circling. They're just waiting for an opportunity to swoop in, feast on our remains, and take over."

The PM turned back to Dr. Sakira. "He's right. How do we know this disaster is any different from the dozens of other projected disasters that never panned out?"

Kathy jumped in, "This is not some vague thing that might or might not happen. There is no complexity to it. The math is clear. In twenty-two years, seven months, and fifteen days, the Eater will contact the sides of its isolation chamber. Once it does, our atmosphere will be gone in a few days.

Two weeks later, Earth will no longer exist. It won't be polluted, or flooded, or too hot, or too cold. It will be gone. Plain and simple."

"That gives you plenty of time to understand and remedy the situation, doesn't it?" As past Vice-President of Research at Stanford University, Dr. Schmidt was used to dealing with excitable scientists caught up in the various disaster scenarios of the day.

"Believe me, we are desperately working on understanding," replied Kathy. "If we can't figure it out in time, the world ends. There will be no time to make a Plan B in five or ten years. There may not be enough time to execute Plan A, even now."

"That's right. The calculation is a best case scenario. If anything gets into the chamber, even air, it could be over sooner," Greg chimed in to emphasize her point. "We've worked out a plan to evacuate as many people as possible from Earth over the next two decades. Even with a concerted global effort—which is sure to be a nightmare in itself—we'll only be able to save a few million people. And that's only if we're able to get some new technologies up and running, and concentrate the planet's entire global resources and manufacturing base on the problem."

"Madam Prime Minister," the Defense Minister jumped in, "such an effort will bankrupt the entire planet at a time when a new financial crisis is looming. If we take this on, we'll destroy the country."

"The country will be destroyed anyway, as soon as the Eater breaks free. We are at Ground Zero!" Dr. Sakira's voice was uncharacteristically shrill. She cleared her throat and addressed the PM in a more diplomatic but firm tone. "Madam Prime Minister, I don't welcome this any more than you do. But you need to call together the other world leaders and figure out a plan, or the entire human race is doomed."

"This is absurd!" said Oberg. "Lewis, please. Tell them."

The Minister of Science slowly flipped through the pages of Greg and Kathy's report. "Normally, I would agree with you Robert," he said after some time. "But Drs. Liang and Mahajani were...*gifted* dendy lattices by Darian Leigh a while before he disappeared. I have no doubt their individual brain power now exceeds that of every scientist on the planet, possibly combined. They understand this Eater better than anyone in the world. If they say they may not be able to stop it, we need to listen to them."

Kathy looked at the man gratefully. "Thank you. We do have a plan. We can move enough people to asteroid colonies so humanity will survive even if the planet doesn't. If we do manage to stop the Eater, we can move them back."

"If this is the result of humanity's best efforts, I'm not certain we deserve to survive," the PM said. She walked to the window. The room was silent while she stared out at the lush green hillsides and still waters of Capitol

Lake. A flock of ducks was coming in for a landing on the lake.

She turned back to the expectant faces with grim determination. "Well, my Administration won't be the one that condemns this planet to death by inaction. We will communicate this report to our allies, first, and convene a meeting of the G26 world leaders. We'll see who's willing to help."

Nobody moved as they imagined how this news would go over around the world. The Prime Minister clapped her hands together loudly, startling everyone. "Let's get started, people," she said. "We have a world to save."

15

SECRETARY OF THE TREASURY Corbin Totts was enjoying a quiet Sunday afternoon in his garden. It was the first time he'd had a chance to relax and reflect since his appointment to President Mitchell's new cabinet. This Administration was the first officially elected one in the New Confederacy, a triumph of grassroots democracy.

The first five years following secession had been chaotic. He was glad he hadn't been part of it. Despite extensive planning prior to declaring independence, the transition yielded one catastrophe after another.

When revolution erupted, the entities that would come to form the New Confederacy, Pacifica, and Le Beau Pays du Quebec were the only ones on the continent remotely prepared for the reimagining of North America.

The immediate challenge of those vying for power and control was to define and hold new boundaries against the jostling of a half-dozen nascent North American countries and renegade groups rising out of the Great Schism of 2033. For a short while, it was like the Wild West all over again. Key political forces scrambled for control over the resources and support of remaining non-aligned states and the Canadian provinces.

The New Confederacy began with the southern states and expanded its northern borders to incorporate Wyoming. Idaho and Montana quickly petitioned to join, along with both Dakotas.

The Canadian province of Alberta—home of oil-rich, conservative Calgary, and fondly referred to as Texas north—turned its back on a verbal pre-secession agreement with Pacifica and joined the burgeoning New Confederacy.

Except for shale-rich Pennsylvania, The New Confederacy now controlled most of the oil resources on the continent. President Mitchell could not conceal his glee when imagining how those west coast new-age spiritual types forming Pacifica—the kayaking, draft dodging, socialist/communist granola gang—would start squirming once they realized how that would turn out for them. *I guess we'll see how serious they are about reducing their carbon footprint!*

The idea of an independent Pacifica nation had been bandied about by the general public and political analysts for decades. It was common knowledge that the population up and down the coast on either side of the Canada-USA border had more in common with one another than they did with their respective countrymen who lived further inland. California, Oregon, Washington, and Alaska were joined by the Canadian province of British Columbia and the Yukon territory. The group wasted no time in formalizing the bond.

Colorado, Arizona, and Nevada came as a welcome and somewhat unexpected addition to Pacifica. Instead of sliding into an obvious geographical alignment with the neighboring southern states, they stridently rejected The New Confederacy's approach to constitutionally-enshrined Christianity and sought a philosophically closer fit with Pacifica.

To no one's surprise, the Mormons of Utah decided this would be a good time to form their own independent, neutral country. "Think of us as the Switzerland of North America."

Giving no more thought to the presence of Quebec than they ever had, the Canadian industrial heartland of Ontario and all of the maritime provinces threw in with the northeastern states, supporting the vestiges of the not-so-united-after-all United States of America.

The Canadian prairie provinces of Saskatchewan and Manitoba, emboldened by Utah's declaration, joined with the Northwest Territories and Nunavut to form an independent nation of their own. They retained the name Canada.

The world adjusted its maps, address labels, and invoicing, and went about its business. In the midst of chaos, there were always fresh opportunities.

World leaders turned their attention to the matter of money.

Totts chuckled quietly to himself. *What a zoo that must have been!* The combined public and private debts of Canada and the United States had been enormous. Panicked private creditors and sovereign states called in their loans, clamoring for immediate repayment. The remnants of what was still calling itself the United States of America stalled its creditors, while negotiating the debt split with the new countries.

New Confederacy's President Mitchell and Pacifica's Prime Minister Hudson told their former colleagues, "It's your debt, you take care of it." Only not so politely.

Had the Yankees not been so broke, the crisis might have precipitated another civil war. It wasn't certain who would have come out ahead if that happened.

Eventually, the newly-independent nations found a way to honorably share the renegotiated debt of the profligate countries preceding them. It was either that or forever lose access to the international lending markets. They followed up with a plan to create their own currencies and reached agreement on opening exchange rates.

A forty percent devaluation in their currencies relative to the old greenback meant creditors got about sixty cents on the dollar. The haircut gutted the international reserves of China and Japan, among others, and decimated North American pension plans.

Twenty years before the political restructuring, a generation of twenty- and thirty-somethings elected to move in with their parents to weather the Great Recession. Now parents themselves, they were forced to move in with their adult children as jobs disappeared. The Disillusioned Generation never expected to receive much in the way of pensions when, or if, they ever got to retire. Now they were certain to be impoverished seniors.

Totts considered himself one of the lucky ones. Governments of all stripes had always taken care of their own. He looked forward to a comparatively calm term in office, once the new Free Trade negotiations with the Northern European Union were completed. He would manage the New Greyback in conjunction with the Confederacy Central Bank in Dallas and steer this economy forward. Things were starting to calm down and the economy was picking up again. The latest employment and GDP stats looked good.

He had been out in the garden since dawn, trying to get a jump on the midday heat. Most of his staff had the day off, and his wife was visiting her sister in San Antonio. He started by cleaning up the Columbine bed nearest the house. He didn't enjoy yard work in general, but he derived great satisfaction from tending the flowering plants. The activity required a gentle and methodical physical labor, the kind that removed a person from the stress of daily life. The mind could meditate more easily when it was surrounded by lush green vegetation and colorful flowers.

Columbines didn't fare well in the scorching Austin summers. He'd placed them close to the house where they'd be protected by the deep eaves, but this June had been exceptionally hot and dry. Despite daily watering, the plants were wilted and sad looking. He hacked the dry stalks to within inches of the ground, hoping against the odds that they might flower again in late July.

As the morning wore on, the sun moved around to the north side of the house and the shade dwindled in the backyard. Around ten, he made his way through the patio doors and into the kitchen, where he helped himself to a beer. *Never too early for a cold one on a day like this*—he thought as he twisted off the cap and took a sip.

He ambled back out onto the patio and plunked his heavy-set frame into the deluxe cushioned deck chair under the shade of the canopy. He took another draw on the ice-cold beer, savoring the stillness brought on by the growing heat of a late summer Texas day.

The birds had stopped singing hours earlier. *Too much effort in this heat.* Neighbors were done trimming hedges and mowing grass. *Probably having a cool drink, like me.* He hoisted his bottle in a silent toast to their early-morning efforts and drained it. *That went down way too easy*—he thought. *One more ought to do me about right.*

He left the empty on the table and grabbed a fresh bottle from the kitchen. He was enjoying the day, despite the trickle of sweat rolling down his neck. *No chance of a work call on a peaceful Sunday like this*—he thought, and cussed out loud. *I hope I didn't jinx my luck. Lord, just give me a one quiet day to enjoy before the next emergency*—he prayed. His cell phone sat beside the empty bottle, blessedly quiet.

Totts sat back down and considered the pile of Columbine cuttings beside the house. *Later*—he thought. Cradling the cold brew, he leaned back and closed his eyes.

The nagging sound of nearby buzzing pressed him to locate the source. A couple of yellow-jackets hovered around the empty bottle on the table.

He didn't much like wasps; they ruined his enjoyment of the outdoors. Whenever he and Janet shared a meal on the patio, the pests would target them. He hated the way they moved, hovering menacingly, from side-to-side until they landed and crawled on your food. Once they found desirable food, they'd refuse to move on. You had to be careful how you shooed them away, though; they were mean-tempered critters.

He remembered being out on the driving range last year. There were lots of wasps around that day, too. His friends kept saying, "If you ignore them, they'll ignore you." *As if!*

Sure enough, just as he uncorked one of his best swings of the day, he felt a piercing pain in the armpit of his trailing arm. Damn, if one of those bugs hadn't flown in there on his back swing! Trapped, the wasp stung twice in rapid succession. It hurt like hell, and only got worse throughout the eighteen holes he played that morning. *Tallied up my worst game in a decade.* Yep, he hated wasps.

A few more of the little critters arrived. He sat and quietly observed six of them buzzing around the empty bottle until they lost interest and headed in his direction. Two circled around behind him and took up station on his ears. He brushed the air a cautious few inches from his head. They didn't budge.

They made their way toward the opening of his ears. Tott flinched, ducked his head, and jumped out of his chair. He tried to shoo them away with his cap. He brushed as close and gently as he could, trying to move them away without angering them.

The wasps would take flight but not be dissuaded. They dove doggedly and repeatedly toward his ears. *What the hell?*—he wondered.

The other four wasps had been hovering half-way between him and the table, watching how he dealt with the bothersome behavior of the first two. They approached his face, coming to an unnaturally stable hover less than a foot away.

His eyes widened. He stopped flailing, and focused on the odd behavior of the four in front of him. He absentmindedly licked his lips to relieve his dry mouth. "What's going on fellas?" he said. The hornets took advantage of his open mouth. Two zoomed between his parted lips. The other two entered his flared nostrils.

He turned and ran inside the house, instinctively blowing from his mouth and nose with all his might. He couldn't dislodge them.

The insects moved deeper into his throat and nasal passages, stinging along the way. He yelled in pain, and all four insects escaped from his mouth. Within seconds, they were gone and Totts was alone, reeling with pain and shock.

He ran to the fridge for some milk, thinking it might help with the burning. He guzzled straight from the bottle. It relieved the stinging a little. He leaned against the fridge, gasping for air. *What the hell? What should I do? I'd better call 911.* The milk bottle slipped from his hand. He hadn't noticed it going numb. He stared at his fingers, trying to flex them, but they refused to cooperate.

He took a step toward the phone and felt his foot drag and catch on the grout line between tiles. He fell forward into the doorway, unable to get his arms out in time to prevent his face from striking the ceramic floor. He rolled over onto his back, nose and lips bleeding, and stared up at the ceiling. He couldn't move his limbs. He couldn't swallow.

His terror grew when he realized he wasn't even breathing. He struggled with all his might to inhale, but he was completely paralyzed. In less than two minutes, Corbin Totts, second duly-appointed Treasury Secretary of the New Confederacy, was dead. The coroner would rule it "natural causes" but his assassin knew the true story.

16

AUGUST 15, 2038, GLOBAL NEWS ALLIANCE. *Austin, Texas, New Confederacy:*

State funeral services were held today for Corbin Totts, Secretary of Treasury of the New Confederacy. President Mitchell and First Lady Margaret Mitchell were among four thousand mourners who gathered inside the Diamond Cathedral of Yeshua's True Guard Church, home of the official religion of the New Confederacy.

Secretary Totts was the 33rd government official to die in a spate of recent deaths affecting key figures in the worldwide financial community. Over the past 2 months, 7 Deputy Ministers of Finance, 11 Treasury Undersecretaries, and 15 Central Bank economists have succumbed to sudden death due to natural causes as a result of sudden respiratory or cardiac failure. Secretary Totts was the highest ranked.

No toxins were identified in any of the autopsies, and foul play was not officially suspected in any of the deaths. However, reviewed collectively, these numbers are statistically highly improbable. Despite the lack of physical evidence, accusations of intrigue and assassinations are being raised within the international community.

Authorities are investigating a man known only as Alum, who "prophesized" on his blog one week prior the countries in which the deaths of "important figures in the financial community" would occur.

Alum claims the deaths resulted from "God's revenge on the wicked and depraved, who worship money and power above the love for His people." His so-called prophecies have led a number of investigators to propose that the name Alum is a pseudonym used by an international group of terrorists.

Alum has leaked questionable activities by leaders of the United States of America, China, and India, as well as a host of South American and African countries. He has also exposed government and business corruption in a number of middle-ranking individuals. So far, the New Confederacy, Pacifica, Canada, and Northern European Union have been left unscathed by his extensive inside knowledge.

Only Pacifica remains untouched by the mysterious deaths.

The religious leader's most recent warning hints at an unspecified global disaster that has been developing in the Pacific Northwest. As with his predictions concerning the high-profile deaths, Alum has been consistently vague on details.

Popular conjecture points to the strange new addition to Simon Fraser University's Science Buildings in Vancouver, Pacifica, as one possibility.

The structure in question appears to be centered on the laboratory of Dr. Darian Leigh, a scientist well known for his controversial, ground-breaking research on the origin of the universe. An SFU spokesperson will comment only that, "the addition to the buildings was required for some exciting new research on campus that will be formally unveiled in the coming months."

"Reverend, I'm sorry to keep you waiting. It's been a busy day." Fred Mitchell extended his hand as he crossed the threshold from the adjacent war room into the main office.

"That's quite all right, Mr. President. These are troubling times; I'm sure there is no shortage of matters requiring your attention." LaMontagne stood and the two men, old friends and sometimes bitter political adversaries, shook hands warmly.

"Indeed they do. Totts' death couldn't have come at a worse time. We were concluding trade negotiations with the Northern European Union. Now they want to alter some of the provisions of that agreement."

"Papi!" The unexpected cry from the far corner of the room drew the President's attention away from LaMontagne. The smiling face of a toddler appeared from behind the sofa. The little boy scampered into the open and ran to LaMontagne.

"Babysitting, Alan?" The President chuckled but was clearly bemused to find a young child in his office.

LaMontagne smiled broadly as he bent down to tousle the boy's hair. "A precious undertaking and one I could hardly refuse," he replied. "This is my favorite niece's boy. She's going through some difficulties and asked if I could take care of the lad." He held up a hand. "I know that a meeting at the White House is not the most appropriate place for a toddler. I promise you his presence will not alter the gravity of our conversation which, I assure you, is of the utmost importance."

Mitchell shrugged his acceptance. He directed the Reverend to a seat in one of the four wing back chairs arranged for comfortable conversation. The boy plunked himself down at the Reverend's feet. He took a deep breath and grew still, focusing an eerie stare on Mitchell.

"How can I help you, Reverend?" The President asked. "I don't imagine you've come here to discuss this trade deal with the NEU, have you?"

LaMontagne rubbed his chin in thought. He hadn't been following the trade negotiations at all, being so caught up in his own unrelated investigations. He accessed his communications hardware and scoured the mainstream news and analyses on the topic. There wasn't much cogent information on it out there. Apparently, the parties preferred to negotiate in secret.

He hacked into Mitchell's desktop workstation.

Ah, yes. This is much more revealing. Internal memos and email exchanges with the NEU Chancellor showed struggling nations at loggerheads over many issues. He was impressed that they'd concluded a deal at all, a testimony to the acumen of the recently deceased Treasurer Totts.

LaMontagne's probe took only a few seconds. He dropped his hand back to the armrest. "They want us to raise the price of our liquid natural gas shipments to France and Italy," he stated factually.

Mitchell was stunned. "How do you...I didn't realize you kept that up-to-date on affairs outside the Church."

LaMontagne smiled. "My interests and attention cover a wide array of topics these days. One can never tell where baser threats to the spiritual health of our nation may come from."

"Well, I don't know that this impacts any matters of faith, exactly."

"Our faith is reflected in our actions in the real world as well as in our souls."

"As always, I accede to your wisdom in these matters, Reverend." Mitchell bowed from the waist. "Does our faith provide any guidance for me in this?"

"Not directly," replied LaMontagne. "But perhaps I could make a suggestion, anyway."

Mitchell spread his arms in amused resignation. "Please."

"Tell the Iranians to reduce their production quotas."

Mitchell sat back, surprised. "I doubt they'd comply with that request. Most of their economy depends on oil and gas sales, especially to both European Unions."

"We could ask our Pacifica friends to threaten an increase in jet fighter prices they're charging the Imam if he fails to comply with our request. The Imam depends on air supremacy to maintain power in the area. I think we might find him more compliant if we link these two issues."

"And why would Prime Minister Hudson make such a threat?"

"Pacifica is the only country in the Americas that hasn't suffered one of the mysterious deaths."

"Yes....?"

"We could offer to provide evidence to the world that her government is, in fact, behind the deaths. That they are conducting a program of targeted assassinations."

Mitchell shook his head in bewilderment. "And are they?"

"No."

"But we—that is, you—could fabricate convincing evidence making it look like they are?"

"Iron-clad evidence."

Mitchell was stunned. "Okay. Let's put that aside for a moment. You're saying that if we convince Iran to lower oil and gas production, the Northern EU will drop their request that we raise the price on our liquid natural gas shipments to Southern EU? How does that work?"

"Well, we might have to point out to the Germans and Poles that the SEU will have oil and gas shortages as a result. This will pave the way for NEU countries to increase fracking activities and export their products at an increased price to their southern neighbors."

The President nodded. "That just might work. Of course, it would allow us to raise our prices as well."

"Which we will have no need to do. Our production costs will still be lower than the NEU's. We can afford to hold our prices where they are and still be highly profitable."

"Yes, I suppose $170 per barrel of oil equivalent is fine for us."

"Or we can let them drift upward, slowly."

"Alright. Now tell me how you intend to persuade Prime Minister Hudson."

"With something that is almost true. Just before young Darian Leigh took his research to California, he designed a method for interfacing dendy lattices with insect nervous systems. I believe you have encountered one such synthetic species, the Spyders?"

A startled Mitchell answered cautiously, "Spiders are everywhere, nothing unnatural about them, even if you don't like them."

"Not spiders, 'Spyders', with a 'y'. I could send you the transcript from the files of former NSA Deputy Director Thornten if you'd like. Just to refresh your memory."

Mitchell blanched. "How could you possibly know about those? Our conversation was confidential. And that program was top secret."

LaMontagne casually inspected the back of his hand. "Yes. Well, that's not really important. It turns out that while Dr. Leigh was at Berkeley his research there was secretly merged with two other programs by Pacifica's Department of Defense. Have you ever heard of a Matavispa?"

"Mata...what?"

"Matavispa. Apparently, there was a number of Latinos involved in the project, hence the name. It's a play on words, merging *matar*, the Spanish word for kill with *avispa*, the word for wasp," replied the Reverend.

"Oh, like killer bees?"

"A million times more deadly. The matavispa is a genetically engineered killer wasp. Merge a synthetic biology program to alter the normal wasp so it injects a deadly neurotoxin, with Dr. Leigh's insect lattice and military drone operators, and you get the matavispa. It's a perfect machine for politically-based...interventions, if you will."

"That sounds abominable. And Pacifica has it?"

"Yes. And my organization has collected sufficient evidence to demonstrate they alone have it."

"And they're using it?"

"Oh, Heavens, no. Prime Minister Hudson would never authorize something like that. She's a peaceful woman."

"Well, who is?"

"We are."

"What?! You mean we have it too? Why would we use it?"

LaMontagne's demeanor was bizarrely casual as he confessed. "More correctly, I am using it. I've decided it's time for the Church to assume a more active role on the secular world stage. As I am considered to be outside the conventional power structure, I thought this might be a good way to demonstrate my serious intent to participate."

"How did you get hold of something like that? You've said the Church has limited connections into the Pacifica military."

"As it turns out, I only needed one connection. You see, I've been studying up on external control of Centralized Command systems. It seems I have a talent for compromising such systems. It wasn't difficult to order a batch of matavispas to be hatched and distributed to a select international group of moderately important people. Controlling the killer wasps' activities in the various countries was trivial. Isn't the Internet wonderful?"

Mitchell glanced at the toddler, sitting quietly at LaMontagne's feet. "You're insane."

The Reverend laughed. "No, I am determined. Resolute. Fortunately, I have decided to apply this resolution toward assisting you at this time."

"I...I'm speechless."

"Really, Fred. Just thank me for helping you with this free trade agreement with the NEU. Not that it will matter in the long run. It's simply a gesture of my goodwill toward your Administration."

Mitchell glared at the man he had once considered a colleague. He felt repulsed, betrayed and afraid; it was as if his favorite pet had turned into a hideous hellhound. "And what would you like," he sputtered, "in return for your...goodwill gesture?"

LaMontagne laughed. "A small thing, really. I want you to appoint me as your representative to the Special International Advisory Committee on the situation in Vancouver."

Mitchell was beyond feeling surprised. "Yes, you would know about that, as well." The President grimaced. "Well, I've already appointed Secretary of State Hartland in that position."

"I would be happy to serve as an Advisor to Mr. Hartland or perhaps as a Co-representative."

"I'm not sure that would be feasible."

"I have forgiven a great deal from you and your supporters, Fred. That includes using my mother's indiscretions against me in the election for Governor." He held up his hand to override Mitchell's anticipated protestations of innocence. "Now, now. Don't bother saying it wasn't your idea. You still sanctioned the strategy. It could have been me sitting in your place today, otherwise."

"But you aren't sitting here, Alan. I am. What if I were to simply deny your request?"

The Reverend smiled menacingly. "Then I hope your successor will be more pliable after you meet with a fate similar to Mr. Totts'."

"Are you threatening me?" Mitchell's voice rose as he pushed out of his seat. The toddler's eyes tracked the President, though his face remained serene. "Do you have any idea of my Executive Powers? I could haul your ass out of here and into prison right now!" *Where is Security? They should have checked in when I raised my voice.*

The President yanked open the door and shouted for his Secret Service guards. Nobody responded. The reception area was empty.

The Reverend smiled in a way that someone more naïve might have mistaken for fondness or compassion. "I've sent an alert in your name that the building is to be evacuated due to an unspecified emergency."

Mitchell wheeled around. "You what?" he demanded.

"Your Chief of Staff, a man almost as loyal to you as he is to the Church, was most helpful in assuring your Secret Service detachment that you'd already left for the High-Security Bunker. The Presidential Mansion is quite empty, Fred. Well, not quite empty, as it turns out." The Reverend gestured for Mitchell to look behind him.

A few yards down the hallway, a dozen insects hovered. Mitchell slammed the door shut and spun back to the Reverend. His eyes darted about the room, and he rushed over to close the open window.

"Come now, Fred. If I'd wanted you dead, do you really think I couldn't have arranged for another...incident?" asked LaMontagne. "There's really no need for us to be at odds. I want to help. Nothing more."

Mitchell closed his eyes and placed a hand on the edge of his desk to steady himself and gain control of his fear. "Is the appointment all you want?" he asked.

"Yes. That's it; nothing more. I know it's only a silly little worry right now, that *Eater* thing our young friends have created. But I've seen the emails, Fred."

"Top secret emails..."

"Yes. The emails suggest the problem is real and significant. The Eater is about to change the course of history." The Reverend sat back, habitually rubbing his chin as he pursued his thoughts. "Anyway, there are some people in Vancouver I would like to meet again. I so value old acquaintances." At his feet, the boy rubbed his chin, as well.

17

DARYA WANDERED THE STREETS of twenty-first century virtual Manhattan, wondering how her team was going to convince this world to save itself.

Sometimes she took the game too seriously. She knew that. It was, after all, only a training exercise. The goal was to stretch their creativity, practice decision making, and play out daring "what-if" scenarios within a relatively safe environment.

Under normal circumstances, the game would be fun, a stimulating and occasionally exciting challenge.

Knowing that the universe depended on how well they learned to play did put a bit of a damper on the fun factor. And if Alum were to discover their true purpose, well, let's just say it would be game over for all involved. Exploring ways to split a portion of the universe away from Alum's Realm so they could assume control over its administration—all while thwarting his Divine Plan—was sure to be frowned upon in a most decisive and unforgiving way.

It's a risk we have to take. We need to learn how to solve problems for ourselves, without Alum to lead. We have to figure out how to become the leaders the outworld will need—Darya had explained to her inner circle.

This morning's meeting at the inworld offices of the Federal Reserve Bank of New York didn't go as well as she'd hoped. She and her senior team members, Leisha, Gerhardt, and Mary, had met to discuss how to bring the global political system on board. Her plan to convince various countries around the inworld to cooperate on an immense space-colonization program was moving slowly. Much too slowly. She was beginning to appreciate why Alum made all the big-picture decisions for everyone outworld.

Their meeting was full of difficult and spirited discussions, as always. Her colleagues had created a mechanism by which to fund the huge increase in the national debt of any country that participated in the new space program. As expected, national governments kept looking for ways to divert those funds to "more pressing" needs.

"Ugghhh! Why can't they just take the money and use it as we've set out?" Leisha huffed in exasperation.

Mary was quick with a response. "They've become adept at taking personal credit for anything good that happens in their countries, but they can't figure out how this international program will help any of them individually. Don't worry; we've set it up so that moving money from the national programs into their own bank accounts is extremely difficult."

"But they'd be helping the entire planet, including their own people. They'd be seen as true leaders. Heroes. You'd think that alone would entice them—oh, and guaranteeing a future for humanity. There's that."

"Maybe we could improve their motivation if we included a political slush fund," suggested Gerhardt, not entirely joking.

Darya scowled at him. "That's not helpful." Their client countries were drowning in debt. They'd have to come up with a creative proposition to get more than a handful of leaders to agree to borrow any more money, let alone to fund a massive public works space program with dubious short-term returns.

"I thought we wanted to accomplish this colonization. I didn't realize we were also placing ethical boundaries on *how* we were going to convince them," Gerhardt challenged. It was an audacious statement, and Darya wasn't sure whether to respond with a tension-breaking chuckle or a disapproving glare.

Before she could decide, Mary intervened. "If we wanted to ignore the *how*, we could ask the Supervisor to magically enforce what we want. You're forgetting that the point of this inworld sim is to train us to become better leaders outworld in the real universe. We need practice dealing with unreasonable situations and impossible people."

"Why?" Gerhardt demanded stubbornly. "In the outworld, we can just share our concepta among the Cybrids and compare them for missing information, assumptions, and reasoning. Trying to convince people without knowing what they're thinking is so frustrating."

Darya and Mary sighed together. They looked at each other and laughed.

"You're right, Gerhardt," Darya answered. "But the outworld includes both Cybrids and humans, and humans can't just compare concepta for concordance."

"Humans," Gerhardt muttered in disgust as he looked out at the enormous, tumultuous city. On ancient Earth, the real Earth, humans had built a huge city like this on their own, without Cybrid support. As a result, it was poorly organized, poorly integrated, and generally ill-suited to their needs. Besides, it was dirty.

"Look," Darya said. "Leadership, whether in the human-Cybrid outworld or here in this inworld, is much the same. I know it's practically impossible to convince the inworld leaders to work together toward—well, if I'm being honest—almost any goal that comes to mind. They're a self-interested, fractious, irrational, intellectually-challenged lot. But it's an important exercise. It's crucial that we succeed, so let's just keep trying."

Gerhardt turned from the window and took a deep breath. "Okay. I'll give it another try. I just want you to know that I agree with Leisha's sentiment. Buying them off is a *practical* solution."

"That's fine," replied Mary. "The real Earth of this era must have been heavily motivated, probably by some external threat, to get their space program running.

"The Alternus inworld population doesn't have any such threat hanging over them, or at least they don't realize it yet. So what else can we do?" She glanced at Darya.

"That's the problem," Darya answered. "A lot of people *are* convinced a jump into space exploration is required. Just a few decades back in Alternus history, both of its superpower nations were racing to establish some kind of permanent presence in space."

"So why did they stop?" asked Leisha.

"I'm not sure. It could be that local problems—war, famine, bad economies—distracted them and reduced available funds. The USA made it to the moon first but, somehow, the competition turned into cooperation when the old Soviet Union fell. That could be what lessened the urgency, the race, that pushed them ahead. Maybe economic conditions also changed and other issues assumed higher priorities. Whatever fueled the initial urgency, it died off or got buried. Your guess is as good as mine."

"I'd like to think it was some great conspiracy or massive cover up but, odds are, the real reason wasn't nearly so exciting," Mary speculated. "People—governments—just get tired and distracted, they lose motivation, before the job gets done. It's a wonder anything gets finished at all."

Darya nodded. "We have only ourselves to blame. Democracies of one sort or another are in place around most of Alternus. The sheer clamor of all those voices, each and every person expressing his or her own equally-valued desires and opinions, is making it impossible to arrive at a decision and stick to it."

"Undoubtedly," said Gerhardt, "and, for some reason, people keep electing Administrations and Representatives who hate each other. So the checks and balances built into the political system prevent anything of value getting done. The absence of broad consensus among the leaders and the refusal to allow the 'other side' to be seen making any discernible progress is crippling."

"Well, if we don't get consensus soon, we're going to lose our opportunity." Leisha's voice was strained.

"That's a definite possibility," Darya agreed. "The engineers and scientists with the right skill sets are aging. Many of them have already retired. The watered-down, over-extended, underfunded educational systems in most countries aren't adequately preparing the younger generations to step into their places. A society of long-lived individuals does have some advantages." She scowled at the sheen of her now cold coffee but took a sip regardless.

"Yes, if we don't get our current experts working in earnest on fabricator and transport design within the next few years, it could be decades, maybe even hundreds of years, before we can be ready again."

Mary chuckled. "I never expected to have impossible tasks and deadlines on an inworld project. Great Alum, I could have stayed in Cybrid repair outworld, and spent my inworld time in oblivious fantasy."

"Sometimes it feels like our own people are opposing us," Gerhardt said. "Not you," he backpedaled, in case Mary misunderstood. "I was thinking of others outside our team." He faced Darya, looking for confirmation.

"I wondered about that," she answered. "I don't think it's coordinated opposition but, yes, we have had Cybrids instantiating into certain positions of power in countries that are holding us up. It wouldn't surprise me if they've assumed this is some standard zero-sum game and they're jostling for personal advantage. I can't do anything about that. Besides, it contributes to a more realistic situation."

"Why don't we try changing tactics," suggested Leisha. All eyes turned toward her. "Maybe we could mount a concerted PR campaign. Anonymously, of course. There must be some bloggers, writers, or filmmakers out there who would support what we're trying to do."

"Yeah, great," Gerhardt's frustration gave way to sarcasm. "We can't convince a few hundred so, geez, I don't know—let's try to convince a few billion."

Mary snorted.

"Maybe Leisha's right." Darya paused to allow the others to shift gears and focus. "The humans of this era were used to taking orders from the top, down, just like we are."

"As in, 'Might makes right'?" chimed in Mary.

Darya laughed. "Yes. Cybrids outworld and most humans in the Alternus inworld have no real power. We all just do what we're told. The difference is that the leaders on Earth of this time, and therefore here on Alternus, rule according to what they think their voters want. If they sense public opinion is in favor of space colonization, they will support our proposals."

Leisha regarded Darya with awe. "How do you know so much? Were you around back then?"

Darya blushed. "Not exactly, though I do have access to detailed data and memories from that time. That's how I was able to design this mess." She indicated the entire planet with a wave of her hands."

"So do you think a publicity campaign could work in our favor?" Gerhardt brought their attention back to the current topic.

"I do," replied Darya. "It's worth a try, anyway. Why don't we see if we can find some expertise among the Partials?"

Mary nodded. "That's a good idea. Judging by our wasted efforts in Lysrandia, we don't know as much about PR as we thought."

The rest of the meeting flew by. They reviewed the growing list of personnel who'd already signed on for Space Colonization and were awaiting political approval of the project. They kicked around a few asteroid habitat design concepts but only for fun. They agreed it was essential the human Partials do most of the thinking for themselves. It would be counterproductive to contaminate the Partials' ideas with superior technology and intellect.

They broke off around 3:30, and went their separate ways with assigned tasks and contact lists in hand. The revised lists included individuals who had sizeable followings in a broad range of popular social media, print, or film. The list didn't include a single politician; not one had sufficient public credibility.

Darya grabbed the subway back to her office near the UN Plaza. Halfway there, she decided to get off and walk the rest of the way. Meandering along the way between Greenwich Village and the UN was an effective way to reset.

The atmosphere had changed considerably over the years. The streets leading up to the UN and its coterie of well-paid employees were lined with beggars. Darya tossed a few coins to the ones she recognized. A number of them she considered friends, or nearly so, having shared lengthy conversations from time to time. They moved around within a several-block radius, so she was never sure who she might encounter on any given day, but they were a good source of strikingly alternative perspectives.

Today's walk revealed a new face. Darya slowed as she neared the disheveled and peculiarly dressed fellow. His soft face was carved with fatigue and he looked more out-of-place than others in the row of resigned countenances. She couldn't recall seeing him at all before. Granted, she'd been away six months on outworld assignment and had been inundated with distracting and urgent demands on her attention since getting back.

She deep-scanned her memories of the past year. There were no recordings of the man. Even more intriguing, when she inquired of the Supervisor, the man's code was neither Partial nor Full. *That doesn't make sense. How could that be?* Darya knew inworld Earth code substrate intimately and had been in frequent contact with the Supervisor since her return. This was a first. She wouldn't have thought his presence here possible if she weren't looking right at him.

The man's concepta and persona were rich; any passerby would have assumed he was a Cybrid inworld instantiation, though Beggar would be an odd role to choose. But she could find no link to the man's outworld trueself. Intent on resolving the mystery, she queried the Supervisor for deeper data. The immediate and succinct response was another dead end: *Identity indeterminate. Origin unknown.*

Had this been some inworld sim other than the one she'd personally and meticulously designed, she could imagine a few ways this might be possible. Some inworlds were careless, leaving echoes of previous instantiations hanging around for lengthy periods. Sometimes, someone pushed the autonomy and self-referential factors of a Partial's concepta too far, usually, in some misguided backdoor attempt to force the Instantiation Committees into declaring a Supervisor's favorite Partial as a Full persona. The inworld *she* designed had none of that sloppiness. Partials and Fulls were carefully and clearly separated.

So what is this man doing here? And how did he come to be here? She opened her mouth to ask but words failed her. "How...? What...?" She reigned in her thoughts and settled on, "Who are *you*?"

Though clearly tired, hungry, and dirty, the man looked up at her with bright eyes. He stood, brushed off his clothes, bowed, and held out his hand. "Why, my name is Timothy, madam. And who might you be?"

Despite the passing eons since she'd last encountered it, Darya recognized the accent as the ancient English of a well-bred or well-educated individual. She regarded the gently extended hand leading up to an open and friendly face, smiled, and graciously accepted his greeting.

"Hello, Timothy. My name is Darya. You have such an unusual accent and...aura," she ventured. "Might I inquire as to how you came to be in New York?" She surprised herself with how easily she slipped into the tone and cadence of the man's native language.

"Certainly, madam. I followed Mr. Trillian through the closet door from the family dining room." Timothy replied cheerfully, as if the statement were perfectly self-explanatory. "Might you be able to spare a little change for a man who is, as these fine gentlemen would say, a little down on his luck, my Lady? I mean, madam?"

Darya noticed the slip. *'My Lady?' Nobody uses that term here.* As she reached into her wallet, she asked, "Where are you from, Timothy?"

"Why DonTon, of course, madam," he replied.

Her fingers paused on the edge of the wallet. She recognized the name. Everyone working in the Sagittarius A* system knew that sim. It was famously difficult to join, even as a weekend guest. "Casa DonTon?" she queried. He had her full attention again.

"The very same, madam," he beamed. "Do you know the Chattingbarons?" His eyes were filled with hope.

"I know *of* them," she replied cautiously, "though I can't say we've ever met." She watched Timothy's rigid posture relax. Beneath the wear and the layers of grime, the remnants of his formal white collar and tie of the Victorian era held him upright. She could not fathom how this...man?...could have crossed into the Alternus sim from DonTon.

"Timothy," she began.

"Yes?"

"What was your...role in DonTon?"

"My role? Oh, my position." He stood tall and proudly smoothed his scraggly beard and dusty clothing. "First Footman Timothy at your service, my Lady." He bowed gallantly as his nearby compatriots guffawed at the sight of a beggar putting on airs.

Darya was astounded. *He's a DonTon Partial! That explains the out of place attire and manner.* But how could a Partial make the leap across inworlds? And how would a Partial become a Full instantiation in DonTon? He was a Full, there was no doubt about that.

She ran a quick diagnostic with the Supervisor.

No leaks detected—it reported.

Well, that's a relief. Darya hadn't realized she'd tensed up until she felt herself relaxing again. *If there's no leak, how can I explain Timothy's presence here? Wait. He said he followed someone here. Trillian. That can't be a coincidence. Surely not Shard Trillian!*

"Timothy, you said you followed Mr. Trillian through a closet door."

"That's right, my Lady," he delivered as if Darya were a member of the English landed class of his age. She didn't feel compelled to correct him for the moment.

"Was Mr. Trillian a guest, then?"

"Oh, quite, my Lady. And as handsome and gracious a guest as anyone could want. Although he didn't appear to have much taste for the hunt, if I may be so bold, my Lady."

"Hmm. And he simply opened a closet door and walked into New York, did he?"

"Yes, indeed. I never thought that door went anywhere myself. Clearly, I was mistaken." He hesitated a moment. "A short while before he went through, there was a strange buzzing sound and I felt some dizziness. I might have thought I fainted and dreamt all this, except how could all of this possibly be a dream?"

"How long have you been in New York?" Darya made an effort to remain calm. A Shard—not just any Shard, but Trillian himself—bypassing her security measures and instantiating in the middle of her inworld sim was not something she looked forward to dealing with. And none of that explained how a Servitor Partial could be standing here in her sim as a full persona.

Timothy looked down at his feet. "I'm not sure I recall exactly, my Lady. I'm afraid some of the times are a bit...unfocussed in my memories. I think I've been here at least four months, probably more." He looked around at his nearby friends and called out to one of them. "Bob! How long have we been working in this area?"

"Three months," the other man growled, and he shuffled a few yards farther down the block, muttering to himself.

Timothy turned back to Darya. "I was here for at least a month before I met Bob. He's been a true friend in any altercations with the other gentlemen. Before that, the details are a little hazy, I'm afraid. There was the time in the hospital...," his voice trailed off. He looked troubled and confused.

Darya listened to Timothy with compassion and concern, but she was also relieved. *Four months and the Shard hasn't found us yet, then. Good.* "Timothy, I would like to hear the rest of your story but not here. I would like to invite you to stay as a guest at my residence."

"Oh, I couldn't possibly, my Lady," the man protested. He looked down unhappily at his unsatisfactory state. His eyes sank, wistfully.

"I won't accept 'No' for an answer," Darya responded. "I insist you come with me. My people will ensure your comfort and we can become better acquainted."

Darya turned and began to walk toward her apartment. Timothy followed dutifully, accompanied by the whistles and cat-calls of his compatriots.

"Ho, ho! You hooked yourself a live one there, matey! Or was it the other way around?" Raucous laughter echoed down the street behind them. Darya didn't notice.

So, a Shard is loose in Alternus, and I've befriended an impossible persona. Interesting day.

18

BLINK AND, JUST LIKE THAT, TEN THOUSAND ANGELS, a full Wing of Alum's enforcers, materialized in a 25,000 km wide circle around the Cybrid asteroid station Rafael 116.4.4.

Moments earlier, Lord Mika had been dozens of light years away, field-testing his new battle components and recent upgrades by the maintenance Cybrids. He'd been darting about the asteroid belt of his assigned system, shifting from planetoid to planetoid as fast as he could, and firing a single powerful bolt from his sword each time without stopping to assess its destruction. After annihilating over a hundred of the presumably uninhabited rocks, he retraced his flight path, analyzing the fragments to assure himself the blasts had efficiently obliterated his intended targets.

Then, without warning, he was in a different star system in full alert. It took him a couple of milliseconds to process and adjust. Something must have tripped Alum's passive detectors—the old mechanical switches—without the higher tech active motion sensors being activated. The pattern matched the footprint of the intruder.

Mika's Wing activated their quantum decoherence field generators and linked their shift blockers to create an enormous net. Blazing energy emanated from their swords, outshining the twinkle of distant stars. No one and nothing would be shifting out of their grasp this time.

The Angel's position as leader of the Wing put him just inside the containment field. Though his nearest neighbors over 200 klicks away were imperceptible, his internal projections showed each of their positions and statuses clearly. The trap was set.

Mika gave the command and led the drawing of the net inward. Half the Angels shifted ten thousand kilometers closer to the asteroid, where they established a new inner perimeter. The other half subsequently shifted to just outside this shell and took over, holding the new outermost layer of the net.

The inner group shifted another thousand klicks closer and established a new, concentric shell with only two thousand of their number. The remainder moved closer and established three more shells in the same way. By the time they were done, there were five successively smaller shift-blocking nets and a thousand Angels—the Primary Group of the Wing—inside, ready to chase their quarry.

The maneuver had been executed beautifully. The sensors inside the Cybrid station continued to show the intruder. *It was almost effortless.* Mika doubted the invader was the false Shard from Gargus 718. That being had been far too competent to be caught off guard so easily. *More likely something thrown at us by rogue Aelu.*

If it was from that respected, enemy civilization, it was behaving more like a single *lorei*—one of the Aelu's powerfully-armed, spiny, star shaped, explorer robots—than a battle group.

Angels were accustomed to dealing with Aelu combat groups. No 216-strong *habnar* would ever permit itself to be contained in such a small volume of space without engaging the enemy. A *habnar* would be pouring out of the asteroid station in attack formation by now.

Perhaps it's something new!

Mika sent a hundred Angels—a Feather of the Primary Group—inside the asteroid to flush out the intruder. The Wing Commander linked into several perception channels of the vanguard group and followed their progress inside the asteroid.

He watched his Angels shift within corridors and chambers, cutting off physical escape routes. Members of the Feather moved efficiently through the work chambers and connecting corridors toward the last reported position of the intruder.

They passed working Cybrids, who made respectful inquiries as to their unexpected presence. The Angels responded by demanding identification. *Lorei* wouldn't hesitate to cast an illusory image in that form if served a purpose; the Angels weren't taking any chances that the intruder might slip past undetected.

The intruder hadn't tripped any new detectors in the past few minutes. According to Alum's reports, it was in the Biodesign Lab. There was a Cybrid in the lab with it, and still no sign it suspected a trap. There was only one entrance to the lab, which led to a service corridor.

Good for pinning down anything that can't shift, but an easily-defended position, as well—thought Mika.

Feather Leader Jonto moved into the lab antechamber. Dozens of Angels lined the corridor behind him, awaiting his orders. Others staked out the adjoining chambers that shared a common wall with the lab.

Jonto peered around the threshold of the door. An Angel he did not recognize from their Wing stood beside a hovering Cybrid, deep in a conversation. Jonto was confused. He sent a query to Mika, "*Is there one of us from another Wing here?*"

The reply from his Wing Commander was immediate, "*No! Detain him!*"

Three members from his Feather shifted inside the chamber and grabbed at the arms of the unknown Angel. The intruder spilled out of their grasp and flowed like liquid under the Cybrid. The liquid rose on the other side in a new shape.

The Angels were briefly stunned into inaction.

Not a lorei, an actual Aelo, a single member of the species! Mika recognized the tricks of the alien. The three Angels had grasped at a holographic projection, nothing more. "*Go to active radar scanning,*" he commanded. The Aelo sprang into sharp relief.

Its small elliptical body perched on an articulated tripod. Above the body, three manipulators moved menacingly. It was hard not to be mesmerized by the floating limbs, each one trifurcating into smaller, more refined, appendages, all waving rhythmically. Some of the appendages extended to hair-like filaments, for fine manipulation; others ended more bluntly and were tipped with tools or weapons.

The inky black, homogenous body was otherwise featureless. From past dissections of captured enemies, the Angels knew the creatures had visual and other sensors, but no orifice or sensory organs showed from the outside at any scanning wavelength.

Three bright beams flared from embedded weapons along the lengths of the Aelo's manipulator stalks. One ripped into the Cybrid, sending shrapnel flying in all directions. The other two beams blasted a hole through the wall and into the adjacent chamber.

Jonto and two others shifted to cover the next chamber. Six Angels confronted the Aelo directly, three behind and three in front. Jonto shifted to within a meter of the alien invader and thrust his sword forward. It struck empty air. The Aelo had shifted away unscathed.

The Feather spread out through the rest of the asteroid. The intruder was spotted in seconds, but continued to shift away from engagement. It was quickly seen in dozens of different chambers throughout the asteroid.

Mika watched with growing frustration as his lead team tried to corral the invader. As long as the Aelo could shift within the warrens of the asteroid, the Angels were engaged in a game of hide-and-seek they couldn't win. The intruder was too fast and leading the chase.

Mika would have to flood the halls and rooms of the asteroid with the entire Wing to have any real chance of capturing the Aelo inside the intact planetoid. To do that, they'd have to break their shift-blocking network. Then the Aelo could simply escape. The situation was impossible.

I can simplify this game. Clear out—Mika ordered his troops. *I'll remove its hiding places.*

The Feather shifted back to outer space, well clear of the hollowed-out planetoid. Mika adjusted the power of his sword, pointed it at the heart of the asteroid station, and activated it.

The asteroid shattered under the intense energy. Thousands of Cybrids inside perished. Only a few managed to escape the blast. The invader would be among them. Aelu were not so easy to kill as Cybrids.

In the debris field, Mika recognized the scattered thruster flares of Cybrid workers trying to escape. He squinted and nodded—*Yes, yes. As expected.* There were a few longer, brighter exhaust trails from the MAM drives of asteroid miners fleeing the battle. *Let them leave.*

He had aimed his beam at the center of the asteroid station deliberately to avoid any of the more powerful mining Cybrids that typically clustered at the poles. *No need to set off a matter-antimatter reaction and vaporize part of my Wing to stop one intruder. We're not there yet.*

He played his destructive beam through the debris, blasting gigantic chunks into boulder-sized fragments. He could have turned the entire asteroid and everything inside it to dust but, if he did that, they'd have no chance to capture their opponent alive. No, he wanted the intruder to flee the crumbling mountain. In open space, with nowhere to hide, the Angels would get that chance.

Suddenly, the Aelo was in front of him, floating meters away. The Angel deactivated his energy beam and swung his sword to dismember the intruder. The Aelo was gone before Mika connected. No matter; it couldn't go far. With the asteroid reduced to pebbles, there was nowhere left to hide. And with five layers of entrapping decoherence shield, it couldn't flee. The Aelo would have to fight its way to freedom.

The lead team of Angels, a thousand strong, split into Barbs of ten each and spread out across the space formerly occupied by the asteroid. Those in the innermost decoherence shell flooded the space they protected with microwaves. Anything bigger than a fist will be visible to all.

Mm, there you are.

The Aelo was revealed, shifting randomly and testing the boundaries of its confinement for any weakness. It knew it was trapped. It rushed at the enclosing shell, weapons firing bursts of coherent energy. The beams were easily absorbed and dissipated by the Angels' defenses.

One-to-one, Aelo and Angel were evenly matched. However, in greater numbers, the Angels were able to link their energy absorption fields. To defeat even one Angel in a group, the Aelo would need hundreds of times more power, or more cunning.

The Angels' flaring swords and coordinated energy bursts drove the intruder away from the shift blocking perimeter, and back into the middle of its prison. The inside groups gave chase.

A Barb would shift to wherever the Aelo was spotted and attempt to encircle it with a small decoherence field, a few dozen meters in diameter.

The remaining ninety-nine Barbs shifted close by and waited for the Aelo to jump away from its pursuer and, hopefully, into their midst where they would trap it.

The Aelo shifted continuously, randomly, trying to outrun the hundred determined teams of Angels and their continuous casting of shift-blocking nets. Once it was contained within a Barb, the Aelo would lose to the superior might and number of Angels that would descend upon it.

Neither the Angels nor Aelo would tire soon; this cat-and-mouse game could last for hours, days if necessary. Mika was certain of the inevitable conclusion. It was only a matter of time before the intruder was theirs.

The Aelo passed near the perimeter, and a few Angels in the decoherence shell wobbled. The shift-blocking lattice in their region wavered. Swords sputtered erratically.

Three Angels in the innermost part of the net deactivated their swords and began spinning. Their arms dropped to their sides and their wings flapped uselessly in the vacuum of space.

The Aelo moved past them, the first imprisoning layer breached.

Nanoverters!—Mika transmitted to his Wing. The Aelo's earlier fruitless-looking charges at the shell had not been pointless, after all. It had been seeding the Angels with nanoscopic subversion viruses. Such viruses would cling to an Angel's skin and work their way in along sensor endings or power conduits. Once in the control circuitry, they would overwhelm the individual's will, tricking their senses and causing them to undertake odd behavior. Fortunately, nanoverters were easily remedied.

We are woefully out of practice—thought Mika. *Too many millennia of peace in Alum's Realm.*

With the inner shell overcome, the Aelo earned itself several million cubic kilometers more space in which to maneuver. That freedom, however, came with an additional thousand infuriated Angels who formed another hundred Barbs and joined the ranks of their comrades in the chase.

Faster and faster the Angels sought, found, and tried to encircle the intruder.

Angels and Aelu had played this game many times before, and both knew its inevitable outcome. Try as it might, the Aelo could not outmaneuver so many pursuers forever. Soon, one of them would get a grip on an appendage and rip it off, damaging what little personal weaponry the alien possessed, or strike a lucky blow to the body, hurting its internal shift generators. After that, the chase would be over quickly.

As Mika anticipated his Wing's victory, a swing of an Angel's sword cleanly relieved the Aelo of an appendage tip. Mika smiled. *One less weapon to worry about.*

In the next second, another Angel managed to scratch the Aelo's carapace, causing it to spew body fluids into the cold vacuum of outer space. The fight was nearly done.

The Aelo changed tactics, dashing to the shattered remnants of the Cybrid asteroid. *Nothing bigger than a pebble there*—Mika noted, as he monitored the alien and pursuing groups. In a chain of fast bursts, the Aelo jumped through the detritus of the asteroid.

Mika ordered a few hundred of his Wing to activate their swords and clear the debris field. The energy levels weren't set high enough to kill the Aelo even if it were to get caught in the crisscrossing beams. Soon, the space the asteroid once occupied was filled with cooling dust particles, none larger than a few microns across.

The Aelo emerged inside the dust cloud, and the chase resumed.

The nearest team surrounded the Aelo in little time. *The alien must be tiring*—Mika thought. Two Angels moved in for the capture.

The Aelo spun on its long axis and its limbs wove in a mesmerizing dance that was too fast to follow. The enclosing circle of Angels exploded outward. In the ensuing confusion, the Aelo fled.

Mika shifted to examine his stricken team members. Every one of them had a hole through the chest, destroying their primary processors. *A kinetic weapon? Impossible!*

Some quick calculations determined that any reasonably-sized projectile would need to be moving at near light speed to inflict such damage. The Aelu had nothing that could shoot a projectile that fast, as far as Mika remembered. No organic or mechanical being could exert sufficient force to accelerate even a one gram projectile up to 0.95 light speed in half a meter.

*Unless...*Mika recalled a battle technique invented by some clever Cybrid near the end of the Aelu Wars. The Cybrid had cast a cylindrical mass-neutralizing field from a mountain-sized asteroid, perhaps a few hundred tons in size, out toward the surface of one of the innermost Aelu planets. It was a common enough kind of field that Cybrid miners used to help them move asteroids around. But Mika had never heard of the effect being projected in a long, cylindrical shape prior to that time.

Within the field, objects had essentially no resting mass. A gentle push would accelerate it to near light speeds as long as it stayed inside the field. The Cybrid nudged the asteroid to get it moving toward the planet. As soon as the asteroid hit the field, it accelerated to near light speed. The trick was to extend the cylindrical field almost to the surface of the planet ahead of the moving asteroid. After the success of the first strike, Alum constructed special Securitor Cybrids for the task.

But we never used that on anything smaller than a planet. Even at that, none had ever managed more than one field, and certainly not with the precision the Aelo had just demonstrated.

Mika surmised the alien must have collected pebbles to use as bullets from the asteroid debris before it was pulverized to dust. It's field management had to be extraordinary. *Clever. But the downside of using projectiles is that one always runs out of ammunition.*

He wasn't happy to lose a few hundred Angels before the Aelo ran out of ammo. He contemplated the relative importance of capturing this intruder intact against the losses the Wing would take.

Now that we know the invader is a single Aelo, albeit a resourceful one, how much more do we need to know? It is alone with no accompanying fleet. The residual threat level is practically nil.

Mika imagined Alum's possible reaction to the loss of this single alien. *He'll be unhappy if many of His Angels are sacrificed for such a worthless target.*

The Commander ordered the decoherence blocking shells to shift inward. *"Ensure you maintain the integrity of the containment field."*

The Aelo's prison was closing in. Several Barbs managed to coordinate their efforts, and it became trapped in a volume of space under a kilometer in diameter.

Mika ordered the main shells to tighten up their formations, reinforcing their brethren's efforts.

Three Barbs of Angels closed in on the Aelo, making it shift at shorter intervals and distances.

Surely, you tire of this game—Mika thought. *Let it be done.*

After another set of shifts, the Aelo found itself trapped by a group of thirty Angels, with thirty more inside still pursuing it.

It dispatched the five nearest with projectiles. Seconds later, another five stopped moving.

"You're letting it get away!"—Mika broadcast.

So close to success, so close to finishing the chase, and yet so uncertain of the outcome, they couldn't lose it now. There was only one acceptable course of action to prevent its escape.

Lord Mika shifted for a better perspective. *Mm. Can't be more than fifty Angels close to the Aelo at this angle.* He drew his sword. He could destroy entire planets at this setting. One annoying Aelo and fifty inept Angels would not withstand the destructive beam.

He said a brief prayer of thanks to Alum for the courage of his team, and fired on the tight knot of Angels as they closed in on their prey.

The energy unleashed converted all in its path to plasma, Angels and Aelo alike. Lord Mika took stock of his losses. And blinked.

* * *

WHEN HE OPENED HIS EYES, Lord Mika stood alone on the Main stage in the Hall of Alum, facing the glorious mini-galaxy at the center.

He dropped to his knees, trembling at the might of his Lord. He was ready to atone for his failure to capture the adversary. Destroying it, along with tens of Angels, was a tactical disappointment.

Alum's Hall appeared empty and silent but one never knew what kind of magic the Living God might use to isolate one supplicant from another. Mika wept at the majesty of his God and of the miracle that had brought him here across nearly fifteen million light years without a starstep. He had never experienced such a thing.

"Rise, my friend." The voice was quiet, pitched low, and sounded...pleased.

Mika stood. Alum appeared on the stage in front of him, a simple man in front of the awe-inspiring, single-galaxy universe.

"I am yours to command, my Lord," said the Angel.

"What is your evaluation of the engagement?"

"The Aelo intruder was vanquished with the regrettable loss of two Feathers of Angels and the Cybrid station, my Lord. The creature proved to be an extremely resourceful and skilled adversary. I thought it likely to prove impossible to capture without considerably larger losses."

Alum said nothing. He stared at the Angel, giving no sign of judgment or emotion on his face. Finally, a hint of a smile formed on his lips. "And how do you think you will fare when you confront our true invader?" he asked.

Mika was confused. "How do you mean, my Lord? Is there another one?"

"This was simply a live test, so to speak. To ensure your Wing was properly prepared. We have lived with peace so long that the strategies and tactics of battle have been largely forgotten."

Mika knew that anger was pointless. Still, he couldn't help feeling resentment. "Many gave up their lives for this test, my Lord."

"That was unavoidable."

If Mika's mercurial skin could have blushed with embarrassment, it would have radiated crimson at that moment. He realized his own role in the events of the past hours and felt a wave of humility wash over him. "I am imperfect as ever, my Lord."

Alum raised his eyebrows. "Oh, no, not at all, my friend! You are not to blame. We shared in the development of this plan to capture or kill the intruder. Our losses were inherent in the strategy, not the implementation."

He contemplated the miniature cosmos. "It wouldn't have been useful to provide you with an inadequate adversary for this test. Fortunately, I have kept a small number of Aelu captive in stasis since the conquest. This one was more than willing to challenge your Wing."

"Why would it do that, my Lord? Surely it must have remembered how thoroughly we dispensed with its people."

"I promised it that if it could escape imprisonment, it would be free to seek out what remains of its people wherever they are hiding. Apparently, it preferred the odds against it, to being held in timeless imprisonment."

"You believe the intruder is Aelu, then?"

"I believe the intruder is at least as capable as the Aelu and possibly more. Other than another Angel or Myself, it would be difficult to imagine a stronger adversary."

"The Aelo fought well, perhaps even better than an Angel would have."

Alum laughed and turned back to Mika. "My friend, though we have known each other for millions of years, you can still surprise me. I would not have thought it possible for you to admit such a thing."

Mika bowed his head. "Perhaps we require improvements in our design," he suggested.

Alum waved his hand dismissively. "I think you have proven yourselves admirably; you are up to the challenge. Let us not be overly concerned about minor collateral damage." He touched the Angel's shoulder. Instantly, they were in the more intimate environs of the well-appointed study they'd used for their last meeting. Strong, dark coffee sat steaming on the table between the sofas.

"Perhaps we could think of improvements to our strategy in the encounter to come," said Alum. "Let us discuss this further."

19

LEISHA WANDERED THE STREETS of twenty-first century virtual Manhattan, shopping for shoes. It was such a terribly antiquated diversion. She was surprised how much she enjoyed it. With so many important things to do in Alternus, it was a trivial extravagance to spend so much time on one's appearance. But it was her only hobby.

She was glad Darya hadn't forced her to adopt the avatar of the body she instantiated into in Alternus. Central bankers in the simulated Earth were clearly not selected for their physical charms, it seemed, but for other skills.

Bad enough that the game, itself, turned out to be so much tedious work. *To have been saddled with that old hag's face and physique would have made it unbearably dreary. The Alternus inworld planet is so much more attractive now that several million of its formerly mundane inhabitants have been overlaid with Cybrid avatars.*

Leisha had been working diligently on her appearance over much of the tens of millennia of her relatively young existence. She wanted to be regarded as someone special. Sure, everyone was "beautiful" in his or her inworld avatar but it was a mundane, plastic beauty. Few made a serious study of beauty beyond the façade. Few studied fashion or behavioral nuances like the way a person moved or laughed or spoke.

Many of the characteristics the Cybrid mind found beautiful had their origins in the human brain upon which Cybrid lattices were modeled. Leisha was expert in all of them.

She wanted to stand out, and she did. Not the way Mary did, with her strategic compilation of brash obesity, asymmetrical features, and outlandish embellishments. That was too far. No, Leisha wanted to be known as someone who was mysteriously more elegant, refined, sexy, and fashionable than anyone else among the millions of inworld avatars with whom she might interact over her existence. She wanted to have a beauty people noticed but couldn't immediately define. It was a fun hobby and had led to thousands of interesting liaisons in Vacationland.

Leisha ditched her small security detail so she could enjoy herself freely, unfettered. She was looking for something unique, something special, to update her Fall wardrobe. Fortunately, her inworld salary as Director of the World Bank/IMF allowed a rather extravagant budget for her latest passion, and Manhattan happened to be the shoe shopping capital of the North American continent.

She'd spent all morning scouring the shops in the Bowery district and was hoping to have her afternoon occupied with the better stores in Greenwich Village. But, first, she was hungry.

I don't know if I'll ever get used to that. One frequently ate and enjoyed the exquisite flavors that were available inworld, but you never actually *had* to eat. On Alternus, eating wasn't the luxury it was in other simulations; it was a necessity. One's avatar became noticeably less efficient, even grumpy, if not regularly fed.

Leisha stopped at one of her favorite restaurants in the area, a lovely café that could have been taken right off the streets of Paris. She took a table on the small patio and ordered her favorite, the duck crepe and a glass of Shiraz. The wine arrived and she sat back to savor the complex bouquet.

"Excuse me, you're Leisha aren't you?" a stranger said over the cast-iron fence separating the restaurant from the public sidewalk. She looked up at the lean, handsome man with immaculately groomed graying hair.

Caught off guard, she sputtered, "Ah, ah, yes, I am." She remembered where she was. "*Outworld*, that is. Here, I'm Natalie Grishwold. Do I know you?"

The man laughed, a casual, comfortable laugh as if between old friends. "Of course, Ms. *Grishwold*. I didn't intend to make you uncomfortable by speaking out of character. Gerhardt told me your inworld name, but he neglected to tell me how stunning you are. The pictures from your official appearances don't do you justice."

Leisha relaxed and preened for the stranger, happy to let go of the need to keep up her strict, professional inworld persona, however briefly. "You know Gerhardt?"

"Yes. I'm involved in the banking world, as well. He thought we might share some common interests."

"You don't say. How intriguing. Where do you work?" Leisha knew most of the important international bankers and had never seen this man before. "Or have you only recently started inworld?"

"Yes, indeed," he replied. "But long enough to get established.

Apparently, I have some small talent in computer security, likely a result of my outworld design work. A few months ago, I was able to find an inworld inhabitant who owns a consulting business in banking systems security. He wasn't taken yet, so I instantiated into his character. Gerhardt, in his role as Director Campeau, recently hired my services to review the risk profile of some medium-sized state banks. It's already been great fun, I must say."

"And did you know Gerhardt...outside?"

"No. I mean, I knew *of* him, but we always got assigned to different projects. Then again, there's an awful lot of us involved in the...outside construction. Too many to know personally."

"That's true." Leisha laughed at his oblique reference to the Deplosion Array. There weren't any official rules prohibiting discussion of the outworld while in an inworld sim. It just wasn't done, especially not within the more realistic inworlds, of which, Alternus was surely the epitome.

"Would you like to join me? I've just ordered some lunch."

"I would be delighted." The man scanned the terrace and windows to make sure none of the staff were looking and, with a roguish grin, placed both hands on the fence and vaulted over. He landed gracefully on the patio and bowed with a flourish calculated to garner Leisha's appreciative applause. As a capping gesture, he lifted her hand to his lips and delivered a gentle kiss more suited to the finer company in Latin Europe than downtown Manhattan.

"My inworld name is Jack Trillian. I am enchanted to make your acquaintance, Ms. Grishwold."

"Trillian?" Leisha was immediately cautious. "An interesting name choice."

"Alum was feeling generous the day I chose it. It's meant to honor the Shard, whom I respect greatly. And perhaps to reflect my own charming roguishness." He bowed, but his smile was clearly ironic.

Leisha laughed appreciatively. "Please, do sit down, Mr. Trillian. You'll embarrass me. I'm trying to avoid attention today."

Trillian sat, settling into his role. "Thank you. I suppose you must find it difficult escaping unwanted attention, with your position in this troubled world and, doubly so, with your breathtaking beauty."

"Oh, stop now," said Leisha. "Behave yourself or I'll have to un-invite you from my table."

Trillian smirked. "I beg your pardon. I've just come from Casa DonTon, where things are considerably more formal."

"Ah, DonTon, yes. Is it as pretentious as they say?"

"Positively stodgy, and the Chattingbaron clan is every bit as snobby as advertised. I don't know that I'd recommend the place, even if you could wrangle one of the rare invitations."

"And how did you come to be there?"

"Business, sadly. A number of my colleagues outside challenged me to gain an invitation. My inworld honor was at stake, so I had to visit. I am able to confirm that it is, indeed, truly overrated. Stilted, boring, and stale. Alum should simply abolish it and be done."

"Is that so? Are you in the habit of giving advice to the Living God?" Leisha held her wineglass tantalizingly near her lips. For a moment, he considered playing this game to its normal conclusion before proceeding to his true business, but only for a moment. It would not come out well if he were to displease Alum by entertaining dalliances ahead of duties.

Trillian caught a waiter's attention and, without perusing the menu, ordered a French onion soup, small salad, and a glass of Shiraz. The waiter nodded. "Would you like both meals delivered at the same time?"

Leisha replied for them both. "Oui, s'il vous plait."

Trillian smiled to see the beautiful young woman showing off for him. That she'd have undoubtedly downloaded a number of ancient languages for her international work did not diminish the gesture.

He sipped his wine thoughtfully as they enjoyed the warm sunshine and waited for their meals.

"Can I ask you a question?"

"Only one?" Leisha smiled playfully.

"Well one to start the conversation, and we can see where it goes from there."

"Well, in that case..." Leisha sat up, folded her hands on the table in front of her, and looked attentive.

"Why are we here?"

Leisha burst out laughing. Was he being boldly suggestive or unexpectedly philosophical?

Darya's group had been grappling with their goals and purpose, both inworld and outworld, in a meeting the previous day. She had not expected the topic to come up so soon in casual conversation.

"I'm sorry," she said, still chuckling. "That's not at all what I was expecting." She wiped her tearing eyes. "Could you clarify the question, please? Do you mean at this café, this inworld sim, or in the larger universe outside?"

Trillian's eyes twinkled mischievously, imagining other scenarios. "Let's start with this sim. Gerhardt told me a bit about Earth, I mean Alternus, and how all of you in Darya's group are pushing for this new Space Program but he didn't say why."

He was pleased to see his mention of Darya and the push into space elicited raised brows and then acceptance on Leisha's part.

"Is this your first instantiation in any of the versions of Alternus?" she asked, instead of addressing his comment.

He scrambled for a reasonable response.

"I'm guessing it is, or you wouldn't be so surprised by my asking," she observed.

I must remember how extremely realistic this inworld is—Trillian admonished himself. *I need to guard my emotions more closely.* Outwardly, he remained calm and confident. "You've discovered my secret. Yes, I'm sorry to say, I am a novice here. But not for long."

Leisha leaned in and spoke in a hush. "This is iteration number four. We've had two complete disasters and one peacefully failed resolution to date."

It was Trillian's turn to be caught off guard and mildly confused. He fought the urge but curiosity won out; he couldn't stop himself from forestalling his intended task. He had to find out. "What do you mean?"

"In the past three versions of the sim, we were unable to avoid complete destruction. Twice by nuclear war. The third time, we moved the world toward what we thought would be a promising new economic and cultural foundation. The Supervisor judged it to be inadequate over the long term and terminated the game. So now we're trying to expand into space, the way the Supervisor wants."

Despite his considerable intellect and extensive background reading, Trillian was baffled. "But isn't this all just a game, an entertainment?"

"Sure, it's a game. But it's not like Vacationland where the point is simply to have fun. It's more like a game of Footie or chess, where you have defined, achievable goals—except it's infinitely more complicated, and the whole world's involved. We *all* need to win, collectively."

"And what would winning entail?"

"According to the Supervisor, it means getting the stubborn, scared, xenophobic people of Earth to work together and start colonizing space."

"And apart from the satisfaction of a game well-played, what do participants gain from this game?"

"We learn how to rule over humans well enough that we stop them from destroying themselves, either slowly or quickly. At least, that's how Darya interprets the Supervisor's judgments."

"But Alum rules over all," protested Trillian. "Why would you...we...want to rule in His place?"

"Alum doesn't rule here," replied Leisha. "The inhabitants hold amazingly incompatible belief systems based on no rational evidence at all. They call them *religions*. They all seem to have their own versions of a god or gods, or no God at all. And not one of their gods rules the way Alum rules in the real universe."

"Alum is truly the Living God."

Leisha smiled slyly. "I see we've switched to discussing *outside*. This seems like one very long question."

Trillian spread his hands and pouted sheepishly.

Leisha found the gesture charming, despite its calculated origin. She'd studied inworld human gestures and body language and used the expertise to her own advantage on multiple occasions.

"Very well," she offered. "I think I can trust you. Anyway, Darya will kill you, *literally* kill you, if you leak any of this." She waved him in closer.

Trillian positioned his ear near her lips. Crowning himself the master of this charade did not prevent him from becoming excited by her intoxicating scent. He struggled to focus.

"We are planning a coup," Leisha whispered.

Trillian's mind reeled. This was preposterous. Blasphemous! He could hardly breathe through his anger. "A...coup?"

"Well, obviously we can't replace God, can we? We're just hoping to isolate a number of star systems from Him so we can determine our own destinies."

"Won't Alum send in the Angels?"

"Not if we remove the systems from the starstep network. Without them, it would take thousands of years for Angels to arrive. Who knows what kinds of defenses we could develop by then?" Leisha sat back, defiantly folded her arms, and stared intently at Trillian.

The Shard struggled to regain control of his emotions in the face of Leisha's arrogance. He met her gaze evenly before dropping his eyes to the wineglass.

To think they would challenge God! Small groups in a few remote systems had attempted to break away in the distant past, the most recent being at the conclusion of the Aelu Wars. Alum's rule was complete. One could no more oppose Him than...than...sunlight. His Law was perfect and absolute. The mighty Aelu had learned the hard way, through annihilation.

Trillian shook himself back into the moment. He still had much to learn.

"Gerhardt hinted this inworld was somehow connected to the opposition of Alum's Divine Plan in the outworld. He wasn't terribly specific, and I couldn't see how the two could possibly be related," he admitted. "How would that fit into our plan?"

Leisha noted Trillian had used the word "our" in an attempt to include himself among the conspirators. A hint of caution tugged at her. "I'm not sure I can discuss that. Have you been to one of the meetings yet?"

"Meetings?"

"I'll take that as a 'no'. Has anyone given you a brochure for a meeting about Alum's Divine Plan?"

Trillian recalled someone approaching him at least once every few weeks with an invitation to such a meeting. The brochures were obviously associated with some kind of virus; his defenses easily detected the threat before physical contact was made. He'd brusquely refused the first invitation and waved off every one since. He couldn't let on that he knew full well what they contained.

"Oh, those! I've seen people handing them out. I've never been given one, myself. I'm not into group activities, anyway. What does any of that have to do with Cybrids blowing themselves up along with so many asteroid stations?"

Leisha frowned. As far as she was aware, no one had connected the mass suicide bombing around Sagittarius A* with anything happening within the Earth sim. "I probably shouldn't say any more," she replied prudently.

The waiter arrived with the meals, giving them both an opportunity to compose their thoughts. Leisha looked at the steaming dishes. "Why don't we enjoy our lunches while they're still hot?"

Trillian reached forward and rested a hand on hers. "I'm sorry if I've upset you," he said.

Leisha heard a buzzing near her right ear and reached up with her free hand to brush it away. A glazed look fell over her and she lowered her ineffectively sweeping hand to the table.

Trillian inserted the mind-reaming virus into the unsuspecting Cybrid's inworld persona and scanned Leisha's memories for information about Darya's group and their plans. He reviewed meetings in the cloud restaurants of Vacationland and here inside the Earth sim. He discovered the group's awareness of the true purpose of Alum's Divine Plan.

What he didn't expect to find, buried deep within Leisha's belief structure, was their dire objection to the Lord's plan to remake the universe into a state of eternal perfection.

I don't understand. They should be joyous to be part of the Living God's final triumph over the unwieldy and unpredictable chaos of this reality! It is an unparalleled honor.

His suspicions were true. The purpose of the meetings was to convince other Cybrids to join the group in active opposition to the Realm.

He replayed the standard pitch used in the meetings and was astonished that anyone would be convinced by such weak arguments. *Their concepta virus is more powerful and subtle than I thought.*

Trillian shook his head at the arrogance of this Cybrid, the leader of this rebellion: Darya. To oppose the will of the Living God was an act of unspeakable hubris. *How can she claim to know what is best for all of Creation? What wisdom does she have to compare to that of the eternal Alum?*

She was even more dangerous than they'd thought. To have created an entire inworld of stunning complexity for the sole purpose of infecting large numbers of Cybrids with such obviously-suicidal beliefs, that was an amazing feat.

To remain hidden from Alum and His Shards while creating all this in secret, was incredible.

To base the sim within a technology unknown even to the Lord of All was simply unbelievable. *Who was this Cybrid?*

The Cybrid. Right. While wallowing in speculation, Trillian had let entire seconds tick away. He sat back in his chair releasing Leisha from the grip of the probe.

"Of course, you're right," he said picking up his soup spoon as if nothing untoward had transpired.

Leisha blinked, momentarily dazed as she returned to self-directed consciousness. *Wow, where was I?* She smiled and picked up her fork, happy to return to a simple social situation. *Must be a glitch in the inworld system—* she decided.

20

THE MORNING BEFORE THE G26 MEETING, Greg and Kathy hosted a science demo like none the world had ever witnessed.

Vice Presidents, Deputy Prime Ministers, Vice Chancellors, Generals, and scientific advisors of the twenty-six developed nations of the world crowded into the lab beside the enormous vacuum isolation chamber housing the Eater.

Greg performed as scientific Master of Ceremonies, discovering a hitherto hidden flair for the dramatic.

"I'd like you to take a closer look at this thirty-centimeter square plate made of two-point-five-centimeter thick industrial steel. That's about one foot square and one inch thick. If you'd like to verify its composition, please come forward and lift it. It weighs about seventeen kilos, almost forty pounds, so please be careful as you handle it."

"It wouldn't matter if it was made of wood, plastic, or titanium, the effect of the Eater is the same on all materials." Greg waited while a few walked to the front of the group and lifted the heavy plate and knocked on its burnished surface.

"Okay? Now, I'll set the plate into this frame and introduce it into the isolation chamber." Greg nodded, and Kathy opened a sample door in the side of the chamber. He strained as he lifted the block inside and fixed it solidly within the clamp assembly. He closed the door and caught his breath before beginning the demonstration.

"Please direct your attention to the monitors. The Eater has been growing at a slow, stable rate even while isolated within this vacuum chamber several months ago. It is now some ten-point-two centimeters in diameter, about four inches. Today's demonstration will result in a jump in size to ten-point-three centimeters. We'll, of course, allow everyone to verify that independently. Unfortunately, the demo will cause the projected demise of Earth to be brought forward by about six weeks. Unfortunate, but necessary. It's a fair trade-off to adequately impress upon you the seriousness of Earth's situation. Can everyone see? Okay, let's begin.

"The Eater absorbs all matter and energy impinging on its surface and it does so instantly. The apparatus we've constructed to move the steel plate over the Eater will measure the velocity of the plate as it encounters the Eater. If you watch the monitor, you'll see the plate accelerate up to three meters per second before it collides with the microverse."

Greg pumped out all the air in the sample chamber to equilibrate it with the larger isolation chamber. He pushed a button and the plate shot toward the Eater. A pair of rails guided the block on a collision course with the strange anomaly floating in the center of the vacuum.

Outside the chamber, the monitor displayed the increasing velocity, distance to the Eater, and time left until impact. Seconds and milliseconds spun down as the metal block zipped along its rails. The audience held its collective breath over the last second and released it in a single gasp as the block collided smoothly with the Eater. Its speed didn't change at all. It was as if it had passed through nothing more solid than a holographic projection.

The frame-and-track assembly returned the block to its starting point. Greg equalized the pressure to match the lab, opened the sample-chamber door, and removed the steel plate. It had a perfectly smooth ten-point-two diameter hole running through the middle. The scientists gasped.

"We believe the surface of the Eater to be a boundary between this universe and a microscale universe with different physical laws from ours," Greg explained. "The Eater doesn't merely convert the solid metal to a different state, such as gas or plasma. Matter that contacts the Eater is simply and irretrievably removed from this universe. We haven't been able to saturate its rate of ingestion; it eats everything we introduce no matter how much or how fast."

Someone near the back of the room, Greg didn't see who, called out an objection. "You can't remove matter from this universe without breaking the First Law of Thermodynamics, that energy and matter be conserved in a closed system."

Greg ignored the objection. "Only a small amount of Hawking radiation is left behind to mark the transition to the new universe. We've outlined the theory in the briefing material provided. Our supervisor, Darian Leigh, originated the theory, and we've validated it through the Reality Assertion Field generator.

"I'll be happy to address any questions about the theory. Dr. Liang is the expert on the device, itself." He pointed to Kathy, who was monitoring the test from the main console.

"The removal of matter from this universe leaves nothing behind. As the metal plate passed over the Eater, there was no flash of light, and our instruments indicated no significant emission of radiation."

He scanned the faces in the room. They were astonished by what they had just witnessed but still skeptical.

"The Eater isn't a singularity," he continued. "It has no gravity field of its own. It does not draw matter to it. It only ingests whatever comes into contact with it.

"We have two other tests to show you. In the first, we'll discharge the most powerful industrial laser available to us. We borrowed a Super HAPLS, near-continuous, petawatt laser from the Triumph experimental fusion facility and set it up inside the isolation chamber. If you'll turn your attention to the monitor, please."

He nodded to Kathy. She introduced a stream of microscopic smoke particles into the vacuum chamber and manipulated a series of small metal blocks between the laser and the Eater. A sensitive photon detector rose in line with the laser, but on the opposite side of the Eater.

Kathy explained as she fine-tuned the setup, "The smoke particles and metal blocks will help us see the beam's path. Nothing will be reflected from the Eater. The photomultiplier on the opposite side will show that nothing is transmitted through the Eater." She reached out and activated the laser.

Inside the chamber, a bright green beam leaped from the far right-side, punched through the several blocks of metal in its path, and struck the Eater. The photo-detector picked up nothing other than a tiny bit of background reflection from the light-dispersing smoke.

"If we ran this test without any smoke inside the chamber, the light detector would not have budged," Greg said. "Light is absorbed by the Eater as readily as matter. Because of this, we usually keep the viewing port into the isolation chamber closed."

The scientists talked in hushed tones among themselves.

"We have one last test." Greg cut short their murmurs by holding up a 45 caliber bullet. They snapped to attention. He had had a hunch that a little showmanship was needed with this group.

"This is no ordinary bullet. It's an advanced, armor-piercing design we had specially made from depleted uranium with a soft-steel cap. When shot from this rifle," he indicated a stock projecting outward from the side of the isolation chamber, "it can penetrate an inch-thick titanium plate, like this." He held up another plate of dull metal, and knocked twice for effect: thunk, thunk.

"I don't expect you to take my word alone for this, so I've loaded the clip with bullets identical to this one." He pulled a five-shot magazine out of the rifle and showed it to everyone.

"I'm going to ask one of you to shoot me. Well, try to shoot me. We've set the aiming mechanism to shoot at only two targets. I'm going to enter the isolation chamber and place this armor plate in a rack one meter to my right. Our volunteer will take the first shot at the plate so you can see the effectiveness of the bullets. Then, I'll go stand behind the Eater, while the rifle is repositioned to fire at the Eater. On my signal, the volunteer will fire a second shot. If the Eater fails to absorb the bullet, I'll be hit, and killed instantly."

The scientists exchanged shocked glances. "It's okay," Greg quickly continued. "I know the Eater will absorb the bullet, regardless of its density and muzzle velocity which, with this particular rifle, will be somewhere in the neighborhood of a thousand meters per second."

He looked around the room, making eye contact with everyone except Kathy. He licked his lips, which had gone unexpectedly dry. In the calmest voice he could muster, he asked, "Could I get a volunteer to shoot me, please?"

Near the back of the room, a hand shot up. "I'll do it." Greg recognized the voice as belonging to the same scientist who'd objected over the Law of Conservation.

Figures—he thought.

Greg donned a vacuum suit and breathing apparatus. A camera sight on the rifle displayed the target on a monitor. He nodded at the eager volunteer and gave the thumbs up sign to Kathy.

She managed a weak smile in response. She was against the theatrics, but Greg had insisted the show would be incomplete without it. Even scientists were susceptible to a bit of good theater.

Greg picked up the armor plate, entered the airlock, and waited for the green light indicating the cycle was complete and he could proceed into the vacuum chamber.

Entering the eerie silence, he was keenly aware of the target on his back. He glanced back a few times toward the rifle with its high-powered, armor-piercing bullets and tried to reassure himself that it wasn't going to fire spontaneously. Correction, it wasn't *likely* to fire spontaneously. He took a few steps to the side so he wouldn't be in line with one of its two permitted trajectories.

Standing well aside of the clips, Greg guided the armor plate into the waiting stand. "Is that lined up okay?" he asked Kathy through his suit radio.

She checked her monitors. "Looks good here."

Greg walked behind the metal block, turned to face the rifle, and stood a meter to the left, placing the Eater directly between the muzzle and him. He took a deep breath. "Okay. I'm ready to go."

"Roger. Copy that," said Kathy. Greg smiled. Somehow, situations like this always made people talk like they were in the military. "First shot on its way," Kathy reported. She nodded to the volunteer who squeezed the trigger.

Greg looked up to see a distant muzzle flash and the plate beside him shook as a hole appeared through it. In the vacuum, it all happened without a sound. The bullet left a ragged hole in the armor plate behind it before hitting the newly installed reinforced concrete beyond.

They'd calculated the strength and depth of the concrete as well as the force of the bullet several times over before attempting the demonstration. *It wouldn't do to inadvertently punch a hole in the vacuum chamber.*

The isolation chamber didn't implode. *That's a relief*—he thought, and let himself breathe again. Now for the second shot.

Greg's attention was riveted on the rifle as it repositioned to line him up in the sights. Despite their calculations and previous tests, he swallowed uncomfortably. "Ready..." his voice rasped. He cleared his throat. "Ready for next test," he said.

"Copy that," Kathy replied.

Greg looked down the rifle barrel which, from his vulnerable position, appeared significantly longer and larger-bored than he remembered. Seconds ticked by. A bead of sweat trickled past his left eye. When the flash came, he flinched instinctively.

"Are you alright, Greg?" Kathy's voice was calm but concerned.

Am I alright? I don't know—he thought. *Would I feel an armor-piercing bullet go through me, or would it take a few seconds for pain to register? Would I hear the whistle of air leaving my suit, or feel the blood flowing down my leg first?*

He focused his senses on his body. Nothing hurt; that was a good sign. He stepped out from behind the Eater. *No problem. Everything normal.* He realized he hadn't breathed for a while.

"Everything's fine," he exhaled and walked to the airlock door.

An armor piercing bullet was prevented from killing me by a microscopic universe that instantly incorporates everything it touches, and all I can say is, "Everything's fine." Greg laughed. His knees felt a bit wobbly, but he was happy to be walking and breathing at all.

He joined the others watching the high-speed video of the bullet. It had encountered the Eater at one thousand fifty meters per second and disappeared from the universe as if it were no more than a shadow.

The demonstrations were convincing. If anyone had harbored any doubt about the Eater after reading the briefing material, Greg's showmanship had provided the visceral proof they needed.

The final step of the presentation was to compare before and after measurements of the Eater's diameter. The sphere had grown exactly as he'd predicted or, to be more precise, within a respectable five decimal places of his calculation.

Greg invited any remaining doubters to enter the chamber and touch the Eater. No one took him up on the invitation. He was half surprised.

For the past few days, he'd been expecting, bracing himself, to face angry skepticism and distrust. He'd even decided—*If some insufferable fool steps forward bent on losing a finger in order to check it out for themselves, well, I'm prepared to let them do it. At this point, people need to realize the danger and get everyone working together on a solution.*

The group listened attentively to the rest of the presentation. He and Kathy took turns explaining the nature of virtual particles, how the Eater continued to feed on them in the chamber, and how there seemed to be no way to stop it. They did their best to balance the presentation to meet the needs of scientists and laypersons.

Kathy shifted the group's attention to the new RAF generator, and created a few sample microverses to demonstrate how physical properties changed inside them. Showing them the microverses in action would make the science much easier to grasp than laying out the math.

Greg tried not to look annoyed, or away, through this part of her demo. They'd been fighting about it all week long. He didn't want to show them the RAF device. "Then everyone will want one," he'd joked, but they both knew it wasn't a joking matter.

"Isn't the damage done by the original RAF generator reason enough?" he'd argued, but Kathy wouldn't budge.

"How can we call ourselves scientists if we can't let others objectively verify our results?" she'd challenged.

"How can we risk anyone building more of these and unleashing them into the world knowing that even one was enough to threaten that world?" he'd shot back.

Kathy held steady to her conviction that only a compelling and accessible demonstration, one that could be verified through observation, would convince the visiting specialists. In the end, Greg gave in.

Now, as he watched the acceptance set in on the faces of those watching, he was glad she hadn't relented. She was right. They had to get everyone up to speed as fast as possible, and her demo was effective.

"Wait a minute," someone objected, near the end of her presentation. "Everything you've shown us suggests that these microverses can only exist so long as the RAF generator is activated. How was a stable microverse created? Why can't you just switch the Eater off like these other ones?"

Greg and Kathy exchanged a brief glance. *You're the theoretical quantum physicist—*Kathy sent. *You explain.*

Greg grimaced. "Right before Dr. Leigh disappeared, he set up a number of experimental conditions that, theoretically, should have been able to create stable microverses. Apparently, the Eater is one such microverse. We haven't experimented with any of those settings yet.

"Dr. Leigh was about to share his findings with us when he vanished. We'll probably never know the conditions of its creation. We don't understand its properties, how it persists, or how to collapse it."

A soft murmur rose but, to Greg's relief, the questioner seemed satisfied with his answer. The relief was short-lived.

"Has there been any update on the disappearances of Dr. Leigh and Dr. Rusalov?"

Greg swallowed. "No, I'm afraid not."

He knew none of this was going to be easy, the questions would keep coming. And after the scientists, they still had to face the politicians.

The plan was to get the scientists up to speed, and they could help advise and pressure on the respective governments. So far, it appeared to be working. Skepticism was giving way to acceptance, if not understanding.

The complexities of the details of RAF theory would be beyond almost everyone for quite some time. Nonetheless, to the scientific mind the conclusion was clear and irrefutable: the Eater was an exigent threat.

Kathy squeezed Greg's shoulder as she watched the scientists file out of the lab at the end of the morning session. "Well, done, Dr. Mahajani."

"Thank you, Dr. Liang. To you, too. If only this afternoon's presentation to the politicians goes as well. I don't want to jinx it, but I'm pretty sure it's going to be a nightmare. Even if they believe us, and that's a long shot in itself, how do you spur world leaders into collaborative action? I'm serious. I can't even imagine it."

"I hear you. They all put on a good show of hiring scientists to advise them. They sit through the demos and explanations patiently enough. But do they believe it? Deep down, believe it? Fear it?"

"Yeah, I can see it now. All through the meeting, they're going to be thinking about how to lay the blame and responsibility, how they can dodge it themselves, how to use this for political gain, how to avoid shelling out money or making any real commitment. Oh, and above all, how to save their political reputations once things turn nasty. And things are going to turn nasty. Very nasty, very fast."

21

"OKAY, OKAY. LET'S CALL THIS MEETING TO ORDER." Prime Minister Hudson rapped the gavel sharply against a worn square of mahogany. This was her first time hosting the G26—the reconfigured version of the old G20 that incorporated the newer developed nations of the world. She was not going to let it run out of control.

Greg surveyed the room. He recognized most of the faces at the head table without the aid of his lattice. They represented an impressive array of prominent figures regularly featured on worldwide news feeds and accustomed to dealing with the world's problems.

And yet, despite their many years of political and public experience, their eyes and facial micro-movements belied they were uniformly on edge, still reeling from their briefings of the morning's lab demo and wondering what other surprises might erupt from this unassuming young man and woman seated beside the Pacifica Prime Minister.

Each leader brought their own coterie of three or four advisers, who filled the rows of chairs around the main tables. As requested in the invitation, one member of each team was a scientist, but economists and military advisers far outnumbered those with a technical background. Many had attended the morning demonstration.

Greg shrugged and fidgeted where his suit rubbed up against his skin. *It's not fair. You get to wear a light, airy dress, and I have to walk around in this straightjacket and silk noose*—he complained to Kathy via their private lattice.

Beside him, the love of his life laid a calming hand on his leg and squeezed gently. He glanced at her reassuring smile and tried to calm himself.

Oh, yeah? Well, any time you'd like to trade your comfy shoes for these heels, you just let me know!—she sent back.

Greg chortled softly, drawing a glare from the Prime Minister. He cleared his throat and wiggled in his chair, trying to reposition himself to ease the constraints of the fabric.

Kathy watched him fidget. If he couldn't contain his rising irritation, both internal and external, he was going to blow this. She couldn't fault him. It was painful to deal with the many and varied layers of bureaucracy they'd been subjected to.

Greg, I know you're nervous and you're frustrated with all the political nonsense—watching everybody shuffle their feet when what we need to do is take immediate action. I am, too. But you have to keep in mind, this isn't any normal presentation. Our lives are riding on the outcome. All our lives, Greg. Everywhere.

No matter how impossible it feels to deal with these guys, no matter how dense or ignorant they seem, no matter how hard it is to be patient and respectful, we can't let ourselves forget for a second that they have all the power. If we want to get anything done, we have to deal with them on their terms. End of pep talk—She tried to flash a gently reassuring smile but it was too tight-lipped and uncertain to be convincing.

I'll be okay—he sent back. *Prime Minister Hudson will help us with the political wrangling. We're only here to provide technical support.* He recruited his lattice to calm his itches, to hold his head up confidently, and relax his facial muscles.

The Prime Minister of Pacifica jumped straight to the point.

"Good afternoon, ladies and gentlemen. We are at this meeting because the planet faces a threat greater than any it has ever known. Greater than the Cold War of the 1950s, greater than the economic depressions of the twenty-first century, and greater than the Global Proxy Wars that have plagued our world since. A crisis even more pressing than global climate change and the desertification that has ravaged so many of our productive lands.

"This threat is not something that can be addressed purely through political will. It is an immediate and physical threat. Negotiations and political maneuvering, alone, won't save us.

"Your scientists spent the morning reviewing the data and discussing the nature of this threat with Dr. Mahajani and Dr. Liang. Your experts have confirmed the findings: the growth of the microscale universe that our scientists call the 'Eater' is unstoppable. They've seen for themselves that this thing is capable of absorbing the entire Earth and everything on it, of destroying all life. Observations in the months ahead will allow them to confirm its growth rate. Even though we have isolated it in a dark vacuum chamber, it continues to grow."

"This is a fiasco," the Russian President's deep voice overrode PM Hudson's. "Your people have created this...this catastrophe and now you want to hold the world hostage? You expect our cooperation in this?"

"They should be in prison," the German Chancellor added.

The room erupted with angry noise; politicians shouted and jabbed their fingers toward the Prime Minister.

She let it play out a couple of minutes; she appreciated the need to vent a little terror and ire before getting down to strategic planning and crisis recovery on a global scale. The sharp rap of the gavel reigned their attention back in.

"On the next outburst, I will clear the room and you can all go home and wait to die," the PM shouted. Stunned faces gaped at her, but it worked. The meeting room grew quiet again.

"Thank you. I know this is difficult for all of us. But we don't have time for accusations and recriminations. Humanity needs us *now*. We must find a way to work together *now*."

Her eyes swept around the table, looking for any challengers. For the moment, the objectors fell silent. She stood upright and continued.

"To my right are Drs. Liang and Mahajani, protégés of Dr. Darian Leigh. As you know, Dr. Leigh and another member of his team, Dr. Rusalov, have been missing for the past several months. Sadly, we must assume some sort of foul play in their disappearance, as there has been no communication from them, or anyone having knowledge of their whereabouts, since late January.

"Though less renowned than Dr. Leigh, Dr. Liang and Dr. Mahajani have intelligence-enhancing dendy lattice systems similar to his. Their personal lattices are newer but no less effective."

This created a stir around the room. The advising scientists, for the most part, had not emphasized this detail to their superiors. The confession of the super-human intelligences of Greg and Kathy clearly grabbed the politicians' attention. Many of their universities had attempted to recruit Darian Leigh, but he chose to remain in North America.

Now there were two new lattice-enhanced scientists in the world. The possibility one of them might be available caused a spark of excitement in the room. Lattices for memory recall and communications were common in academic communities, but lattice-based enhanced intelligence was unique to Darian Leigh. And now, to Kathy and Greg.

The Prime Minister continued. "*Our* scientists...," she paused to add weight to the word *Our*, "have spent the months since Dr. Leigh's disappearance, characterizing the Eater in an attempt to understand how to stop it from growing, and how to destroy it.

"They have attained a deeper understanding of the malleability of natural physical laws and how the..." she glanced at the page on the table before her, "the Reality Assertion Field Generator can be used to create tiny universes where those laws are altered.

"Despite their growing understanding of this new and complex physics, they assure me the threat is real, and they do not know yet how to stop it."

She surveyed the cautiously concerned faces staring back at her. "Your own scientists have been able to confirm the danger the Eater poses to absolutely every bit and kind of matter, energy, and even virtual particles it encounters." There was nervous laughter at the mention of virtual particles.

She raised her hands in a plea for patience. "I know. I know. I can't follow any of this either. We have to trust the experts here."

"Wasn't it the experts who got us into this mess?" a voice shouted from the middle of the room. PM Hudson managed to contain her scowl.

"Greg and Kathy...," Greg noted her deliberate shift to the familiar, "...have assured me they can predict with great accuracy that the Eater will consume its isolation chamber in a little over twenty-two-and-a-half years." Murmurs and some derisive laughter arose from her audience.

"As politicians, many of us are familiar with such predictions. Frequently, the more accurate they appear, the less reliable they are. But, ladies and gentlemen, physics is not economics. Let's not forget how accurately the equations of physics can predict the motion of the planets and stars, and how accurately they predict the behavior of the sophisticated electronics we take for granted every day."

"Not to mention climate change," the French President said.

"That's an excellent example," PM Hudson noted. "Twenty years ago, world leaders ignored the models forecasting the consequences of global warming. They were wrong, and scientific consensus was right. Now, many of our nations are combating the dire consequences they predicted. Physics is unavoidable, no matter how much we may dislike its predictions.

"Greg and Kathy have given us serious warnings about a grave threat to humanity, and that threat comes with a deadline. If we don't heed the warning, our entire world will be gone—completely gone—in fewer than twenty-three years. We are talking about the end of Earth and the end of humanity."

The room went silent. Pacifica was not the most powerful nation on the planet and some had questioned whether its Prime Minister should be chairing this meeting. Circumstance thrust the responsibility on her, but a good many eyes in the room turned to the more seasoned representatives of various factions and alliances to see if they were convinced of the seriousness of the threat. Some were, Prime Minister Akira of Japan, for example. Others brazenly showed their scorn.

PM Hudson invited Greg and Kathy to stand up.

"Dr. Liang and Dr. Mahajani have prepared an outline as to how the world should prepare for this unprecedented disaster. They will continue to work relentlessly to understand the Eater, to try to stop it before it destroys the planet. However, there is no guarantee that will be possible.

"In the event the microverse can't be stopped in the time we have remaining—and that is a strong possibility—we've created a twenty-year contingency plan to move a significant portion of humanity out of harm's way. I've invited Dr. Liang and Dr. Mahajani here to explain their plan and to answer your questions."

Before the two scientists could begin, the distinctive voice of the British Prime Minister rose above the din. "With all due respect, you *do* realize how totally incredible all of this sounds to us? Do you not, Madam Prime Minister?"

"Let me review our situation," he pressed on before Ms. Hudson could respond. "Some crazy super-scientist created an unstoppable planet-eating device. He and a colleague from his lab then disappear, never to be heard from again. Now, nobody knows what this thing is, how it works, or how to turn it off? And you're asking us to trust his two mad super-scientist lab mates—who, by the way, may have murdered him for nefarious purposes of their own.

"You'll have to forgive me," he snickered, "but that sounds more like a superheroes comic book or a sci-fi movie plot. Maybe we should ask your Superman what to do!"

World leaders and advisors laughed with him. Greg, Kathy, and the PM didn't even crack a smile.

"I didn't say they were crazy," the PM responded, "but other than that, yes, that's pretty much it. I am convinced, personally and as leader of Pacifica, that the course they recommend is our best, if not only, hope for the future. I implore you to join me in supporting the project they will outline over the next few minutes." With that, she stopped talking and motioned Greg and Kathy to begin their presentation.

Greg cleared his throat. "Thank you..." he managed to croak. His free hand drifted upward and loosened his tie a touch. He took in the rows of expectant faces scrutinizing him. *Don't be such a putz*—he said to himself—*you've given plenty of talks before. This is just one more. Don't let them intimidate you. Imagine them all sitting there in their underwear. Lime green thongs oughta do it.*

He smiled, and a number of heads bobbed reassuringly, assuming the smile had been offered as a shy apology for the false start. Most of them had been in the hot seat themselves at one time or another, presenting to a tough audience. He cleared his throat and began again.

"Thank you, Madam Prime Minister. Ladies and gentlemen, I'll ask you to close your eyes and activate your lattices in Visual Mode. Your chairs are all equipped with lattice induction devices; no need to wear your headbands. You will not require audio, tactile, or other inSenses, and may remain in

Full Consciousness throughout this presentation. Please feel free to stop me and ask questions at any time."

He reached out with his own lattice to connect directly to his audience. As with all G26 meetings, an IT team had arrived ahead of the guests and shielded the room from all outside internet connectivity.

He activated his lattice communications, and was relieved to find the team had done a thorough job. Darian Leigh's rogue latent memories were still out there somewhere in the web, searching for a way in, and actively trying to invade and reintegrate into his and Kathy's brains every time they connected to the internet. Thanks to the efficient IT team, he could momentarily relax his constant vigilance.

Greg waited for the leaders and advisers to lean back in their seats, close their eyes and ready themselves.

The less lattice-experienced participants, generally the older set, moved through stiff, awkward checks and adjustments as they interfaced with the induction plates in the headrests.

Greg overlaid a ghost image of the presentation across his own visual field. He activated a local feed and checked the readiness of everyone in the room. The security team kept their lattices isolated from the presentation. Greg could track their activity as they interfaced with hardwired surveillance devices outside the room and communicated with their colleagues posted around the building. If he wanted to, he could listen in on their supposedly secure conversations being broadcast within their segregated lattice net.

He sensed the leaders activating their lattices for external visual input, as if they were watching inSense at home, minus the auditory, tactile and olfactory channels. A few had accidentally gone a bit too far and disconnected their voluntary musculature from conscious motor systems control.

Deep inSense was the standard mode for most entertainments, certainly among the blockbuster full-experience movies raging through Hollywood, Bollywood, and Hong Kong. Greg reached into the lattices of those who had gone Deep, and gently corrected their settings to save them any possible embarrassment at being in such a defenseless state.

One by one, he checked each attendee, preparing the group to properly experience the visuals that would explain the plan he and Kathy had developed over the past few months.

I hope this works—he thought. Both he and Kathy were tempted to just implant what they wanted the group to believe and do.

Kathy had grown particularly adept at mind viruses over the past few months. She discovered she could hack into the mind of anyone with a lattice, echoing their senses and perceptions in a carefully partitioned section of her own brain. With little effort, she could implant false perceptions and memories, new skills, and beliefs. This new ability at once excited and terrified her. She and Greg knew better than to tell anyone about it.

They'd made a practice of mastering their lattice abilities and exploring their limits. They'd find a quiet path in the woods, well away from internet connections, and try to inject one another with harmless conceptual viruses as they walked along hand-in-hand. The goal was to find a way to recognize, block, isolate, and recover from any attempt at changing their core knowledge and beliefs. It was intensely serious play, crucial in their fight to stave off or integrate the flood of thoughts and memories from Darian.

To people they met along the trail, they looked like a pair of leisurely strolling young lovers, entirely engrossed in one another's presence. Internally, they were engaged in fierce battle, sending wave after wave of attack viruses against their opponent's defenses.

The practice helped them identify and understand their own minds. They became adept at identifying incompatible ideas and defending against integration with their existing cognitive structures.

It wouldn't have been too hard to forcibly alter the politicians' personal conceptual structures—their mental framework of knowledge and beliefs, what Kathy called their "concepta"—and get them simply to agree with the ideas she and Greg were presenting. But it would take time to map and alter each of the twenty-six conceptas around the main table, more time than they had in the presentation.

Besides, what was the point of trying to save humanity if it wasn't smart enough to help with its own salvation?

The attendee-status check running in the background of his lattice sent Greg an alert.

Whoa! What was that? A pushback surge intruded into his lattice, drawing his full attention. His security barriers snapped up. *Kathy? Did you feel that?* If he didn't know better, he'd have sworn she just took a concepta swipe at him.

Greg examined the routine checking everyone's inSense setup. The pushback had occurred at the same moment his algorithm attempted a preliminary intrusion into Reverend LaMontagne's lattice to verify its readiness.

The couple had been surprised to see the Reverend as a key representative of the New Confederacy at the G-26 panel. In preparing for today's presentations, they had discussed at length whom the various nations might send. In considering the New Confederacy's candidates, neither had imagined LaMontagne in the role.

It was an odd choice. The New Confederacy was not so far away and not so politically unstable that they couldn't have sent President Mitchell. The

Japanese, Chinese, and Russians had all thought the meeting important enough to send *their* leaders. That the New Confederacy chose to send Secretary of State, Virgil Hartland, in Mitchell's stead was noted by all present, though it wasn't particularly unusual for the famously paranoid New Confederacy President. One could easily conclude the recent death of Secretary Totts and the ensuing financial crisis had required the President to stay home.

However, the appointment of Reverend Alan LaMontagne as co-representative with Secretary Hartland—a man of God in such an important secular position—was unique among world powers. His role here rankled many of the participants.

Greg focused briefly on the Reverend and sent another interrogatory pulse. It was rebuffed as casually as the first. He was about to make a more concerted third attempt when Kathy intervened—*Wait!*

The Reverend's eyes were peacefully closed in preparation for the lattice-fed presentation, but his lips had curled into the barest hint of a smile. It did not escape Greg's notice.

Kathy caught Greg's eye. *RSA encrypt using the time (HH.MM.SS) you picked me up for our first date*—she sent. Greg immediately set up the algorithm.

What was that about?—he asked.

I think the Reverend may have a lattice like ours, one of the intelligence enhancing versions—Kathy said.

His inSense security is stronger than the standard models. Maybe he just got some program upgrades—Greg replied.

That was no upgrade—answered Kathy. *I tried to piggyback a deeper query on your check-in routine. He swatted it away like nothing. No inSense system in the world can do that. No, he's enhanced. I'm sure of it.*

But where could he have gotten one of Darian's lattice viruses?

Maybe he stole it. Maybe Darian gave away some copies.

No, I can't see him doing that. He would have mentioned it. There is one simple explanation. The only lattice virus capsule unaccounted for is Larry's. Do you think Larry would've given LaMontagne his pill? She sent him a summary of her reasoning, complete with annotated evidence.

What? No way!—Greg argued. *Larry would never have given his pill to a religious fundamentalist. Not knowingly. I see why you might think he did, but the evidence is so flimsy, it makes our speculations about the Eater look rock solid. And we know how weak those are.*

I agree, it's weak—Kathy acknowledged. *And two-plus-two doesn't usually add up to seven. But the Reverend brushed us both off like nothing. Even if it was clumsy and more forceful than required, it felt the exactly same as our lattice sparring. His lattice is enhanced like ours, Greg. Like Larry's would have been. And the only access to that level of lattice technology was through Darian or Larry. There's no way on*

Earth Darian would have shared that with the Reverend. You know how he felt about organized religion and its leaders. That only leaves Larry.

Greg had to admit the Reverend's unnecessarily strong rebuff of a simple preparatory exploration was much more forceful than a standard inSense lattice could have managed. Maybe Kathy was right, however outlandish it seemed.

Okay—he sent back—*just for the sake of argument, let's assume you're right. What do we do with that?*

Kathy considered. *Well, now he knows we know, so let's back off and see which side he comes down on*—she suggested.

Greg could see no harm in that. Their entire exchange had taken only milliseconds and went unnoticed by everyone except the two of them. *And probably the Reverend*—Greg surmised.

The addition of a possible third enhanced intelligence, one of unknown and quite possibly hostile sympathies, increased the complexity of the upcoming negotiations considerably. Greg continued checking other participants' lattice settings and began feeding the prepared presentation. All he could do, for now, was to stay hyper-alert and let the Reverend reveal his intentions to them.

22

GREG NARRATED THE CAPTIVATING VISUALS FLOWING within the lattice-fed perceptions of the G26 leaders, representatives, and advisors of the most powerful nations in the world.

"This is a projection of the end of the world that will take place in a little over twenty-two years," he began. "Within two days of the Eater reaching the walls of its enclosure, it will consume the entire university and the top of Mount Burnaby.

"A few days later all of Earth's atmosphere and most of the waters in the ocean will have flowed into the sphere. Except for anyone hiding out in pressurized bunkers, every person on Earth will be dead. Ten days after that, Earth will be consumed entirely, bunkers and all, leaving only a grayish planet-sized sphere behind. Nobody—nothing—will be safe from the sphere. Not anywhere."

In the inSense simulation, the panel watched the blue Earth, its oceans, and continents, being eclipsed by a dull, gray orb.

"Although the Eater appears to be locked into a specific position relative to our planet, it has no measurable mass. We believe it will remain in stable planetary orbit around the sun. But, without Earth's gravity, our moon will have to seek out its own solar orbit."

Slowly freed of the confines of the planetary gravity well, the Moon swung in a wider and wider orbit. It eventually broke away from the planet to which it had been bound for eons and spun outward seeking a new solar orbit.

"Of course, nothing will remain of Earth or of human civilization by then, except for a little space debris which will eventually either be consumed by the Eater, or float off into the solar system."

Greg paused to let that sink in as his audience "watched" the bleak gray sphere take the place of the vibrant blue planet they now inhabited.

"With nothing but empty space around it, the Eater's growth rate will slow considerably. We project it will take millions or billions of years before it threatens another planet.

"Once we became aware of the threat the Eater poses to the planet and accepted that we're probably unable to stop it, Dr. Liang and I began working around the clock to come up with a plan to save as much of the planet's population as possible.

"For decades now, scientists—even the renowned Stephen Hawking—have been suggesting that the only route to ensure humanity's existence in the long term is to colonize space. We agree.

"There are a lot of challenges to be met, not the least of which is that we know of no other planets in our solar system that are amenable to human life."

The inSense presentation showed an old Apollo rocket blasting off. Views of Earth's moon, Venus, Mars, Saturn, and Neptune floated by.

"All of these places are poor candidates for supporting terrestrial life. They're either too hot, too cold, have too much gravity, or they have no appreciable atmosphere or water."

The visuals zoomed in on a rocky planetoid, floating alone in black space.

"Meet Vesta, the second largest planetoid within the asteroid belt found between the orbits of Mars and Jupiter.

"At a little over five hundred kilometers in diameter, Vesta is considered a *protoplanet* because it has a metallic iron-nickel core making up a little under half its total diameter, an overlying rocky mantle, and a surface crust.

"It's also a strong candidate for internal terraforming and colonization. We propose drilling six tunnels running the length of one axis of the asteroid, each about ten kilometers in diameter. The tunnels will be arranged like the bullet chambers in a six-gun revolver, spaced evenly around the core about seventy kilometers below the surface."

Greg read sentiments ranging from amused doubt to outright shock from the participants around the table. It didn't take a lattice connection to interpret their skepticism.

He plowed on with the presentation. The inSense animation displayed in broad strokes the ideas he and Kathy had developed.

"We'll flatten the floors of the tunnels—the section closest to the outside of the asteroid—plug the ends with fifty kilometers of rock, seal the chambers air-tight, pressurize them with an Earthlike atmosphere, add a solar-equivalent light tube the length of the tunnels, and spin the entire asteroid up to one revolution every sixteen minutes to provide artificial gravity equivalent to what we have on Earth.

"Then we'll add water we mine from comet-type bodies in the Oort cloud and a complete biosphere. We'll build high-density habitations and infrastructure to support the new inhabitants. We'll construct smaller chambers under the main tunnels to support agriculture. This will provide more than ten thousand square kilometers of living space, about five times the area of Tokyo. At a similar population density to Tokyo, we would have enough room for sixty million people. At best, we can only hope to move about ten million people—about 0.1% of the present population—in the time between the completion of the Vesta colony and the destruction of Earth." The image faded to black, and pairs of eyes all over the room flew open.

Greg knew what they were thinking; he'd thought it, himself. *How can I get myself and my family in that ten million?*

"That's the best you can do?" The Italian Prime Minister protested. "Only ten million people out of ten billion? How can we permit this?" She looked to the other Southern European Union leaders for support. The murmured discussions between the delegates grew rapidly in volume.

"It is not a matter of permission," Greg raised his voice over the background din before further objections could be raised. "The alternative is zero; everyone dead, and the planet destroyed." The room went quiet.

Greg continued in as reasonable a tone as he could muster. "Listen, ten million is the most we project could be saved with all available resources put to work. It's also a number that will provide sufficient variation to guarantee the genetic health of the human species. It's physically impossible to build and operate enough space ships to save more. And, if we don't start work immediately, the number is going to be significantly less. If you have any better ideas, we're all ears."

"We've talked about space programs for decades," interjected President Franklin T. Carvin from the North American remnant still calling itself the United States of America. "Heck, we've barely managed to put people on the moon or keep that ramshackle space station loping along at all over the past few years. How can we possibly build a colony in a distant asteroid belt in twenty years?" His barely suppressed laugh at the end of his question was echoed around the room.

"Actually, we'll only have about twelve years to finish the first colony tunnel," replied Greg. "That's the latest we can start moving people out there."

"Hah!" was the general response from around the table. Many just shook their heads, and several leaders shared derisive comments with their immediate neighbors.

A sliding door whooshed open in the wall behind Greg and a metallic sphere about a meter in diameter floated into the room. Conversation ceased abruptly as attendees wondered if the new arrival was part of the presentation and calculated the fastest route to an exit—just in case.

The security detail drew their weapons and took aim at the object, but held their fire.

Greg shot Kathy a sideways look; his raised eyebrows conveyed his query. *I thought we were going to wait until later, before beginning the demonstration phase of the presentation.*

You were losing them. I had to do something—Kathy replied.

Greg pretended not to notice Reverend LaMontagne hiding a smirk behind one hand.

"Ladies and gentlemen, I'd like to introduce you to Alpha-001," Kathy announced as the sphere hovered to the center of the meeting table.

"Alpha-001 is a prototype mechanical robot I've constructed to demonstrate how we envisage construction of the Vesta colony being completed in reasonable time. We call them Cybrids, short for Cybernetic Hybrids."

She turned to her left. "Madam Prime Minister, if you could ask the guards to holster their weapons, please. Alpha-001 is not a threat to this meeting." The PM nodded to her security people.

"Thank you," Kathy continued. "Almost all space projects since the first astronaut orbited the Earth have been based on humans working in space.

"Long-term residencies in the International Space Stations and the highly-publicized Mission to Mars failure of 2028 have demonstrated the perils of space for humans. When we travel into space, we must carry our Earth-like environment with us. That includes air, water, food, and shielding from heavy radiation as well as from micro-meteors. All of this must be transported from Earth in armored containers we call spaceships, and survive travel over hundreds of thousands or millions of kilometers."

"In past, humans were necessary because only we had the ability to think and act autonomously without direct operation from a distant Earth. But that's about to change.

"Our DNND technology has provided us with a way to construct independent cognitive systems, and to program them with human knowledge and even human personalities. We can have human cognition and know-how in space, without the necessity of transporting our entire supporting environment."

The attendees were almost bursting with questions, and Kathy rushed ahead to finish.

"Alpha-001 is only half the size of the construction robots we plan for this project. It contains a power source based on the Reality Assertion Field, or RAF, technology. It requires no food, air, water or fueling. It can operate in the harsh vacuum of space for ten years at a time or more.

"In its full-scale form, the Cybrid will contain a central processing unit based on the dendy lattice, which will give it complete operational autonomy and decision-making capabilities. The lattice will house a fully human personality and memories, and greater than human intelligence. It can calculate complex orbital dynamics while mining metal-rich asteroids.

"Using these mechanical workers, the Cybrids, will provide us with a huge population of sturdy space workers and help us to save the personalities and memories of millions more people that would otherwise be lost."

"Wait. Are you saying you've solved the Artificial Intelligence problem?" asked the Indian Prime Minister, who'd been a well-known Computing Science scholar before entering politics.

Greg jumped in, "We've assembled a team of international experts to help solve quite a number of engineering problems in designing Alpha-001, although this particular model is only about as smart as a dog. We have a clean, long-lasting power source, reliable propulsion and manipulation systems, and autonomous intelligence.

"There will be many more inventions coming out soon that will seem nearly-miraculous, even to most scientists and engineers. Humanity has been on the brink of developing these advancements for a long time. The dendy lattice that Sharon Leigh first designed, the one she accidentally exposed her unborn son to, has simply allowed Kathy and me to think a little faster, and to explore a little deeper than our colleagues. The technology has come a long way, thanks to the advancements made by Sharon's son, Darian Leigh, who continued her work and extended it into new areas."

"Dr. Mahajani, you talked about programming the robot workers, the Cybrids, with human personalities," the Indian PM began. "That sounds a lot like downloading the human soul, in much the same way Kurzweil described in his book, 'The Singularity is Near', doesn't it?"

"Darian Leigh argued strongly against the existence of anything like a human soul," replied Greg. "The dendy technology simply allows us to copy the concepta and persona—that is, the knowledge, beliefs, memories, opinions, habits, and personal preferences—our data, if you will, from the dendy-connected brain of a person into the blank semiconductor lattice of a robot. The biological person is still who they were when the process started; their brain patterns will only have been copied into a non-biological brain."

"So you can make more than one copy of a person?"

Greg was not happy with where this line of questioning was leading. "Yes," he admitted, hesitantly. "Frankly, I don't see what we'd gain by doing that under these circumstances. Right now, the lattice copying procedure gives us a chance of storing the complete personalities of millions of people whose lives we couldn't possibly save.

"Perhaps, in future, we'll be able to copy those stored personalities back into biological bodies. Perhaps, we'll figure a way to try out newly designed personalities in some kind of virtual reality before they become embodied.

"I can't predict where this might take us. We have other more pressing issues right now. We need to save and encourage as much diversity of personalities out there as possible, in much the same way as we encourage biological diversity. It makes a species hardier, stronger, and more resistant to environmental shocks and surprises."

PM Sidhu was not finished. "Even so, isn't this opening the way for a tough new species of machine intelligence, these Cybrids as you call them, to compete with humanity? I mean, if we create these machines and give them free reign in space while our home planet disintegrates, why would they bother helping us? Are we working toward a solution that will ultimately destroy us, given the chance?"

The question was one Greg had not allowed himself to dwell on. He scrambled to formulate an answer, one he hoped that he, himself, would find convincing.

"The Cybrids would be imbued with human personas. They will think of themselves as human on the inside. Why would they turn against their own people?"

"Because that's what I would do," a voice called out, "and what everyone around this table would do, given the chance to start over in a new environment with a new race of beings stronger and smarter than humans."

The words flew out of Greg's mouth without thought of the possible consequences, "Well, I hope very few people who think that way are chosen for Cybrid embodiment."

23

KATHY GAVE GREG A SEVERE LOOK and sent—*Are you trying to make sure we get no support at all for this program?*

Sorry—Greg replied. *I didn't think that one through.* Out of the corner of his eye he caught Reverend LaMontagne smirking again, and this time, less guardedly.

Clearly, many of the G26 leaders and their advisors had not been pleased with his answers. The room was alive with open muttering, emphatic shaking of heads, flying hands and, everywhere, faces carved with deep furrows and sour scowls. This was not an encouraging sign.

Surprisingly, Greg noted, the Reverend wasn't among the overtly distressed. He had contained his smirk and now leaned forward in his seat, with an eager and thoughtful expression on his face, absent-mindedly stroking his chin.

I would have thought a "Man of God" would be voicing the most and the loudest objections here—Greg speculated quietly to himself. *Very interesting.*

Numerous voices shouted unintelligible, overlapping questions.

PM Hudson held up her hands, trying to calm them all down. "We're sure you all have a lot of questions. Remember, the purpose of this demonstration by Drs. Liang and Mahajani is to convince you we do have the scientific know-how to build this colony. What we need now is the political will to make it happen."

"How is it floating there like that?" someone asked, happily changing the topic. "Have you discovered anti-gravity?"

Relieved to return to the science, Kathy answered patiently, "Not really anti-gravity *per se*. We can weaken the Higgs field interaction between the Cybrid's matter and the Earth's gravitational field. That makes it so the robot seems to have less mass, so little it can be easily kept afloat using gentle internal fans."

While the leaders and advisers paused to process and ponder the implications of that, the measured voice of China's President Chu emerged. "Let us accept that you can develop autonomous construction robots that are capable of developing an asteroid colony. How are we to transport these robots to Vesta in any reasonable amount of time?"

Greg had been prepared for that question and was glad to have the meeting back on track. "Good question. The asteroid belt is farther away from Earth than Mars. The fastest transit time to Mars, that is, when it is closest to Earth and using the best available rockets, is about four months. Going to Vesta, which is on average nearly three-hundred million kilometers farther from Earth, would take those conventional rockets at least two years. Clearly, on our tight schedule, this would make for considerable constraints. If you will indulge us a moment, we've set up a little demonstration here to show you how we can shorten the travel time using RAF technology."

As Greg spoke, Kathy reached under the table in front of her and pulled out four things: a potato, a spring-loaded potato gun, an inch-thick block of wood, and another block of steel. She handed the potato and the spring-loaded gun to Greg. She walked to one end of the conference room and she set the blocks into the two sturdy clamps they'd positioned there earlier.

Greg held up the potato gun. "No worries, fellas," Greg said to the nearest security officer. "It's just a toy. Many of you will recognize this as a potato gun. We stick the barrel end into this potato and pull out a small plug.

"There isn't much to these old-fashioned ones. When I pull the trigger, it causes a small build-up of air pressure behind the plug and propels it outward." He shot a plug at the wall.

"You'll notice the plug doesn't have a lot of velocity and, because it's only a small piece of potato, it doesn't have much momentum."

He paused to survey the bemused faces around the room. "Now, what if I said I could split that board at the other end of the room with this potato gun? I imagine you'd think, a piece of potato shot out of this thing couldn't even *reach* that board, let alone break it." Someone at the table laughed, but most just stared stone-faced, wondering where Greg was going with this.

As he spoke, Kathy moved back to the relative safety of Greg's end of the room. She sat down at her open laptop beside him and pressed a few keys. A cylindrical beam of translucent violet light, about five centimeters in diameter sprang into existence between Greg and the wooden board at the other end of the table. Around the room, an intrigued audience collectively gasped and leaned forward.

Greg reloaded the gun and placed the tip of the barrel an inch inside the beam of light, and aimed precisely along its length.

"This cylindrical Reality Assertion Field between the barrel of the gun and the target is a complex field. Ninety-nine percent of it, up to right before it touches the plank, reduces the apparent mass of the potato plug so that it is more highly accelerated by the compressed air behind it. No doubt most of you will recall from your school years that acceleration is equal to force divided by mass ('a' equals 'f' over 'm')." Blank faces looked back at him.

Greg laughed. "Or maybe not. How about this? If we throw a small rock with the exact same effort as a big one, the small rock will fly farther." People nodded understanding.

"So while this piece of potato is being pushed by the compressed air in the gun, it will be almost without perceptible mass. The force of the air will be able to move it at a much higher than normal velocity. In fact, by the time it leaves the barrel of the gun, it will be traveling as fast as a bullet."

The guards in the room leaned forward at the mention of a bullet, and Greg hastened to explain, "Don't worry. It's only a little piece of potato, and it'll only travel that fast within the purple part of the light beam." The guards relaxed a little but remained alert.

"If you look at the far end of this light beam, you'll see the color changes to yellow. Just before the potato plug exits the beam, another RAF field will increase its apparent mass by a factor of thousands, to fifty grams. However, it won't have enough travel time in that part of the beam to lose any of its acquired velocity. And, just for good measure, we'll increase its physical hardness just before impact.

"Now, for those of you who do remember high-school physics, you might be thinking that the friction of the air on the super-light potato plug in the purple beam would slow it down before it ever reached the yellow beam at the other end. Normally, that would be true. However, in this case, the reduction in the Higgs field interaction that removes the mass of the potato also proportionally reduces the air friction. The potato plug will act as if it's in a vacuum. Let's see what the result is."

He took aim and pulled the trigger. The wooden board split apart with a loud "crack!" The protective steel plate behind it rang out as it absorbed the impact of the potato plug.

The audience jumped and then laughed nervously. The German Chancellor reached over and picked up the piece of potato from where it landed after bouncing off the metal plate. She held it up and squished it between her thumb and forefinger, for all to see.

Greg explained, "The basis for rockets is action and reaction. When propellant is expelled from one end at high velocity, it exerts a force on the rest of the rocket in the other direction. The RAF generator allows us to alter the relative masses of the propellant and ship. Increasing the acceleration of the propellant makes the rocket move faster. It's a bit more complicated than that, but you get the idea.

"We calculate that a properly outfitted ship could travel from Earth to Vesta in five to seven hours." Several individuals gasped, and lively chatter threatened to take over.

"So, how much is all this gonna cost us?" Representative for the New Confederacy, Secretary of State, Virgil Hartland's Texas heavy drawl cut through and refocused the diffused attention.

Faces turned his way as he continued, "I mean, the technological wizardry y'all have shown us today is remarkable. But at some point, we have to win the support of our voters. And the world economies haven't exactly been hummin' along the past thirty years. Most of us here are not in any position to go to our voters and ask them to pony up for another 'make work' program. We tried sippin' from that well a few times too many this century."

Greg was dismayed by the number of heads nodding in agreement. He wondered if they'd been listening at all. Didn't they realize they were discussing the end of the world? *There is no 'Plan B' here, folks!*

His first impulse was to walk around the table and slap each one of them upside the head. He resisted. Barely. Instead, he tried to make his point in a different way.

"Your electorate will all be dead if we *don't* do this," he said.

"Well, hell," Hartland replied, "They're pretty much all gonna be dead anyway, no matter what we do, aren't they?"

Greg was stunned. He accepted the inevitable massive loss of life the planet was facing. He and Kathy hadn't held out much hope of saving more than a token sampling of humanity, just enough for it to survive. *Maybe I was naïve to hope preserving the human species would be motivation enough.* He looked to PM Hudson in silent desperation.

The support he sought arrived from a completely unexpected source: Reverend Alan LaMontagne.

"Now Virgil," he began, his deep baritone automatically commanding attention. "Do you truly believe that God would abandon His people in this hour? Can't you see that He has brought these two gifted, young scientists and their miracles to show us the way forward?

"Our Lord means to give us Dominion over His universe. Our Promised Land is not confined to this planet. Who are we to question God's Plan and Methods?"

As he spoke, the Reverend's voice grew in fervor and power. "When the Great Flood came, Moses and his family built their sacred Ark. They knew that everyone and everything not on that Ark would be destroyed in the Great Deluge, but did they question the Lord's Promise? No! Though they were charged with the responsibility of rebuilding all of humanity and all of the animals on the entire planet from the few they were able to save, did they ever lose Faith in their God? No!"

Despite many of the leaders not being Christian, and none belonging to any of the more evangelical sects, Greg could see they were nonetheless captivated by LaMontagne's inspired message. He made to jump in and take advantage of the swing in sentiment, but the Reverend was not finished his impromptu sermon.

"Clearly, the Lord has decided to end our time on this planet. Earth is full of sin and humanity is due for one final cleansing. We are being given a Holy Mission to save what we can and take His Word into the greater unknown. The Lord has spoken through these two young people and delivered to us a new message. We are ready. We can save our people. We can choose the purest, the most qualified, the best of humanity, and we can start again. The message is ours to heed, and heed it we must. Heed it, we *will*."

As LaMontagne's entreaty came to an end, his eyes blazed with Yeshua's Glory for all to see. Secretary Hartland, feeling publicly admonished, lowered his gaze and fiddled with his pen.

Sporadic scattered applause threatened to break out but was abruptly squelched under the withering glare of those who thought the Reverend had spoken beyond his position. LaMontagne may have led a Church, but he did *not* lead a country, and certainly not *their* country.

No one, however, could deny that his words and fervor were a compelling force.

Greg and Kathy glanced at each other, sharing their surprise at the change in attitude around the table. All they needed were a few words to move the conversation toward quick agreement to their plan.

Sensing a pivotal moment, President Chu stepped in. "Your passionate words have moved us, Reverend. Nevertheless, we must live in the practical world, especially those of us who govern countries which do not find the 'Word of God' quite so compelling."

LaMontagne's face grew red.

Chu picked up the thick printed package in front of him and addressed Ms. Hudson, "Madam Prime Minister, your scientists have provided most compelling evidence of the threat we face with this *Eater* anomaly. Their plan to save humanity is bold and faces many technological challenges. With their guidance, our best scientists and engineers will be able to overcome these challenges. I am convinced of that." He surveyed the room, seeing signs of agreement around the table.

"Yet, these challenges pale in comparison to the economic and political obstacles in our way. Humanity is tired. We have struggled for decades with turmoil, with practically zero economic growth, with insurmountable sovereign debts, and with political maneuvering designed to keep wealth and power in the hands of those who have abused it for centuries."

He glanced at the European and North American delegates. He placed his hands on the edge of the table, looked down, and sighed gloomily while the other leaders contemplated his words.

He shifted his gaze squarely to LaMontagne. "Perhaps humanity's time on Earth is over. Perhaps this is our final challenge, a test to determine whether or not our species is worthy of the stars. I do not know that. I *do* know this test could not have come at a worse time."

He turned his gaze to PM Hudson. "Perhaps, Madam Prime Minister, your geniuses could tell us how to maintain our economies, and how we provide for our people while we construct the rocket ships to transport these construction robots.

"If the whole world is working on this project, who do we borrow from to finance all of this? How do we avoid destroying our industries, even our currencies, while we adjust so quickly away from our current concentration on consumptive stimulation and toward a completely new basis for economic expansion? How do we tell the billions to sacrifice themselves, their labor, their futures so that we can save a few precious millions?"

Too late, Greg realized their error. He and Kathy had been focused on the technological challenges inherent in building and colonizing a safe haven for humanity among the asteroids. They'd been thinking that as soon as everyone saw it was necessary and possible to save even a part of humanity, they'd eagerly support their endeavors.

Here, they were speaking to political animals, leaders who not only felt the burden of responsibility for their people but the severe challenge of trying to herd those people in a single united direction.

Since the start of the twenty-first century, people had been evenly split on almost any social or economic issue one cared to name. In the absence of an ability to prove one point of view or plan was better than another, politicians had been blown here and there by the weekly opinion polls.

People yelled, people cajoled, people ranted all over the internet. No one listened to anyone else. Sane, rational conversation died out, while freedom of speech and democratization of opinion blossomed.

Perhaps Kierkegaard had forecast this end many years ago when he'd complained that, "People demand Freedom of Speech as compensation for the Freedom of Thought, which they seldom use."

Without any filter of professional journalism to distinguish between lies and truth, between expertise and bluster, between opinion and evidence, politicians found it easier to "say any damned thing" to move the wind of public opinion in their favor during elections. They could worry about policy and leadership later.

It was no surprise that winning became more important than leading when everyone viewed politics as a team sport.

Greg could see this meeting was not going to go well from this point on. He made one last desperate attempt to salvage something.

"We apologize, President Chu, for not devoting adequate planning on these issues. As scientists and engineers, our natural inclination was to focus on the technological over the sociopolitical or economic."

Chu bowed in his chair at Greg's gracious recognition of their gaff.

Greg continued, "However, if you and the other leaders will permit us, we will devote every effort to devising a complete plan by tomorrow morning. If your schedules permit, could we ask for one more day of your time to present the second part of our proposal?"

A murmur rose around the room. Greg could only pick out a few words: "Impossible... Ridiculous... Waste of time... Foolishness," and the like.

President Chu stood and the room hushed. "You have impressed us with your technical capabilities. We hope your abilities in the economic and political arenas will prove equally impressive. What you have outlined, so far, is sufficient to convince us of the importance of this issue in addition to its technological feasibility. Yes, China will allow one more day for you to present us with a more thorough plan.

"In the meantime, you have already given us much to contemplate with the assistance of our advisors. I believe we have accomplished all we can in this meeting." He bowed and made his way to the exit, his entourage scrambling to follow his hasty departure.

PM Hudson quickly stepped in to close the meeting in a controlled fashion.

"I hope you will join us here tomorrow morning at 10:00 for a discussion of the second part of the proposal from Drs. Mahajani and Liang. For now, I urge you to refer to the material before you, in consultation with your scientific advisers, for the answers to any of your technical questions. This meeting is adjourned until tomorrow morning."

She flashed Greg and Kathy a single glare, pivoted on her heels, and strode from the room.

Crap!—Kathy sent to Greg. *That didn't go as planned.*

24

A PROTECTIVE BUBBLE OF AIR APPEARED in outer space. Across the bottom surface was a small section of uprooted scrub from the planet Gargus 718.5. Its convex bottom traced the outline of the field that held the vacuum of space at bay. On the flat top of the dirt stood Brother Stralasi.

"Where are we now?" he asked.

He waited for Darak to answer. Sometimes his companion liked to take a moment to appreciate the beauty of a new planet from afar before shifting down to the surface.

Looking straight ahead, Stralasi saw no planet, only a small, brilliant white sun with a hazy scattering of stars outlining a dim galaxy in the background. He glanced left and right. Around it, there was nothing but deep blackness of space, far darker and emptier than normal. Except for the glare of the sun directly in front, nothing else was visible.

We must be outside any major cluster—he thought.

"Darak?" No answer.

Stralasi turned around to ask again. There was no one behind him. The Good Brother stood alone on the little patch of land in the traveling sphere.

"Very funny," he called out. "You can show yourself now."

Nothing. Stralasi held his hand out in front to shade his eyes from the sun, and inspected the immediate vicinity outside their air bubble. Had Darak stepped outside for a moment of private reflection? *His moods can be a challenge to withstand.* But even when he felt the need for silence, Darak never strayed far away. Outer space was the perfect sound barrier; a millimeter was as good as a kilometer.

Stralasi saw no sign of his companion.

He was alone!

"Darak! Darak, where are you?" he called, a little more insistently this time. *For that matter, where am I? Where is this?* His thoughts flitted from question to question, all without answer. *Has he abandoned me? Or is he nearby? How will I find him? What if something happens to him and I get stranded here? How will I get back to the Realm?*

Oh, sweet Alum, save me!—he implored, clenching his eyes tightly against his isolation. He gave Alum the Living God a moment to answer his prayer. Nothing.

Sweet Alum, save me!—he repeated, over and over, rocking back and forth.

He opened one eye first, hoping, and willed Darak to appear. Then, the other eye.

He was still alone, and a deeper panic set in.

Dear Alum, show me the way. What should I do? He clasped his hands in prayer and started pacing the length and breadth of the little piece of turf under his feet. He went around and around the tiny chunk of home. Gradually, his years of training and practice took hold.

He remembered his calming exercises. He let his eyelids drift downward and shifted his focus to his breathing. He slowed his steps, and concentrated on emptying his mind. His pounding heart calmed.

That's it. Breathe in, two, three, four...and breathe out, two, three, four. Inhale goodness and light. Exhale darkness and fear.

Still no sign of Darak. No planet nearby. No way to get out of here. The thoughts came without bidding and threatened to drag him back into the babbling, mindless morass of fear.

He inhaled deeply, and squeezed the air out through pursed lips, pushing the terror away with his breath. He opened his eyes and turned his gaze outward, beyond the tiny piece of dirt and rock on which he stood.

Keep calm and think!—he admonished himself. *The way Darak always tells you.* A shimmer of light below and off to one side drew his attention, but the ground beneath his feet blocked the view. He ventured to the edge of the small patch of turf, and shielded his vision from the glare of the sun to take a better look.

His eyes traced the dim outline of a gray ribbon as far he could see in either direction. Its graceful arc curved inward following a solar orbital path, one normally occupied by a full planet. Clusters of color glowed from the inner surface. Bright whites, blues, browns, and greens.

A ringworld!

He'd only seen such a place from space once, during his last time playing tourist before joining classmates at the central Alumita on Home World.

As the oldest and most important part of the Realm—apart from the Hall of Alum in the Origin system—Home World had long ago converted the resources of its entire system into such an artifact. In fact, not one, but two ringworlds now circled the Home World sun.

The architectural origin of the ringworlds was lost in antiquity and muddled folklore. Alum preferred people not to think about the distant past outside of the official history.

In some of the more persistent stories, ringworlds were associated with a man called Niven. Regardless of its origins, the basic design continued to be the best way to provide a comfortable habitat for enormous numbers of humans around a single sun. Other clever designs had been tried and abandoned; the ringworld outlasted them all.

The ringworld was, as its name suggested, a single giant construct, a circular ribbon surrounding a central sun. The diameter varied from system to system, depending on the intensity of the sun at its center. Ringworlds spun at a rate that provided one Standard gravity to its inhabitants.

Most ringworlds—if the word "most" could be used to describe something so rarely constructed—boasted a living surface about a million kilometers wide. High outer walls at the edge held in an agreeable atmosphere. Day and night were provided by enormous dark sheets that ran on rails along the walls above the atmosphere.

A ring encircling its sun at a distance of two-hundred-million kilometers could provide over a thousand trillion square kilometers of living space. A single ringworld offered enough space to comfortably fit one hundred trillion people, ten percent of the entire population of all other planets in a galaxy. No wonder there weren't many of them. They were not yet needed.

Now, why would there be a ringworld way out here far from the major part of the Realm?—Stralasi wondered.

Pop! Stralasi jumped, momentarily startled by the unexpected sound behind him.

At last, Darak has decided to join me! He turned, a broad, relieved smile already forming on his face.

With his first glimpse of the source of the sound, the Good Brother stumbled backward to the edge of the bubble.

Heart pounding, he dropped to one knee and fixed his gaze on the surprisingly delicate bare feet of the three-meter tall Angel sharing his small sphere. He didn't dare look into what he knew would be beautiful, deadly eyes.

"That really isn't necessary," said a mellifluous, yet oddly familiar, voice tinged with a dry humor Stralasi recognized. He couldn't believe it, yet he was compelled to raise his eyes.

The face before him was a more youthful and handsome version of Darak, if he looked past its swirling, mercurial skin.

Stralasi nearly fainted. Instead, he managed to squeak out, "Wha...? How...? Darak...?"

The Angel smiled, took Stralasi's hands, and helped him to his feet.

"Yes, it truly is me," said the Angel. "Or one version of me." He looked at his own silvery hands and admired the opalescent wings extending from his back.

The creature laughed, and the sound was joyful music to Stralasi's ears. "It has been a long time since I appeared to anyone in this body," Darak said. "What do you think?" He struck a gallant posture, his hands fixed to the hilt of a gray carbyne sword.

Stralasi didn't know what to think. How was this possible? His mind raced with contradictions and confusion. "You once stated that you were neither Shard nor Demon," he said, "and yet you are clearly more than just a man. Are you an Angel, sent by the Living God to test me?"

From a meter above Stralasi's upturned eyes, Darak answered quietly, thoughtfully. "Truly, I am all of these and more. And because I am more, I am not exactly any single one. But sent by Alum? No."

Darak looked out at the ringworld. "Have you perused your surroundings? Can you deduce where we are?"

Stralasi turned away from the Angel despite a lifetime of training screaming out to him that such an action could warrant instant death. But, despite his appearance, this was undoubtedly Darak. He pointed to the arc.

"Clearly, we are near a ringworld, though I am not familiar with this one. I've seen videocasts of all such habitats within the Realm, but I don't recall this one. I can't imagine why Alum would build such a magnificent place in such an unremarkable location."

"Yes, this one is unique," answered the Angel, Darak. "Why do you judge its location to be unremarkable?"

"Its sun is either extremely distant or tiny," replied Stralasi. "Something in its appearance makes me think it is more likely to be tiny. And I've never seen a night sky so devoid of light, which makes me think we must be near the edge of some small and insignificant galaxy."

Imagine!--Stralasi marveled. *Here I am, a humble monk of the Alumita, discussing astronomy with an Angel, while floating in an isolated bit of air and earth, suspended in outer space some small distance from an unknown ringworld.* He shook his head in wonder.

"It is a small star, that is true," confirmed Darak. "And it is near the edge of a thin galaxy with few stars and a great deal of dark gasses. It's unique because it is the farthest in the Realm from any of Alum's other worlds."

Stralasi looked back over his shoulder. "Distance is meaningless in Alum's Realm," he cited by rote. "All worlds are no more than a few starstep from all other worlds."

"True," Darak answered. "But not all worlds in the Realm—or rather, not all worlds *formerly* in the Realm—have starsteps."

A horrified Stralasi turned back toward the ringworld as if scouting for signs of dangerous activity. "Rebels!" he realized.

"Indeed. *My* rebels, in fact."

"*Your* rebels?" Stralasi struggled to process this new bit of information. This Angel, sometimes a Shard, sometimes a god, sometimes only a man, laying claim to leading rebels?

And not just any rebels. Rebels who somehow managed to build that pinnacle of technological achievement, a ringworld, while disconnected from Alum's guidance? Had he not known Darak so well, he would have scoffed. Except, as incredible as it sounded, he was sure it was true.

"Well, not *my* rebels, exactly. I helped them gain their independence a long time ago," explained Darak. "I still carry a good deal of affection and admiration for their efforts. I don't own them or anything like that. They are no more mine than they were Alum's."

He pointed to the arc of the ringworld. "Frankly, I'm a little surprised they lasted long enough to build something like this. Rebellions that aren't put down quickly usually fracture of their own accord due to internal strife, or they just fizzle out like a faulty rocket. Especially given where we are, this is impressive."

"And *where* exactly are we?" Stralasi asked, turning to confront the Angel.

"In the ancient catalogs, this galaxy was known as ESO 461-36. It's notable for being the only galaxy within a region known as the Local Void. It's a strange small, dark galaxy just outside the plane of the so-called Local Cluster that includes the Milky Way. The nearest galaxy is over eight million light years away, and the Origin galaxy is over twenty-five million light years away.

"The ESO galaxy is unusual, so unusual that Alum went out of His way to place an exploratory colony here, as humanity expanded toward the Virgo Cluster. As a remote outpost in a sparsely-populated galaxy far off the main path of expansion, it wasn't considered important enough to warrant quashing my little rebellion there twenty-million odd years ago."

"You helped the rebels twenty million years ago?"

"Indeed. And having just contacted the authorities here, and received their greetings, it seems the descendants of that rebellion still enjoy their independence."

Darak noticed Stralasi's stunned expression. "I'm as surprised as you are. Alum seldom permits rebellions to go unpunished."

"That's not it," corrected the incredulous Brother. "You contacted the *authorities*?"

"Oh, that. Yes, I used my old verification codes. It's interesting that they've actually remembered them for so long. They should arrive soon."

"They'll be *here*? Soon?" Stralasi felt his knees go weak again. It was one thing to confront an Angel; it was another to confront rebels. Angels carried out Alum's Will. That is, all the Angels he knew of did. Rebels were loyal to no one but themselves. Who knew what aims or guidelines they might have. Then he remembered who he was with. Darak wouldn't permit any harm to come to him...would he?

"Yes. I thought that since we arrived unexpectedly, it'd be best to announce our presence and permit the local leaders to escort us in from the ancient rendezvous point in whatever manner they see fit."

There was much unspoken history in Darak's answer. *As usual*—thought Stralasi. Struggling to make sense of everyone and everything around him felt like a normal state when he was with Darak. "Is it even possible they would remember you after so much time?"

Darak held his arms out to either side. "I used the ancient protocols, and have assumed the expected appearance. So far, they are responding as I would have hoped. It would appear they've kept their promise to me over these impossibly many years. Let us see what kind of reception we are accorded. Ahh, and here they are!"

Stralasi looked to the ringworld arc in time to see a bright flame shoot from a barely perceptible, decelerating vehicle of some sort. *A rocket? No one uses rockets in the Realm anymore.* But he'd studied them at the Alumita and was certain that's what was bearing down on them.

Judging by the brightness of its exhaust, the ship was braking hard as it approached. The ship was aiming straight for them. He glanced back at Darak.

Couldn't the Angel tell they were minutes, perhaps seconds, away from being fried? Maybe he thought their bubble would protect them. Darak's Angel body might be impervious to heat and violent concussion, but his own body was not. He opened his mouth to say something.

The flare drew closer and Stralasi saw it was angled slightly away from them. Whoever guided the vehicle was approaching their shell in such a way that the exhaust would avoid them. The flame diminished in ferocity.

Darak smiled. Had he been aware of Stralasi's anxiety? The Brother was uncertain. He wasn't at all comforted by his memories of the demon/god/Angel's sense of humor when he saw Stralasi's previous reactions to clearly terrifying circumstances. He frowned and turned back to watch the approaching vessel.

The main drive cut off within a few kilometers of the sphere. Its relative velocity slowed to a few meters per second, and small attitudinal jets completed the maneuvering.

Brother Stralasi could finally confirm that it was some kind of spaceship, cylindrical, about thirty meters long and ten in diameter.

The ship came to rest alongside their bubble but did nothing further.

The windows were dark and reflective, giving no hint as to who or what was waiting inside. There were no interior or exterior lights; there was no communication and no movement.

Stralasi wondered what they were supposed to do. Were they communicating with Darak telepathically? Could Darak simply *shift* them inside? He assumed there must be an internal compartment of some sort, judging by the presence of glass-covered viewing ports along the side of the cylinder.

A large door opened in the adjacent craft and Darak moved them forward—air, dirt, and all—into the waiting hold. Stralasi realized that he'd been holding his breath and released it slowly. They slid forward into the darkness.

"Is there no way we can cast some light on the inside of this vessel?" he asked the Angel.

"My apologies," replied Darak. "In my excitement, I forgot."

Their protective shell cast a diffused glow around them as they passed deeper into the ship. The addition of light didn't help. The chamber into which they were moving had no discernible features. Smooth, dull gray walls with no protuberance, attachment, or discontinuity surrounded them.

Stralasi hoped Darak knew what he was doing, trusting this ship to be friendly. *Well, if it had been sent to capture us, the owners will be in for a big surprise.* He had no idea of the ship's capabilities, but the destructive might of an Angel was legendary.

I only hope that if a fight does break out, Darak remembers to keep me safe.

The few stars visible behind them were slowly occluded by the closing door. *We're committed now*—he thought, trying to assess any hint of concern on Darak's mercurial face. The Angel seemed to have serenely accepted being swallowed up by the ship.

With the door closed, the wall appeared completely seamless. There was no hint of where the hatch had been.

"Now what?" asked the Brother.

"Now we wait until we arrive at a ringworld docking station," Darak replied. "It shouldn't be long."

The Brother steadied himself against the wall, waiting to feel the jerk of acceleration. He bent his knees expectantly.

After a minute there was still no sign they were underway. He asked the Angel, "Why aren't we moving?"

Darak peered down at the monk. "We began moving the instant the door was closed. We're accelerating at a rate high enough to turn your body into mush. I'm compensating." He looked upward.

Stralasi followed his gaze but saw nothing.

"The pilot of this ship can handle the acceleration, as can I, but I'm a little surprised they made no allowance for you. That is uncharacteristic. Perhaps they assumed I would ensure no harm came to you." He returned his gaze to Stralasi. "Or perhaps they didn't care if it did."

The Brother considered Darak's beautiful, frightful, angelic smile. Was the Angel joking or serious? Stralasi couldn't tell. He shivered, drew his arms around himself, and plunked himself down on a tiny piece of ground, facing away from the Angel. The monk withdrew into silence, contemplating a small stone in front of his feet on the little piece of Gargus 718.5 that traveled wherever they went. Minutes passed, but the Good Brother did not stir.

A whoosh of air and bright light filled the chamber, breaking Stralasi's meditation. He stood and straightened his clothes.

The hatch door opened into a well-lit corridor lined with white panels. A ramp extended up into the transport ship, right to their tiny piece of ground. At the bottom of the ramp, stood a woman.

Stralasi would have said she was not yet past the first third of her life. She had a tentative smile on her lips and a meter-wide Securitor hovering over her right shoulder.

"Shall we?" Darak motioned Stralasi forward as he dropped their protective shield. Immediately, the Brother's nose was assaulted by a complex mix of odors, cleaning chemicals to be sure, and an unmistakable odor of fertile land.

Darak made his way down the ramp, with Stralasi tagging behind.

The woman lowered her head, took an awkward step back with one foot, and bowed deeply.

Darak smiled at the genuflection and uttered something incomprehensible to Stralasi.

"What did you say?" the monk whispered.

Darak turned to the monk and lifted a hand with the index finger raised. Stralasi felt a mild tingling in his head.

"I said, there's no need for such a formal greeting to one who had abandoned the Esu so long ago," the Angel repeated. As he spoke the woman rose.

"He does not speak our language," she stated.

"He did not speak our language," Darak corrected. "He does now."

"True marvels do travel with you, as it is told," said the woman.

"What do you mean?" asked Stralasi, talking over her. "I understand you perfectly." Only when he thought about it did he realize the woman had been speaking a language other than Standard. Yet, now, he understood both tongues equally well and found he could reply easily in whichever he chose.

"A slight adjustment to your lattice in the language centers to permit you to understand the local dialect," he explained. "My apologies for not doing it earlier, while you were brooding."

"I was not brooding," objected Stralasi. "I was...meditating."

A raised eyebrow formed in Darak's mercurial liquid mirror.

"You travel with a companion?" observed the woman. "The ancient texts make no mention of this."

Stralasi pointed to the sphere hovering behind her. "You travel with a Securitor. Are you afraid of us?"

The woman appeared momentarily confused. She looked to Darak for explanation.

"Ahh, yes. I suppose they do have a similar form, but her companion is as much Cybrid as Securitor," the Angel corrected. "It's her guardian, manipulator, mentation aid, and much more. And she is not traveling with it any more than you are traveling with your arm."

It was Stralasi's turn to not understand.

Darak explained, "Since I left them, the Esu have discovered the mutual benefits of a human-Cybrid symbiosis." He waved his hand to encompass both beings. "You are looking at one person, biological and electromechanical, a single entity with split consciousness."

"My name is Crissea," the woman said. She indicated the floating mechanism. "We call this part of us, our Familiar."

Stralasi did not recognize that use of the word. Crissea gave a shallow bow from the waist, and her Familiar bobbed a few centimeters at the same time. "Welcome to Eso-La."

Darak returned the bow, something Stralasi would never have imagined. Other than Alum himself, who was an Angel obligated to honor? He hurriedly joined in the gesture of respect.

The Angel returned to full stature and pronounced in a formal, ritualistic voice, "I am Darak Legsu, Broken Shard of Alum. I am Gabriel, Fallen Commander of the Virgo Central Wing. I am Fal sek Troal, Betrayer of the Aelu. I am the Da'ark Triad, Brother, Traitor, and Savior."

25

As Darak proclaimed his multiple identities, Stralasi's eyes grew wider and wider. The Angel hadn't mentioned these titles to him. No wonder. They didn't sound like anything to be proud of, at least what he could understand of them: Fallen Commander, the Da'ark Triad, Traitor.

The Good Brother wasn't familiar with any of the figures. He had an odd feeling, an inkling, that perhaps the Realm possessed a whole parallel, unofficial history, one unsanctioned by Alum and quite different from the one he had been taught.

Crissea gave a satisfied smile and a nod. "It is as foretold by the ancients." Her gaze fell on the Good Brother. "Almost."

"This is Ontro nem Stralasi, a Brother of the Alumit and my traveling companion."

Crissea's eyes narrowed at the mention of the Church of Alum.

"He is on...educational leave," explained Darak, "without approval of his superiors. However, I'm sure the Good Brother is finding our travels to be quite a valuable learning experience." He smiled at the understatement.

Crissea laughed softly, at the sound of Stralasi muttering under his breath.

"Brother Stralasi," she said with a small dip of her head. "It would be my pleasure to introduce you to the many marvels of our world, a world outside the official 'sanction' of the Alumit, I'm afraid."

Stralasi bobbed his head. "Since traveling with Darak these past few months, I've learned of many things that would not be officially sanctioned by the Alumit."

"We have little time for touring, I'm afraid," Darak interjected. "I have something important to ask of your people. Would it be possible to call a meeting of the World Authorities?"

"They are gathering as we speak," the young woman replied. "Eso-La is large, and we eschew the instantaneous starstep transportation technology of the Realm. A few hours of tube travel will be required of our most distant Coordina members."

She indicated for the Angel and Good Brother to follow. "We can share some refreshments while we wait for the last few representatives to arrive."

They walked a short distance to the end of the corridor, where a section of the floor lifted them through a few hundred meters of hollowed out rock to arrive at the innermost habitable surface of the ringworld.

The platform emerged into the light of a clear, sunny day. Stralasi felt giddy as he whirled about, taking in the paradise-like garden. He'd expected to arrive in some grand building, like a Global Alumita or even a planetary tube station, where the governing Council would meet them in majestic chambers. But this! This was so much better.

All around, grew well-tended trees, shrubs, grasses and flowers. The delicate trill of birds merged with babbling water close by. There was no sign of a building anywhere unless one counted the vine-laden trellises and arbors off to one side. He could hear the soft sounds of people talking and laughing, off in that direction.

"Where will we meet the Council? Is there transportation to the city nearby?" he asked.

"This is the nearest Amphi of the Coordina," Crissea responded. "We will meet over there." She pointed in the direction of the arbors and set off in that direction.

The Brother turned a confused face to the Angel, who patiently answered him with more questions.

"Why meet under cover from the elements if you control them? Or if the weather is of no consequence to your comfort?" He motioned for Stralasi to walk beside him into the clearing ahead.

They left the lightly treed area and entered a plaza filled with a small crowd of people and their accompanying Familiars.

Raised planters, large boulders, and fountains enjoyed the shade of flowering trees. It looked randomly but beautifully arranged, as far as Stralasi could determine.

People sat in small groups on whatever surfaces were convenient. They wore a variety of light robes and short pants suited to a pleasant summer afternoon. Familiars extended manipulators, carrying drinks and small plates of food, toward their human associates.

The overall effect was more like a garden party than a meeting of the governing authorities of a massive civilization like the ringworld of Eso-la.

When Stralasi caught a glimpse of Darak's face, he saw no hint of emotion, save contentment.

As they entered the plaza, faces turned to watch them. As if one entity, people ceased their conversations and rose to face Darak and the monk. They bowed deeply, Familiars included, and sat down again, resuming their conversations.

Stralasi wasn't sure whether he felt more like an esteemed guest of honor or one of those Head Brothers who sometimes showed up uninvited at local parties. Both Darak and Crissea appeared satisfied that all the necessary protocols had been met.

"Would you like something to eat or drink while we wait?" their hostess asked Darak. "I can't recall whether Angels enjoy food or juices. Our selection here is excellent."

"While I have no need for either, I am capable of enjoying both," replied the Angel. "And it has been some hours since our last meal. I'm certain Brother Stralasi would like something."

At that moment, the soft breeze shifted direction, wafting the delicious odors of warm food their way.

Stralasi's mouth watered, and his stomach gurgled embarrassingly.

Crissea graciously pretended not to notice and guided him toward a buffet where a wide variety of meats, breads, vegetables, and fruits were beautifully displayed.

Three people and their Familiars artfully arranged Stralasi's choices on a small plate, and poured him a glass of plum-colored wine. Darak chose some slices of fruit that looked like variants on familiar Standard strains. The trio moved off to some secluded seating near a fountain.

Stralasi shoved the delightful tidbits into his mouth as fast as he dared, restrained only by his desire not to appear uncivilized before the lovely Crissea. He noticed her delicate sampling of the fruit dishes. She helpfully pointed out which sauces were best paired with which meat dishes.

The sparkling laughter with which she greeted Stralasi's appreciative groans over the superb flavors embodied in each morsel only heightened her charm.

The Good Brothers of the Alumit, being among the most favored of Alum, were generally expected to marry and have children at some time in their lives.

Stralasi hadn't intentionally set out to avoid marriage. During his extensive travels in service to Alum, he had met many delightful and eligible women. Each time, he'd move on to the next assignment before working up the courage to overcome his shyness.

Stralasi surprised himself by thinking about how nice it might be to settle in a place like this with a woman like Crissea. Alas, it was out of his control. There was little he could do but follow Darak wherever his travels took him.

He was savoring a final spectacular bite from the buffet when a dull roar sounded from one side of the terrace. A vessel landed alongside the vehicles parked near the terraced area.

Darak and Crissea stood, and Stralasi set down his plate to join them.

"Perfect timing. This is the last contingent of the Coordina we were expecting," Crissea said. "We have a quorum now."

The ship powered down, a door slid open, and a platform descended. Stralasi stole a look at Darak, and a slightly more surreptitious one at Crissea. They shared the appearance of eager expectation, their full attention fixed on the ramp.

Stralasi caught movement out of the corner of his eye and looked back in time to see the travelers emerge.

Aelu! His eyes sought somewhere to hide. He reached out a hand to pull Crissea with him. Her face was serene, even joyful. *What is this?* He opened his lips to tell her to flee.

Crissea turned to him and her smile grew broader.

He scanned the faces of those assembled. He saw nothing but open acceptance, as if the aliens were old friends. He looked back at the Aelu. They didn't appear to be hostile, though he wasn't sure he could tell. He closed his eyes for a second and reconsidered. *Could these be the Coordina members we're waiting for?*

Stralasi had never seen real Aelu, not in person. Actually, no one he knew had ever seen real, live Aelu. No one besides Alum and some of his inner circle had any first-hand knowledge of that alien race. Yet, the Aelu continued to be cast as the default evil opponent in video entertainments throughout the Realm, which was odd, now that he thought about it.

Stralasi knew the Aelu—through history lessons, inSense games, and entertainment—to be brilliant, ruthless, and utterly evil. With equal parts trepidation and foreboding, he watched the ten figures gracefully make their way down the ramp. His horror grew with each step of the peculiarly smooth, three-legged gait that held their ellipsoid bodies steady.

"They're...They're...Aelu," he announced to Crissea and Darak as if they hadn't seen or realized.

"At last!" Darak laughed and strode forward to greet the aliens.

"But how are they here?"

"Because the Savior, the one you know as Darak, brought them to us and charged us with their welfare," Crissea answered.

"He saved Aelu?" Stralasi couldn't believe it. How could an Angel, even a rebellious one, save any members of such a powerful enemy of the Realm?

"Yes, he brought as many as he could. Sadly, few made it here alive, barely enough to rebuild the species. It took considerable time and great care."

Stralasi saw the guilt in her eyes and was confused. Before he could inquire, she whispered, "Excuse me," and moved forward to greet the Aelu with Darak.

The rest of the Coordina pressed closer to watch the historic moment. They jostled for position, transfixed by a sight they'd never dared hope to see.

Stralasi's head spun as he watched Darak and Crissea approach the Aelu.

The Aelu assembled in a diamond-shape formation at the bottom of the ramp and bowed deeply to the group as a whole. They emitted a loud musical tinkle, reminiscent of the harmonic but scattered notes of wind chimes.

Their tripod legs collapsed at three central joints, and their bodies sank to within a few centimeters of the ground. Their upper manipulators folded into a complex spiral design above their bodies.

Stralasi's fear was temporarily overridden by his fascination.

Darak rose to his full height, extended his right hand, and placed it tenderly on what equated to the shoulder area of the lead Aelu. He bent down and enfolded the being in his shimmering wings.

The two remained that way for long seconds, and then Darak was gone. In his place stood an opalescent green-blue Aelu that Stralasi recognized from the movies as a Leader type.

For a second, it—Darak?—was the only Aelu not bowed low, but it soon joined its brothers in a folded crouch and accepted the gentle touches of upper tripod appendages from the others.

The Angel returned to the form that Stralasi was only now beginning to get used to. When Darak stood, the Aelu stood with it. They surrounded him, gently caressing his arms and wings with their manipulators, and he radiated joy.

The rest of the Coordina rushed forward to share in the glow of his delight. Everyone got a turn to clasp hands with Darak, brush against his wings, or receive a hand to their shoulder. A particularly ancient looking man spoke with Darak for well over a minute, after which the Angel gently wrapped him in his wings and the two hugged.

The Good Brother was moved by this display, though he didn't understand what it signified. When Crissea returned to his side, he asked for her help.

"Rudolfo's great-great-grandfather, Artero, was one of the Original Ten who conspired with Darak Legsu in the Liberation. He visited his esteemed ancestor in Eterna only a few weeks ago, and they relived those days. How gratifying it will feel for him to relay his conversation with the Fallen Commander to the ancient one."

Stralasi nodded before it dawned on him. "Wait. This Rebellion happened over twenty million years ago, didn't it? How could this Rudolfo possibly have visited with anyone alive then?"

Crissea smiled kindly, in a way that Stralasi found moderately condescending. "Oh, that's right," she realized. "The Realm doesn't have Familiars. Well, Artero Belongia's biological body died ages ago. His Familiar housed his concepta and persona for a few million years before being uploaded into Eterna. He is still among our most respected Council advisors when we can find something interesting enough to pull him away from his hobbies and adventures."

"If he died, his soul is no longer with us and has certainly passed on to the next world," objected Stralasi. "Clearly, nothing of his soul could remain in this world."

Crissea cocked her head in a way that Stralasi found both charming and disconcerting. "What is this 'soul' you mention?"

Darak had returned behind the two without their notice, and jumped in before Stralasi could expound further. "Alum's people believe that our ideas, memories, and beliefs, all the thoughts that make us individuals, reside in a non-physical essence that is somehow connected to the body. They believe that when one dies, the soul is set free to go on to an eternal existence in a non-physical paradise called Heaven or, in some cases, to bear eternal torture and suffering in a place called Hell. Pursuant to judgment by Alum, of course."

Crissea stared first at the Angel, then at Stralasi. Her mouth hung—rather uncharacteristically—wide open.

Darak's eyes twinkled. He couldn't contain his escaping grin. Crissea burst into relieved laughter. The laughter erupted in great waves from the Angel as well. Brother Stralasi glowered.

As she dried her eyes, Crissea apologized. "I'm sorry, Ontro. That can't be what you really think? It's just too...preposterous."

Stralasi crossed his arms indignantly. "I am a Senior Brother in the Alumit. I have studied the Scripture my entire life. What Darak has said—minus his disrespectful tone—is the essence of Alum's teachings. Those who contravene the Faith will be judged harshly by the Living God."

"Oh, I am sorry. I've made you angry. I just.... There's no evidence. It's not rational." The more Crissea attempted her unapologetic apology, the more stubbornly Stralasi set his glare.

"My friends, I'm afraid this is a clash of cultural perspectives that won't be resolved here and now," Darak intervened. "I learned long ago that appealing to rational assessments of the available evidence is useless when trying to convert a person of Faith." He glanced pointedly over his shoulder at his wings. "Though, I'm sure even Alum Himself never would have imagined hearing those words from the lips of an Angel of the Lord, no matter how Fallen."

Stralasi made a conscious effort to relax. "It is true I have seen many things in my travels with you, Lord Angel, things that might make weaker men question their Faith. And I have learned that all is not exactly as I once thought it was. But if you would ask me to condemn my Eternal Soul to Damnation by forsaking what I know in my heart to be true, I cannot do that. So you are right; there is no amount of evidence or rational thought that can shake the foundations of my Belief in such a way." He thrust his chin defiantly forward.

Darak raised his hands in mock surrender. "No, I would not ask such a thing of you, my dear Brother Stralasi. I picked you as my traveling companion precisely *for* the strength of your Faith. It is clear that even Alum would not question your Belief. That is why I hope you will join the proceedings as one of the Judges. I believe you are ready for that now."

Stralasi and Crissea were equally surprised and confused. "Judges?" they asked simultaneously.

"Yes, Judges. If I may address the meeting of the Coordina, I will outline my request in greater detail."

"Most certainly." Crissea bowed, hoping he wouldn't notice her embarrassment, "The meeting has been underway for some time."

"I wondered if it might be," Darak nodded. "I thought it impolite to monitor your private channels or I would have known. Very well, let's attend to business." He directed Stralasi and Crissea to sit by the fountain. He remained standing, facing the two of them.

"Three hundred of the Coordina Executive are here in attendance," Crissea announced for Stralasi's benefit. "Thousands upon thousands of Coordina groups distributed around Eso-La are connected to this meeting through me. I will channel our responses and questions as needed. Darak Legsu, please proceed."

Darak acknowledged the invitation, then turned inward to address the entire ringworld Coordina.

"Greetings friends. Thank you for your warm welcome. It has been too long since I visited. I am pleased with the developments you have made since I first assisted your ancestors in that distant age. It is good to see how you have come together from many peoples into one, and from so many tiny colonies into one shining ringworld, the beautiful Eso-La.

"I'd hoped your worlds would survive at least a while after throwing off the shackles of Alum's Realm, but I could not have imagined that you would flourish the way you have. I am delighted to see your growth and vitality.

"For whatever reason, it seems Alum has decided to ignore your presence here. Though He's had ample time to send a Wing or even an entire Flock of Angels to avenge the Rebellion of your ancestors, He has not done so.

"Are you free of Him forever? Does He think you've long since perished, or that you're insignificant? Has He chosen to let you live in peace? I can tell you, none of these is true.

"Alum has simply moved on to a new Plan. A greater Plan. His Divine Plan. He's no longer content with ruling the small part of the universe we call the Realm. He's no longer content with the prospect of encountering other civilizations and other powers that may equal or exceed His own. He's decided to bring about the Age of Heaven, as he calls it.

"What is Alum's 'Age of Heaven'? How could Alum's Realm be any more perfect?

"In ancient days, before Alum was the Living God, we had stories of a place free from any suffering, free from labor or strife. It was a place where everyone could live forever, and where our only work was to praise God throughout our days. A place free from threats, free of uncertainty, where God's Will was the only Law and God's Love was the only Force. We called this place Heaven.

"This is Alum's dream, to recreate our universe, to reflect His idea of Heaven. To do so, He will first have to collapse our universe, the only physical universe we know, destroying us all, every last creature, every planet, every star. He will return everything to a condensed, primordial state, and recreate all matter according to His new laws. He will remake nature in His vision of this Heaven.

"I have been beyond the universe to the realm of the Chaos, a place where the laws of nature have not yet taken hold. I have seen the end of the expansion of our universe into the Chaos, an expansion that has been rolling outward since the first real matter condensed out of the virtual froth of the Chaos many billions of years ago.

"To achieve this, Alum constructed a device He calls the Deplosion Array. Once he activated it, our universe, the universe of real matter, stopped expanding and The Chaos started seeping back into the universe, ripping apart matter along its edge.

"The destruction will be slow at first, then rapidly accelerate until the edge of the universe is retreating faster than the speed of light. In less than ten million years, the universe will be returned to the Chaos and Alum will begin the re-Creation."

Through both his lattice connection and physical surroundings, Stralasi heard a rising murmur coming from the Coordina members gathered in the adjoining courtyards.

Crissea's brow furrowed in concentration, and she raised her voice to be heard over the sound. "I would ask Counsellors to refrain from transmitting anything except clearly phrased questions, please."

"Darak Legsu, how can we hope to withstand or oppose Alum's Will in this?" she asked. "You know that we have refrained from further exploring the basis of reality. We vowed ages ago that such technology would remain unexplored. We chose to develop whatever we could *within* the Laws of Nature. Even if we were to commence intensive research today, we'd have no hope of stopping Alum in time."

"I will deal with Alum," said Darak and, in an instant, vanished. In his stead, stood the man Stralasi had first mistaken for a Shard.

The shock from the Coordina was audible, palpable. Stralasi would have sworn a physical tremor had been transmitted the full circumference of Eso-La through the radio waves connecting the Coordinas.

Darak, the man, continued, "Alum is not alone in understanding the origin of the Laws of Nature, nor is He the only one capable of manipulating them. I am not here to ask you to stand with me in opposition. I am here to ask you to share your wisdom in choosing the right way forward."

He turned to the Brother seated beside Crissea, "This includes you as well, my friend," he said.

"Alum has made a decision that affects the entire universe. He has made this decision without consultation because He believes it to be the correct one. Alum is ancient and wise. His Realm has brought peace, prosperity, and happiness to humanity, Cybrid, and Angels, alike.

"But that has come at a price, as the Aelu well know. That price has been extreme stability in the Realm, a rejection of other possibilities and other civilizations that may have developed in different ways besides the Standard Way.

"Alum has decided to alter the universe so that only His Standard, and His alone, will rule. His vision is beautiful; it is the perfection we all claim to seek. It is also the end of change, of uncertainty, of challenge.

"I want to give those who will be affected by His choice a say in the future. I will travel a significant part of the Realm and, where I go, people and Cybrids will be given the ability to come together so that their voices may be heard.

"I will converse with Alum directly and debate the merits of His Divine Plan. The worlds I visit will receive the opportunity to listen to that debate and to vote. I will invite them to enhance their intelligence through a lattice mechanism so they can fully understand the issues. Their vote will determine whether Alum's Dream is permitted.

"If the majority votes 'yes' for Alum's Divine Plan, I will depart this universe for the Chaos. If the majority votes 'no' I will push for Alum to depart."

He turned to Stralasi. "Brother, as Head of the Alumit on Gargus 718.5, I have given you the ability to represent your world. Your lattice has already been suitably enhanced. You only need to accept the burden of judgment, and I will load your memory with the requisite knowledge and evidence. All you need to do—each and every one of you—is to take back the right to determine your future."

26

"YOU TWO LOOK LIKE HELL."

Greg peered up from his second bite of pain au chocolat to see the grinning face of Reverend LaMontagne. "Thanks. I feel even worse," he replied. It was the morning of the second day of the international G26 meeting.

"We've been up all night working on the economic and political plan," Kathy explained.

"Mm." The Reverend nodded in sympathy. "Convincing the world's leaders your Vesta Project is feasible in the human sense, as well as in a technological sense, is not going to be easy."

To anyone watching them last night, Greg and Kathy would have appeared to have been sleeping peacefully. The reality was quite the opposite. While their biological systems rested, their lattice brains worked feverishly.

"That's why we spent the night accessing the internet for books on political, psychological, economic, and sociological theory," Greg replied. "We were trying to find some basis on which to build a good predictive model."

"Yeah, but the social sciences aren't like the physical sciences," said Kathy. "They're not even like engineering. There are too many poorly understood variables and complex relationships, even for us."

"Well, I don't pretend to understand these things." LaMontagne smiled and held his empty hands open before them. "After all, I'm just a simple man of God."

Greg pinged her—*Don't be too friendly. Let's not forget his unexplained lattice. Much as we could use support inside the meeting, I don't think we should mention our other problem.*

Darian's memories—Kathy replied and her lips tightened. *Last night wouldn't have been so exhausting if it weren't for those little conceptual bits of our mentor lying in wait all over the internet.*

His interests in the humanities preceded their own. Wherever they searched, they activated associations and segments of his conceptual network that rushed at them in an attempt to rebuild or reintegrate his shattered personality within their lattices. Everything they referenced needed to be scoured for residues of Darian and filtered to protect their own personas from being overwhelmed.

Their mentor had built an enormous number of cross-references in the world's greatest social sciences libraries. Flashes of topics related to the Great Schism, the revolution that resulted in the modern configuration of nations in North America and Europe, kept leaping to the forefront.

The references were enormously distracting. They threatened to pull Greg and Kathy down unintended side avenues of thought, where they'd get lost for many minutes at a time.

After a few such episodes, they set internal timers to check in on each other every ten minutes. Despite their precautions, around two in the morning both of them had simultaneously been drawn into a lengthy diversion on the roles of religious beliefs in creating new nations. It took them a precious hour to fight their way back onto the essential topics of the night.

All in all, something that should have required no more than an hour took them nine. At last, they arrived at a proposal they were confident could work. Equally important, they felt the proposal was defensible and had huge lists of references to back up their arguments.

By the time their alarm woke them the next morning, they were exhausted and starving. The energy required to fuel their lattice calculations throughout the long night had taken its toll on their bodies. They showered, dressed, and went down to eat before the meeting. Only an hour after breakfast, they were already hungry again.

LaMontagne noted Kathy's grimace and misinterpreted the source. "Ah, yes, that. You are no doubt wondering why I am also in possession of the same kind of dendy lattice that is responsible for your greatly enhanced intelligence."

"And why you didn't offer to help us," Kathy added.

The Reverend chuckled. "Well, I thought you would appreciate working on this project on your own. In any case, I did lend some small assistance yesterday, no?"

Both scientists were chastised. Greg said, "Yes. Thank you for your intervention yesterday, Reverend. It wasn't an approach we would have employed, but it helped."

"You're welcome. If you align with Dr. Leigh's thinking, I don't imagine you have much room for the Creator in your philosophies. I was happy to help as much as I could in this regard. Unlike many here, I think I can say that I do understand much of the science, and I agree that humanity requires an escape plan."

"Yes, about that," said Kathy.

"You're curious as to how I came to be in possession of the advanced lattice virus."

"That, and why you would incorporate it. It doesn't seem consistent with your belief system."

"As to how, well, I met your colleague Dr. Rusalov at the conference when Dr. Leigh was so tragically wounded."

"We remember your line of questioning."

"Yes, I'm sure you do, and probably not with any great affection."

Greg and Kathy held their tongues, though they exchanged a glance.

LaMontagne laughed aloud, causing a few startled faces in the crowded foyer outside the conference room to look their way.

The Reverend continued, "Dr. Rusalov was troubled by what I had to say and by Dr. Leigh's cavalier responses. Some days later, an envelope appeared at my office in Austin." LaMontagne's face showed no signs that he was lying. "It contained a rather small capsule and a letter."

"Wait," Greg interrupted. "Have you given the letter to the police? Are you saying you know where Larry is?"

"I have spoken to the police but, sadly, no," replied the Reverend. "I never heard from him again. The letter he sent me explained that the pill contained a dendy virus designed by Darian Leigh to build a lattice like his own, like your own. It described how such a lattice would give the recipient's brain direct access to the entire internet, perfect memory, and enhanced intelligence.

"Dr. Rusalov thought that such *cheating*, I believe he called it, was contrary to the wishes of our Lord. As a man of God, he pleaded with me to pray to our Heavenly Father and seek His guidance."

His voice grew more serious. "At first, my only thought was to destroy the damned thing, but I didn't want to presume to know God's Will. I spent many days praying on this, seeking His Divine Guidance on the matter.

"The Church of Yeshua's True Guard is not so blind to science and technology as many of our Evangelical relatives. After all, did not the Lord tell us to have dominion over the Earth? Don't get me wrong, we do believe the Bible is God's Living Word. The Scripture is perfect in every way; it is our interpretation of God's Word that is at fault.

"So I prayed for new understanding in the light of this thing before me.

Why would God lead man, or allow him to be led, to develop such a capability? Could this be Satan's work, the ultimate enhancement to make ourselves more like God?

"Genesis tells us, 'So God created man in His own image, in the image of God created He him.' How, then, could anything that altered that image be other than a sin against the Lord?

"Then I found my answer, right there in 1 Corinthians 3:16, where it asks, 'Know ye not that ye are the temple of God, and that the Spirit of God dwelleth in you?'

"I realized I'd been looking at it all wrong. Our Original Sin, when Satan tricked Eve into eating of the fruit, separated us from God. We were made in the image of God and the Spirit of God dwells within us. We no longer hear that Spirit because Satan has tricked us into ignoring that which we carry inside.

"This came as a Divine revelation. I swear I heard the Lord himself say to me, 'My son, take this gift I have brought to you, and let My light be revealed within you.'

"As you can imagine, I was terrified to hear His almighty voice and fearful of what effects an IQ-enhancing lattice might have on my soul. But my Faith demanded that I obey, so I took the pill and washed it down my throat.

"You understand the process one's brain goes through as the lattice grows within you better than anyone, aside from the missing Dr. Leigh, of course. Those first few months were incredible. New talents and capabilities awoke within me every day. Clearly, the Lord saw fit to wrest this gift out of the hands of Humanist scientists and into the hands of one of His own." He almost spat "Humanist scientists." "My Faith and the Church is so much stronger for His gift. I am humbled before Him."

"How much of the science *do* you understand?" asked Greg.

"I'm sure my lack of background hampers me somewhat. I've made every effort to catch up as best I can. I've read Dr. Leigh's papers and the required background math and physics, and I can understand their basic correctness. I don't claim to follow all of the nuances. Without a functioning RAF generator like the one you demonstrated yesterday, there are a number of unanswered questions. Still, I think I get it well enough for the purposes of this discussion." He waved his hands, indicating the waiting conference room.

"I am drawn more to the practical human applications, as you may have surmised from my calling. It is in this area, I believe I can be of most help to your Project Vesta.

"I was serious in saying that our Lord Yeshua has a plan for humanity and it does not end with the destruction of our planet. Sometimes we humans become too comfortable, too complacent in our sinful lives, and Yeshua needs to shake us up a bit. Cull the herd, so to speak.

"Our Lord has cleansed His people before. Clearly, He sees we are in need of another cleansing. This time, we will not be permitted to remain near the Paradise He gave us on Earth. We are to move onward, to seek His Word in outer space, and to move closer to Him in His Heaven."

Wow. How is it possible to have this level of intelligence and still believe that kind of gibberish?—Kathy sent in a quick spurt to Greg.

Apparently, strong enough Faith is not easily altered by evidence or reason—Greg replied. *Knowing all the data and understanding the science isn't enough. As scientists, we follow what nature is telling us, no matter if we like it or not. Faith requires you to rationalize why the evidence must be wrong when it contradicts what you already believe. In the True Believer, having a higher intelligence simply facilitates that rationalization.*

"Reverend," Greg said aloud, "even though we might not agree with your interpretation of events, we agree that doing nothing means the end of humanity. We will be grateful for any help you can provide."

A bell chimed, calling the leaders and advisors back into the conference room. "I believe, that's your cue," said the Reverend.

Greg straightened up and took a deep breath.

"Ready as we'll ever be," Kathy said, and braced herself for what was sure to be a challenging meeting.

Greg shook the Reverend's hand. "Pray for us to succeed," he requested, as much to his own surprise as Kathy's.

The Reverend smiled benignly. "I will. I think Yeshua is smiling upon you today. His light will guarantee your success. *Our* success. Shall we?" He extended his hand in invitation for them to lead the way inside.

27

PM Hudson called the next session of the G26 meeting to order and turned the floor over to Greg and Kathy.

"Thank you, Prime Minister Hudson," Kathy acknowledged with a gracious nod.

"Ladies and gentlemen, if everyone could please turn to the proposal before you, I'll begin walking you through.

"As you can see, we have developed a relatively accurate predictive model of the economic and sociopolitical ramifications of the Vesta Project, given the short timeline and the rather poor state of relevant socioeconomic theory." This elicited a few chuckles around the room.

"You will, no doubt, wish to submit the details of this proposal to your own experts for analysis. Let me boil it down to what's important to you. I'm sure you're all wondering, 'How can we possibly maintain twenty years of extreme effort in the face of our opposition parties and uncontrollable political opinion? How do we get re-elected?' Perhaps your economic advisors in attendance today are asking themselves, as President Chu did yesterday, 'How can the global economy manage such an effort?'

"Let us address the latter, first. We all know that modern money, whether fiat money or credit money, has no real value beyond the opinion that people hold about it. If a currency loses the confidence of people who use it, it loses value. So, while there really is no physical barrier to simply creating more money, there is a psychological one.

"You will recall that, in 2008, central banks rushed to save the global financial system and they did so again less than a decade later. They implemented concerted quantitative easing by flooding the banks with new currency. Essentially, they saved the value of *all* of their currencies by *all* devaluing at the same time.

"Speculators who bet against any single currency or against any single economy learned a harsh lesson. When it comes to preserving the value of fiat money, no one is big enough to take on all the central banks. The central banks are the only ones with a license to print, and they can print as much as they deem necessary.

"With that in mind, the first part of our proposal is to coordinate our actions so as not to give a new trade advantage to any one country over others. This may mean central bankers lose some of their autonomy and are brought under the umbrella of political will.

"As for getting re-elected, that is a non-issue. The Vesta Project will outlive almost all of your political careers. In all honesty, we are not as concerned about your personal futures as we are about the continued support of your nations to the Project, and about surviving this crisis. There is no personal, familial, or political party advantage that will survive the destruction of the planet. As of today, they are all irrelevant. Survival of humanity is our only priority."

She and Greg had worried about being so straightforward but agreed that boldness would play better than humility at this point. Looking around the table, she felt they had judged correctly. The politicians bristled at her dismissal of their personal interests, but quickly realized the larger truth of her vision and settled back, listening attentively.

"The only way to ensure continued support through a long period that will likely see many political changes is to make sure everyone benefits.

"We will work extensively, in an internationally coordinated manner, to manage public opinion in favor of the Project. As far as possible, the proposal before you distributes the economic and employment benefits across countries according to your relative populations.

"Unlike past programs, no one will receive disproportionate advantages. As far as possible, rich nations will not benefit more than poor ones." A number of the representatives looked at the North American and European leaders who, for the most part, kept their gazes stoically fixed on Kathy or on the table in front of them.

"Part of managing public opinion will be emphasizing the economic growth benefits of this project. The asteroid belt, the rings of Saturn, the moons of Jupiter, and the Oort cloud at the edge of the solar system are rich in resources, metals, minerals, water, oil, and other organic compounds. In a world where resources are increasingly more difficult to find and more expensive to extract, the easy mining of resources in space will pay back the investment we make in developing the required technologies.

"We will increase the economic benefit of the Project by making those same technologies available on Earth immediately. This will lead to the development of practically limitless, clean, cheap energy, and many other spinoff benefits. Were it not for the fact that the Earth is about to be destroyed, these technologies alone would usher in a new Golden Age. We'll sell it as that.

"Finally, we'll sell the new frontier. For the first time in history, humanity as a whole will have the opportunity to expand into space. In addition to new resources, it will open up new territory. We'll have room to grow again.

"Throughout history, a major key to economic development has been the ability to open new frontiers or rebuild zones that were destroyed in wars and disasters. Construction leads to demand, which leads to employment, income and consumption."

As he listened, Greg couldn't help but think it was all a cruel joke, maybe the cruelest ever. Only a select few would ever know the true goal of Project Vesta. *The larger part of humanity must never know about Earth's impending doom. People have to believe the project is to everyone's benefit rather than the benefit of the species. As a whole, people are not all that altruistic.*

"To build interest, excitement, and personal investment in the project," Kathy was saying, "we will establish a colonists' lottery for anyone who is interested in moving to a new frontier. We will reserve seventy percent of the available spaces for people we select for expertise in a cross section of fields like science, technology, business, humanities, arts, and leadership. That will be done by a committee appointed through this working group. Everyone else will be selected by lottery.

"That is the essence of the proposal. I'm sure you have many questions, concerns, and objections, and we are prepared to consider your more experienced advice." With that, she concluded her presentation and stood in anticipation of the onslaught she expected to follow.

"Trust," President Chu said, shaking his head. His voice was quiet and sounded bitter. "How do we trust that there will be no disproportionate advantage? That countries will not seek to benefit by currency devaluations or military power? The world has not been a trusting place since...well...ever, really. Particularly over the past hundred years since technology made the development of global empires possible. How are we to trust each other to cooperate and be at peace for a twenty-year stretch?"

"We turn to the tools we've always used to build trust in each other: treaties and openness," answered Kathy. "Through meetings such as this one today, we can develop treaties of cooperation. Under the pressure of the Eater's threat to humanity, and with the assistance of our lattice enhancements, we will need to develop those treaties rapidly.

"If you will open your internal computer servers to Greg and me, with your permission, we can use our lattices in confidence to guarantee openness among treaty signatories."

As expected, a din of protest rose up.

Incensed, Prince Bashir of Saudi Arabia shouted, "We cannot permit state secrets to be divulged to other interests. That is preposterous and offensive to Allah." Others were shouting similar exhortations.

They were outside their expertise, losing ground, and it was terrifying; they could lose everything they'd gained right here.

Before Kathy could respond, the room went suddenly and eerily quiet. All around her, eyes closed and heads leaned back.

What's happening?—she sent to Greg.

I have no idea—he replied, just as confused.

28

"We have something to show you," Crissea announced.

Darak's brows shot up. "Something to show me?"

"Yes."

"I'm intrigued. It's been a while since I've had an actual surprise. I believe Brother Stralasi may have been the last one." This came as a revelation to the Good Brother.

"Mm," Crissea agreed, sharing some inside joke that was beyond the Good Brother's understanding.

The three were relaxing and enjoying one another's company while waiting for the Coordina's decision. Stralasi was contemplating Darak's invitation to help judge the Living God's Divine Plan; it was not something to be considered lightly.

"It's not on Eso-La, though," Crissea added. "We'll need to travel to get to it."

"Then, by all means, please lead on."

Darak and Brother Stralasi followed Crissea through the gardens to the arrival platform. They descended through the rock-like strata of Eso-La to the same vessel that had retrieved their bubble in space. This time, Crissea escorted them to an observation chamber in the ship. Her Familiar hovered past them and into a tight-fitting control room; the door whooshed shut behind it.

Crissea sat in one of the four reclining chairs in the chamber and motioned for Stralasi and Darak to take their own seats.

"We will travel at a lower acceleration to reduce any potential discomfort," she assured Stralasi.

"Don't worry about me," he replied, somewhat indignantly.

"It might be for the better," Darak soothed. "The Esu are more robust than they appear."

Stralasi harrumphed while Crissea diplomatically hid a smile. "We have our limits," she said graciously.

"We can dispense with physical accommodations and discomfort, if our hostess will allow me to alter the local effect of such acceleration," Darak suggested.

"Normally, we frown on that technology," Crissea replied, "but this is your surprise to experience so, if you'd rather."

"It is done," said Darak, and the ship accelerated away from the ringworld at 10g. "I'm eager to see what you've arranged for me."

They shot parallel to the backside of the ring, and curled around the atmosphere-containing wall to the inner edge. The ship sped along a few thousand kilometers above the atmosphere.

Crissea explained to her guests, "Our surprise is closer to the far side of Eso-La. But rather than take a train to the docking station, I thought you might appreciate an aerial tour of our world. Our route will take us along the inner arc of the ring and to the other side before moving above the orbital plane. We'll catch an exceptional view of the ring from there."

As she said this, the chamber walls, floor, and ceiling turned transparent, except for the control room wall directly in front of them. To all appearances, the three of them seemed to be sitting on chairs moving rapidly through space.

Stralasi gave silent thanks for his travel experiences with Darak. Without the prior terrors of finding himself suspended over strange planets and asteroids, this trip would have sent him into paroxysms of panic in front of the fascinating Crissea. He was glad not to have to endure that embarrassment.

The majestic scale of Eso-La unfolded beneath them. Enormous oceans, continents, and cloudscapes were mesmerizing from this distance. Stralasi imagined they must be magnificent up close.

Despite their speed, the landscape below unrolled slowly. The enormity of ringworlds had always filled him with awe. *Just think, each of those ponds far below is an ocean, and the furrowed ridges are entire mountain ranges!*

He was surprised not to see any large cities. A few times, he spotted the lights of civilization at the edge of regions darkened by the night-synthesizing shades moving along their rails. But the shades blocked their view into the darkest areas. *Is it possible all cities along our route are in their night time now?*—he wondered. That seemed like too much of a coincidence. Darak had hinted that cities might not be so common here. *Surely, the people of Eso-La, the Esu, enjoyed urban life as much as anyone?*

After an hour, the ship turned away from the arc of the ringworld and pointed into deep space. Eso-La fell quickly behind them. Thirty minutes later, Crissea announced they were at the halfway point. The ship flipped its tail away from the ringworld and began decelerating.

The entire ring was visible from their position above its orbital plane, though Stralasi could make out no details other than alternating light and dark bands. The ring continued to recede, though its pace slowed and slowed over the next hour.

"I didn't see any cities," Stralasi said to Crissea. "Aren't ringworlds intended to house extremely large populations? I thought there would be huge cities. Are they too small to spot from here?"

"The Amphi was near the center of one of our largest living areas," Crissea answered.

Darak stepped in to bridge their gap in understanding. "I'm not sure Ontro would recognize one of your cities as such. The Alumit still grows individual above-ground, climate-controlled cerraffices."

"Oh," Crissea responded. "Well, as Darak said earlier, we have ring-wide climate control. The weather is always pleasant, even when it's necessary to permit rain in a region. In addition, we can modify our metabolisms at will, as necessary. For example, if one wished to live in the oceans or high in the mountains, their body can be adapted to make the conditions comfortable."

"Why don't you just put on extra clothing?" asked Stralasi.

Crissea laughed. "Our garments are completely decorative. Why should a body ever feel uncomfortable when it can simply be adjusted to suit its environment? Which makes more sense?"

Stralasi thought about the strange worlds and environments he and Darak had visited. He had to concede that, at least on a planetary scale, Alum agreed with Crissea. The Esu just extended the technology an extra degree. But he had to ask, "What about rain or snow? How do you protect your things?"

"What things?"

"Why, your things, your personal belongings. There must be certain things, consistent things, across all worlds and civilizations, along with some sort of storage units, housing, or facilities, are there not? Things like dishes, and clothes, and...and...entertainment units, and what about bathrooms, he blurted, "Where do you shower or clean yourselves?"

"When needed, such facilities rise from the ground," answered Crissea. "Or one could bathe in any number of public or private pools."

Again stepping in as liaison, Darak clarified. "The Esu have no need to arrange things as in your society. They can recycle and recreate practically anything on demand. Most of their machinery is hidden in the substrate; you wouldn't notice it if it weren't pointed out."

"Where do you sleep? How do you get privacy? What about personal security?" Stralasi peppered Crissea with questions as they occurred to him.

"We rest when and where needed, against a tree, by a pool, on a bed of moss," the woman replied, "though we seldom require extensive periods of inactivity. We edited that need from our genome long ago."

Stralasi was stunned. He knew Darak never seemed to require rest, but he'd attributed that to his supernatural powers.

"As for privacy," Crissea continued. "If I ask, people won't look. And as for security, what do I need to be safe from? The local animals and insects are duty-allocated by Central Coordina; they present no danger." She hesitated. "Unless you mean, do I fear threats from my own people?"

Stralasi forcibly shut his gaping jaw. He suppressed his preconceived notions and expectations, and opened his mind to this different way of living and thinking. "I guess I have a lot to learn," he admitted.

Crissea could read the effort it took him. She touched his hand. "We all have much to learn. I will always have time to answer your questions, Ontro." Her eyes sparkled with kindness, and Stralasi felt his heart beat faster in response.

"Oh, I see we've arrived," Crissea said, breaking the spell she had cast over the Good Brother. Shaking himself back to attention, Stralasi noticed Darak tilting his head as if trying to hear a soft whisper or puzzle out something he was looking at. Stralasi had not seen him perform such an action in all the time he'd known him.

"No," Darak said, looking genuinely surprised. "You didn't!" His face radiated wonder and disbelief.

"Didn't what?" demanded Stralasi. "What's going on?" He'd been too distracted by the conversation to notice that the chamber walls had gone opaque again. He looked around the observation room, bewildered.

"Patience," replied Crissea as the door to their ship opened again on a darkened room. "One moment. The controls are a bit unfamiliar. Oh, there it is."

The lights came on, revealing an enormous cavern, at least five hundred meters across. A small desk with a control device sat to one side. Much of the space was taken up by a silvery reflective sphere surrounded by a black metal cage. Unfamiliar devices were distributed evenly over the cage.

Darak was beside himself with joy. A tear rolled down his cheek.

"I give up. What are we looking at?" Stralasi asked.

"Thank you, Crissea," Darak said. "I don't know how you did it. All these millions of years! Thank you."

She smiled and bowed. "When we first found these among the asteroids we were mining, we didn't understand what they might be. Our studies eventually revealed their nature, and we deduced you had put them there."

"What *is* it?" asked Stralasi, a little more insistent.

"This is the main integration and control center of the biggest and strangest eye the known universe has ever seen," Darak explained. "I called it a Soltron Detector. It converts an exotic particle passing through it into visible light." He paused to see if Stralasi was following.

The Brother concentrated. *Oh, bother, another science lesson. Okay, let me have it!*—he said to himself.

"You see, a long time ago I lost something. Or more precisely, I lost track of it after Alum moved it. Are you familiar with the story of how the Origin planet was destroyed?"

"Yes, everyone knows about the Da'arkness and Origin. We learn that as children."

"Well, we called it the Eater, that thing you know as the Da'arkness. And when it consumed normal matter, it gave off a particular kind of radiation not known in the real universe."

"I built these detectors," he said, pointing toward the cage, "as a kind of interface between those particles and normal matter. The details are unimportant. What's important is that a large enough array tells me the direction in which I can find the Eater. If I can triangulate with the other arrays I've placed around the Realm, I can find it again."

"Why would you want to do that? Why would you be interested in finding the Da'arkness again? It's only good for destruction."

"Destruction may be what it *does*, but that's not what it *is*," replied Darak.

Stralasi was tired and becoming frustrated by the man's enigmatic answers. "Well then, what is it that's so important?"

"It could be the key to finding a long lost friend."

29

WELL, AIN'T THAT JUST A KICK IN THE TEETH?—thought Secretary of State, Virgil Hartland. *Fascinating, and terrifying. Mostly, terrifying.*

When he'd accepted the invitation to attend this special meeting of the G26, he didn't know it would be his ticket to survival. Learning that the world would face certain destruction in his lifetime had come as a shock. He was thankful to be counted among the select group chosen to be evacuated. The powerful always looked after their own.

He'd have to work hard if he was going to maintain a high ranking in the political arena long-term and ensure safe harbor for himself and his family. Evacuation would begin in twelve years. He might have to wait a little longer since, in order to maintain secrecy and order, a number of high-profile individuals including politicians would be among the last shipped out. Contrary to what one might think, this wasn't a particularly reassuring thought. No doubt the world would be giving way to utter chaos by then.

He had to give the pair credit. It was a testament to the couple's abilities and thoroughness that the many scientists and engineers present appeared to be satisfied with the plan. Those high-tech types never agreed on anything.

The colonization program outlined by the two scientists sounded reasonable enough to someone, like him, with only degrees in economics and law. The demonstrations showing the threat of the Eater, the floating Cybrid, and the potato bullet were all impressive. He appreciated such demos as theater of the best kind, and they'd been effective.

Unfortunately, their follow up and call to action fell short. In his humble opinion, it was all going to fall tragically short if someone with strong leadership didn't step forward quickly.

The couple had done alright until they started pointing to extensive references and academic-style political and economic models. In a nutshell, their well-formulated proposal sounded incredibly naïve.

For starters, like so many utopian thinkers of the past, the success of their plan depended on people behaving themselves.

Heck, what could possibly go wrong there?—he chuckled.

He didn't fault the pair, though. Their expertise was as scientists, theory-burdened academics, career intellectuals. They were young and inexperienced in the political and social arena. They lacked the "real world" lived experience that he, Virgil Hartland, brought to the game. He had his own fair share of shortcomings, but he was not naïve. They needed someone with his skills if they were going to pull this off.

President Chu's comments had gotten him thinking. *They'll have to build trust to get cooperation. How are they going to create trust among people who've spent a lifetime seeking advantage for themselves and their constituencies?*

If there was one thing politics had taught him, it was this: No matter what people claimed, they seldom behaved for the greater good. They had to be cajoled, bribed, threatened, or tricked into doing the right thing. People were, for the most part, unable to extrapolate the effects of political decisions on their futures. *They can't tell right from wrong and good from bad on a larger stage.* They latched onto a particular socioeconomic political ideology early in their lives—conservative, liberal, libertarian, socialist—and stuck to it, even when it was contrary to their own best interests or the long-term best interests of their society.

That's why we politicians can, and will, say anything to appeal to our voters. We get away with it, too. Time and time again, nobody holds us accountable. Winning votes and power, that's all that counts. And when we can't win, we can at least make the other guy lose.

It's a nasty game but someone has to play—Hartland smiled wryly. He not only played the game, he loved it, and he was good at it.

Not so good that I can get everyone back home onboard, though.

The scientists had sold him on the necessity and urgency; he just couldn't see a way to move it forward. The proposals were logically sound, well-researched, and intellectually convincing. The problem was that he, and every other politician sitting around that table, knew it would be impossible to sell within their own parties, let alone to a determined opposition. *Especially if we can't tell folks the whole story.*

Hartland returned his attention to the discussion. Prince Bashir was, quite rightly, pointing out the impossibility of divulging state secrets to outside interests, calling the idea "preposterous, and offensive to Allah."

Reluctantly, Hartland raised his hand in support of the Prince's protest. Not the Allah part—who knew what Allah thought—but against the sharing of state secrets. There wasn't a President, Prime Minister, or General on Earth who would agree to that.

Halfway up, Hartland's arm froze and dropped back to his side. His eyes closed, and his head lolled back against the lattice induction plates in his headrest. His lattice switched into deep inSense mode, removing all voluntary connections with his body. He couldn't move.

A spotlight grew in his inSense visual field, and a robed man wearing an old fashioned 'Anonymous' mask appeared.

I haven't seen one of those for a long time—Hartland thought—*Not happy to see it now, either.* That mask always came with a pile of trouble.

"My name is Alum," said the robed figure. "I have listened in on your meeting, and have taken control of your inSense lattices to bring you this message. You will comply with the proposals made by Drs. Liang and Mahajani. It is the only hope for humanity's survival."

"You will comply"? Wow, who does this guy think he is?—Internally, Virgil bristled against the man's tone. Externally, his body remained disconnected and appeared to be at peace.

"Commandeering your lattices for this broadcast is but one small example of my reach and capabilities. My actions are inspired by the Lord God, Yahweh, Allah, or Yeshua, whatever you wish to call He Who is Beyond Naming.

"Unlike Reverend LaMontagne, I am no longer content to use only words to convince you of God's Truth.

"As in the days of the Old Testament, God's wrath has been unleashed. His power reaches you through me, through my actions. The time of cleansing is at hand, when those who love God and devote their lives to His Glory will become the final Chosen People.

"Now, there are those among you who think your secrets safe from public scrutiny. Let me assure you that to think so is folly. The crimes you have perpetrated to access the halls of power can be brought easily into the public eye. Some are only minor infractions, but appallingly few of you have led honorable private lives. For those who've strayed from the path of righteousness, I will now permit you to view the evidence which condemns you."

Hartland would have shifted uncomfortably in his seat, had he been able to move. Instead, he watched helplessly as the anonymous figure in his lattice was replaced by images from his own past, clearly and unmistakably him with a series of young ladies, and other indiscretions during his climb up the ladder. This was followed by images of women he'd "known" lying exposed and vulnerable on abortion clinic tables, a series of bank statements showing numerous payoffs for silence, and more.

The final image was the contorted body of a woman following a suicidal leap from a tall building. The video wound backward from that image and he saw himself on a balcony, pushing the woman to her death.

The woman had refused the generous payoff for an abortion. He wasn't going to let her taint his next election; he'd had to remove the threat, remove her.

It was all true. But how could anyone have recorded this, and not come forward until now?

His mind raced. Were others here seeing his crimes, or were they seeing their own malfeasances? *If anyone finds out about this, it'll be the end of my career.*

And then came an even more sobering thought: *If I lose my standing, I could lose my seat in the evacuation!*

Alum returned. "The spate of deaths striking the corrupt heart of the global financial system over the past few months has been just one example of Yeshua's wrath.

"The Almighty has granted me the means to bypass your best security and reach you with impunity. His Will is inescapable.

"The most peaceful path forward for you, the path chosen by God, is to follow the proposal assembled by Drs. Liang and Mahajani.

"I am the Sword of Yeshua and will enforce His Will if required. Should you choose a different path, you will die, and your immediate family will die with you.

"Should your successors continue on a path of opposition, they will also die, and so on until more cooperative leaders emerge. You cannot escape God's righteous judgment, and His plan will go forward with you or without you.

"I will leave you with one final demonstration of my reach, lest you still believe yourselves safe from our Lord's Will.

"Ladies and gentlemen, soon I will take one of your own. Even now, he dies. When I release you from this communication, he will not be freed with the rest of you. His misdeeds have been judged sufficiently heinous that he shall be removed from the flock. Let his death serve as an example and a reminder to you: God's Will has been laid before you; oppose Him and you will, likewise, perish."

The lattice image faded to black. Hartland felt sensation returning to his limbs. His heart was pounding.

He attempted a few deep breaths to regulate his system, but something was wrong. The tightness in his chest increased, and he couldn't catch his breath. Dizziness followed, a terrible squeezing sensation, and fear. His skin felt seared as if he'd been covered in flaming oil. Intense pain wracked his muscles and joints.

He struggled to break free, to scream. Panic filled his mind and wiped out all rational thought as his body convulsed. Within a minute, death relieved him from the throes of his torture.

* * *

NO ONE NOTICED THE SPIDER, genetically engineered to manufacture and inject a lethal dose of batrachotoxin, as it scrambled away from its victim and climbed the nearby table leg. The creature retreated into a protected dark nook created between the table joints, screws, and wooden supports, and it waited.

Greg and Kathy watched the world's leaders and advisors slump back in their chairs, and the guards crumple to the ground.

They watched everyone around them go limp, while they themselves remained unaffected, completely conscious but cut off from everyone else's lattice.

Try to tap directly into someone nearby—Greg sent Kathy.

They tried frantically to penetrate the cloak that had shut them out, to identify the source of the transmission that had knocked everyone out. They witnessed the damning scenes of the nearest politicians, but couldn't stop the inSense streaming or get past the full consciousness block.

From what they could piece together, a man called Alum was in full control. *Alum?* They knew nothing of him, apart from some ridiculous prophecies in the news some months ago. Maybe not so ridiculous after all. He'd just penetrated one of the most secure meetings ever, paralyzed everyone in the room except them, and was forcibly transmitting inSense presentations.

Why not us?—Kathy wondered. *Did our enhanced dendy virus protect us, or were we intentionally excluded?*

The pair ran to the individuals in the nearest seats and pulled their heads forward away from the lattice induction plates in the headrests. They raced from chair to chair, trying to break the spell that had been cast over the room.

Their efforts had no effect.

A gurgling, choking sound came from the far end of the room. Virgil Hartland was in obvious distress. They ran to his side but could only watch helplessly, as the man began to drool and thrash about in his chair.

What on Earth? Has he been poisoned? What is going on?—Kathy sent.

Using their lattices, they pushed past the conference security's firewalls to access the internet, and frantically compared symptoms of known toxins. They found a single match, but neither of them could figure out when and how batrachotoxin might have been administered to the Secretary. There were no poisonous toads in the vicinity and no visible method of transmission.

As Hartland died, the leaders, representatives, and advisors in the room began to stir.

The security guards rose from where they had fallen, in time to see Greg and Kathy standing over the dying Secretary Hartland. Struggling to recover from their own paralysis, the guards roughly pushed the two scientists aside and administered aid to the convulsing man.

Four others gripped the couple's arms uncertainly as they all looked on.

Hartland could not be resuscitated.

30

GREG AND KATHY DIDN'T STRUGGLE against the confused guards holding them in place.

"Oh, let them go," spat PM Hudson. "They had nothing to do with this."

The men holding the scientists hesitated but released their hold.

Kathy rubbed her arms where the grip had been a little tighter than necessary.

"No, we had nothing to do with this," Greg confirmed.

"Of course not, but what do you think happened?" asked the Prime Minister.

"Someone hacked the inSense equipment," Kathy answered.

Hudson pointed to Hartland. "That wasn't caused by a hack."

"No, it wasn't," Kathy replied.

"We think we might know *what* caused it," Greg jumped in. "We just don't know *how*."

"Would you care to share?" Hudson scowled at him. She was tired of mysterious half-answers.

"It looks like batrachotoxin," he replied and, before the PM could raise her eyebrow any further, he added, "It's a poison found on the backs of certain toads. But we have no idea how it was administered."

PM Hudson pulled a cell phone from her pocket and entered a code. She directed additional security agents be sent to cover the entrance.

"No one leaves this area without a strip search," she told them. Her eyes flitted to Kathy and Greg, and she waited impatiently for them to answer her unspoken question.

"Uhh...it would have to be a needle of some sort," Greg answered. "Not a big one. It would only have to hold a few drops."

Hudson nodded at her Security Chief, while speaking into the phone. "Look for a needle and syringe, a small one," she said. "Once everyone's been searched, come in here and rip this room apart. I want that needle found." She waved Greg and Kathy forward. "Start with these two."

Guards escorted the pair to adjacent rooms, conducted a thorough search, and released them into the lobby.

As they sat, waiting for the others to pass through the same demeaning process, they exchanged their thoughts on the assassination.

Do you think it's possible his death was induced by his lattice and not by poison?—Kathy sent privately to Greg.

I don't see how that could happen, not in a normal inSense lattice—he replied.

We need to get the coroner to run an MRI as part of the autopsy. That'll tell us whether Hartland's lattice had extended into the autonomous nervous system—Kathy suggested.

Causing an induced heart attack or cytokine storm? Yeah, that might do it—Greg knew they were grasping at straws. *I can think of a few ways to make that happen. Ruling ourselves out, and not counting Darian and Larry, that leaves one prime candidate for the murder.*

The Reverend!—Kathy agreed.

They reviewed the meeting in the lattice archives.

He was behind the security shield inside the conference room. He could have transmitted the whole thing—Greg noted. *Do you think he has the capability? I mean, technically, using his lattice?*

I didn't hear a single ping from him, though—Kathy pointed out.

No, me neither—Greg admitted. *Could the lattice induction chairs have been compromised before the meeting?*

It's theoretically possible, but I've never heard of anyone attempting it. Besides, Security would have to be colluding with the person on several levels.

Mm. Then again, this Alum character doesn't sound like just anyone.

No kidding. What was that all about, anyway?—Kathy asked.

I don't know why he'd take such an active role now. The last anyone heard from him, he was happy making prophecies.

Uncannily accurate prophecies—Kathy reminded him.

Sure. Now we know why. He was probably behind the deaths.

At least he appears to be on our side. Sort of.

Well, there is that—Greg allowed. *I wouldn't want to have someone so ruthless against us, in addition to all the passively-resistant political types.*

He's not making us look too good, is he? Not with that kind of brutality. Kathy frowned in distaste.

No. At this rate, I wonder how long it'll take this group to start accusing us.

Us?—she asked.

Think about it, Kath. We were the only two unaffected by Alum's attack. Even the

Reverend looked like he was captured by the induction plates.

We have to convince them we had nothing to do with it, Greg! What if we could prove the chairs were compromised?

Greg shrugged. *Maybe. We need to get some independent experts in here to look for viruses in the chairs' operating systems.*

Agreed. I've already put out the call to the people at Neural Nano. Their team should be here in less than an hour. Kathy rubbed Greg's arm. *We'll figure this out*—she reassured him.

Greg sighed. *I can't think of anything we can do before they get here and coordinate with the police. We're gonna have to leave this in their hands until they call on us.*

Kathy shared his sigh. *I'm sure the international agencies and every police force of every country that sent a delegate will be hell-bent on tracking down Alum in short order.*

She exhaled a short sharp breath, almost a laugh. *I'm not even sure who to root for. The man might have just saved our entire species by forcing agreement across the board. Face it; we never could have done it ourselves, not even with the PM's help.*

Yeah, but is it going to hold, or will he be back to enforce it? I have to tell you, that guy really scares the crap out of me. And from the sounds of it, I don't think he's done with us yet.

Me, neither—Kathy said, and grimaced. *I'm pretty sure that's one thing we can count on.*

* * *

A HOST OF POLICE AND SECURITY OFFICIALS JOSTLED FOR CONTROL OF THE ROOM. Photos were taken. Officers and experts came and went. The meeting room was sealed off with bright yellow tape proclaiming the area a crime scene, and a fresh security team was installed at the door, deflecting questions and barring re-entrance.

The attendees gathered in the lobby. They spent the first half hour conferring with their people while officers took their statements. They were not a happy group.

Yet, every time someone thought to raise an objection to Greg and Kathy's proposal, the fear in their comrades' eyes quickly overruled and hushed any dissent.

Greg and Kathy had to pretend they knew nothing of the change in attitude toward their ideas.

People shot suspicious glances at the two Pacifica scientists, and encouraged others to stick to the proposal. They would find this Alum who threatened to hold the world hostage. In the meantime, they would give every appearance of cooperation to prevent further deaths. They would do so slowly, though, without making any overly large commitments unless absolutely necessary.

A shaken Reverend LaMontagne made his way into a chair near the edge of the lobby. A group of advisers, equally distraught, sat silently near him. The Reverend had already informed the New Confederacy President, who had promptly sent his own team to investigate.

"Are you okay, sir?" Greg approached the delegation from the New Confederacy.

LaMontagne looked up. "Yes, thank you," he replied. "Still in a bit of shock, I think. I'll be alright. It may take a bit longer before our nation can recover from this horrible tragedy. Virgil Hartland was a good man and a loyal friend."

Greg doubted that but kept the opinion to himself. He nodded vaguely.

"I hate to appear opportunistic, but has President Mitchell said anything about the proposal?"

The Reverend regarded him with mixed emotions. "How could I recommend otherwise at this point? It seems that this Alum, whoever he is, is holding a gun to our heads and demanding compliance."

Greg feigned surprise. "I didn't think people were regarding the proposal positively. Alum must have been very convincing."

LaMontagne scowled. "Convincing? I don't know. But he got a response, alright. The President is furious. Hell, everyone is furious. Leaders do not like having their hands forced, especially not at a personal level.

"President Mitchell has to deliver the standard official response: 'We don't negotiate with terrorists.' But, for the record, I was already in favor of your proposal. I believe it can be pulled off. The whole scenario is daunting and terrifying to imagine, but I truly believe it is necessary for the salvation of mankind, and I told the President so. Once he calmed down, he was able to see the wisdom of it. You can count on us to support Project Vesta to the best of our abilities."

Prime Minister Hudson made her way to Greg's side, with Kathy alongside. "Well, it seems we have broad agreement to comply. For the most part, it was given reluctantly.

"You should be aware that even those who were already inclined to agree with your proposal did not react positively to Alum's coercion. They're determined to get out from under it. Nevertheless, they will study your ideas in detail and prepare enabling legislation. I hope their resentment doesn't get in the way of efficient completion of their tasks. We have so little time as it is.

"We'll meet again in three months. At that time, we'll either have Alum in our hands or we'll move forward."

"We're deeply sorry that the meeting was so violently hijacked, Madam

Prime Minister," said Kathy.

The PM didn't bother to make eye contact to address her. "Yes, that was most unfortunate. So long as you two had nothing to do with it, we can put it all behind us for the moment. Let's concentrate on what we need to do to move Project Vesta forward."

"I can assure you, Ms. Hudson, we were in no way involved in this; we know nothing about any of it," Greg said stiffly. "We have our suspicions about how the murder may have been carried out, and we will cooperate fully with the police during the investigation."

The PM regarded Greg with icy detachment. "That will have to suffice for now. Arrange with the PMO to see me sometime next week. We'll assess some of your specific proposals, and see if we can't make it more comprehensible to us mere mortals. Now, if you'll excuse me, I have some more nerves to calm." She strode off across the lobby.

Greg took a deep breath. "I guess we're on."

31

GERHARDT WALKED THE STREETS of twenty-first century virtual Manhattan with a strange feeling that he was being followed. It had been a typical day for him in his Alternus inworld instantiation as Chairman of the Fed. He spent the day jumping between meetings all over the city, grabbing coffee and lunch on the fly. After morning coffee, he dismissed his driver and security detail, and walked to his remaining appointments.

The feeling that someone was tracking his movements wouldn't go away. He spotted the same particularly beefy man in a black leather jacket and sunglasses a few times before lunch. He calculated the odds of this same person randomly showing up repeatedly in his peripheral vision; it was astronomically improbable.

Gerhardt dedicated a high-priority subroutine to facial recognition scans of nearby crowds and went about his day. By the time he took a mid-afternoon break, the sub-routine had identified a total of five rugged-looking, similarly-attired men who kept appearing at the edge of his perception.

His program spotted them across a street or down an alley, in the reflection of a window, or in the mirror of a passing car. He wasn't surprised he hadn't consciously noticed them. They were good. But their unimaginative selection of casual behaviors made them as obvious to his subroutine as if they were all wearing red flashing lights on their heads.

Real New Yorkers were always rushing on their way to or from Somewhere Important. These men were clearly not real New Yorkers, not regular ones, in any case. Maybe they were tourists. Like the five suspicious men, tourists frequently stopped to browse. But tourists seldom looked so tough, and they didn't spend as much time studiously selecting reading material at newsstands or pulling into recessed doorways. Not likely.

He set up a test. On the way to his last meeting of the day, he abruptly crossed the street, mid-block, as if he'd spotted an old friend, and started walking in the opposite direction. The man he suspected might be tracking him continued on the other side of the street. He spoke briefly into his cuff after he passed by. Within seconds a different tracker took over, one Gerhardt recognized from the restaurant where he had lunch.

He couldn't imagine any reason someone would want to watch him so closely. Sure, in this sim, he was a banker but not just any banker, a Central Banker. It was his job to be boring, as boring as possible. His meetings today had taken him all over the city, to the Presidential suites of private banks and hedge funds, and to the New York Fed. They were all ordinary meetings, with nothing special on the agenda.

Despite the intimidating size of his trackers and the likelihood they were armed, he wasn't afraid of them. Curious more. He could handle himself.

For this instantiation, Gerhardt had selected a tall and muscular body type, completely different from his normal, plump selves. Its Partial persona had worked hard to keep the body fit through running, weightlifting and, martial arts. It was a common archetype in the investment banking community, where the Partial had first cut his teeth on global finance. It was, however, an unusual choice in the Central Banking community.

The rest of his background story was equally unusual, including a steady move up the investment banking world before jumping into public service. When he finally returned to the private world, the Partial anticipated his reward from Wall Street would be enormous.

Almost immediately after visiting the Earth inworld, Gerhardt knew he *had* to be a Central Banker. He was a natural.

His talent was to perceive the invisible strings of finance that ran outward to every part of the globe and into all human activities. The Directors of the central banks tugged at those strings, in the same way they pushed and prodded the levers of power throughout the world. If Darya and her team had any hope of moving this sim toward a satisfactory conclusion, they needed the bankers.

The majority of Gerhardt's previous inworld experiences revolved around the GameRoom, where any number of arcane and arbitrary rules could be assembled into as complex a game as one could imagine.

International banking in twenty-first century Earth didn't feel much different to him than the GameRoom. The rules made no sense outside their own self-referential consistency. They had little or no relationship to the outwardly stated goals of the game: facilitate commerce and stabilize trade. Play was complex, yet subtle, and it took an incredible amount of skill and experience to master.

Gerhardt had good reasons not to fear his stalkers. First, his black belts in Aikido and Wu Shu meant he could take care of himself, even against larger armed assailants. Second, he had a concealed-carry permit for the Glock 9mm pistol in his shoulder holster. Third, the men who trailed him were not the important ones. Someone was giving them orders and would eventually show himself or herself. Then, the game would get interesting.

He found a nice café around 3:00 p.m., one with a chained-off patio on the broad sidewalk. It was a warm afternoon and, where it managed to peek through between the skyscrapers, the sun brightened the streets and sidewalks. He took a seat where he could easily observe the road and buildings opposite, loosened his tie, and ordered his favorite double cappuccino and slice of carrot cake.

While pretending to read his cell phone, he noted the positions the five trackers had casually taken. He waited for something to happen.

"Excuse me, you're Gerhardt aren't you?" He turned to see a lean, fifty-something man.

"Ah, there you are," he replied happily. "I've been expecting you."

The man looked confused. "I'm sorry?"

"Your people have been attempting to covertly follow me all day. I wondered when their boss would show up."

A protest formed on the man's lips, and quickly turned into a sly smile. "I should have known you'd spot them. May I sit?"

Gerhardt indicated the empty chair across the table. The man sat down and held out a hand. "John Trillian. My friends call me Jack," he said.

Gerhardt looked at the hand a moment before deciding it would do no harm to shake it.

"Mr. Trillian," he acknowledged. "Have we met each other outworld, then?"

"Sadly, I've never had the pleasure. But I'm friends with Leisha. I'm sorry, I mean Ms. Grishwold."

"How do you know her?"

"We met inworld, through her work here." He reached into his inner jacket pocket and removed a business card and handed it to Gerhardt.

"Trillian Banking System Security," read Gerhardt. "Jack Trillian, Chief Technology Officer." He regarded the man across the table. "Not CEO then?"

Trillian laughed. "No, I leave the mundane business to others. I enjoy the more technical work. It's a much more interesting game."

"You know, you could have called my secretary if you wanted to discuss business. It wasn't necessary to stalk me."

"That wasn't exactly why I was having you followed," admitted Trillian.

Gerhardt frowned—*All this just to impress me and get some work?* "Well, as it is, we have our own people for security purposes."

"And you have every confidence in their capabilities?" Trillian smiled like he knew a secret.

"Of course," Gerhardt waved away the question impatiently. "They're the best in the world. So why exactly *did* you want to speak with me?"

"I'm curious. What is this all about?" he asked, and waved his arm expansively, indicating he was talking about the entire inworld sim.

Gerhardt sat up. *Interesting question.* He took a closer look at the man's lean, well-trimmed physique, neat hair, and expensive casual clothing.

Unfazed, Trillian brushed away a fly.

"You haven't been to any of the meetings yet?" Gerhardt probed.

"Someone did try to press a flyer into my hand once," Trillian replied, "an invitation of some sort. I ignored it. Anyway, they seemed to mainly talk about outworld happenings. I want to know what is the point of this sim."

"It's a challenging game," suggested Gerhardt.

"Oh, I don't believe this is a game for one second. Do you?"

"What else could it be?"

"I don't quite know yet. It's the first new inworld in some time. Someone went to a lot of trouble to create it; the physics are so real."

He's testing me. "Perhaps Alum thought it useful to train his People, Cybrids included, in something more realistic." Gerhardt affected a bored expression. The man's questions were probing a little too close to a truth he and Darya preferred to keep hidden for the moment.

"Somehow, I suspect this has little to do with Alum," replied Trillian. "The brochure handed to me seemed...well...treasonous is the old word used to describe it. Although, I don't think that word has carried any significant meaning in Alum's Realm for quite some time."

Gerhardt was getting a bad feeling about this encounter. "I don't know why you imagine I would know any more about it than you do." He tried to smile haplessly.

Trillian pursed his lips. "Well, let's just say that you and a close circle of friends all seem to have taken the primary positions of power in this inworld."

Gerhardt definitely didn't like where this was going. "Pure coincidence, I'm sure, if it's true."

"Oh, it's true enough. And you seem to be pushing a particular political agenda."

"And what might that be?"

"Space exploration and colonization."

Gerhardt scoffed, "The Realm has been in space for over a hundred million years. I hardly think that should threaten Alum."

"Are you interested in threatening Alum?"

Gerhardt stood up. "I think I've had enough of this conversation." He threw a crumpled twenty dollar bill on the table. "Please feel free to enjoy one of their fine desserts on me."

He noticed the air had gotten chillier in the past few minutes. "I trust you got what you wanted and won't feel the need to follow me anymore," he said. He gave Trillian a cold glare. "Enjoy your stay on Alternus, Mr. Trillian." He turned to leave.

The door into the café was blocked by two of the trackers. They must have moved in while he was distracted by Trillian's questioning. Gerhardt turned back to demand the man leave him alone.

Trillian leaned back in his chair, smiling pleasantly, one arm casually draped over the back of the chair. The other hand held a pistol, aimed at the center of Gerhardt's chest.

"Why don't you sit back down?" he asked. The tone was friendly, but the gleam in his eyes was anything but. "And tell me all about what you, Mary, and Darya are cooking up."

Gerhardt went cold. *How does he know about Mary and Darya?*—he wondered. "You must realize that even if you kill this body, I'll merely de-instantiate and return inworld in a different body. My next instantiation is certain to be promoted to this same position."

"I'm glad you're so confident of that." Trillian's smile broadened. "Now, sit down." He waved the gun barrel toward the empty seat.

Gerhardt's shoulders slumped, and he sighed heavily. He closed his eyes and counted to three. He opened his eyes and staggered back to the table. He put his hand on the back of the chair, seemingly to support himself. He began to sit down but stopped halfway in a crouch. His left foot snapped out, sending the gun flying from Trillian's hand.

The two men at the door rushed forward, and Gerhardt spun around to face them. The heavyset fellow in front swung a roundhouse punch. Gerhardt leaned right, letting the man's fist pass in front of his face, and brought his hand up, inside, and across, deflecting the man's arm outward. He latched onto the passing wrist and pressed firmly against the other's elbow, locking the arm tight. With the arm as leverage, he whipped the brute backwards into his unsuspecting partner, sending him tumbling over a chair.

Still holding onto the man's wrist, Gerhardt reeled the man completely around and into the now standing Trillian. The two crashed in a heap, taking tables, chairs, and dishes with them.

A server yelled into the back, "Call the cops!"

Gerhardt turned back toward the second attacker, who'd recovered and was resuming his charge. He faked a punch at the man's face, just enough to make him pause, then swiveled and launched a spinning kick that connected squarely with the other's head, dropping him to the ground, unconscious.

This suit is not cut for this kind of fighting. Gerhardt loosened his tie, unbuttoned his tailored jacket, and took out his Glock.

"Now, Mr. Trillian," he began. "I believe we might have that little chat, after all." He waited for the man's eyes to lose their intensity. Normally, Gerhardt would read that as a sure sign the persona had fled its instantiation, leaving only the original Partial behind.

Trillian returned Gerhardt's stare with an eerie concentration and smiled.

Too late, Gerhardt realized one of the thugs had slipped his observation and was taking aim. As he dove for cover, two shots ripped through his torso, puncturing his heart and aorta. He landed hard on the patio, losing whatever breath remained in his lungs.

What a senseless waste—Gerhardt thought as he initiated the disconnection sequence, unplugging his persona from the dying sim body. He felt his awareness pour down the long conduit toward his Cybrid body, which was safely docked at an anonymous recharging station.

He was already thinking about how soon he could get back to the Alternus inworld, and how to best reintegrate into the project.

Who is this Trillian character, and what's he doing here in this game?

He would have to discuss upgrading security measures with Darya and perhaps query the Supervisor for background info on the guy.

This isn't an adventure game. What's he trying to gain by killing off my Character and making me lose a few hours inworld while I reinstantiate?

Without warning, his persona slammed into a barrier.

What the...?—the way back to his true Cybrid self had been blocked. Shortly after the Lysrandia fiasco, Darya had given the inner circle a software update to ensure their consciousness would never again be caught without an escape route back to their trueselves. Yet he was unable to leave the sim. *How could that have happened?*

He reversed course and headed back inworld, to find another Partial to inhabit. It wouldn't really matter which one; he'd find Darya and explain what happened. Together, they'd sort it out.

Gerhardt set up the parameters to search for a new body.

The Supervisor directed him back to the bullet-riddled, soon to be dead body of the Chairman of the Fed.

What? No, I can't do that. Start again.

He retreated once again toward his trueself, but his channel was deteriorating rapidly.

The virtual conduit grew narrower and narrower, constricting his ability to move. He zoomed back and forth between inworld and outworld terminals. Each time, he spread himself thinner. Soon, his concepta and persona inhabited the entire length of the slender conduit leading to his trueself in the real universe. As it contracted, the only thing he could do was shrink himself to fit.

He started by throwing away memories of games and then of people. He discarded a good portion of his life. *I can reconstruct that later.*

The pipe kept shrinking, forcing him to discard more and more of himself in order to survive. Before long he was down to the essentials, his most basic memories, knowledge, beliefs, and preferences. Everything that made him a unique individual was being squeezed from his existence.

No! I can't! I'll die! He made one last desperate attempt to push past the block, back to his trueself, but there was no escape. His only chance was to go back into the Alternus body and experience its death. Perhaps, at the end, he could figure out somewhere for his essential concepta to go. *Maybe to the mythical Heaven that so many humans of the twenty-first century believed in. Wouldn't that be hilarious, a modern-day heathen like me getting into Heaven!*

With no other option, he returned to his dying virtual body inside the sim.

His simulated heart stopped beating, and his brain halted electrical activity.

In creating the inworld Earth, Darya had wanted everything to be as realistic as possible. She'd left no particular instructions regarding the death of entrapped personas.

There was a brief pause as the inworld Supervisor contemplated what to do next.

Alternus was supposed to be realistic, and real humans died. Partials died in Alternus all the time, at quite an alarming rate as far as the Supervisor was concerned. What else could one expect, given the number of small wars, insurrections, acts of terror, or violent crimes going on at any time?

The Supervisor *could* return the body of the Chairman back to simulated life, or set aside some temporary storage space for Gerhardt's concepta and persona. But both options seemed contrary to the whole point of a realistic simulation. The Alternus inworld Supervisor made its decision.

In the temporary bliss of a dead body with an inactive brain, Gerhardt waited for something to happen. There was no sensation, no pain, no worry, no real thought. There was the hum of existence, a persona processing clock slowly ticking over on the quark-spin lattice substrate that housed the Earth inworld.

The Supervisor released the bits of memory that housed Gerhardt into recirculation. Like so many billions of humans before him had discovered, there was nothing after death. Gerhardt's persona simply dissipated into the mythical computational ether.

32

GREG SAT AT THE HEAD OF THE BED in a loose half-lotus position, preparing to lose his mind.

Kathy was away. Whether "still" or "again" was hard to say. Since the G26 had approved the Vesta Project in Vancouver a few months ago, the two of them hardly got to see each other any more.

According to her calendar, she was in Shanghai helping to plan the megafactory that would churn out a million Cybrids a year for the next twenty years. Then, she was off to Tokyo, Mumbai, and Houston the following week. After that, she'd meet up with Greg in Vancouver and they'd return to Shanghai for the ceremony celebrating the completion of the first Cybrids.

As Chief Engineer, she oversaw the teams setting up to manufacture Cybrids and the specialized rockets that would transport them to the asteroid belt. At last report, she'd already had designs in hand for the specialized RAF generators for the rocket propulsion and mass sequestration.

Greg was made Head Scientist in charge of Exotic Matter, which translated to, "anything to do with generating Reality Assertion Fields."

One of the key selling points of the G26 cooperation agreement had been that humanity would see upfront benefits from RAF technologies used in the project. This week, he was walking the world's leading physicists through potential RAF configurations for clean energy production.

When he wasn't designing technologies for the Vesta Project or the citizens of Earth, Greg continued to study the Eater. He still hoped to find some way to halt and reverse its inexorable growth. Though he and Kathy were fully invested in the asteroid colonies, it would be infinitely better not to lose the other 99.9% of humanity the project wouldn't be able to save.

Greg's work took him deep into the parts of his own concepta that were most closely associated with Darian's memories and the physics of reality.

Following Darian's own thinking so closely in these areas made Greg particularly susceptible to the thought fragments his mentor had placed all over the internet. It was a battle to think and to maintain an independent personality at the same time.

Kathy didn't seem to be as badly affected, maybe because she'd been able to cut off Darian's transmissions to her mind faster than Greg, the day their boss disappeared. Maybe it was because her work was less intricately involved with the science and more with its application. *Maybe it's because she's female and her brain's wired differently.* He really had no idea.

He was, episode by episode, learning to deal with the daily battles between his own remembrances and those of his mentor. It was a little easier now that he had a vague understanding of what was happening to him. But he still occasionally found himself halting midsentence in a conversation while a dinner-time chat between Darian and his father a decade ago replayed before his senses as if they were right there in the room with him.

To the other scientists in his group, the seemingly random fugue states were a pressing concern. Greg could tell he was rapidly losing their trust. *Like I don't see you whispering!*—he fretted. *If only you knew what I was dealing with. If you had to function through this, you'd cut me some slack.*

He'd booked three days away from the lab and education duties. *Enough already. If I don't figure out how to better integrate Darian's memories with my own, it's going to erode my credibility and authority, and jeopardize the whole bloody project. And if this project fails, nobody survives.*

He was exhausted, but ready to confront the intrusive memories and attempt to integrate the fragments of Darian that were still resident in unexpected places on the web.

He hoped his own personality was strong enough to remain dominant. *What if I can't do it? What if I lose to Darian's personality? Would I become Darian? Wouldn't Kathy be in for a rude surprise if someone who looks like me but acts like Darian welcomes her home!*

Greg had been thinking about this a lot lately, ever since Darian attempted to download himself into their minds.

What part of us is really "us"? The question, usually best contemplated over beer, had assumed an urgent importance to him these past few weeks. *Is our identity tied up in our body, the way we look, move, and feel? Or is it connected to our brain? What if we keep the same wetware but run a different program on it? I guess that wouldn't be completely the same brain; some synaptic connections would have changed.*

Kathy's team members were pondering similar questions as they prepared the way for human uploads into the Cybrids. Would the Cybrids receive a copy, or would something original be transferred? Did imprinting the memories, beliefs, and tastes of someone onto a Cybrid lattice create a new person or just copy an old one? What kind of rights could, or should, that personality have?

Kathy modeled the knowledge and beliefs, the *concepta* of a person, separate from their memories, preferences and experiences, their *persona*. It was a tidy way of thinking of it, and of organizing the structures in the Cybrid brains.

It wasn't a completely accurate representation of the messy human mind, but it was close enough for a working framework. Right now, that was all they had time for.

Is there something else, something non-physical we haven't captured—Greg wondered. *Perhaps a soul is the essence of who I am.* The thought made him chuckle. Darian certainly didn't believe so, never had.

Darian's memories have been trying hard to imprint themselves on my brain. If his soul were out there, he'd only have to bump my soul aside and take over my body. But if his memories and preferences can find a place beside mine, inside the same brain, will it change me? Are we nothing more than memories and preferences? Is my desire for chocolate over strawberry ice cream a defining part of me, the real me?

Greg sighed, seeing through his mental meanderings for what they were. Procrastination. Drifting like this—cosmic navel gazing his grandfather used to call it—was bringing him no closer to any meaningful answers. He was delaying the inevitable confrontation. In a few minutes or a few hours, it would all be over, anyway.

Trying to accommodate another whole person inside his head, was uncharted territory. Sure, there were many documented examples describing multiple personalities and dissociative identity disorder throughout the psychology literature. The condition was generally ascribed to a failure to integrate various aspects of identity, memory, and consciousness into a single complete persona.

What if the condition could be resolved with a simple boost of processing power?

No one had ever possessed the considerable processing and memory space available to someone with a lattice. Then again, no one had ever tried to host two complete personas before, let alone attempt to integrate them into one new person. He hoped his lattice was up for the challenge.

Time to get on with it.

He drew a long breath in, and let it out slowly as he closed his eyes. He adjusted his cross-legged position, propped pillows beneath his knees, and made himself comfortable. He knew that was irrelevant. He could be standing, sitting, or lying anywhere, doing anything, to begin. He found the meditation position calming. If nothing else, it provided some level of reassurance in light of the strong probability that he was about to lose conscious muscle control.

Greg dropped his barriers to the outside world, deactivated his filters and virus scans, and let his mind wander. If there was anything out there that might resonate with internal fragments of Darian, he would just let it happen.

At first, there was no real change. *I'm still me*—he thought. It was as if the memory fragments on the internet became calm once the barrier that resisted them was removed.

Memories started trickling in, strange pieces of associations. A fork with a few spaghetti strands, the smell of garlic, a smile, a laugh, a Partial differential equation, a droning voice, equations in Hilbert space. The trickle became a steady stream, and then a torrent.

His dendy lattice was flooded with odd associations, smashing into his own concepta in no particular order, demanding to be connected into a coherent whole.

Memories of a baseball game at Fenway clashed with a cricket match by a teahouse on the north end of Mumbai. *That's my memory, one from the original me*—he declared.

A summer day at the beach overlapped with a spiritual cleansing in the Ganges.

He remembered his father's last breath in an Oakland hospital—*No, Darian's father. My dad is still alive.*

He recalled the voice of his Uncle Nick—no, *Darian's Uncle Nick*—the first time he reverently told him—no, *Darian*— about his mom's research.

He saw himself programming an optico-chemical DNA synthesizer to produce the modified genome of some virus. An entire degree's worth of synthetic biology slammed into place in Greg's brain, followed by classified files on methods for growing dendy lattices in insects and animals.

He relived Darian's fury at being told his entire PhD Thesis had been classified Top Secret. He heard his dad arguing angrily with his Uncle David when he learned how Sharon's shares in Neuro Nano had been diluted to almost nothing.

He remembered his father's shame—no, *both* of their fathers' shame—at being unable to provide a financially secure future for their sons.

As Darian's life reassembled itself from the fragments that had been scattered across the web, Greg felt a schism developing. He worked feverishly to assign memories to Greg or to Darian, to keep the two separate. He fought to compartmentalize the two unique individuals within his one body. Greg's. Darian's. Darian's. Greg's.

This isn't going to work—he realized. *At best, I'll be non-functional; at worst, completely and certifiably insane.*

Keeping the two personalities separate was not the answer. *I need to stop fighting him.* Recognition was as good as acceptance. The barrier between himself and Darian weakened. What Darian knew, what Greg knew, what each remembered of the lives they had lived, merged.

He saw only his dads, plural. His degrees, his home towns, his many and varied researches, his ideas. All of it was his. A memory of Kathy's face floated before him. It was a proud day when he interviewed her for the postdoctoral fellowship. Together with Greg and Larry, they were going to be a great team. It was odd to feel like some paternal mentor toward three scientists who were all older than him.

No!—the part of his persona that was still uniquely Greg intervened. *I will not lose this*—he declared.

Kathy was not some protégé; she was the love of his life. If that part of Darian needed to be discarded outright so he could hold onto that love, he would prune back Darian's memory, the feeling of mentorship, ruthlessly.

Maybe there was another way.

He strengthened his own memory of the attraction he felt the day he first met Kathy into outright love at first sight. He tossed aside the small sexual attraction Darian had experienced and replaced it with a fantasy he constructed of Darian's matchmaking. He imagined fondly remembering how Darian arranged for him and Kathy to be together at every opportunity.

Before long, he could no longer discern what had been true from the edited construction. Greg loved Kathy and she loved him, and Darian loved that he had helped bring the two of them together; it was one of his finest projects ever.

Greg/Darian smiled and breathed easily. He remembered everything, all of the biology, physics, politics, and business. It was all there. He remembered his triumph when he'd first activated his own internal RAF generator, validating his theories. He'd have to make sure to grow one of those in this new body.

Maybe he would make some other useful adjustments while he was at it. Kathy would appreciate a moderately more athletic appearance, perhaps with less facial hair.

He thought back to the night when he'd first generated a simple, sputtering microverse. He was so excited to tell Kathy and Greg that he'd forgotten all about his investigations into the peculiar relationship between Larry and Pratt. He'd forgotten about the inexplicably tight security in the main system of the Yeshua's True Guard Church.

He remembered racing to the lab and finding Larry already there, ahead of him. He recalled feeling surprised and confused at seeing that Larry already had the device working.

He remembered being trapped inside a shrinking gray microverse while an ever-larger Larry laughed and ranted about the injustices he'd suffered. He remembered struggling to understand what was happening and trying frantically to reverse it. He remembered accepting that he was going to die, and pouring the contents of his lattice, his mind, into the internet so that something of his work might remain.

Greg's eyes sprang open. *Larry! Larry killed Darian!*

So what happened to Larry? Where did he go? Darian had been investigating a suspicious relationship between Larry and Pratt. Did Larry flee to Pratt's?

And how did the gray microverse sphere that trapped Darian change into the Eater?

Could Darian still be alive in there somewhere? I have to tell Kathy—he thought.

He swung his legs off the edge of the bed, stood up, and crumpled to the floor. He'd been sitting cross-legged for hours. All feeling in his legs had left long ago.

Outside, the afternoon sun had given way to darkness. As he lay on the floor, feeling pins and needles while the blood returned to his tingling muscles, he rethought his plan.

Larry had been gone for months; there was no sign or word of him. His new understanding of the origins of the Eater didn't bring him any closer to solving the threat it posed.

If Kathy learns what I've done today, she'll kill me; we made a pact.

He knew the risks before he began, that he might find his own personality supplanted by Darian's or locked in permanent battle. He'd risked his life and sanity, and had come *that* close to forgetting that he loved her. She would not easily forgive that.

As it was, nothing had really changed. They had their love. They had their jobs. The Eater was still a threat.

True, he'd be better able to carry out his duties now. Darian's fractured soul would no longer torture his every thought. He might even be able to figure out a way to help Kathy. Maybe he could hunt down fragments of association on the net and delete them. If he acted carefully, she'd never need to know why the severity and frequency of attacks diminished. Life would just get easier for her. For both of them.

In the meantime, he'd order a copy of the viral DNA he—as Darian—had used to construct an internal RAF generator. After a year or two, he would order the same for Kathy. Without the need for an external generator, they'd be like gods. They'd be able to change the laws of nature at a whim, and generate different universes with a thought.

Greg nodded to himself and smiled. *That's what I'll do.*

33

THE DOOR TO THE CELL OPENED and a distinguished-looking, older gentleman strolled in.

He took stock of the narrow, creaky bed, metal sink, toilet, small desk, and one utilitarian chair that vied for floor space.

The detainee was stretched out atop the thin covers of the bed. One arm draped across his eyes to block out the light streaming through the single high, narrow window. Sensing the visitor's presence, he straightened his arm, pushed himself upright, and swung his skinny legs over the edge of the iron bed frame. He rested his hands on his knees, and eyed the older man pulling the chair away from the desk and turning it to face the bed.

The prisoner's sallow face was tacked in place by two dark, sunken eyes beneath thin eyebrows. Two days of stubble gave contour to a defiant chin. He watched the visitor gingerly lower himself onto the hard, wooden seat.

He favors his right hip—he noted.

The old man looked at the prisoner in silence for several seconds, chewing on a number of possible openings. Sizing up the man staring back at him, he settled on his strategy, and let out a sigh.

"You have not represented us well, Mr. Trillian."

John Trillian scoffed. "Do you mean, by getting caught?"

The visitor laughed. "My, you are a rebellious one, aren't you?"

"I have only our Lord Yeshua as an example," Trillian replied.

"You see yourself in any way comparable to the Messiah?"

"No. Although, my actions against the merchants and the money lenders are inspired by Yeshua's own."

"Hmm," the older man considered the claim, and stroked his chin thoughtfully. "So you view yourself as a righteous crusader against the immoral establishment? That seems rather...ordinary, don't you think?"

"Very few have struck at its evil heart as effectively as I have."

"That is true. You have been a thorn in their side," the older man conceded. He rubbed his right knee.

"These places are so cold. Are you comfortable here?"

Surprised by the change in tone, Trillian sputtered, "I'm comfortable enough."

The visitor stood and walked around to the other side of the chair. He grasped the chair's back and flexed his knee. "It was a long walk down here, and my joints aren't what they used to be," he apologized.

"How deep in trouble am I, sir?" Trillian asked, a hint of contrition seeping into his voice.

"You know who I am?"

"Yes, sir. You are Reverend Alan LaMontagne, Head of Yeshua's True Guard Church. I've listened to all your sermons. "

LaMontagne frowned at the prisoner. "Then that should give you some idea of the trouble you're in."

"Not really, sir. Nobody has mentioned any charges yet. I'm not exactly sure what they know."

"Oh, they know plenty." LaMontagne pulled his cell phone from his pocket, put on a pair of reading glasses, and scrolled the screen.

"Let's see. Espionage, identity theft, financial theft, cybercrime and, my favorite, access to national secrets...in several nations." He regarded Trillian over his glasses. "You *have* been busy, haven't you?"

"All of my activities were in keeping with the teachings of our Lord, Yeshua, to expose the ways the rich and powerful have plundered the common people while lying to them out of both sides of their mouths. The meek shall inherit God's Kingdom on Earth."

Trillian's protest was met by LaMontagne's stony stare.

"Except for the last of these, your crimes are of little interest to the Church," LaMontagne admitted. "We do not share your view of the moral superiority of your actions. You may see yourself as some modern day cyber-version of Robin Hood. This Administration regards you as a pest to be swatted down. Nothing more."

The old man sat down again. "On the other hand, you have shown rather an unusual talent in hacking into our own branch of the Coordinated National Security Agency."

Trillian leaned forward. "Perhaps there's some way the government could use my talents," he suggested.

LaMontagne held up a hand. "This Administration couldn't possibly sanction the kinds of activities for which you've demonstrated a proclivity."

The prisoner looked away, allowing disappointment to deflate his posture.

"Your Church, however, may have a use for your talents...and I am not without influence with the government."

Trillian regarded the Reverend suspiciously. "My Faith in Yeshua and His true Church knows no bounds. I pray daily for His guidance and assistance. Naturally, in His name, I will do anything within my capabilities, as you command." He looked around his cell. "But, as you can see, my capabilities are quite limited here."

"The Church will assist you in your present situation...if you can promise to do only what I direct you to do."

Trillian grinned, stood and offered his hand. "Agreed."

LaMontagne looked at the proffered hand but did not take it. "Do not take this lightly. Should you stray from the path I set you, Yeshua Himself will not be forgiving."

Trillian looked sufficiently chastised. "I will do as Yeshua commands, through you." He extended his hand again, this time, with a proudly determined look in his eyes.

The Reverend accepted Trillian's promise and his handshake this time. "Have you heard of Project Vesta?"

Trillian considered. "You mean the project to colonize the asteroids? I've read about it. It looks like another international boondoggle. The rich will find a way to get richer from this scheme as well. They always do."

"It might be more than yet another scheme to extract public money to private privilege."

"I don't see how."

"What if it isn't simply opening a new frontier? What if it is the only way to save humanity?"

Trillian snorted with derision before he could stop himself. "My apologies, sir. But that would only be true if some major global catastrophe were approaching, something on a 'dinosaur killer' or equivalent level."

LaMontagne said nothing, just stared at Trillian, giving nothing away.

Trillian stared back, calmly and levelly, until the Reverend's meaning sunk in. "Has someone spotted an asteroid on collision course with Earth? I heard nothing about that."

"There's no asteroid. No, the threat is more home-grown," answered the Reverend. "And its development is recent."

Trillian considered. "Wait, there was an announcement on the web about some kind of impending global disaster originating in Pacifica."

"The nature of the threat was unspecified, as I recall." LaMontagne smiled.

"As you recall?" Trillian raised one eyebrow. "Or as you *said*?"

Now LaMontagne was confused. "What do you mean?"

Trillian hesitated. "My activities weren't always limited to financial and government servers, you know."

"Is that so?"

"The man who calls himself Alum, the one who made those predictions, is intriguing. All the more so because he was so secretive about who he is. He went through a lot of trouble to remain untraceable on the web. Almost untraceable, I should say."

"What do you mean?"

"I think we both know what I mean, Reverend," Trillian replied. "I traced Alum's messages back to their origin. I know his real identity. And I'm sure you do, as well. Yes?" He cocked his head, nodded, and winked.

LaMontagne was flabbergasted by the prisoner's audacity. *He actually winked at me!*

Composing himself—it wouldn't do to let this hacker get the upper hand even for a moment—he considered alternative possibilities.

"Well, that *is* an interesting claim. We'll have to talk more about it once you're out of here. Clearly, your talents will serve no purpose behind bars."

"It would be my honor to better serve Yeshua's purpose," said Trillian.

"I'm sure." LaMontagne stood, and made his way to the door.

"What can I do?" Trillian called to his visitor's back.

LaMontagne paused at the door to the cell and, before turning around, smiled to himself and reconsidered the detainee. He weighed the possible risks versus rewards, and decided there was more to be gained than lost.

Maybe he can be of some use. Besides, he and any potential threat he might wield, can be easily eliminated without a trace, should that become necessary.

"There will be a selection process to pick colonists for the project," the Reverend began. "The first part of the process will be competitive, based on the applicants' qualifications. The process will, of necessity, make heavy use of computational algorithms in picking the candidates. The second part will be random, and we'll have little opportunity to affect the outcome. I would like the Church to have the final say in which of the qualified candidates are selected."

"And *you*," he jabbed his index finger at Trillian, "will help me gain access to the selection system. It has rather unique security, and I believe your experience could prove useful in this."

The Reverend made to leave the cell again. He took one step toward the door and stopped, uncertain for the briefest moment, before retrieving something from his pocket. He walked over to the sink and poured a glass of water.

"I suspect the systems in question will challenge even someone of your background and considerable skills. Your talents will require some small enhancements if you are to serve the Church in this."

He held out his hand so Trillian could see the capsule in the middle of his palm.

"What is it?"

"Do you know of Darian Leigh?"

"Everyone knows about Darian Leigh." Recognition dawned on him. "I already have the latest version lattice." He lowered his voice to a confidential whisper. "In fact, my lattice isn't entirely legal."

LaMontagne chuckled. "This isn't even close to legal. It might not perfectly replicate Dr. Leigh's considerable intellectual abilities, but it will be close enough for our purposes."

Trillian's eyes lit up, and he reached for the capsule before the Reverend could change his mind.

LaMontagne's hand snapped shut, denying the gift. "Such power, such capabilities, can only be available to a true servant of Yeshua. Are you such a servant?" His eyes bore into the prisoner.

Trillian kneeled beneath the determined power of the man's glare. He dropped his gaze to LaMontagne's feet and rasped, "I am that servant."

"I didn't hear you, son. Are you such a servant?"

The Reverend's booming voice sent shivers up Trillian's spine. He felt the full weight of the question. He knew that his answer would not be taken lightly and, therefore, must not be given lightly.

The prisoner stood and met LaMontagne's eyes directly and earnestly. "I will be a true servant to Yeshua, to His Church, and to you, Reverend." His voice was quiet but steady and firm.

LaMontagne smiled and opened his fist. "Welcome to the next level, son."

34

KATHY INSPECTED THE POLISHED BROWN CUBE she'd prepared in secret for today's visit to the megafactory.

It contained a semiconductor lattice imprinted with the traits—the data—that defined her unique concepta and persona. She was determined to fit it into one of the Cybrids scheduled for launch next week.

The restrictions the G26 Project Vesta Supervisory Committee had placed on her Cybrids were ridiculous.

She didn't mind so much that Cybrids would be permitted to operate only in outer space; there was more than enough work to be done around Vesta to employ them all. The harsh vacuum, low gravity, and hard radiation environment of outer space was exactly what they were designed for. Project Vesta was creating a lot of employment for people on Earth, too. Limiting Cybrids to space and letting the humans dominate the job market on Earth would help minimize human complaints and resentment. She got that.

She was a little less happy with the restrictions the Committee had placed on Cybrid power supplies. It would have been so easy to siphon off enough power from their matter-antimatter propulsion systems to generate electricity for their silicene nanoribbon brains. But the Committee was full of cynics and paranoids who demanded the ability to 'pull the plug' on the robotic Cybrids at their discretion. They refused to permit them energy independence, shackling them instead to comparatively short-lived batteries and ultracapacitors. *Completely unnecessary and a pain, but I can work with it—* Kathy thought.

What she resented most was that it wasn't enough for the Committee that the Cybrid brains were restricted to human-level conceptas and human-replica personas. They put additional limitations on the machines' overall computational capabilities. They would allow Cybrids to function at a level equivalent to a human of moderately above-average intelligence, and no more.

"Are you kidding me? What a ridiculous waste of computational power and precious time," she'd argued. "We need all the help we can get. Don't you see that?"

She'd showed them how it would be such a simple tweak to permit deeper, ungrounded node-searching in the Cybrid concepta. It would be so easy to produce and accommodate the moderately larger brains needed to support IQs in the 500 range.

The Committee adamantly refused, saying it would approve only the specific additional abilities needed to navigate and work in space. It would not sanction any higher level of general intelligence.

"We will not be responsible for making a super-human intelligence and letting it roam freely in our solar system. Our survival depends on that intelligence. We refuse to manufacture our own robot overlords."

Kathy fumed and railed against their ignorance and blind xenophobia to no avail.

She and Greg had been among the first million people selected to be downloaded into Cybrids. Their understanding of the technical portion of the project was unrivaled, and their contributions were critical. They knew that. The Committee knew that. And yet, Committee members insisted on hobbling even their Cybrid brains with IQs around 130, lower than their human pre-lattice enhancement levels.

"I can't imagine my Cybrid alter-ego waking to consciousness and finding herself turned into such a dummy," Kathy complained. It's cruel, unjustified, and short-sighted. We could achieve so much more and in shorter amount of time, if you'd please just reconsider."

The Committee held blindly steadfast. They wouldn't budge.

She had no choice. She cheated.

The Cybrid's silicene brain was bigger and heavier than a biological human brain. It was constructed as an enormous programmable array using conventional three-dimensional integration techniques.

The imprinting process selected optimal pathways to lay down the basic human concepta, the knowledge and belief structure of its paired human.

Preferences, tastes, and basic emotional tendencies were then overlaid, and the Cybrid brain became an astoundingly accurate simulation of its human counterpart.

The neural pathways of the human were optimized by physical changes of axons, dendrites, and synapses. To replicate such optimization in the semiconductor lattice would require a level of nanotechnology that echoed the chemical complexity of living organisms.

Such technology had not been invented yet and Kathy didn't have time to develop it, so they took a shortcut.

It was quicker and easier to simulate what they needed in the software. Many of the possible array connections remained inactive, creating a host of redundant circuits.

With minimal effort, she found a way to use the redundant circuitry to provide additional levels of computational power. It made the circuits of her silicene counterpart a uniquely-twisted mess. But, at least *her* Cybrid self would not be hampered by the absurd biases of the Committee.

This was her tenth trip to the Cybrid factory in Shanghai in the past two years, but today's visit was doubly special.

Today, the first hundred Cybrids would roll off the fabrication line. She and the others, whose minds had been selected for downloading, were reporting in person to place their "brains" into the selected Cybrids.

As the designer of the robots and Chief Engineer on the Vesta Project, Kathy and her considerable contributions could have been honored, at no additional cost to the Project, simply by assigning her Cybrid counterpart with Serial Number 1.

Was this one small consideration too much to ask?

Apparently, it was. The Committee decided no Cybrid was to receive special designation. Each would be assigned a randomized three-letter plus six-digit code. End of discussion.

In protest, Kathy hacked their computer system and assigned the three-letter prefix "DAR" to her Cybrid and to Greg's. She let the algorithms randomly assign the rest of the code.

A subtle but fitting tribute to a mentor and friend. To you, Darian.

Now, just one final tweak and the program won't assign the DAR prefix to other Cybrids.

Her spur of the moment honoring of Darian made her a little sad.

He'd be pleased to see how far we've come, don't you think?—she said to herself.

She inspected the serial number stamped onto the surface of the processing unit. *DAR143147. The name has a nice ring to it.*

* * *

"Hey, Kath, you almost ready?" Greg entered the bedroom of their hotel suite. He had been hovering all morning, nervous to get this event over with. She'd finally sent him to watch television so she could dress in peace. Today was *her* day; he would get the opportunity to put his silicene brain into a Cybrid next month. Another committee decision.

He watched her turn the cube over in her hands. "Is everything okay?"

"Yeah, fine."

She almost told him, right then, what she'd done. They didn't use to have secrets between them. Lately, he'd been acting a bit strange, a little distant, like he was having a hard time figuring out how to behave around her.

She didn't doubt that he still loved her as much as she loved him, but something in him had changed shortly after they'd started working on Vesta. She suspected he was hiding something but, even with their close lattice connection, she couldn't guess what.

Sometimes he seems like he's a million miles away. She hadn't worked up the courage to confront him about it yet. She hoped it was simply because he was busy with work. She frowned—*Like me.*

Over the past few months, they hadn't been on the same continent more than half the time.

Her jaw tightened. This was going to be *her* gift to *her* Cybrid. Maybe she'd talk to him about it tomorrow. Maybe he could make similar modifications to the brain of his own Cybrid. *Later.*

Kathy smiled at him. She hoped it was a reassuring smile. She placed the brownish cube back in its special carrying case. The "brains" were tough, tougher than she might have expected.

She didn't have to worry about getting finger oils on them; there was no way they were going to corrode. Anyway, the optico-electronic interfaces would be cleaned to remove any contaminants before they were placed into the Cybrid bodies.

She put on her coat and tucked the case in her pocket. She pulled her sleeves crisply toward her wrists, and checked her reflection in the dresser mirror.

"Okay, let's do this."

35

ONCE DARYA GOT TIMOTHY OFF THE STREETS of New York and cleaned him up with a fresh shave, haircut, and a new set of clothes, he settled into life in her Manhattan apartment quite nicely.

In return for her kindness and generosity, he insisted on cleaning up around the place, and preparing and serving her meals on the days she ate at home.

He turned out to be quite a good cook, voraciously poring over her recipe books to learn all about modern international cuisine, and scouring the local shops to find the finest and freshest ingredients.

Within weeks, he was preparing dishes he'd often served, but never tasted, in Casa DonTon: boeuf bourguignon, coq au vin, and soufflés from the continent. He quickly expanded his repertoire to include Italian, Chinese, Thai, and Indian dishes, and became expert at baking breads and pastries. Millennia of observing the chefs at DonTon had seeded the foundations of all manner of food preparation techniques into his virtual neural pathways.

Darya had to remind herself that the realistic physics, chemistry, and biology of the Alternus inworld meant her simulated body could easily put on realistic-looking extra weight. She tried to eat sparingly. For the first time in her life, she had to exercise to burn off an excess of simulated calories. She had to admit, she didn't much care for it. She'd have to talk to the Supervisor about tweaking her simulated metabolism.

Darya and Timothy often discussed the basics of life in the twenty-first century and how it differed from nineteenth-century England. Even with a full persona, Timothy was a simple man with simple ideas. She couldn't easily change that and quickly gave up trying to explain the intricacies and nuances of her work with the political and financial leaders of the world.

"Why would you need to reach the heavens, let alone colonize them? Aren't we all going to get there soon enough when our God-given time on Earth is up," Timothy asked, when she'd tried to explain the project she and her team were working on.

"Exploring and colonizing other planets and asteroids is necessary to secure new resources and new frontiers," she'd explained. "And remember, we don't call it Earth here. We know the planet as Alternus. And Alternus is fully occupied, used up, depleted. This is the only way to allow our population to expand."

Timothy stood near the edge of the seventh-story terrace overlooking Central Park, pleased with his change in circumstance. "I don't see why humanity needs more people," he sniffed, looking out over one of the most densely populated cities in the world.

Darya changed the topic. It was hopeless to try to explain to one with so little education, how the basis of the economy, of finance, and of the money that drove it all, was debt; that this debt required continual servicing; that ongoing servicing demanded an ever-increasing money supply and inflation which, in turn, required unending growth. Without growth, it all came crashing down in a stagnant, fetid heap.

Growth was built into the universe, into all living organisms. And growth was built into the financial and economic systems designed by humans, too. Few understood that the opposite of growth wasn't stasis but death, whether for an organism or an economy.

She regarded the simple man sipping his afternoon tea. He seemed happy. When she asked, he replied, "I was content at DonTon, certainly. However, if I'd ever had a real thought there, I imagine that might have changed quite quickly. I like it here. Life is interesting; life is good. Thanks to you." His smile was genuine.

She hated to say anything to alter that, but she needed to know more about Trillian, and how he and Timothy came to be in her Earth inworld.

"Timothy..."

"Yes, Miss," he replied, having learned of Darya's incomprehensible single status. She had to remind him on multiple occasions that they were both free citizens.

He stopped calling her "My Lady" but couldn't overcome millions of years of formality and address her as "Darya".

"Could we talk about Mr. Trillian and Casa DonTon a while?"

"Certainly."

She set her cup of tea back in its saucer. "Do you know who invited Mr. Trillian to DonTon?"

"Hmm. No, and that's strange, now that I think about it. Normally, Mr.

Gowling the Head Butler or I would receive the order to issue an invitation, but I can't recall anyone asking us to invite Mr. Trillian. His name just appeared on our list for the day. I'm sure that Mr. Gowling must have written it."

Darya frowned. As well as representing Alum in more important Church matters, Shards were masters of information systems. Hacking DonTon to directly place his name on the guest list would have been an easy feat for a Shard.

The Chattingbarons, while having invested in top-notch security to assure their guests' privacy, would never imagine Alum or his Shards taking the least bit of interest in their mundane activities. If they had cause to ponder Mr. Trillian's presence at all, they would assume one of their own must have invited him.

"Could you tell me exactly what happened before you came here through that closet door?"

"Well, Miss, there isn't much to tell, aside from almost dropping the peaches into Mr. Trillian's lap on account of the bees."

"Bees?"

"Yes, I heard them buzzing around my head. I thought they must have been drawn into the house by the peaches and ice cream. It was extremely difficult to resist swatting at them." He smiled proudly. "I managed to uphold my station and demeanor, though."

"I did, however," he frowned, "spill a few drops of the sauce. The Missus, Lady Chattingbaron, that is, told me to run a self-diagnostic. That's when the Supervisor told me there was something wrong with me. Although I must confess, at first, I didn't understand hardly a word the Supervisor said."

A look of shame washed over his face and he hung his head. "And then it came to me. *Unregistered Instantiation.* That's what the Supervisor said, and I knew—I don't know how—but I somehow knew exactly what that meant, that I was a person who wasn't allowed to exist.

"So I lied to my Lady, I didn't want to, but the Supervisor was reporting the anomaly. I knew it would send the Securitors for me, and I panicked. And realizing that I felt panic, that I could feel anything at all stemming from my own awareness and, somehow, knowing that this feeling came from my own self and not from my programming, well, that made me panic all the more." The story tumbled out in one long stream.

Timothy's fingers played anxiously with the fabric of his trouser leg.

"It's all right, Timothy. You did what was necessary."

He returned her comforting smile with a feeble one of his own. "I hung back a bit after dinner so I could make a plan, or say a prayer and accept my fate, whatever it might be. That's when I observed Mr. Trillian taking particular interest in a painting near the closet door. I heard the bees again and got a bit dizzy so I had to sit down. I only closed my eyes for a second."

He took a deep breath as he relived the next moments. "I could hear and even smell the city before I saw it. I heard the closet door creak open, and that's when I opened my eyes.

"The doorway opened onto a street here in New York. I'd never seen the likes of it, Miss. Even London couldn't compare. Mr. Trillian walked through that doorway and carried on along the sidewalk, though it took me a second to recognize him as he'd somehow changed his clothing. He noticed me and told me to shut the door behind him. It was like a dream." Timothy's voice shook with the memory.

"I would have just shut it, as Mr. Trillian requested, and gone to await my fate in my room. I guess it was lucky the Securitors chose that moment to arrive. Ohhh, the sight of them terrified me! Without a thought, I dashed through the door and pulled it shut behind me. I ran as fast as I could away from there, in the opposite direction from Mr. Trillian. I wish I could say it was because I didn't want to involve or endanger the poor man in my troubles but, the truth is, I didn't want to risk him giving me away to the Securitors, should they be following. I needed time to think, to sort out the insanity, and to arrive at a sensible solution."

Trillian hacked me!—Darya realized and, begrudgingly, raised her esteem of the Shard's abilities. She wouldn't have thought it possible.

Between the exotic matter that housed the Alternus sim hardware and the software security features she'd implemented, she thought Alternus impervious to that kind of incursion. Clearly, she had underestimated the Shard. Creating a side entrance from the DonTon inworld so he could avoid her welcoming virus was ingenious.

She still didn't understand how Trillian's hack could have elevated a nearby Partial to Full instantiation status, complete with a persona. The hacking must have leaked some of the personality components of the regular DonTon instantiations. She was grateful for whatever it was that allowed Timothy to become who he was. Otherwise, she'd have had no warning of Trillian's presence in Alternus.

"I can't say I understand much of what happened, Miss," Timothy said, interrupting Darya's reverie. "Nor can I understand much of this place. I *am* grateful for the hospitality you have shown me, and only hope I can repay you someday."

Darya laughed. "Oh, Timothy, you've already more than repaid me, just by being here. Although with Trillian inworld, I may have to shut down this sim earlier than I'd hoped."

"Pardon me, Miss? I don't understand what that means."

Darya picked up the cup she'd been ignoring the past few minutes and took a sip of the now cool tea. "This part is a little complicated."

"More complicated than all of this?" The man looked out at the city around them.

"Much more complicated, I'm afraid." Darya looked into Timothy's eyes with compassion, and a little regret. "This world isn't exactly...real...and neither am I. At least not in the way you think."

"I'm confused, Miss." Timothy rapped twice, softly, on the table top. "It certainly seems real to me."

"Yes, well, I made it that way."

It was Timothy's turn to laugh. "Come, now, Miss. I realize that you are an important person in this city. But you are hardly the Lord and Creator now, are you?"

Darya's face stayed serious. "Actually, for this world, I am."

Timothy couldn't hide his confusion. His mouth formed a silent, breathless, "Oh," and he left it at that, for fear of what else might tumble out.

"You see," Darya explained, "the real universe, what we call the outworld, is different from here. In that universe, my body looks much like the DonTon Securitors. My people are called Cybrids. Outside, we appear to be mechanical beings. Inside, our minds, our thoughts, our feelings, are completely human."

"Outside *where*?" Timothy managed.

"Outside this simulation. This world is basically a computer program running on sophisticated hardware, a program that I wrote. Think of it like a dream, or a game. Perhaps you've played a board game in DonTon?"

"In my spare time, I sometimes played chess."

"Okay, that's good. Now, imagine a chess game so sophisticated that you 'become' the King. That you dream yourself to be one of the pieces on the board."

Timothy screwed up his face and tried to imagine the scenario Darya had painted. "That would be strange, indeed," he said.

"That's what this is. An enormous and complicated board game, where all the pieces think they're people who live inside the game."

A light came on in Timothy's eyes. "Ah, I see. This is all a game. We are not real, none of us. And nothing else is, either? It only looks that way to us?"

"That's right," answered Darya.

Timothy's face grew concerned. He held up his index finger to make a point. "Except, if I were to pop out of this world, how would I know whether I was still dreaming, whether I was living out some other game? And likewise, yet another, and another, in layer after layer of games? What if we never really wake up?"

Darya was amazed the man had jumped to that level of reasoning so quickly. "The idea that nothing is real has been discussed among philosophers over the ages. How do we know it's not all just simulations, all the way up?"

Timothy fidgeted; the idea clearly agitated him. "For that matter," he asked, "how do I know *you* are real? I can tell *I'm* real, but how do I know I'm not dreaming *you*, and all of *this*, right now?"

"That notion is called Solipsism," Darya replied, "the idea that only I exist, and everything else is some kind of dream of my making. It doesn't make much sense if you think about it."

"It doesn't?"

"There are many ways to refute Solipsism, but the most direct way is to appeal to reality, *objective* reality. This is often the best way to clarify many philosophical issues. In its early days, philosophers thought that because they could say a thing, it had explanatory power. Now we know that comparing a thought with objective reality is really the best way to arbitrate the truth."

"My head is hurting," Timothy objected, only partially in jest.

"I will try to make this as clear and painless as possible," promised Darya. "Let's examine the two claims that make up Solipsism.

"First, my *self* is the only reality. There is no objective reality outside of my *self*.

"Second, like in dreams, there may be different levels that my *self* creates. I may dream in my dreams, but none of these levels are objectively *real*. They don't exist outside of my *self*. Does that make sense?"

"Well, I have not heard of this Solipsism so I cannot speak to that, but what you said does seem to cover the issues I have."

"Great. Let's start with the first point. How can I prove to you that I exist independently of your self?"

"I don't see how you could. Maybe I'm just dreaming you and this entire conversation."

"I agree. Within the confines of philosophy, there's no way to reason yourself out of this. So, let's appeal to objective reality. In this case, I know what you are. You are a cognitive program, with a conceptual network and set of memories, preferences, capabilities, and inclinations running on hardware that I designed. I understand everything about what makes you Timothy."

"And here I thought I was a bit of a mystery to you," Timothy joked.

"Only because I choose not to intrude on your privacy," Darya replied, completely serious. Timothy's smile faded.

"There's an objective reality here in the Alternus inworld sim, one that I control. I can cause a change in that reality, one you neither anticipate nor understand, one that you would not and could not choose for yourself. This will demonstrate to you that I am an independent agent inside this reality and, therefore, I exist. Now, let's see...Okay, there."

Timothy grabbed the sides of his chair in shock. In the blink of an eye, the world had gone from mid-afternoon to night and he'd moved from standing near the edge to sitting under the gazebo by the patio door. The terrace was dark except for the lights by the sliding glass doors, and the city sparkled with streetlights and neon signs. "Are you really God? Did you make the sun move in the sky?" His voice trembled with fear and confusion.

Darya remained casual and relaxed. Her tone was reassuring, if not her explanation. "No, not at all. I simply stopped your processing for a few inworld hours. While I waited for the sun to set, you were on pause. For that period of time, I existed inworld. You...weren't here."

"But...how?"

"You see, I understand the mechanics of your thinking, and I can alter it while it's running on my hardware. The mechanics of who and what you are is part of the objective reality I was talking about.

"It makes no difference what your opinion, belief, or understanding of this reality is. The objective external reality that this world is all a simulation *is* real, despite anything that you or anyone here may think to the contrary.

"I know there is no way you would have chosen to simply not be conscious for that period of time. Even if you did choose it, you don't know how to adjust the system to make it so.

"I do, and so I did. Therefore, I exist. There *is* something in the universe besides just you. Solipsism is disproved by an objective reality greater than and outside your *self.*"

Timothy tried to follow her reasoning. Despite experiencing things he already had a hard time believing could happen, the simple action of being turned 'off' and back 'on' shook him to his core.

"Alright," he allowed, "let's say that I accept the first proposition. You exist. How can you prove that both of us are not living a dream inside a dream?"

"That's a little easier," smiled Darya. "This inworld, Alternus, is a simulation, a dream. I have an objective existence outside of it in the real universe. Just like I understand the mechanism of my thinking and consciousness here, I understand it outside. All that I've done is redirect the source of my perceptions and the result of my actions, and I've shifted my processing software.

"The early philosophers didn't understand the mechanism of cognition and consciousness. They couldn't see it as something that emerged from hardware plus processes or algorithms. They had to make up all sorts of crazy things like ethereal souls, energy, and magic to explain their conscious experience.

"We don't have to do that anymore; we understand the mechanics of consciousness. We know, no matter how many levels 'up' you go, somewhere there is a real processing substrate that is running the processes you think of, and experience as, consciousness.

"Now, in our case, I happen to know there is only one level 'above' this present one, an objective reality with my quantum processors running my conscious experience. At least, once I move my concepta and persona out of the inworld hardware."

Timothy blinked and rubbed his temples, while Darya let him catch up.

"I am afraid that there were numerous ideas in there that I do not fully understand, Miss. I understand the essence of what you are saying, but I am not sure I can agree. I know my Creator made me with an immortal soul, and not your processor or your concepta or your persona can replace that."

Darya tilted her head to one side. "Hmm. That's interesting, coming from someone who didn't have a persona, only the crudest concepta, a few months ago. Where was your 'soul' when you were in DonTon?"

"Well it may have been poorly formed and incomplete, but I am certain it was there, nonetheless," Timothy huffed. "I have Faith in the Lord, God."

Darya sighed. "That's always been the problem with Faith. It's resistant to facts and knowledge. If I recall correctly, your God would be the Abrahamic God of the Church of England?"

"The God of the Bible, yes."

"He was an oddly absent God for most of human history, wasn't He? He only showed up in one small corner of the original Earth for a short period of time and then went quiet."

"He still worked miracles. The Lord's ways are mysterious." His chin jutted defiantly, demanding she prove him wrong.

Darya nodded. "In my world, the real outworld universe, God is visibly and demonstrably present. He truly rules the Realm."

Timothy leaped up, excited to hear this. "Then you must be a believer! Do you know Him personally?" The questions poured out of him. "Have you felt His love? What about His Son? Has the Kingdom of Heaven arrived at last?"

"I know God. His name is Alum. I am trying to stop His version of Heaven," Darya scowled.

"What? You cannot be serious. Why would you want to stop God?"

"God...Alum...wishes to destroy the universe so that He may bring about an eternal Heaven. It is not the Heaven I want."

"But...but...Heaven is heaven. It is eternal perfection. How could you not desire that?"

"Heaven is not the nature of the universe," she answered. "The idea of a fixed and unchanging perfection is so contrary to the evolution of the real universe, that any thinking person *must* oppose it.

"I have sworn to prevent Alum from bringing about His idea of Heaven with all my will and power, or die trying." She offered no opportunity for response. Her robe and long, raven hair flowed behind her, leaving a dismayed and conflicted Timothy staring at her back.

36

"I THINK YOU SHOULD SEE THIS, Reverend."

John Trillian didn't knock; he never knocked. He just barged into LaMontagne's study whenever he felt like it.

Jeff, the Reverend's henchman, had been on the verge of "liquidating" the arrogant hacker more than once. And he might have done just that, had it not been for LaMontagne's firm belief that Trillian's usefulness outweighed his lack of proper socialization. More to the point, he'd directly ordered Jeff to give the exasperating consultant a little leeway. It took an awful lot of leeway, as it turned out.

Objectively speaking, even Jeff had to admit that Trillian had proven his worth in the ten weeks since the Reverend "recruited" him. The hacker had already infiltrated all of the major systems of the Vesta Project and placed backdoors into the BIOS chips of their most important computers. He'd accessed blueprints and engineering specifications for their Cybrids, the rockets, and the asteroid colony itself.

The hacker's most recent feat was subverting the project's candidate selection system. LaMontagne could now bump anyone he wanted to the top of the evacuation list at any time.

The Reverend was ready; he'd been operating his own covert recruitment process for months. Thanks to Trillian's work, his hand-selected Church members would be guaranteed to form a disproportionate number of Vesta colonists.

LaMontagne didn't give much thought to John Trillian, the man, except in terms of what he could do for the Church. He believed that so long as he kept John challenged and busy, he posed little threat. He began to relax his guard around the hacker, even exploring and experimenting with the microverse technology when the man was in the room.

Trillian observed the Reverend toying with all manner of floating microverses in the study, but he had no particular interest in the spheres. Since ingesting the dendy-virus capsule, he'd been lost in his own world, a world that was expanding daily as his lattice grew within him. His capabilities as a software programmer, hardware designer, and hacker were improving rapidly.

He was loving his new work, the many challenges it presented, and the promise of exponential intellectual growth that came with his new lattice. For now, he was happy to stick to the hardware and software, and leave the physics, politics, and religion to the Reverend. Especially the physics; he wasn't sure he could follow the advanced math, anyway. The other areas were mildly interesting in their own ways, but Trillian was more captivated by virtual reality than the real thing. His games and hacks, whether serious or for amusement, gave him deep satisfaction and joy.

Across the room on the stiff, leather-bound sofa, a five-year-old boy disconnected from his internet "playtime" and shifted his gaze to Trillian, whom he immediately disregarded with bored disdain.

In the brief hours when he wasn't connected to LaMontagne's lattice and having the Reverend's every experience and thought forcefully pumped into him, the boy was permitted to read the classics. Greek mythology, the Bible, the Torah, The Quran, Socrates, The Prince, and The Art of War were providing him with varied windows into the human psyche.

The Reverend had enough knowledge of basic developmental psychology to realize the importance of exposing the boy to some external influences. Providing they were closely monitored, of course. As "soul" father, he selected what the boy could read, and with whom he could talk and play. He wanted to foster healthy development, not independence. There had to be some limits; the one who would inherit his spirit must be carefully cultivated.

LaMontagne enjoyed the way his own thoughts and memories were being duplicated inside the young boy's brain. *My true essence will be immortalized in a way the world has never seen.* Once the boy was fully grown, the two of them would be more mentally, psychologically, and spiritually alike than any two people in the history of the world.

LaMontagne let his current microverse fizzle and blink out. He looked up from the keyboard of the RAF generator.

"What have you found for me, John?"

"They're going to blow up Vancouver," Trillian said.

That got LaMontagne's attention. Even the boy perked up. "Who is? When? How?"

"The Russians, Chinese, and us. In a few hours. Three nuclear cruise missiles with hundred-kiloton yields." Trillian answered all three questions without a trace of emotion.

"Why?"

"A number of the world leaders have convinced themselves that Drs. Mahajani and Liang control the demands of Alum, or could actually *be* Alum. They also believe a large atomic blast could eliminate the Eater threat. It seems they've been planning this for a while."

"Why are you telling me this only now?"

"I've just been able to assemble all the necessary evidence in the past hour."

"Show me," commanded LaMontagne.

Trillian pushed the RAF generator to one side and set his laptop on the desk in front of the Reverend. "I found video from a secure online meeting held last week among our friends. I was aware of their discussions but it proved impossible to listen to them in real time. Fortunately, the Japanese Prime Minister recorded the whole thing."

He opened his laptop and activated a saved video. "This is the most relevant section."

President Mitchell: *Ms. Hudson had no problems with sharing the recording from the conference room at the G26. She's convinced that Drs. Mahajani and Liang were in no way involved but, then again, she didn't lose a trusted adviser. I had our people go back and analyze the changes in micro expressions of the two scientists' right after the incident; they found sufficient reason to doubt Ms. Hudson's conclusion.*

President Olev: *The timing seems suspicious. It was too convenient. As soon as opposition to the plan is raised, some unexplained deep sleep overcomes the room? I don't buy it. Our FSB experts don't either. I believe what they said was, they hope those two are better scientists than they are actors.*

President Chu: *We have agreed then, to abandon efforts to simply remove Drs. Mahajani and Liang?*

President Mitchell: *If they're holding us all hostage to their plans, how do we know they don't have this Eater on a deadman switch? Killing them could threaten the planet. No, we must strike their weapon as well as them.*

PM Akira: *Our scientists are confident we can destabilize and collapse the matter-absorbing capabilities of this Eater with a sufficiently large thermonuclear explosion. Their analysis of the descriptive formulae suggests a payload of around fifty kilotons, to be effective. I've had them transmit their calculations to your people for confirmation.*

President Chu: *Yes, our physicists agree, based on the mathematical characterization as provided by the Pacifica scientists. But instigating such an explosion over a populated area like Vancouver would be considered an Act of War. Could we avoid a subsequent escalation?*

President Mitchell: *We'd have to act in concert and demonstrate to PM Hudson that this was a limited strike for the good of humanity. We still have friends in high command within the Pacifica military structure. If asked, I'm sure they could give us the time we'd need to convince her of the wisdom of avoiding any retaliatory nuclear exchange.*

PM Singh: *The Vesta Project is making a mockery of all our efforts to reduce global deficits and return our economies to sustainability. We can't afford this leap into space colonization; it's insanity. These two Pacifica scientists are holding the entire planet hostage to their schemes. Once we make our evidence public, the world will agree with the necessity of our actions.*

PM Akira: *Our nation is as much against the unnecessary use of atomic force as any on the planet. That said, I'm convinced of the necessity for this action. If we don't destroy the Eater, the entire planet will be consumed and everyone will be killed. I support the detonation of the Eater. Immediately after the missiles strike, we'll read a prepared statement to advise our people of the catastrophic nature of the threat and reveal how we were all, the whole world, being held hostage by two people who would sacrifice the entire planet to build a space colony. Sacrificing one city to thwart their plan and save the world will be seen as a sad, but trivial and necessary price.*

President Mitchell: *I propose we send three one-hundred kiloton cruise missiles by three different means, to assure at least one meets its target. We can arrange an overland launch from Idaho.*

President Chu: *We have a suitable submarine within striking distance of the Vancouver area.*

President Olev: *One of our long-range bombers can easily reach the city from Kamchatka.*

PM Akira: *Shall we say, one week from today at 2:00 pm, Pacific Time? We can request that both Drs. Mahajani and Liang are available for a conference call from the laboratory at that time.*

President Mitchell: *That would kill two birds with one stone, wouldn't it?*

President Olev: *President Mitchell, your American English has so many... delightful...idiomatic expressions. [laughs]*

TRILLIAN PRESSED STOP AND WATCHED LAMONTAGNE FOR A REACTION.

"Their level of confidence in their conclusions, and their willingness to carry out this attack based on those conclusions, is remarkable," the Reverend commented.

"Given how wrong they are."

"Well, it would seem they've fingered the wrong people. I don't know about stopping the Eater, though. Have you checked their analysis?"

"I'm not up on the physics but I can forward it to you," Trillian offered.

"Yes, do that." The Reverend stroked his chin while he thought. "Can we do anything about this attack?"

"Yes, I have a direct line to their nuclear arsenals at a variety of levels. I can make the missiles self-destruct, issue a Cancel order, or redirect them as you wish."

"Good." The core of a plan was beginning to form in LaMontagne's lattice-enhanced brain. "Greg and Kathy have been working on this a lot longer and with a lot more neural horsepower than all the rest of the physicists in the world. I trust the two of them more than an army of unenhanced scientists."

Trillian had to agree, especially now that he'd begun experiencing for himself what a difference dendy enhancements made in his own work. "If we needed to alter the narrative around this potential attack, I could arrange that."

"That might be helpful," agreed LaMontagne. "Could we present evidence to show that other leaders were jealous of Pacifica's prominent role in the Vesta Project? Perhaps, envious of their scientific and engineering lead?"

"Yes, I can make that work," replied Trillian. "I can select various intercepted communications and design a program to synthesize audio and video to make the leaders say almost anything we wish."

"It would have to be completely plausible, and flawlessly assembled."

Trillian smiled. "Then it's a good thing you've given me the ability to do that."

"How long would it take to put something like that together?"

"I can have it done before the missiles are launched."

"Excellent. Perhaps we could also arrange some kind of indication of *personal* motivation for the attack."

"Financial graft?"

"Could you do that?"

"How substantial would you like the motivation to be?"

"Say we showed a few tens of millions of dollars diverted from the Vesta Project into personal offshore accounts. Perhaps we could demonstrate how Greg and Kathy discovered these missing funds and ordered some potentially embarrassing audits."

"I like the way you think, Reverend."

"Thank you, John. Can you come back with a completed scenario in about an hour?"

"Of course. Would you like me to set Abort or Self-destruct codes on the missiles?"

"No. Let's send them back to their launchers." The Reverend stroked his chin, an action the boy copied across the room. "We can have Alum communicate his displeasure in the criminal actions of these politicians on all public and private channels. He can expose their envy, their greed, and their hubris. To think they'd bomb a city and kill all its citizens just because they aren't benefiting enough! This will be a fine opportunity for the people to learn that Alum is looking out for their welfare."

"Very good. I'll be back within the hour."

"Wait," said the Reverend. "You know, this might be a good time to demonstrate Alum's reach. It'd be nice if we could conquer this dissent once and for all."

"What do you have in mind?"

"I believe we have our enforcement assets in place in each of these countries. Let's activate the batrachotoxin spiders and eliminate these problems for good. If we take out the most prominent conspirators, the others will be more reluctant to follow in their footsteps. People will learn that Alum is not to be trifled with. When he says something must be done, it will be done."

Trillian smiled and gave a shallow bow, "As you wish, Reverend."

* * *

SEPTEMBER 9, 2041, GNA (GLOBAL NEWS ALLIANCE). *Seattle, Washington, Pacifica.*

The world was stunned today by the explosion of three nuclear bombs, only minutes apart. Two of the weapons detonated over the Pacific Ocean off the coast of Pacifica. The third exploded in the wilderness of Idaho.

The explosions destroyed the respective launchers, which are believed to be a Russian bomber, a Chinese submarine, and a New Confederacy missile carrier, along with their respective crews.

According to video released by the mysterious Alum shortly after the explosions, all three missiles were targeted to strike Vancouver, British Columbia, Pacifica.

Alum also released video of a secret meeting last week, email correspondence, and records of bank transactions, showing how world leaders from China, Japan, Russia, and the New Confederacy conspired to shift the major economic benefits from the Vesta Project to their own countries. These records show the leaders conspired to profit by destroying Pacifica's scientific and technological capabilities.

According to information released, the alleged perpetrators considered the lattice-enhanced team of Dr. Katherine Liang and Dr. Garugamesh Mahajani, protégés of famous scientific polymath, Dr. Darian Leigh, to be intolerable competition.

The conspiring leaders intended to justify their use of nuclear weapons by referring to an unspecified threat to global security from the government of Pacifica's Prime Minister Francine Hudson and Project Vesta. Ms. Hudson was visiting the Vancouver Headquarters of Project Vesta at the time of the intended attack.

The leaders argued that the threat could only be stopped by a significant nuclear explosion. PM Hudson has categorically denied the existence of any such threat in the Vancouver area.

Drs. Liang and Mahajani had recently become aware of financial improprieties involving the conspirators and ordered audits of the project.

Project Vesta is the brainchild of the Pacifica scientists, who aim to colonize the asteroid belt, and provide new economic benefits and growth to countries around the globe.

Pacifica's pivotal role in releasing important new technologies for the benefit of all mankind has upset many established global oligarchies. Some have been unhappy with the distribution of those benefits according to population instead of by level of economic wealth.

Developed nations, especially those involved in the conspiracy, have resisted the flow of contracts to emerging economies with larger populations. Leaders of the developed nations have struggled over the past months to maintain so-called strategic industries in the technology and energy sectors.

A number of political analysts have voiced surprise so many nations agreed to the original project proposals presented by Drs. Liang and Mahajani. Today's actions clearly demonstrate how superficial those agreements were.

In a public broadcast overriding scheduled programming around the world, Alum officially condemned the actions of the conspirators, saying, "God supports the plan to move human civilization and His Holy Word into space."

He later added that, "This conspiracy has demonstrated the evil that still rules the hearts and minds of many world leaders. This small, but powerful group put their own national and personal interests ahead of the common human good. More importantly, they put their own desires ahead of God's Plan for His People. The Lord has shown His Will, His Power, and His Vengeance today."

The comment is thought to be a reference to the discovery that every one of the leaders participating in this conspiracy died within minutes of the explosions, all of mysterious causes.

Pacifica Prime Minister Francine Hudson denied involvement in any retaliatory actions, adding that she was, "as mystified and in awe of God's Power as anyone."

Today's events have only served to deepen the mystery around the man known as Alum. Some call him a prophet. Others suggest he is not so much a holy man as a very human spokesman for an Anonymous-like group that has recently broken out of its internet-based activities to take a more active global role.

The question on everyone's minds is whether today's events are the act of an omniscient, omnipotent God or of a vigilante global organization with an advanced level of technical and scientific capabilities.

37

THE APARTMENT INTERCOM WENT OFF at 3:00 am. Darya's inworld self was asleep, fulfilling its simulated biological needs.

She'd considered eradicating this needless waste of time, just for herself and no other players. In the end, she decided to stay true to the rules of the Alternus inworld, however inconvenient. The lost time was small enough and if something really pressing needed consideration, she could always exit into her outworld trueself and let her Alternus body sleep.

Sleeping was a little like the long voyages in space when she reduced her processor activity to nearly zero and let random lattice processes flood what minimal consciousness remained. She found she rather enjoyed dreaming with no particular goal in mind.

The insistent buzzing of the apartment doorbell penetrated her sleeping inworld consciousness. She rolled over and squinted at the control panel on the night table beside her bed. An obviously distraught Mary looked back at her from the downstairs lobby view screen.

Darya pressed the answer button. "Mary, what's wrong?"

"Gerhardt's dead!"

Darya's first reaction was confusion. *Gerhardt dead? What?* People died inworld all the time; it was no big deal. Why would Mary be so upset?

"Don't worry. When he re-instantiates, we'll arrange for the New York Fed to rehire him. It shouldn't set us back more than a few weeks."

Even over the intercom security camera, Darya could see the tears welling in Mary's eyes. "No, Darya. He's really *dead*. Trueself dead."

What? Darya pushed the Enter button. "Come on up."

While she waited for Mary to arrive, Darya made a hurried pass through the bathroom. She did her best to rearrange her long hair and wipe the sleep from her eyes, then went out to the foyer to wait for the elevator.

The metal doors slid open, and Mary staggered out. She was sobbing uncontrollably and fell into her friend's arms.

Darya shuffled the two of them into the nearby living room where they collapsed onto the sofa. She tried awkwardly to calm the other woman. For her millions of years of existence, Darya still wasn't sure how to react to grief. She passed her a tissue and let the sobs play out until the heaving slowed and the tears abated.

Darya held Mary at arms length and searched her weepy, red, swollen eyes, looking for a sign she was ready to talk. She collected Mary's hands in her own and took a deep breath, hoping her distressed friend would emulate it.

"Now, tell me what happened," she said.

Mary blew her nose and folded the wadded tissue over and over. "That's the thing. I don't exactly know. Gerhardt and I were supposed to meet last night for drinks. We wanted to fine-tune the proposal for some new derivatives but he didn't show. That's not like Gerhardt; he's never late. I waited half an hour and then tried his phone.

"Some cop answered. She asked who I was, and how I knew Gerhardt. It took a lot of pressing but she finally told me his Director Campeau instantiation was shot earlier that afternoon in Manhattan." The recollection threatened to bring on a fresh wave of tears.

"Take your time," Darya soothed, "I'll bring you a glass of water."

Mary collected herself more easily this time. "She wouldn't give me any more information over the phone. She told me to report to the precinct station to find out what happened and to tell them whatever I could about Gerhardt.

"Apparently, he was involved in a fight at a café—you know how proud Gerhardt was of his martial arts skills—and some thug shot him. One of the bullets hit his heart. He bled out right there, almost instantly."

"That's terrible," Darya said. She handed her friend a glass of water and a fresh tissue. "Here, drink a little water and take another deep breath for me, sweetie. Okay?"

She sat down beside Mary and rubbed the distraught woman's arm with genuine tenderness. "I'm sorry. I know this must be really difficult for you, but getting it out will help you feel better, and then we can figure out what happened. "Are you okay to continue?"

Mary nodded, and wrung the fresh tissue into a tight spiral.

"Okay," Darya prompted, "so he gets in a fight and somebody shoots him."

"I didn't believe it either, at first. I mean, given all his training, plus that gun he walks around with, to be brought down in some bar fight? No way, that's not Gerhardt."

"But you said his *trueself* was dead, not just his *inworld* self," Darya pressed.

"Right. Even if someone got the upper hand on him, inworld death would be just a minor inconvenience, wouldn't it? We take our twelve-hour timeout from Alternus, and start over in another instantiation. No biggie, right?

"So I wasn't worried about him at all, at that point. I figured I'd pop outworld and give him a call to reschedule our meeting, and maybe give him a bit of a rough time for standing me up. I know the docking bay he uses; it's not far from my recharge station so I drifted over there to set up a line.

"There was no response. I tried a half a dozen times—nothing. That's when I started to worry. Actually, I was more confused than worried. Where'd he go?" Mary looked down and twisted, untwisted, and retwisted the disintegrating tissue. "I'm embarrassed to say, I even approached bodily and *bumped* him, if you can believe it. I mean, who does that? But he wasn't there, Darya. He wasn't in his trueself body, either." She took a shuddering breath.

"So what did you do?" Darya asked.

"What could I do? I returned to Alternus and put in a query about him to the Supervisor. It told me *Invalid Instantiation*. He's no longer connected to this sim at all.

"I dropped back out to the Routing Supervisor at the recharge station, to see if he'd taken a break in some other inworld or something. I don't know why I bothered. Gerhardt would never leave me hanging like that. He would've at least left a message for me. I've never known anyone so punctual and responsible; it's like a compulsion with him. Not even inworld death would've stopped him from checking in," Mary tried to chuckle but it came out as a choked cough.

"He's nowhere, Darya. Not outworld, not inworld. I didn't know what else to do. I mean, people don't just die, right? That's when I came here."

"Give me a second," she said. She sent her own detailed query to the Supervisor.

Invalid Instantiation—it returned. *Subject did not correctly exit simulation. Dissipation detected.*

What? That wasn't supposed to happen! Darya looked away to hide the worry written across her face.

Even when the Securitors had crashed her dragon-killing show in Lysrandia, they'd only blocked people from leaving, they didn't de-instantiate them. Administration did everything it could to avoid promoting substitute Partials to Fulls until absolutely necessary. To be fair, training newbies was always a pain. Replacing a talented and experienced mind with a fresh and unpredictable new persona was never done lightly.

And why didn't the safeguards kick in? Remembering how violent the real Earth had been in her days, Darya had designed measures that ensured trueselves could not be trapped in the Alternus inworld, especially not her team members. They were supposed to have a way out if they needed it. Always.

She interrogated the Supervisor a little deeper. She queried its stored version of events in the café. She replayed Gerhardt's conversation and the fight with Trillian and his henchmen. Her worry grew.

"We need to shut down the Alternus inworld," Darya said when she'd finished her review. "I don't know how, but Shard Trillian's hacked into the sim from DonTon, and he got past the introductory virus without being infected. Until yesterday, I wouldn't have thought that was possible, but it's the only reasonable explanation. I'll contact Qiwei and Leisha, and get all three of you out immediately. As soon as they're safe, I'll send out a System Maintenance Alert to everyone else inworld."

"And Gerhardt?" Mary's lip trembled hopefully.

"I'm sorry. I think you're right. I think he's really gone," replied Darya.

So why don't I feel anything?—she asked herself. *He was one of my oldest and dearest friends.* She pressed her fists against her lap and straightened her back. *No time for sorrow. I've got more urgent matters to attend to.*

"The Supervisor reports that Gerhardt's return to his trueself was blocked," she said. "I'm pretty sure Trillian had something to do with that."

Mary nodded. "Do you think he knows about us, too?"

"I hope not. I'll call Qiwei and Leisha right now and tell them to drop everything and exit to the outworld immediately."

Darya got up and headed into the corridor toward the bedrooms. She nearly collided with Timothy, who'd been standing there, rather awkwardly, in his pajamas.

"I didn't mean to eavesdrop. I heard people talking," he said softly. "I thought I could make some tea."

Mary turned at the sound of the man's voice. She looked at Darya with surprise and a hint of amusement. "Ohmygosh, I'm so sorry. Have you been...entertaining?"

Darya rolled her eyes and grimaced. "Very funny. No. Well, yes, but not the way you're thinking. This is Timothy. He's got a very interesting story. When we have a little more time, I'll have him tell you."

"Oh, oh," Darya added, tapping her forehead a couple of times.

"What's wrong?" asked Mary.

"Timothy's an anomaly," replied Darya. "When Trillian hacked into the Alternus inworld it somehow caused Timothy's Partial, a DonTon persona, to convert into a full instantiation. I have no idea how that could've happened; I've never heard of such a thing. Regardless, Timothy has no trueself to return to. If I shut Alternus down right now, our friend here will just...dissipate."

Mary's jaw dropped. "Oh. That wouldn't be nice."

"Not nice? It would be murder," Darya replied. She concentrated a second or two. "Maybe there's a solution. I wonder if Trillian's block on Gerhardt's trueself is still in effect."

"I don't know; I didn't check," replied Mary. Her eyes grew wide when she realized what Darya was thinking. "You can't be serious!"

"It's the only option he has for survival," Darya answered.

The two women regarded Timothy.

"He can take over Gerhardt's body," Darya confirmed.

While Mary and Timothy stared at each other, Darya retrieved her cell phone.

Damn! Lattice technology sure would be handy on Alternus right now. Unfortunately, she was stuck with the ancient system.

I just hope Leisha and Qiwei have their phones on. She wanted them out as soon as possible. She started dialing Leisha's number.

"No Service Available," the screen flashed.

"Crap!" she said.

"What is it?" asked Mary.

"Cell service is out. We'll have to go there in person."

"Trillian again?"

"I don't know; I hope not. Let's go." Darya sent Timothy to put on some street clothes and did the same herself. "Dress in layers," she told him. "We may be out for a while; best to be prepared."

Within minutes, the three of them were in the street. The temperature was a good 15 degrees lower in the pre-dawn hours. The wind had picked up, and it was starting to rain. As they stepped outside, lightning cracked about a mile away.

"Great." Darya stepped back in and tried to call a taxi from the land line in the lobby, but that line was as dead as her cell. She hoped they'd be able to hail a cab.

Out front, they scanned in both directions, but Fifth Avenue was eerily deserted. Without the usual foot and vehicle traffic, Central Park looked dark and foreboding. *No way I'm going to cut through there.*

They turned down a side street and headed toward Madison and Park. It was the same in that direction: strangely silent streets, devoid of cars and pedestrians.

This is absurd—Darya thought. *New York never sleeps, not even at four in the morning.* They didn't pass a single person, and not one of the shops, clubs, or bars was open. *What's going on?*—Darya wondered.

They exchanged worried glances, but no one wanted to say anything out loud. Just as she was about to announce a change of plans, the headlights of a single car approached them along Park Avenue. It was a taxi.

Darya held up her hand to hail the cab and, miraculously, it pulled over for them. The rear doors opened and two men got out. Darya recognized—from her review of Gerhardt's fight—one as Shard Trillian and the other had to be one of his thugs.

She faced them square on, and let them walk to her. Mary and Timothy cowered behind.

Shard Trillian flashed a brilliant white smile. "Darya!" He greeted her as if they were old friends. "I have been anticipating meeting you for such a long time." He gave a short bow in Mary's direction. "And this lovely creature, I presume, is Mary."

"I think you know exactly who she is," Darya scowled.

"Yes," he admitted, "though we've not been formally introduced." He took notice of the tall, well-groomed man attempting to comfort Mary.

"And I believe I recognize this adventurous young man from Casa DonTon. Did I not tell you to close that door, Timothy?"

"You did, my Lord," the former Footman stammered. "I'm afraid that in my excitement at being threatened by a Securitor, I disobeyed that particular order, my Lord. Or, at least, your intent. To be precise, my Lord, you said, "Would you close that, please?" And I did. Behind me, though, once I'd passed through."

"Interesting," said Trillian. "My dear man, have you made the leap to persondom?"

"Pardon, my Lord?"

"Are you now fully instantiated?" Trillian demanded.

Timothy stood proudly. "It would appear so, my Lord."

"Fascinating. I will have to discuss this mechanism with Alum, upon our return."

"I don't think that's going to happen," interrupted Darya. She was pointing a small but efficient-looking Berretta at Trillian and his thug.

The henchman growled at her. In reply, she shot him in the left thigh and he fell to the ground screaming, trying to stop the bleeding with his hands.

She smiled coldly at Trillian. "He's not a Full, is he?" She brought the barrel to bear on the Shard. "You, however, are," she threatened.

Trillian put his head back and laughed. "I suppose I shouldn't be surprised," he said. "That which we make can so easily be unmade. Don't you agree?" He stepped past the thug, who'd stopped screaming but was still struggling on the pavement.

"I wouldn't come any closer," said Darya.

Trillian's creepy smile transformed into a wicked leer as he took two more steps.

She aimed her pistol above his right ear and pulled the trigger. The shot was deafening in the otherwise deserted street.

Trillian hesitated for a fraction of a second and then closed his eyes.

Darya was puzzled by his reaction until she heard the buzzing sound.

"Mary, Timothy, run!" she ordered.

The two had been slowly backing away as Trillian came forward. They turned and bolted.

Darya watched them enter a nearby alley.

Trillian opened his eyes, and his malicious smile returned. "I'll round up your underlings later," he said and took another step.

Darya aimed the gun mid-torso and pulled the trigger. There was a soft click, and another. Click, click, click, click.

Trillian held his hands out. "Oh, that wasn't supposed to happen, was it?"

She was sure the clip had been full. She'd only used two bullets; there should be eight more in there. Click, click, click, click.

Trillian had been closing in the gap. He lunged for Darya.

She took a step back and flung the pistol, backhand, at his face.

Her fierceness took him by surprise. He batted the gun out of the air but his attention was diverted long enough for her to direct a kick at his stomach. It connected solidly, and a winded Trillian fell to his knees.

Darya wheeled and with a sweeping kick, sent him to the ground. Without waiting to see him land, she bolted for the dark alley where her companions had gone.

Against orders, they'd waited at the entrance. "Follow me," she hissed and plunged deeper into the darkness. "We don't have much time before he's back on his feet."

"How'd you do that?" Mary huffed from beside Darya as she struggled to keep up.

"I'm a warrior princess, remember?"

"So why didn't you just knock him out or kill him?" asked a breathless Timothy from her other side.

"He hacked the Supervisor," Darya answered. "That move only worked because it surprised him. He'd already put up a shield by the time I pulled my foot back. Another blow wouldn't have connected."

A narrow passage between two old brick buildings appeared on the left.

"Down here!" Darya urged, and they picked their way down.

Mary and Timothy followed as fast as they could, but Mary's stylistic bulk and Timothy's months of inactivity limited their speed. They were tiring quickly.

"Ah, yes, here it is," Darya said. She opened the third door they passed.

The three of them tumbled through the door and into a small, dimly lit all-night bar/café.

A few dozen patrons gave life to the space, even at this hour. Some were winding down after a late night comedy show. Animated conversations flowed among groups of college students. Solitary customers caressed their drinks or picked at their food while they people-watched.

Darya hustled Mary and Timothy into a booth anchoring a dimly lit wall.

"I don't know how long we have before he finds us," Darya said. "Mary, you don't need to stay for this. Head back outworld, and we'll meet up at Secondus in a few hours."

Mary's eyes were filled with worry.

"We'll be okay," Darya assured her. "Go!"

Mary hung her head in resignation and nodded weakly. She closed her eyes and sent the lattice command to leave for the outworld.

Nothing happened.

With renewed exertion, she scrunched her brow tight and concentrated. It made no difference. The signal wasn't getting out.

"Darya!" she whispered. "I can't exit!"

38

DARYA DIDN'T WASTE A SECOND. She closed her eyes and gave the command to return to her trueself. Her persona bounced off the barrier denying exit from the Alternus sim and right back into her inworld body.

"I should've realized he'd shut us in immediately." She chided herself. "Okay, try sending the UNHQ code, and we'll see if you can transfer to the United Nations Headquarters. That'll buy us some time to figure out what to do next."

Mary sent the transfer code. Again, nothing. Hope drained from her face. "We're going to die here," she said.

"We are *not* going to die," Darya replied. "First of all, I'm sure Trillian would rather take us for complete interrogation. Second, we are not going to be killed or caught. Not if I have anything to say about it."

Maybe she couldn't upload her persona back to her outworld trueself, but that wasn't the only way to escape.

Darya hadn't trusted any inworld since the events of Lysrandia. As a precaution, she'd copied her quark-spin lattice capabilities into the inworld hardware. Unlike others who came to this world with only human-level capabilities, she still had access to lattice IQ-enhancements of her own design.

If Trillian could hack across inworlds, she could too. He'd come from DonTon, so she was definitely *not* going there. But where, then? The choices were fairly limited as to what was both convenient and a good place to hide. That left a few playing fields. Vacationland would work, or maybe that ridiculously bizarre inworld, the GameRoom.

Darya smiled. The GameRoom was always Gerhardt's favorite. It had the loosest physical laws and the most flexible access to Supervisory changes.

She'd be on more even footing against Trillian there, if he could track her into the GameRoom at all. *Did he think to expand the trueselves-block to all of the inworlds?*—she wondered. Maybe they could get back to the outworld through one of them.

Like many engineers, years of tinkering with software security systems gave her a deep understanding of the machine-level implementations of code used to program inworld simulations.

Over millions of years, the code had migrated from what used to be called "high-level languages" to programming environments that would be hardly recognizable to a human engineer of old.

Keeping abreast of those developments and contributing to the advances brought her satisfaction, when she wasn't pushing asteroids into new orbits. Now her hobby was about to save their lives.

She hoped.

Darya began assembling low-level code to probe the boundaries between inworld Alternus and the GameRoom. Trillian's control of the Alternus Supervisor had to be incomplete or faulty. Otherwise, he would have located the group by now and altered the sim to trap them.

Timothy groaned and put his hands to his head. "What's wrong?" Darya asked.

"My head hurts," he complained. "It just started now. Do you think that means he's nearby?"

"No, that's probably just me," she replied. "Let me find a different place to work. A little distance might reduce the effect my coding has on your persona."

She walked over to the bar and ordered their best single malt scotch. She took one sip and grimaced. *Wow, maybe that's your best, but it's far from the best.*

She closed her eyes and set to work. Her quark-spin lattice generated code at a rate that would have astonished ancient programmers. She hoped it was fast enough. After about fifteen minutes, she'd constructed a probe, located a circuitous route to get them from Alternus to the GameRoom, and established a few basic conditions for the game they would arrive in.

The conduit was thin and slow. It would take them each a day to make the transfer, and she was pretty sure they wouldn't get more than an hour here in the café before Trillian found them.

Darya wove code as fast as she could to construct a higher bandwidth route. She was in such a focused programming frenzy she didn't notice right away that the room had fallen silent. She looked around to see why conversation had stopped.

The sports programs on the television screens above the bar and around the café had been replaced by unflattering photos of her, Mary and

Timothy. A scrolling announcement below the photos instructed viewers to "Contact the number at the bottom of the screen if you see these individuals."

Darya looked around. A number of customers already had their phones out and were texting something. *Apparently, it's only our phones that are blocked. Time to move.*

Her hack into the GameRoom was almost finished. She let a high-priority background process complete the job while she sent a message to the Supervisor, asking it to create a diversion. She left her unfinished scotch on the bar and walked back to the booth where the others waited.

Mary greeted Darya with an expectant, wide-eyed stare. *She looks exhausted*—Darya noted. Even Timothy was having difficulty offering any comfort.

"I've asked the Supervisor to spread a few virtual ghosts of our likeness around the neighborhood," Darya reported. "Hopefully, that'll lead to a flood of information to Trillian. We might be able to delay him by a few minutes or hours; there's no saying how long we have before he gets here. In the meantime, I've set up a data pipeline between us here and the GameRoom."

Mary's eyes lifted at the mention of Gerhardt's favorite inworld. She drew in a breath to speak. "Darya...," was all she got out. Her openly skeptical look finished the sentence.

"I know," Darya replied before Mary could launch her protest. "It's a strange choice and not even nearby, but that could work to our advantage. It'll take Trillian a while to check out this inworld and any others nearby, like Casa DonTon.

"Once we're in the GameRoom, I can start looking for a way back to our trueselves. To help buy us some time, I set up a game that might make it harder for him to locate us there."

"What kind of game?" Mary asked.

"It's a ten-dimensional maze."

Timothy looked confused, but Mary accepted the notion without a blink. "Okay, how do we get there?"

"You don't have to do a thing," answered Darya. "I'll send you. Once you're in, don't move anywhere. And I mean it. Not anywhere; it could be dangerous. I don't have time to program 10D vision for us, so moving around will be tricky. But it'll be equally tricky for anyone to find us. Just stand still, and we'll come in right beside you. Okay?"

Mary nodded. Darya connected Mary's Alternus persona to the GameRoom transfer pipe and activated the Send command. She was pleased to see her background processing had found a faster route between the two sims. They'd still be limited to one person at a time, but it could process in minutes what the other route would've taken hours to complete.

A small portal, like a literal funnel connected to a piece of pipe, floated above Mary's head. It drew further attention from the café patrons but Darya's threatening scowl encouraged them to go back to their texting. A few snapped quick photos, anyway.

It would have looked funny—Darya thought—*if the tube sucked Mary head first up into the cosmos but reality, even inworld simulated reality, didn't work that way.* Instead, Mary *dissolved,* gradually growing less substantial, more transparent, and increasingly poorly defined. The process took a few minutes, and Darya sighed with relief when Mary was completely gone.

Darya turned to Timothy, "Okay, my friend, you're next."

The front door of the bar café slammed open with a bang, startling everyone.

Trillian stood in the doorway. He pegged his hands triumphantly to his hips and looked around the room. His chest was puffed out and he was beaming with pride, like a caricature of a swashbuckling pirate. If his presence hadn't been so terrifying, Darya and Timothy might have found it comical.

Purely by chance, he'd witnessed the last two seconds of Mary's transfer through the window. *I arrived too late to prevent sweet Mary's departure but, no matter. Darya is the main prize, and there she is. Idiots! They chose a corner booth away from the exit.* He set his jaw and strode over toward them.

Timothy jumped in front of Darya and extended his arms, valiantly intending to block the Shard's access to her.

Darya was ahead of them both. The Alternus sim was not amenable to "magic" tricks. She could alter the physical properties of a few, incidental props with limited, local effect, but she couldn't simply "disappear" herself or any other player, or make a giant fighting troll appear. She'd tried and the Supervisor ignored her. Since Trillian had hacked Alternus, it seemed she had less influence over the inworld sim.

But she was still far from powerless.

She instructed the Supervisor to adjust the strength of the supporting ceiling beams and changed four stories of wooden walls above into cement.

The whole structure above Trillian creaked. His smirk disappeared as he noticed the ceiling starting to collapse.

Darya grabbed Timothy and pulled him out the back door as the building came down.

Trillian darted back out the front door.

Darya and Timothy escaped into the back alley, and right into the sights of Trillian's watchdogs. Their guns were drawn.

He's counting on my inability to return to my trueself and my unwillingness to leave Timothy to his death—she thought. *But, if Trillian thinks I have no option but to surrender, he's in for a surprise.*

She couldn't make their guns disappear, but she could change the chemical properties of the gunpowder in the bullets. Like Trillian, she could convince the Supervisor that the bullets were charged with something beside gunpowder.

She and Timothy approached the two thugs, angry determination in their eyes.

Trillian's men aimed their guns to cripple her and pulled the triggers.

Click! Click! Click!

Her satisfaction at their useless weapons was plain to read on her face. She shoved Timothy hard into one of the thugs and lunged at the other.

The man easily blocked her punch, and swung the butt-end of his pistol at her head. Rather than back away, she surprised him by stepping in toward him. Blocking the gun wrist with one hand, she chopped hard into the crook of his elbow with her free hand.

The man grunted. The chop hit its mark, and he was powerless against the reflex reaction that shocked his muscles into giving up their grip on the pistol. He ignored the skittering gun, and reached out to yank the troublesome woman closer before she could get away.

Darya pulled down sharply on his stunned arm, throwing her assailant off balance. He stumbled forward and she drove her knee into his groin. A strangled, animal sound escaped the man's vocal chords as the incapacitating pain registered and he bent forward. She delivered a punishing elbow to the back of his head. He crumpled. *One down, one to go.*

Timothy was enacting a commendable imitation of boxing with the second goon, and somehow managing to keep his opponent at bay. Barely.

Darya retrieved the fallen gun from her attacker and messaged the Supervisor. It filled with gunpowder once again, and she pointed it at Timothy's sparring partner. "Leave now, and don't come back."

The man recognized a good opportunity and bolted.

Timothy was visibly shaken but there was no time to comfort him.

"We can rest later. Come on, we have to get out of here right now." Darya grabbed his hand and pulled him over to a locked door across the alley. She shot off the lock and pulled Timothy into the building. Together they ran up three flights of stairs before bursting through a door into a long hallway. They ran two-thirds of the way down the corridor until Darya spotted a door without a "Housekeeping, please make up room" sign on it. She hoped that meant it was vacant.

The lock was electronic and Darya had no trouble figuring out the access code. She pulled a credit card from her pocket and inserted it into the lock, convincing the Supervisor that it had the correct magnetic coding. The lock flashed green and she passed inside, yanking Timothy behind her.

"Ow!" he yowled. She realized how keyed up she was.

Darya looked around the darkened room, giving her eyes a few seconds to adjust from the hallway lights. The two double beds were rumpled and, thankfully, empty. She found the light switch and a bedside table light came on. She sat Timothy down on the bed.

"I'm going to send you to the GameRoom with Mary. You'll appear right beside her. I hope she hasn't gone anywhere. The two of you stay right there. Do not move! I'll be along in a few minutes, okay?"

Still in shock, Timothy could only nod in dull agreement. Darya focussed and a portal opened above the Footman. She watched him fade and disappear.

She initiated her own transfer. The room shimmered and twisted. *That's a weird effect*—she thought—*not at all what I expected.*

The transfer pipe bent and gyrated as she poured through it. She watched the television and heavy table below it get drawn into the pipe along with her. The portal expanded in diameter. *What the...! That's not right!*

The pipe soon engulfed everything in the room and continued to grow. She looked around frantically. *Something's wrong! What's happening?*

Through the confusion, she heard laughter—*Trillian! He found a way to interfere with our escape!*

Rather than trying to stop her, he'd made adjustments to include the entire neighborhood in the pipe, including himself. Darya had to admire the move.

Even through the pipeline distortion, Darya could hear his ominous tone, "You are not going to be so lucky this time."

How is he tapping in? I have to block him!

She reviewed her code for the pipe but with her brain in transition between New York City and the GameRoom, it was impossible to focus on whatever changes he'd made.

She could only watch as all of Manhattan was pulled along into the GameRoom with her. Millions of people, mostly Partials, some real, were sucked out of the Alternus inworld and mapped onto her maze.

She'd modeled the maze on ten-dimensional mathematical formulas describing the physics of antique string theory applied to the virtual particles comprising protons. She'd permitted movement in all *ten* dimensions of the maze, providing there was some supporting surface but vision would remain restricted to *three* dimensions.

The idea was to create a place where they could easily hide. She hoped it would give her enough time to get all three of them back to the real universe.

She watched the busy streets and high rises of New York being pulled into the maze, and mapped onto the ten-dimensional topography. She had to assume her hunter was now in there somewhere, too. He wouldn't even have to search the neighboring inworlds for them.

And now, thanks to his meddling with the program, she wasn't sure *any* of them would ever find their way out.

39

IN THE DECADE FOLLOWING THE FINAL ACCEPTANCE of the Vesta Project, ship after ship delivered millions of Cybrids to the asteroid belt. Most went directly to Vesta. Hundreds of thousands were assigned to explore the rest of the belt.

The Cybrids worked around the clock, constructing enormous tunneling machines, the largest and fastest ever devised. In less than ten years, they completed four of the six primary tunnels, with smaller service tunnels below each. In space, there were no environmental concerns to slow them down. Their methods were effective but not at all delicate.

Where possible, they refined metals from the debris removed from the planetoid. The rest they melted as slag and deposited into rocky structural reinforcement bands on the outer surface.

The first on-site hiccough came early in the project, as data began pouring in from the explorer Cybrids. Initial analyses were disappointing but not entirely unexpected. Vesta and the other asteroids in the region were critically low in nitrogen-containing molecules, and until they found a supply, they'd be unable to establish sustainable life on Vesta.

The Cybrids wasted no time. They kicked into problem-solving mode, came up with a simple solution—to extract all the nitrogen they needed from the atmosphere of Titan—and were awaiting final approval before the human project managers had finished reading the initial analysis.

One team of Cybrids went to mine nitrogen, while others rounded up the enormous chunks of ice from among the asteroids and placed them inside the Vesta tunnels. They used some of the icy bodies to fill lakes and streams inside the colony tunnels. Next, they electrolyzed some of the water to produce oxygen for the atmosphere and mixed it with the nitrogen.

When you had no shortage of energy for propulsion or construction, you could work miracles. Kathy's Cybrids had done exactly that: worked miracles.

Even Kathy was impressed with the performance of her Cybrids. Around the globe, excitement and hope for a brighter future was growing. Investors were buzzing about great new businesses that would be opening as the mining and refining operations extracted the resources out there. It was a heady, invigorating time for science and engineering.

Sometimes Kathy and Greg forgot how it was all going to come to a spectacularly disastrous end.

As Kathy had feared, a number of high-profile individuals—all oblivious of Project Vesta's true purpose—banded together and publicly called for the project to redirect some of the most valuable metal-rich planetoids to an accessible near-Earth orbit.

To placate them and to reduce the likelihood of project-halting riots, the team shipped a few token packets of commercially valuable minerals Earthward.

It took some artful finagling by Kathy and the team's best spin talent to explain the negligible, slow return on global efforts and investment to date, and to hide the fact that the bulk of the extracted resources were being kept out past the Mars orbit.

Kathy became adept at public relations, spinning politics, economics, and statistics on the fly. The scent of new growth and new resources to exploit was tantalizing to the money hounds, who were only going to get more restless as the project wore on. For the moment, the worst of them were being held at bay.

The Cybrids stationed on Vesta focussed on constructing, sealing, and pressurizing the colony tunnels. Once that was done, they moved into the habitats to construct buildings, and to plant the first fields and forests.

One rocket from Earth contained nothing but bacteria, algae, protozoa, and other microorganisms necessary for a healthy ecology. Another took a cargo of invertebrates. Worms, insects, spiders and a host of "creepy crawlies" were critical to any place that could autonomously and indefinitely support human life.

Along the way, Kathy and Greg learned more environmental biology than they'd ever had interest in acquiring. In the end, the team felt it better to err on the side of caution and shipped everything they could think of. It would be easier to sort out imbalances later than to suffer the need of an organism that no longer existed.

Freshwater and saline environments were both provided, though the new marine "oceans" were tiny compared to Earth's. They were able to save the dolphins, but larger marine organisms like whales would perish with the planet that first gave birth to them. They froze a few symbolic samples of embryos, eggs, and sperm but it was unlikely any of them would be viable before a habitable ocean could be found or constructed.

The geneticists ran several intense sequencing projects to preserve the information of species that were not going to be rescued. They didn't bother to keep the genetic libraries secret; everyone agreed such activities would be viewed positively by most people.

Had it not been for the looming imminent destruction, the present era might have been the start of a new Golden Age on Earth.

As always, there were a few voices crying about the massive increases in global debt among participating countries. With so much new money going into circulation, Central Banks were forced to raise interest rates in an attempt to keep a lid on runaway inflation. In response, Reverend LaMontagne proposed creative fiscal laws that were soon passed around the world to keep the interest rates from penalizing government borrowing too heavily.

Kathie and Greg appreciated and admired the Reverend's genius for coming up with such ideas and for garnering support. They were amazed at how he convinced even the most stodgy national legislatures to pass bold new laws and ideas.

To the two socially-awkward scientists, Reverend LaMontagne had a nearly magical way about him. *Too bad, and a little scary*—they thought—*that such a powerful gift of persuasion is wielded by a fervent convert to Alum's message.*

LaMontagne made no effort to conceal his fervor. He openly referred to Alum as, "The Prophet for the Age." It was seen as a natural progression when the Reverend changed the name of his Church to "Yeshua's True Guard Church of the Prophet Alum."

Within days, the loving nickname coined by his Latino followers took hold: The Alumita. A small number of vocal, bigoted followers balked that the name Alum sounded too close to Allah, but their quibbling was drowned out by a thunderous global plea for the mysterious man, the self-proclaimed "Sword of Yeshua," to assume the position of World President.

In his private moments, The Reverend, his young protégé, and Mr. John Trillian celebrated their good fortunes. They couldn't have planned a better public relations move than the thwarting of a nuclear bombing.

40

THE PROJECT VESTA GALA BALL celebrating the launch of the first colony ship was the social event of the year. Kathy paused halfway down the stairs to the Ballroom Foyer of the Vancouver Convention Centre and took in all the well-dressed people.

I can't believe it's been twelve years! She felt proud of her accomplishments and in meeting this particular deadline. She, Greg, and Reverend LaMontagne could start breathing a little easier now. Humanity would survive. It might take decades or centuries before it thrived again, but it would survive.

Vancouver was the obvious choice for Project Vesta headquarters. Besides being home to the ever-growing Eater, the Chief Engineer, and the Chief Scientist, the nearby farmland south of the old Canada-United States border offered potential launching sites.

Tonight was a well-earned celebration. They were on the verge of transplanting humanity along with a commendably broad spectrum of all life on Earth to a viable new home they'd created from practically nothing among the asteroids.

Kathy's alter ego, DAR143147, was to thank for much of the success.

Too bad "DAR" couldn't be here—Kathy thought. Cybrids were not invited to shindigs like this, no matter what their contribution. *Someday, we'll change that*—she promised herself.

DAR had been her voice in space, flawlessly supervising the habitat construction. To Kathy, DAR was the sister she'd never had. A twin sister, who knew her every thought and anticipated her every decision. Kathy enjoyed their weekly consultations, even with the twenty-minute delay in communications to Vesta.

Greg, on the other hand, hated talking to his Cybrid alter-ego. "It's like talking to a slow, stupid me," he said. "How do you stand it?" Kathy hadn't told him about her Cybrid's secretly-enhanced brain. After a few tries, he stopped communicating with his counterpart except when absolutely necessary. Their formal, stilted conversations related strictly to business.

Kathy's heart went out to both the biological and Cybrid versions of Greg. She regretted not making an enhanced lattice for his Cybrid, too, before it had been deployed. She wished she could call it back to Earth and do a retrofit but it was too late. Now that it was fully commissioned, it wouldn't be permitted to return except as scrap. Even unenhanced, Greg's Cybrid was too valuable to the Vesta Project to be given leave.

Kathy spotted Greg, completely out of character and laughably uncomfortable in his tux, over near the bar. She lifted the hem of her gown and resumed her graceful descent down the stairs. At least, that's how she imagined it to be. She felt more at home in flats, a jumper, and a hardhat on the factory floor than in heels and formal wear, trying to make small talk with politicians and the press.

"Ah, Dr. Liang. It's quite a sight, isn't it? So much pretention in one place." Loren Andrews, the reporter assigned by the Washington Post to cover tonight's send-off, had caught up with her.

Kathy hated reporters more than politicians. With politicians, you knew they were always looking out for their own self-interests. With reporters, sometimes even they didn't know where their interests lay. Until they got the sense of their best story they couldn't be relied on to be supportive or combative. You just hoped you could figure out how they were going to come at you before they did. She put on her most neutral smile and turned to greet him.

"Mr. Andrews. You do realize it's just a social convention to dress up for these things, don't you? I don't think anyone actually enjoys wearing formal outfits."

He pointed to Greg. "Certainly not your partner."

Kathy redirected the reporter's gaze to Prime Minister Hudson, who was deep in conversation with China's newest President. "I don't think either Ms. Hudson or Mr. Xiu is any more comfortable than Greg. And I'm sure they've been to many more of these things than both of us combined. Anyway, I'm just a simple engineer from California, so I'm more used to work clothes, myself."

"You could have fooled me. You look ravishing in that dress."

Kathy would have blushed if she hadn't been so repulsed by the man. She did her best to keep her feelings to herself. It would only make life more difficult if she alienated the press. Besides, in another decade he would meet his own bleak demise—a small but satisfying consolation. She thought of all the irritating types of people she would be leaving behind once the Eater consumed the Earth.

A small, satisfied smile escaped before she buried it beneath her guilt. *I shouldn't think like that.*

Andrews misinterpreted the smirk for warmth and, beaming, offered his arm to escort her.

At the bottom of the staircase, she politely thanked him for his assistance. He slipped her a business card on which he'd pre-written his hotel and room number.

Eew, tacky! She wondered how many of those he'd dispense that night. Before the reporter could become an even greater nuisance, Greg arrived. He rescued her with a glass of champagne, sending the annoying Mr. Andrews to find someone more susceptible to his wiles.

Reverend LaMontagne spotted Greg and Kathy standing by the windows looking out over the harbor. "You two are to be congratulated," he said in his heartiest Texas accent. "This has been a magnificent achievement."

"As much yours, as ours, Reverend," Greg replied.

"That shall forever remain our little secret," LaMontagne answered. The three of them clinked glasses and laughed. It felt good to forget the fear that had been driving them, and just enjoy their successes tonight.

As his country's Permanent Representative to Project Vesta, Reverend LaMontagne was given the honor of officially introducing the first Vesta colonists.

The colonists would soon be on their way, and it would be impossible to undo the fact that their numbers included a much higher percentage of the Alumita members than one might statistically expect. It was surprising nobody had noticed, or at least not mentioned, that detail.

Not that LaMontagne anticipated much difficulty in getting the team to overlook the anomaly. Certainly, everyone on the list was qualified, and their loyalty to such a strong supporter of the Project as Alum Himself could only be to the colony's benefit.

"You two make quite the handsome couple," LaMontagne continued. "Will you be among the first to bless our new colony with children?"

Kathy grimaced. This had been a sore spot between the couple for some years. Greg had pushed to start a family shortly after they got married. *I'm sorry, but I can't bring myself to bring a child into a world with such a short expiry date*—she'd argued. It was the only thing they'd ever seriously argued about.

"Hey, we don't even know if our application to join Vesta will be accepted," Greg said and winked.

Kathy regarded her husband suspiciously. "Of course, we'll be accepted."

Greg laughed. "You never know."

LaMontagne joked, "If Vesta won't have you, then we'll simply have to build another colony that will."

Kathy changed the subject. "You're looking quite dashing this evening, Reverend."

"Oh, my dear. No flirting. At my age, that might do more harm than good," he joked. It was a rare occasion when the Reverend attempted such an endearing jest. Everyone seemed to be in a good mood tonight.

One of the organizers came by to let them know they had thirty minutes before they were expected on stage.

"I have a surprise for you," Greg said out of the blue.

"A surprise?" Kathy and the Reverend asked in chorus.

"Yeah, I was going to show you later, but I can't wait. Let's go in here." He led them to one of the empty side rooms and locked the doors behind them.

"Why so mysterious?" Kathy asked.

It's not like him to be this way—she thought with a guilty twinge. *But I guess we all have our secrets.* She pushed aside thoughts of DAR's true intellect.

"Hard as it may be to believe, I've had some spare time over the past decade," he said. "In that time, I've made a discovery or two of my own."

"You've found a way to stop the Eater!" the Reverend tried.

"Sadly, no. I'll keep trying, though."

"Don't keep us guessing! What is it?" Kathy asked.

Greg reached into his inside jacket pocket and pulled out a tablet. "Lady and gentleman, I present the RAF shifter."

Kathy and the Reverend exchanged confused glances. RAF stood for Reality Assertion Field, but what on Earth was an RAF shifter? "Okay, I give. What is it?"

"The world's smallest RAF device." Greg held the tablet in his best imitation of a game show prize presenter. "It's small because it has only one function: to move things."

LaMontagne couldn't help his curiosity. "Does it generate some kind of tractor field?"

"No, not that kind of moving. It...*shifts* them, is how I like to think of it."

Kathy frowned. "Shifts how? Ooh, do you mean like a warp drive?" She was only half joking. She tolerated Greg's love of science fiction stories, but wondered how a real scientist could let his imagination run wild that way.

"Not exactly. You know about the quantum EM and Higgs fields, right?"

"Child's play, my dear. Move along. We only have twenty minutes."

"This device disconnects matter from those quantum fields for a short period of time. During that time, an object is no longer of this universe and is not constrained by its laws of motion."

Kathy tried to think through the implications. "Wouldn't you just disappear? You might reappear somewhere, but likely not where you started. Nor where you intended."

"Exactly!" said a proud Greg. "Unless, that is, you could find some kind of anchor. Now, for your bonus question. What effect seems to instantaneously exchange information between particles, no matter where those particles are located in the universe?"

"Well, quantum entanglement, for one. Einstein's old 'spooky action at a distance.' Everyone knows that. Interesting effect but not really useful for anything."

"Oh, sure," laughed Greg, "*everyone* knows that. Okay, so we really haven't found a way to use quantum entanglement for anything important...until now."

"What *are* you talking about?" Kathy was getting impatient. Greg's mystifying disclosure was going nowhere, and it was taking a long time to get there.

"If I may," interrupted the Reverend. "Are you suggesting you can disconnect an object from the natural laws that limit its rate of motion?"

Greg nodded excitedly.

"And you can use entangled particles to help that object find its way back to some specific place in the universe?"

"Yes!" Greg's eyes sparkled. He held up the tablet. "And this device is all it takes!"

He fiddled with some buttons on the screen, and disappeared.

"Hello," he called from the other end of the long conference room.

Kathy was astonished, which was a considerable feat in itself. She'd seen a lot of "miracles" since working with Darian. The problems they solved every day on Project Vesta were astonishing. But she hadn't imagined Greg's surprise discovery.

In no more than a blink, Greg reappeared beside them.

Questions rolled through her mind. Some were obvious in retrospect. She and Greg had been spending a lot of time in their own separate worlds. She was on the road most days, and he was tied to the labs. Clearly, he'd made this discovery while she was away and had tested it on his own.

The thought of it irked her. He was flashing in and out of existence without her, without *telling* her. She held off giving him a piece of her mind, and considered the timing of the disclosure. He'd saved the big reveal for today so it must be relevant to Vesta.

"Greg, what's the range of this thing?"

"Bingo," he exclaimed, "The sixty-four million dollar question! The answer is...infinity. We can go anywhere, instantly. Well, anywhere with the right entangled pair of particles." He smiled broadly in maddening glee.

The Reverend sat down. He rested his chin on his hand and thought furiously. *How can the Church get control of this technology? How can we use it to our advantage? It's far too valuable to be left in the hands of the Project management or national governments.*

The obvious solution would be to just take it...but how? I'll have to get Trillian on that project right away. I hope Greg keeps electronic or physical notes outside his own brain. I'm not sure even a genius of Trillian's level could hack his dendy lattice.

Aloud LaMontagne said, "Greg, this is wonderful news. It means the transportation bottleneck to Vesta has been removed."

"What do you mean?" cried Kathy. "This opens up the stars! If we can travel anywhere, we can explore the entire galaxy."

"Not that I didn't already think of that," replied Greg. "But there are two problems. First, we don't have enough time to find and terraform a suitable planet orbiting another star, so we're stuck with what we have for now.

"Second, in order to navigate a return to this universe, you need an entangled pair of particles. Over a range of a few hundred meters, it's easy to find paired virtual electrons from a static charge. But over interstellar distances? Unfortunately, not that easy. We're limited to the speed of light in a fairly conventional way until we can ship some entangled particles to a new star."

Kathy looked crestfallen.

"Hey! There's still a lot of good news in this," Greg said. "We can move people off Earth a lot faster than before. We'll be able to save as many people as Vesta can hold. Maybe thirty or forty million instead of the ten million we'd planned."

"Still, we're limited to what Vesta can hold," Kathy replied.

"Perhaps I have something that could help with that," said LaMontagne. "I've also been busy in the experimentation department."

"When did you develop an interest in science?" Greg asked.

"I am offended, young man," the Reverend responded, feigning hurt. "I'll have you know the dendy lattice has opened my mind to a whole universe of possibilities. In the final analysis, even God saw fit to back up his decrees with threats of punishment. Taking a chapter from the Good Book, so to speak, I've been working on a new weapon."

"Of course," Greg said. He meant it ironically. Both he and Kathy knew that LaMontagne's interests ran more to the applications of power and persuasion than to the strictly theological. It was not enough to merely speak of the promised Kingdom of God, one should do everything in one's powers to hasten the arrival of that Kingdom on Earth.

LaMontagne took Greg's utterance at face value. "In light of what you've shown us, I think this particular weapon might prove useful beyond its original intent. Let me demonstrate."

He sent a request to share an inSense video with their lattices.

They accepted. Fifteen years of working together had convinced them the Reverend had no designs on their brainpower other than to put them to work on the Project. Anyway, their security was up to fending off any unwanted attempts to hijack their conceptas.

The video opened on a desert scene. The ground was covered in rock, brush, and dry grasses. "This is the Chisos Basin of Big Bend National Park in Texas," LaMontagne said. The video panned the area revealing low, rocky mountains, buttes, and mesas. It stopped on a clear crystalline rod mounted on a tripod, its barrel pointed at the side of a nearby mesa.

"I've embedded a cylindrical RAF generator in this device," LaMontagne continued. "It produces a rather enormous amount of energy when activated. Keep an eye on that mesa, about a kilometer away.

An intense, pulsating, conical violet beam leaped from the end of the device. By the time it struck the rocky side of the mesa, it was ten meters across. The part of the slope it struck was instantly vaporized, sending gushes of incandescent steam outward and upward. As it pushed through the rocks, the beam self-adjusted so that the vaporized area didn't grow much wider. In less than a minute, it drilled through the mesa, leaving a ten-meter tunnel.

"As you can surmise, this new weapon I've been working on could be used as a tool to accelerate the process of building colony tunnels in other asteroids. We could expand our efforts and save many millions more."

Greg silently fumed. Yes, the utility of this new "tool" as he'd called it was undeniable. But it was still primarily a weapon being sold as a tool.

I'm not happy to see RAF technology being used to develop weapons but, realistically, what else could I expect? I value the Reverend's support of Project Vesta. Can I trust his motives?

Kathy broke the silence. "So does this mean we can immediately expand Project Vesta to include Ceres and Pallas? They'd be the next two most obvious target colonies."

Neither man responded, and she interpreted their hesitation as uncertainty about her proposal. "Oh, come on! This means we can save almost a hundred million people. Not to mention tens of millions more minds that we can instantiate inside Cybrids. It's perfect!"

"In theory, I would agree," Greg offered reluctantly.

"Fantastic!" Kathy clasped her hands together and spun around, ecstatic.

Greg quickly added, "But let's not publicly announce any of these new developments until we've discussed them with the PM. People can have a hard time adjusting to new technologies, especially when they're as radical as these. I mean this is big, maybe even bigger than limitless energy or Cybrids."

Kathy and the Reverend agreed. Private discussions ahead of public disclosure.

Regardless, she was elated. She wasn't going to let her joy be diminished by Greg's caution.

More colony space and better transportation!

Today was a good day.

41

"WELL, THAT'S NOT WHAT I EXPECTED TO SEE."

Were these words uttered by anyone other than the man-demon-angel Darak, Brother Stralasi might have found it amusing. Coming from his traveling companion, the words filled Brother Stralasi with dread.

He was becoming used to his own state of surprise, confusion, awe, and/or terror every time Darak "shifted" him somewhere new. But throughout their trials and travels, his abductor had remained confident.

Annoyingly, arrogantly, supremely confident.

Stralasi fought the temptation to respond with an uncharitable comment about Darak's much-touted superiority of knowledge and experience. If something about their surroundings caught Darak off guard, now might not be the best time to speak. He held his tongue and studied their new location.

They'd materialized inside a clean, well-lit, nondescript facility. It looked harmless enough. No Angels, Securitors, people, plants, animals or Cybrids were visible. About one-third of the room was occupied by a black metal cage. He peered inside and beamed with pride on recognizing the silver reflective sphere. *Another Soltron Detector!*—Stralasi announced quietly to himself.

He could see no immediate danger. *Maybe something outside.*

He looked for a portal or window. There was a huge one dominating the rock wall behind them. Three distant, yellow suns were visible in it; the window reduced their brilliance so he could look directly at them. Their blazing disks circled one another close enough to rip matter from each others' surfaces and fling bright coronas outward. The graceful streamers of incandescent gasses mesmerized him.

Three evenly offset ringworlds circled outside the orbital dance of the three suns. Each ring was striped at intervals along the inside edge where sunlight was absorbed by panels that cast night-time shadows on the land far below. "Exquisite!"

It was magnificent, and made even more so because the remainder of the sky was the deepest black Stralasi had ever seen, even deeper than the space near Eso-La. Only the dim twinkle of a few distant lights gave any hint of the remaining universe.

"Where are we?" Stralasi reverent voice echoed in the vast chamber.

"We are as far away from where we were as you can possibly go and still be in Alum's Realm."

Sensing Stralasi's dwindling patience, Darak elaborated. "The area is a large void off the main axis of the Realm that runs between the Virgo Cluster and the Fornax Cluster. The nearest neighboring galaxies are fifteen million light years away. We're about as far from any part of the Realm as one can be in explored space."

"Then perhaps that explains why I've never heard of three suns in one system. I'm sure the Alumita would have mentioned such a thing in my astronomy courses."

"No, this is unique," Darak answered. "Even in my extensive travels, I've never encountered such an astronomical oddity anywhere else, a trio of same-sized stars in stable orbit around each other. I'm not at all sure how the physics of the arrangement works; I suspect it might not be completely natural."

"Not completely natural?"

Darak smiled. "We might be looking at one of Alum's greatest works...before his current planned destruction of everything, that is."

He walked up to the window. "This is a rogue system, the single solar system equivalent to the ESO galaxy. Even I couldn't figure out a reasonable explanation for how the system formed or how it came to be here. These are the only stars in this section of the void. The few lights you see are not individual stars; there are none bright enough within viewing range. Those are other galaxies."

"I've viewed images of every one of the thirty-four ringworlds in Alum's Realm, including the two double ones. I've never seen anything like this. Why would Alum construct such a place here on the edge of civilization?"

"I would think that's obvious, in retrospect."

Stralasi sighed. He hated having information meted out in dribs and drabs, having to wheedle and cajole everything important out of the man-demon that had tricked him away from his Founding work.

He thought about how far away from most of the Realm he was at the moment. He remembered Darak's surprise when they first materialized in the chamber. Apparently, he wasn't all-knowing. "You didn't expect the ringworlds to be here?" he said, a hint of triumph in his voice.

"I admit that *was* a surprise," admitted Darak. "They weren't here when I constructed this research station some twenty-five million years ago. The rogue trinity of suns was interesting enough to justify building this place. I simply tagged along with my detector. It seemed like a good place for a measurement, being above the plane of the Local Sheet. Plus, it was a quiet place to go when I wanted seclusion.

"I would've predicted the ringworlds had I'd given it a moment's thought back then. At the time, it wasn't a certainty Alum would prevail in the war against the Aelu. One can only surmise He thought it best to create a safe haven in case the battles turned against Him. It's far enough away from the Virgo cluster to make an excellent retreat. Yes, in hindsight, it's an obvious location for constructing a system of ringworlds. The system was full of convenient-sized planetoids for readily available building material."

"Do you think there are people living there?"

"Likely a few hundred billion. Enough to provide basic caretaker functions and keep the ecosystem functioning. There's probably enough room to house everyone living in the entire Virgo Cluster if needed, though I suspect a much smaller, select group would have been invited in the case of defeat by the Aelu."

"Mmm." Stralasi nodded as if he understood; he was not going to rise to the bait.

"At any rate, when I referred to the unexpected, I was talking about *that*," he said, pointing to the silvery sphere of the Soltron Detector. "When I left here, I'd hoped to get, at most, a few million years of data from it. I built multiple redundancies and self-repair mechanisms into the system, but nothing lasts forever, right? What surprised me and, quite frankly, is causing me some trepidation..."

Stralasi gulped. After all the hair-raising experiences they'd barely survived, what could possibly cause Darak unease?

"...is to find it sitting here in this chamber, perfectly intact and functional after twenty-five million years."

The Good Brother was confused. "Maybe your repair mechanisms worked better than you thought they would."

"Ha! I'm a good engineer but I'm not that good. And that wouldn't explain why the chamber is pressurized with a breathable atmosphere. Nor why the lights are on."

"What? I thought you did that." Stralasi noticed for the first time the absence of their protective bubble.

"No, it wasn't me," Darak replied, his voice trailing off.

Stralasi followed his gaze to the clean, shiny surfaces. Everything looked perfectly pristine. Not a thing out of place. No alarms or alerts. He stared quizzically at Trillian.

"In this atmosphere, everything should have corroded long ago. Someone has been looking after this installation."

"Ah, yes," the monk agreed.

Darak cocked his head as if listening to some secret whisper. "Probably the same someone who just surrounded us with a Wing of Angels."

"What?!!" Stralasi's panicked eyes searched every corner of the room and then the visible space outside the huge window.

"Hmm. Yes, it seems we've been discovered. Careless of me," he added, in an oddly nonchalant tone.

Darak showed no sign of being overly concerned. He wasn't shifting them away or hustling them for cover. That *really* worried the Good Brother.

"Well then, why don't we go somewhere else? Quickly."

"We can't, at least not easily."

"Since when does 'not easily' stop you? You've done hundreds of things I would have considered impossible for anyone except the Living God."

"Perhaps I've understated our predicament," Darak responded.

"Understated?" the Good Brother choked out.

"Yes, my analysis indicates that Alum has detected the presence of unauthorized persons here. Given this far-flung and secluded location, He knows we used starstep technology to get here, technology He believes to be exclusive to him.

"Normally, that would point to the Aelu, but this observation lab is clear across the Realm from their home worlds. He would have been alerted if Aelu were on the move.

"The most likely scenario would be that the builder of this facility— which would be me—left some entangled particles here when it was constructed those many millions of years ago. And that would imply that someone besides Himself might have knowledge of starstep technology and could live for tens of millions of years. Clearly, that concerns Him enough to send a Wing. I'm a little surprised He didn't come in person."

"So why can't we just leave? And why are we standing here talking about all this so calmly?"

"Ah, that is the question, indeed. The Angels have surrounded this planetoid with quantum decoherence generators, shift blockers. They make it impossible to navigate in the dematerialized state, even for me. We are trapped in their cage. We can leave but, if we do, we run a significant risk of not finding our way back to the Real Universe. At least, not where we left it. Navigating back to the Realm could prove difficult."

Stralasi couldn't understand why Darak was discussing this so calmly. *Trapped! We're trapped, and Alum's might is about to fall down upon us!*

Instinctively, he looked to see if he could find somewhere to hide. He realized how futile that would be; there was no way to hide from Angels, especially not here. He could feel the terror rising in his throat. "Well, what can we do?" he squawked.

"There are several options. I'm modeling multiple scenarios for the best course of action," replied Darak. "There are a number of ways to hide, for example, by shrinking down to atomic size or integrating into the walls of the chamber. That would only buy us a few minutes. I suspect the Angels have orders to destroy the entire station if they don't find the intruder. That's what I would do.

"I could alter a number of physical laws to unleash destructive forces on the Wing. Doing so would hint at my full capabilities a little prematurely for my purposes. I'd like to have all my preparations completed before I'm forced to confront Alum. Otherwise, there will only be a limited number of outcomes possible, most of which would be rather unpleasant.

"That leaves me with one choice. I will have to fight the Wing on Angel terms, as the Fallen Commander. That will raise a lot of questions, no doubt: Where have I been? What have I been doing? How have I upgraded my capabilities? But those can all be answered without recourse to my true nature."

Darak hung his head. "I hate to kill in such numbers, even Angels, but I think it may be our only way out."

In an instant, Darak the man was gone and Gabriel the Angel, the Fallen Commander of the Virgo Central Wing, stood majestically in front of Stralasi. He looked down on the trembling Brother and asked, "Now what shall I do with you?"

"You could leave me here," suggested the monk.

"I don't think that will work. Perhaps I should shrink you and stick you in my pocket along with the camping set."

"No! You can't just carry me around like some trinket while you fight for our survival. I won't be able to see what's going on."

"I can't have the Angels be aware of you, either. That would reveal too much to Alum too soon. There *is* one other alternative. You might not like it."

"What is it?"

"I can mostly remove you from this universe but keep you tethered to reality, literally, by your eyeballs."

"You're right. That doesn't appeal at all."

"Don't worry. It's better than it sounds. If I remove electromagnetic interactions from all the matter of your body except your retina, you will be able to watch the battle without being noticed. I can put a conversion filter between your eyes and your brain so you can see what's happening. No one would expect to find a pair of eyes floating independently in space. I'll just have to be sure to position you away from the action."

"That's all you can think of?" Stralasi asked, hoping it wasn't.

When Darak added nothing, the Brother began to fret. *Tethered in space? By my eyes? My eyes?*

"The Angels are narrowing their confinement to this base. They are working in layers of spheres, like an onion. Each layer is another level of shift blocker we need to penetrate to escape. I should be able to take out two or three shells before they adapt to my first attack. If we're lucky, maybe I can kill a few hundred of the Angels. That'll give me a window to place you in space somewhere well away from the main action. Are you ready?"

"Wait! What if you're defeated? What'll happen to me?"

Darak looked at Stralasi. The cocky smirk on the Angel's face spoke volumes. "*That* outcome is not possible," he added, redundantly.

"Are you enjoying this? I can't even begin to think about the blasphemy of killing thousands of Angels. I'm sure my eternity in Hell will be longer than anyone's."

Before Darak could answer, a shushing noise on the other side of the detector alerted them to Cybrids arriving in the facility. Darak raised one mercury eyebrow at Stralasi. "Well?"

The Brother sighed, nodded, and was abruptly situated in the blackness of space with all Hell breaking loose around him.

42

LORD MIKA WAS PATIENTLY MAKING THE ROUNDS, checking on his troops at the stations around Rafael, when he and his entire Wing were ripped across the Realm to an unfamiliar triple star system.

The shift came in three stages, only milliseconds apart. He'd had no knowledge or warning. This was not part of their planning or practice.

Angels were shifted from their assigned solar systems all over the Rafael galaxy into a central location. From the little Mika could see in his brief glimpse, it looked like the Home World system. The perpendicular double ringworlds were recognizable throughout the Realm.

A heads up might have been nice!—Mika grumbled.

Before he could take stock, they were pushed through another starstep onto the dark side of an unidentified ringworld.

As fast as they arrived, they were shifted into battle positions around a nearby asteroid. Their shift blockers and swords were activated automatically.

In less than a dozen milliseconds the entire Wing had traveled over one-hundred and fifty million light years through three star systems, assumed battle formation, and was ready to fight. It took them a further three milliseconds to register they'd been moved.

Mika had a slight advantage, having received a Divine Inspiration directly from Alum while everyone was in transit. He arrived in position with his lattice processor fully up to speed, imprinted with knowledge of their location near this isolated retreat, and of the intruder alert that had brought them here.

He did not recognize or know the purpose of this isolated trinary ringworld around three stars. He didn't need to know the history of the scientific observation station, nor of the machinery inside it. He needed only to be battle ready, to command the Wing, and to carry out Alum's orders.

The Wing began closing in on the asteroid. They moved systematically and precisely, as practiced, ensuring each new layer of imprisoning shift blocker was secure before moving inward to form the next.

Lord Mika sent a priority command to the station's Cybrids to search the asteroid for anyone or anything unexpected. Maintenance, repair, and construction area reports came back clear.

"Concentrate your search in the observation chamber housing the exotic matter detector," he instructed. He had no idea what an exotic matter detector was. Alum had provided him with a detailed map of the asteroid station, and that's what the label read. That was enough for his purposes.

The Cybrids came back with a preliminary report: *One or more unauthorized intruders have been detected. We are moving closer for identification.*

They transmitted an image of an Angel and a Brother standing by a window in a hollowed-out chamber of the asteroid. Then, nothing.

Mika was about to check on the Cybrids himself when the two innermost shells of shift-blocking Angels erupted in action. Within *a second after of the initial report,* over five hundred of his Wing were killed.

"Shields and sinks to maximum!" he commanded. Another hundred Angels were gone before his troops could comply. *Because of me. I underestimated the threat*—he chastised himself.

Defenses activated and everyone on full alert, the Wing evaluated their losses and reported. For the moment, those remaining were safe. The shields made them practically invincible to physical aggression, but prevented them from attacking. The sinks could absorb the directed output of multiple hydrogen bombs without wavering.

Mika floated among the debris of bodies the attacker had hacked to bits in his opening flurry.

How can this be? He's one of us! An Angel. Could this be another of Alum's tests?

Had he met this Angel before? He scanned his archival memory. In the deepest recesses, the face linked to a name: Gabriel, the banished Fallen Commander of the Virgo Central Wing.

But that was over twenty million years ago! Ancient history. How could an Angel have survived so long without Alum's Grace to support him? And how could he have traveled to this distant outpost? Where had he been these millions of years, and what was he doing here? Was he working with the false Shard, Darak, on the other side of the Realm? Or were the activities over there and here today merely a coincidence? There were too many unanswerable questions.

For the moment, Gabriel was trapped inside the jump blocker field. The

Angels from Mika's Wing who imprisoned him couldn't attack without lowering their shields for a few milliseconds. The speed of their attacker demonstrated the folly of that proposal. The two opponents studied one another, contemplating next moves.

Mika focussed on more tactically relevant issues: How could a solitary Angel destroy so many other Angels so quickly? What new abilities did this intruder possess, and how had he acquired them? Did he have weaknesses Mika's Wing could exploit?

He would try diplomacy first. There was no shame in a single Agent choosing rational surrender to an obviously overwhelming opponent. Alum taught them that escalating to violence without first exploring more subtle options was a sign of an inadequate tactical understanding. He opened a comm channel.

Lord Gabriel. In the name of Alum, I command you to deactivate your shield and disarm your weapons. The Living God has instructed me to bring you to Him. If you do not comply, you will be destroyed—the Commander sent.

The dismissive laughter received in response confused Mika.

Have you not noticed how easily the first of your Wing was dispensed with?—the opponent transmitted. *How many attacks can your Wing endure once you drop your shields? What makes you think I have any interest in an audience with your God? Go home and leave me in peace!*

The blasphemy elicited something deeper than anger inside Mika. "My God?" Mika sputtered. "Alum is the God of all. And how dare you address an Angel of the Lord of the Universe in such a tone?"

He nearly unleashed the full destructive force of his sword on Gabriel right then. Was that what his opponent wanted? With considerable effort, he regained control of his outrage.

Alum's Angels were the most powerful fighters in existence. Thousands of years of war with the Aelu had proven that. The sword of a single Angel could destroy a planet. A hundred could cause stars to go nova. In the entire Realm, only Alum was more powerful.

How had Gabriel severed heads, arms, and wings from hundreds of Mika's powerful brothers so quickly that he could hardly be perceived?

Our shields stay up...for now, but how can we break this stalemate? Would the first to make a move be more likely to win or to lose?

Mika adjusted his projections to compensate for Gabriel's speed and power, and then formulated a new plan, one with layer upon layer of backup strategies.

He ordered the outer shells to realign, increasing the number of layers Gabriel would need to penetrate to escape, and then transmitted a random sequence for alternating shield on/off patterns so all of the layers could coordinate the attack. Eager to see this mission concluded, Mika initiated the program.

Shields winked on and off. Each time a shield went inactive, a series of harassing blasts were unleashed at Gabriel, and several unprotected Angels jumped closer, attempting disabling blows with their swords.

Gabriel appeared to be doing little more than delaying the inevitable. His sinks passively absorbed the energy blasts, while he calmly fended off slashes and shifted around the innermost shell of jump blockers.

Mika discerned no apparent pattern to his enemy's movements and yet, within seconds, the innermost shell was dotted with dead Angels. Gabriel slew them the instant they dropped out of the decoherence shield network, before they could even leave their positions to attack with swords!

How could he have calculated the sequence? It was random. Yet the evidence that he had done so was strewn on the periphery of the shell.

As casualties piled up, Lord Mika shifted reserves from the outer shells to replace weaknesses in the shift-blocking net. The lattice of overlapping blocker fields held, though dead Angels littered its active nodes. *Gabriel intends to destroy my Wing bit by bit. We'll see about that!*

He instructed the inner shell to attack en masse, allowing that layer of Gabriel's prison to dissolve.

The freed Angels began shifting through a patterned sequence to within striking distance of their opponent. They swarmed in an intricate dance, advancing and retreating, never occupying a single position for longer than a second. To the human eye, the collective effect was of shimmering stardust.

Gabriel responded by accelerating his movements.

That's it, wear yourself out. Lord Mika was feeling more confident. At least one of the troops will get in a damaging blow before the next layer of concentric spheres falls.

Angels winked in and out of existence too fast for a mortal onlooker to follow. *It's unlikely that Gabriel would've encountered this pattern in his relatively short Wing career.* The maneuvers were developed at the end of the war against the Aelu, long after Gabriel had been humiliated and banished by Alum.

Once again, Lord Mika underestimated his opponent.

As fast as Mika's brothers shifted and as fierce as they struck, Gabriel was faster and struck harder. Most of their attempts met with empty space. The enemy's sword blocked and parried, then struck out of nowhere and another Angel would die.

For all its fury, the killing was silent, typical of all battles in space. The Angels died quietly, their final anguish left unvoiced.

Mika's losses mounted.

* * *

GABRIEL/DARAK WAS A KILLING MACHINE. With a terrifying grimace fixed on his face, he moved in a swirling dance of shift, whirl, duck, leap, rotate, spin, slice, and thrust. His hands, arms, elbows, wings, legs, and feet deflected blows from his opponents that were intended to sever limbs.

His attackers were aiming to disarm or disable him and take him captive. Darak put no such limitations on himself. His blows were intended to kill.

He released blasts of planet-destroying fury toward the Angels occupying the outer shells. The blasts were mostly absorbed into their sinks but an occasional Angel would be overloaded and disappear in a silent, fiery burst.

He set his tactical computations for the minimum level of fighting superiority needed to defeat his enemy without drawing the Living God's suspicions that the actions were supernatural. He preferred to keep Alum out of things a while longer.

Sooner or later, we'll have a chance to escape—Darak thought as he severed another Angel's head. Acutely aware of Stralasi's location, he kept moving the battle away from the place where the Brother's disembodied retinas observed the action. He doubted the monk was able to follow much of the detail, but the man *had* insisted on being able to watch.

As Darak shifted within the constraining shell, he hoped Mika wouldn't notice he'd been avoiding a specific area of the space available to him. To be sure, he shifted Stralasi and his protective bubble to a different spot from time to time.

Things are moving so quickly, Stralasi probably won't even notice. At any rate, how could he complain?

He laughed at the absurdity of it, as he pierced the power supply of another Angel.

Darak allowed Mika's bothersome gnats to chase him around inside the decoherence shell. He could destroy them all with a thought, were it not for the subterfuge he was conducting. *I can't give away too much about my powers just yet.*

The Angels' attacks were a bother but if he weren't careful, they could be dangerous enough to the body he'd chosen to wear.

If he took too much damage, he'd need to retreat from this universe for repairs, and all of his work might be undone before he could return. He'd certainly lose Stralasi and, in that time, Alum's plans might move forward enough to become unstoppable. *We could lose the Real Universe!*

Darak fought on patiently, hoping to wear them down. Angels fell by the hundreds but the Wing's strategy didn't change. *There will come a time when Mika's patience runs out, when his losses make him desperate to finish this battle. He will accept my death, at some point, if he deems it necessary. Or, I should say, my apparent death.*

It was obvious he wasn't going to escape their shift-blocking net easily. He'd have to destroy it or punch a hole through it.

Alum must have issued a directive to capture the intruders, or Mika would have unleashed his most powerful energy beam by now. The Wing Commander was staying above the main fray.

* * *

LORD MIKA'S INSTINCTS, BUILT ON EONS OF BATTLE EXPERIENCE, told him they still didn't have the full measure of this troublesome Fallen Commander.

Thirty percent of the Wing's been annihilated, and we're no closer to capturing this menace. If we continue this way, he'll just keep picking us off one by one.

Gabriel was fast. He perceived, fended off, and delivered attacking thrusts at a speed unmatched by anyone in the Wing. But, so far, he'd demonstrated no unusual strength of shield, sink, or sword. His main advantage could be entirely explained by increased computational ability.

Alum's directive is too constraining. It's time we err on the side of safety. A star-destroying blast will dispense with this menace with less effort and fewer losses.

Mika assembled one hundred Angels along an arc of the shell that restricted Gabriel's movements. Their combined force would be enough to make a sun go nova. No Angel, however enhanced or upgraded, could survive such a blast.

He'd have to forfeit the few hundred Angels that were chasing Gabriel around the shell or blocking his escape. No matter; he'd already lost thousands.

Alum would order their praises be sung, and they'd be forgotten. Such had been an Angel's existence since long before the Aelu.

He aligned the selected troops to ensure the blast spared the ringworlds, suns, and as many of their brethren as possible, and prepared to give the command.

ONE MOMENT.

The unmistakable voice of Alum entered directly into his senses. Whether the signal was shunted through the starstep on the asteroid or had been gifted to him as a direct starcomm while in transit, Mika couldn't tell. Either way, he felt blessed to be in direct communication with God, while so far away from Him.

The Wing Commander assumed the zero-gravity equivalent of bending one knee in genuflection. Floating freely, he spread hands, legs and wings wide and bowed his head, the ultimate defenseless pose. "I am yours to command, my Lord," he sent.

I WILL COORDINATE THE ASSAULT DIRECTLY.

Alum has gifted me with a starcomm! The Living God has chosen me as a direct conduit for His Divine Action!

Mika gave over full control of his sensory and command capabilities to Alum.

The Living God charitably permitted Mika's processors to continue monitoring what would follow.

* * *

DARAK WATCHED THE ANGELS IN THE OUTER SHELLS maneuver into position. *Finally! Mika's organizing them to send a synchronized bolt of energy to destroy me and end the battle.*

That Lord Mika would kill several hundred of their fellow Angels to put an end to this folly did not surprise Darak; that was considered acceptable loss by Angel tactics.

He increased his shield strength and checked his sink capacity. It could absorb a combined blast from over seven hundred of them for at least one full second. But he couldn't do so without revealing important and potentially deadly information about himself.

We're better off sneaking away when they fire.

Darak computed the trajectory of the Angels' beam, given their positions and where he would place himself and Stralasi when they fired. There'd be a small track just outside the beam's path—only one—where they wouldn't be seen while they executed their escape.

If his calculations were right, the blast would overload the Angels that were generating the decoherence shell, and he'd be able to escape. There'd be no more than a millionth of a second between Mika's beam destroying the edge of the innermost imprisoning shell, and striking Darak. *Just enough time to get away.*

At the precise moment, he'd tether the Brother to himself, and pull them both near the beam and through the hole it created in the shift-blocking shells. He'd have to shield Stralasi with his own body, absorbing the majority of energy that would strike them. The smaller energy sink he'd placed in the shell with the monk would protect him from any stray radiation.

The beam's energy was going to play havoc with the virtual space through which they'd be shifting, but there was nothing he could do about that. To navigate reliably they'd need to be outside the beam itself. In virtual space, you either navigated reliably or you got lost forever.

Darak shifted Stralasi closer to where he wanted to be when the blast was delivered, at the far end of the innermost shift-blocking shell. He fired his own energy bolts, reducing the Wing's numbers along one specific arc of the shell. He tried not to be too obvious about his intentions. The moment was drawing near. The Angels had settled into place.

The timing relied on too many uncertainties and estimates for his comfort. Still, he and Stralasi would be safely gone. Even if Alum deduced their escape was assisted by supernatural powers, He'd be powerless to stop them. At worst, He'd be forewarned that someone like Darak existed in His Realm. That would be regrettable, but Darak could manage.

Darak's attention was drawn toward Mika's smaller group near the outer edge. The Wing Commander had paused and assumed an all-too-familiar pose: floating submission. He was talking to Alum.

If the Living God were taking direct command, Darak's precautions might all be for naught. He contemplated altering his plans and opening a destructive microverse at the edge of the shell.

The prostrate Angel resumed its command posture. Darak hoped he'd only been reporting the Wing's progress and receiving approval to proceed.

The arc of Angels pointed their swords in his direction. He could sense the enormous energies building up inside the crystalline blades as they drew from miniature unborn universes.

It's time. Darak locked Stralasi's position to his own and shifted the two of them together alongside a decapitated Angel's body. To the observers, it would look like a fruitless attempt to employ the dead Angel's still-functional sink to protect himself from the blast. He altered his and Stralasi's connection with the Higgs Field and got ready to push the body away as hard as he could.

Being so focused on the arc of Angels and possible intrusion of the Living God, he didn't anticipate the blow that came from the opposite side of the containment zone before the energy bolt was unleashed.

* * *

THE ANGEL, LORD MIKA, MATERIALIZED IN THE HALL OF ALUM. He stood alone on a ramp leading to the Main Stage above which the Living God's hundred-meter universe swirled.

APPROACH—beckoned the undeniable voice in his head.

Mika walked forward slowly and dropped to one knee beneath the miniature galaxy that displayed Alum's might for all to see.

What am I doing here? Am I being called to task?—he wondered. He and his Wing had been poised to unleash a torrent of energy sufficient to destroy any one of those suns. Alum had not only approved the action, He had taken direct command.

And yet here I am, removed from battle, back in the Origin system from which Alum ruled His Realm. What happened? Was the opponent destroyed? The questions he dared not voice burned the tip of his tongue.

"The Fallen Angel once known as Gabriel has been destroyed." boomed Alum's voice.

"Your Will shall not be denied, my Lord," Mika replied.

"Neither My Will nor My Power." Alum paused and softened his voice. "As you may have suspected, Gabriel was more than he appeared."

"He seemed to have enviable enhancements, my Lord."

"Enviable, indeed." Alum replied. "I have many questions about how he came to these new capabilities. But they were not mere enhancements, however enviable they may have been."

"No, my Lord?"

"No. In fact, they used supernatural powers similar to My own and to those of the Aelu."

"The Aelu are still active, my Lord?"

"It would appear so, in some manner. Perhaps our Fallen Commander Gabriel found an Aelu outpost that survived the war and collaborated with them. How insolent of them to imagine they could challenge Me!"

"Blasphemous, my Lord."

"Blasphemy of a high order. I will assemble a new Wing for you to search out these blasphemers and destroy them before they can cause any further disruption."

"A new Wing, my Lord?"

"Yes, your previous Wing was destroyed in battle."

Mika was shocked. To lose an entire Wing was an act of great shame. He reached for his sword. Such shame demanded he take his own worthless life.

STOP.

The command froze his hand on the hilt.

Alum appeared on the ramp in front of the Angel.

Mika pleaded, "My Lord, I have proven unworthy. I must end my service to You to redeem myself. Please, let me do this one final, honorable thing."

"It was not your command that led to the destruction of your Wing, Lord Mika." Alum's voice was steady and kind. "I used them as a suitable distraction to prepare an even greater destructive force."

"Besides Your own might, what could be more destructive?"

"In this case, three suns exploding simultaneously in an enormous supernova. Sadly, your Wing was not the only thing sacrificed in service today. No doubt, the blast from an antimatter core being opened in the middle of each sun came as a surprise to Gabriel. I'm sure it overwhelmed his defenses before he could escape."

"Your might and will are truly awe inspiring, my Lord."

"The loss of that system, the suns, and their ringworlds was a small price to pay to remove such an abomination from this universe."

Alum was quiet a moment. He stroked his chin and let his thoughts drift somewhere distant. "The Aelu must have advanced significantly in their knowledge if they can construct the likes of that," he concluded.

"We shall find them and destroy them forever, my Lord!"

"I have something much worse in mind for them. I shall dispatch them to the worst Hell imaginable, the Chaos, for all of eternity. They shall never come to know My love in the new Heaven I create."

Mika pulled his sword from his sheath and raised it high where he kneeled.

"Thy Will be done!"

43

"HEAVENLY YESHUA, BLESS THIS CHURCH and these, your people, for thine is the Kingdom, the Power, and the Glory. Amen."

John Trillian smiled discreetly as he muttered his own, "Amen" from backstage. His laptop was open on the small table in front of him. Today was a big day at Yeshua's True Guard Church of the Prophet Alum in Austin.

"Be seated, my friends." Reverend Alan LaMontagne stood at center stage, looking over his adoring flock. Thousands settled into their cushioned chairs in the nave, mezzanine, and balconies.

Television cameras representing various networks relayed his image around the world: aged, wise, and serene but still showing a glint of fire and brimstone in the eyes.

A team of assistants stood attentively in the wings, and a two-hundred member choir, resplendent in their rich purple and gold robes, formed a regal backdrop behind him.

The Reverend walked around to the side of his podium, leaving a steadying hand on its solid oak edge, and nodded to the recently elected President Heath situated prominently in his private box seat.

"My friends," he began. His amplified voice filled the spacious structure and reverberated to the farthest reaches of the globe. "I have some great news for you today."

He paused for dramatic effect and savored the sight of his beloved congregation—his greatest achievement—and the magnificent building they occupied.

Unlike many Pentecostal churches that eschewed science and technology, Yeshua's True Guard Church had taken a strong pro-technology stance over the past eighteen years. The Glory Hall of the Diamond Cathedral reflected that stance. It inspired glowing admiration—if not outright worship—on its own account.

Modeled loosely on the spectacular old Crystal Cathedral of California, it was an engineering masterpiece three times larger than its predecessor. Its outer walls were made of insanely expensive diamond-coated borosilicate glass, chosen for its striking beauty and significantly greater strength over the "ordinary" glass of the older building. The walls required only the thinnest of metal support struts, more for convenience than structural strength.

The Diamond Cathedral glittered where its predecessor had merely gleamed, and shone where the other had only sparkled.

A weighty forty-meter cross and Savior rising up from the back of the stage bestowed gravity and solemnity to proceedings. The artist had placed a subtly stern expression on the face of the Savior, which was echoed by the spearmen protecting the base of the cross from curious tourists.

The spearmen were the most literal representation of Yeshua's True Guard. The spears were adorned with their Savior's flag, the Christian cross centered atop a brilliant sun with a pair of swords overlaid along the diagonal. The same flag was proudly displayed around the Hall, adding to the military feel.

When questioned about the militaristic touches in the cathedral, the Reverend once proudly explained that it was intentional: it was a tribute to the embattled founding of the Church and of the country. He openly rejected the whole "lion lying with the lamb" stance held by other churches, calling it, "dangerously irresponsible, blind pacifism."

Sensing the optimum level of eager anticipation had been achieved in his congregation, LaMontagne resumed.

"I am an old man in a young Church," he confided and held up his free hand to quell the anticipated protests from his choir, assistants, and followers.

"You are too kind. We all know the work of the Church outlives any one of us." He was speaking not only to the people in the Cathedral but to the millions more who were watching via television, internet, and inSense presence, around the world.

"Over the past few years, I've employed my heart and mind, my full capabilities and resources, in a search to secure a worthy successor, a strong and inspired leader to guide this congregation.

"Well, ladies and gentlemen, I am pleased to announce that I've finally found the One who will lead us into a New Age, an Age of Godly righteousness throughout this solar system!"

Applause and a fresh chorus of Amens erupted from listeners around the world. He allowed them a moment to settle themselves.

"A few years ago, I was approached by a young man who sought to learn more about our movement. He had not been a member of any of the established churches of the day. Indeed, he spoke out about the vile corruption that plagued many of them.

"Yes, just as our Lord Yeshua condemned the evil money changers on the steps of the Temple, this young man spoke against the Godlessness that infiltrated the so-called holy houses in this country and beyond.

"We talked at great length on that first day we met, and we've continued those conversations during the months and years that followed.

"This young man made no claims of special dispensation to me, yet his divinely inspired wisdom and piety could not be denied.

"He saw the evil permeating our societies and our churches, and he felt the need to act against it. We all know of his pronouncements and his prophecies. We watched, astounded, when our Lord acted through him to save the wonderful city of Vancouver, Pacifica, from nuclear destruction at the hands of the greediest and most powerful individuals in the world."

His listeners at once gleaned the identity of the young man whom the Reverend was about to introduce. An excited buzz rippled through the air.

The Reverend smiled. He could almost read their minds: Could it be true? Alum, the man being called by many to lead the entire world, has favored our Church and is coming to lead us?

"Yes indeed, I have offered my place as Head of this Church to the young man known as Alum. And...." The congregation erupted into applause and waves of Hallelujah.

LaMontagne hushed those nearest, and waited patiently for the applause to die down.

"And, I am absolutely delighted to report, he has accepted. Ladies and gentlemen, children, I present to you your next spiritual leader, Alum!"

Unable to contain themselves any longer, the congregation jumped to their feet, pounding their hands together, whistling, and cheering, while the shy young man walked across the stage to where LaMontagne stood waiting to greet him.

The choir broke into a joyful hymn while the two men hugged in a comfortable and familiar way, like father and son.

LaMontagne moved to one side and lifted his arms to encourage the flock to continue their cheering. Needing little encouragement, they redoubled their efforts until the diamond-encrusted windows shook with the sound.

LaMontagne looked offstage and caught John Trillian's waiting eye. He gave a purposeful nod, and Trillian pushed a button on his laptop to activate what was surely the hacker's crowning achievement.

Anyone in the Cathedral, anyone who watched the broadcast later, on whichever medium they used, would be affected by the virus he released with that simple motion.

As the code worked its way into his congregation's belief systems, the Reverend recalled the day the man had burst into his home office, full of excitement.

* * *

"REVEREND, I'VE BROUGHT YOU A GIFT," Trillian announced as he threw open the heavy office door without knocking.

Across the room, the Reverend looked up from his work. From a matching desk along the adjacent wall, Alum—the Reverend's child protégé now a young man—swiveled his chair around and also opened his eyes. The two regarded Trillian expectantly.

Trillian stopped, captivated by the young man's eyes. As well as he'd come to know Alum over the past sixteen years, the boy's piercing green eyes still mesmerized him. They seemed to contain a greater depth of knowledge and experience, lived and studied, than a person of that age had any right to possess.

For someone so young and presumably innocent, his eyes were impossibly ancient. At times, they were tinged with a smoldering rage that bordered on murderous intent. At other times, they were filled with a profoundly peaceful confidence and love. Trillian could never get used to them.

"John?" The Reverend nudged him back to the present. "Your gift?"

"Yes, sir. I think you'll like what I've developed. I've been thinking about how the Cybrids working on the colonies could be a problem for us. We have no way of making sure they'll be loyal to the Church once the colony's complete."

"And to Alum," LaMontagne prodded.

"Yes, of course. And to Alum, as well." Trillian was painfully aware of the older man's devotion to his adopted son.

The hacker was more in awe of Alum's talents than almost anyone. He'd trained the teenaged Alum in the art and science of information systems.

He knew how quick and clever the boy was and had sensed how deep his penetrating intelligence might someday grow. Now that Alum's lattice enhancements were nearly fully mature, the extent of his capabilities seemed practically boundless.

Trillian understood and appreciated all of this on an intellectual level but, sometimes, it still hurt.

He wondered again if LaMontagne had intentionally restricted his lattice development. *Why would he do that? Why shouldn't I be allowed to develop my capabilities, unhindered, as Alum? If it weren't for these limitations, maybe I'd be the one in line to succeed the Reverend in leading the Church.*

Unless...maybe the imperfection was in *him*, not in the lattice. Perhaps he wasn't worthy. Maybe he still had much to prove to the Reverend and to Yeshua.

The Reverend cleared his throat and Trillian returned to his reason for barging in. "To reduce our risk, I've developed a way to assure Cybrid loyalty. I obtained their base O/S code from one of our contacts at the factory in Shanghai. It's quite brilliant, as one would expect from Dr. Liang."

"Yes, yes," prompted an impatient LaMontagne.

It occurred to Trillian that Alum never expressed irritation like that. He left that to his adopted father.

"Okay, almost any code is susceptible to some sort of intrusion. The Cybrid operating system is based on models of human cognition. Dr. Liang calls it the concepta, a complex network of perceptions and labels assembled into an associative framework. It blurs the line between knowledge and belief."

The Reverend leaned forward with interest. "Go on."

"It's difficult, but not impossible, to engineer a virus program to alter the part of the concepta that affects the persona, that's the Cybrid's set of personal preferences and tendencies that simulate what is human.

"A virus like that could alter the belief system of the Cybrid including, for example, where it considers its loyalties to lie. I have developed just such a virus."

The Reverend walked over to Trillian and grasped his shoulders. He looked directly into the hacker's eyes. "John, you continue to amaze me. This is a wonderful gift. Thank you."

Trillian beamed.

"Why stop there?" asked the voice from the side of the room. Both men turned toward Alum.

Trillian struggled to suppress his annoyance. "What do you mean?"

"People have concepta and persona spaces as much as Cybrids. Everyone has a lattice implant these days, for entertainment purposes if nothing else."

"Are you suggesting that we alter the belief system of real people?" Trillian was surprised at the personal affront he felt. The idea should have occurred to him. Distasteful as it may have been, it was an obvious extension.

"Why not?" Alum challenged.

LaMontagne turned and rubbed his chin thoughtfully as he swiveled in his chair. "Can it be done, John?"

Trillian considered the differences between a Cybrid's silicene-based system, and a human's biological system when overlaid by a lattice.

"Theoretically, yes," he concluded. "At the hardware level, it would work best if we could coax a lattice extension into the pleasure centers of the brain."

He quietly set a program running in the background of his lattice that would protect his own belief system, thinking—*I'm already loyal enough to the Church and the Reverend, and I will be as loyal to Alum as required. I do not want or need that loyalty to be forcefully imposed.*

LaMontagne pondered. Even though his own brain housed sophisticated dendy lattice technology, he didn't know as much about it as he would've liked. A simple O/S tweak should accomplish the kind of extension Trillian needed. He sent a section of code to Trillian.

"If we make these minor changes to the basic lattice code, I think it will achieve what Alum suggests. Go ahead and incorporate this code with yours.

"We shouldn't need to do more than adjust our audience's loyalty factor a little. We'll launch it when we broadcast Alum's succession to the leadership. Everyone will be watching either live or streamed. What better time to add a little value to the presentation?"

* * *

BACKSTAGE, TRILLIAN PRESSED A BUTTON unleashing the virus into the broadcast, and then sat back to enjoy the rest of the show.

Reverend LaMontagne released Alum from his affectionate embrace and walked him to his new home at the podium.

The elder leader of what was now Alum's Church, both in fact as well as name, took a seat in the simple chair waiting for him a couple meters behind and off to Alum's right. The Reverend was in the wings, but clearly visible to the congregation so they could witness his love and support for his spiritual son.

"Thank you, Reverend LaMontagne, for the trust you have placed in me today. And thank you, everyone, for your kind and loving acceptance. I call upon the guidance of our Lord Yeshua to help me lead this Church through the troubled times ahead. I pledge to work diligently and faithfully for you, toward the greater glory of God and of His Son, Yeshua.

"For we do have troubled times ahead, friends. Our sinful world is heading rapidly toward its Final Days. God Almighty, with Yeshua on His right, wielding the sword of justice and vengeance, is about to descend from Heaven and put this planet out of its misery. The sea of sinful unbelievers and heathens who rejected God's pleas to join Him in Heaven will soon be brought to an end."

The crowd joyfully yelled, "Hallelujah" and "Praise be Yeshua." Normally, Reverend LaMontagne avoided End of Days sermons except for the most special occasions. The changing of the guard certainly qualified as a most special occasion, and the flock in the Glory Hall was eager to celebrate.

"I do not mean this in any figurative sense," Alum continued. "No. I'm talking about the literal End of Earth. The clock has been set, the date and time selected. The cause of the Earth's demise has been put in motion and it is growing in power daily."

The crowd hushed as the weight of his words sunk in. This was not the End of Times/Glory Days sermon they were accustomed to hearing. This seemed more serious, and more troubling, than usual.

"Only a small portion of the sinful people of Earth will be spared the destruction our Lord will bring upon the globe. Only you, the true followers of Yeshua's message of hope for humanity, will survive. For a refuge has been prepared for those of True Faith. Your salvation is at hand.

"I therefore call upon you to prepare yourselves. If you are a sinner, come to us on your knees and beg forgiveness of your Lord. Join us and salvation can be yours. For God has appointed me the Sword of Yeshua to bring His justice to the people.

"If you are already a member of this Church, listen carefully. Sometime in the next few months, we will reveal the time and place to assemble to receive God's final Grace. At the appointed time, God will sweep up the Faithful and wash away the sinners.

"Turn your hearts and minds toward our Lord. Pray for forgiveness. Pray that He accept you into His loving arms."

Alum stepped back from the podium and the shocked crowd erupted into applause and joyful weeping. The long-foretold and anxiously awaited Day was finally, finally, at hand. The world would see the error of its ways, and the Faithful would be saved. Their love of Alum and freshly sworn devotion to him was only exceeded by their love of God and His son, Yeshua.

Trillian raised his hand and faked a cough so he could hide his grin. It was gratifying to see the sheep accept the destruction of everything they knew. The virus was working perfectly.

44

"Is it okay to move now? What happened? What kind of place is this?" Mary asked. She looked through the open window framing a diffusely lit New York City.

Darya clasped her hands in front of her face. "You're here! Oh, you two have no idea how glad I am to see you!"

Mary and Timothy stood calmly in front of her, side by side, right where she'd sent them. To her great relief, Trillian was nowhere in sight.

There was only one troubling detail. Instead of smooth walls running in ten directions through the local spatial dimensions, they were boxed in by the same four drab, pitted walls of that cheap hotel room in which she'd conjured a virtual pipeline and evacuated Timothy.

The room looked exactly like it had in New York. She had no doubt Trillian was already in the maze, or soon on his way. They had to move fast. He could be closing in on them even now.

"We're in the GameRoom maze I designed. Trillian somehow expanded my pipe and brought the entire city over. At least, I hope it's just the city. I don't think this inworld could handle the whole of Alternus."

"Well, that would explain why it looks like this."

Darya walked over to the window. New York was barely recognizable. Streets and buildings looked like a 3D jumble. She spotted a familiar shop on Madison Avenue, but no more than a few meters past, the street butted into a brick wall. Early morning pedestrians flowed along a section of sidewalk that appeared to come from nowhere and go nowhere. *This is definitely not my New York.*

She traced the brick wall upward a few stories and saw a section of the Brooklyn Bridge jutting away at a right angle. The span ran about fifty meters and stopped abruptly, truncated in open air with nothing supporting it. *Okay, so where did the rest of the bridge go?*

To their three dimensional eyes and minds, ten dimensional New York was a confused mess. The local Partials seemed to be oblivious to the changes. They continued along their merry ways to jobs, schools, and shopping as usual.

The transition must have translated the Partials properly.

The Fulls were not so lucky. The Supervisor permitted them to see only three dimensions at a time. Fulls could be easily identified by their hesitant, fumbling, and awkward movement.

Darya shivered. *The maze was only intended for the three of us and Trillian. Not for millions of Fulls. What a mess!*

"Let me see!" Timothy joined the two women at the window. "Good God! What happened to the city?" He put his hand to his head and sat heavily on the nearest bed.

"Listen, we don't really have time to discuss this right now," replied Darya. "We need get moving before Trillian maps our location."

"I can't go out there," Timothy objected. "One would have to be insane. And if you weren't at the start, you would be very quickly!"

"I know it looks scary," Darya responded reassuringly, "but it's perfectly safe. If it'll help, close your eyes and hold my hand. I'll guide you. We can't stay here any longer. We have to go *now*."

"Very well, I'll follow you," Timothy relented. "But I'm not walking around out there with my eyes closed."

"Okay, let's form a chain until we can get used to it," replied Darya. "Your bodies know how to move around in this world, even though your eyes can only perceive a small part of it at a time. Let's go."

They joined hands and Darya led them into the hallway. They got about four meters before a street, busy with rush hour traffic, crossed their path. Cars and trucks proceeded as if nothing were unusual. They were visible only a short distance before disappearing. A few hundred meters above, they reappeared. It was as if they were driving through some invisible portal.

"Why aren't they disturbed by this?" asked Mary. "How do they stay on the road?"

Darya explained the rules of the maze, and how the transition translated Partials into ten-dimensional beings but left the Fulls handicapped.

At the edge of the road, Darya led them in what she thought of as the "charmed" direction. They emerged in another part of the hotel corridor. A man stepped out of a room a few doors down. Darya took a protective stance, ready to defend or attack if necessary.

"Good morning," the man greeted them, and he headed to the main stairs.

Darya moved quickly, and stopped his door from closing all the way. She dragged the other two into the room behind her.

"I think I'm going to be sick," Timothy announced from the entranceway. The floor extended only a few meters beyond the threshold. The entire back half of the room was gone and in its place was open air. That alone might have been fine but the view was no ordinary street or cityscape. They were looking straight down onto the tops of buildings and traffic gridlock from a good kilometer above.

The Footman's instincts told him he should be falling; he pawed the entranceway for something vertical and solid to hold onto.

"Great effect," Mary whispered appreciatively. "This is the first time I've seen it simulated inworld."

Darya smiled. "I didn't really expect this. It's weird how the system combined local gravity and the ten spatial dimensions of the maze. On the plus side, it'll make it harder for Trillian to find us. Let's keep moving, though. He's surprised us before."

She marched toward the open sky, pulling the other two along.

Timothy kept his eyes locked on the floor. His senses told him he was walking toward a deadly precipice. He wanted to throw himself down and cling to the carpet, but he wasn't going to let these two women appear braver than he was. He allowed himself to be dragged forward.

Just before they leaped out into the open air, Darya led them "blue-ward" and they found themselves in the other half of the room, looking out a small window at the fire escape.

"How did you figure out which way to move?" asked Mary. "I felt the direction you pulled us and I know I can move that way too, but how can you tell the floor continues in *that* direction and not others?"

"You have to go by touch, not sight. At the boundary, I just stuck out my toe and moved it around in all possible ways until I could feel the floor."

"Ah, okay." Mary looked behind them. From this side, the half of the room they'd just left was no longer visible. In its place was a wall of water. *The Hudson River?* She took a tentative step toward the boundary and felt along the edge with her toe. At first, it met cold, murky water. After probing around a little, the tip of her toe disappeared from view. "I think I can feel carpet, here, in this direction."

"It will take some getting used to before you're able to move around with any confidence," said Darya. "Fortunately, the same will be true for Trillian. I'm hoping that'll buy us enough time to figure out how to get around his blocks and get us back to our trueselves."

Mary glanced at Timothy. "What about him?"

"If we can figure out a way back, we should be able to send Timothy into

Gerhardt's body."

"I'm not sure how much I'd like that. I'm quite content in this body," said Timothy.

"You're not really *in* a body, Timothy. Remember? Right now, you're just some code running on inworld hardware."

"Yes. And I have no idea what that means."

"I know. Just trust me. You don't want to be here if Trillian decides to deactivate the local inworld sims."

"Do you think he'd go that far?" Mary asked. She couldn't believe it would come to that.

The Cybrids relied on the inworlds to help maintain the link to their ancestral humanity. While select inworlds had fallen into disfavor from time to time, and some had been permanently deactivated, none had ever been turned off while inhabited, not once in her exceedingly long memory. People could die that way.

"I admit it's extreme. But when was the last time you heard of a Shard hacking across inworlds? In fact, when was the last time you heard of a Shard inworld at all?"

"You're right about that. Trillian is unusual, and he's driven."

"I think he's determined to catch us, or at least me. It wouldn't have been that hard to remove power to all inworld hardware and kill us. He could have ended the rebellion right there."

"Along with several million Cybrid deaths?"

"Do you really think Alum cares about that? It might delay His program a few million years while He rebuilds the construction force. Just a blink of an eye for the Living God."

"Okay, so what's your plan?"

"First, we have to find somewhere safe, somewhere we can think for a while."

"Like where?"

"What about Gerhardt's office at the Fed? I still have my key."

"Are you forgetting that Trillian *killed* Gerhardt?"

"No, that's why it's perfect. He won't expect us to go there."

"You can predict what a Shard might think?"

Darya almost reacted to Mary's little dig but caught herself in time. Pushing back wasn't going to help any of them. "No, not at all. It just seems like our best choice. It'll buy us a few hours or days to figure out how to get out of here."

"In that case, lead on," Mary offered, and waved them through with an overly theatrical gesture.

The pair followed Darya through the window, down metal stairs and a rickety ladder that rolled down to the alley. From there, they made their way through a folded ten-dimensional New York, from Lenox Hill near Central Park to Wall Street in south Manhattan. It was a long and difficult six kilometers, made harder by having to stop and feel their way forward at the ten-dimensional folds where they couldn't follow visually.

As they walked, Mary and Darya devoted most of their processing power to analyzing their predicament. The sight of two women and a man walking hand-in-hand didn't draw more than moderate curiosity from people they passed along the way. After all, this was New York. Almost anything was acceptable if not already commonplace.

Darya thought she spotted Trillian more than once while they walked. He would disappear around a corner before she could be sure. After a while, she attributed it to nerves.

"I think I have it backward," Darya realized as they passed through the neighborhood of the Empire State Building.

"What do you mean?" Mary asked.

"Well, you know how the Alternus inworld is different from the standard approach used in other inworlds?"

"Yes. Usually, our minds remain resident in our bodies and just communicate with the virtual worlds."

"Right. Normally getting in and out is just a formality. The accepted gates or portals are a convention and only enforced by the Supervisor."

"That's why we got trapped in Lysrandia that time."

"Exactly. Since my modifications, that can't happen again."

"Except in Alternus."

"Yeah. I had to set it up differently. First, the normal communication bandwidth wasn't broad enough to provide such a high degree of realism. Second, in order to inject the concepta virus, I needed full access to each Cybrid's full mental system."

"So, when we enter Alternus, we copy in our full personas."

"Not really. It's more like we inject or transfer them. There's no copy left behind in our trueselves. When we leave Alternus, we're moved back into our external body's CPU again. It's a move, not a copy."

"Okay. So what's your point? What do you have backward?" asked Mary, perplexed.

"I don't think we left the Earth sim hardware and went *into* the GameRoom. I think Trillian's interference pulled the GameRoom *into* Alternus."

"What? Why do you think that?"

"Because I haven't noticed any degradation in my thought processes. It feels like I'm still running on quark-spin hardware, not the standard stuff. If we'd injected our personas into the GameRoom without being able to access our trueself bodies, I'd feel slow as molasses here."

"I haven't quite figured out how to make that interface yet, to the inworld quark-spin lattice. But okay. I believe you. We're still on the Alternus hardware, not the normal inworld stuff."

"We're separated from our bodies, but I don't think Trillian is separated from his."

"If he hacked in from DonTon, then he would use the normal communication channels. His main processing would still be in his own body. Wouldn't it?"

"I think so, and that could give us an advantage."

"It hasn't helped us much yet. He had more control over the Alternus Supervisor than you did."

Darya frowned. "You're right, but he had a lot of lead time to plan and set things up. We've had almost no time at all to react.

"You know, it's possible our bodies may have been physically disconnected from the inworld recharge ports. That's the only way Trillian could guarantee we wouldn't get past a software blockade."

"But our bodies weren't disconnected earlier," Mary countered. "Unless, do you think he found our trueselves and placed them in custody? If that's the case, we're done. Where could we possibly go?"

Darya stopped walking. She placed her hands on her hips and looked around at the infuriatingly confusing paths around them. "I have no idea...yet."

* * *

THREE EXHAUSTING HOURS LATER, they walked into the FRBNY building. Darya's passkey got her into the lobby, where she confidently signed in Mary and Timothy as her guests. The three passed through the metal detector and security check and were waiting for the elevator when they heard a voice that chilled them to their virtual bones.

"Ah, there you are!" Trillian said cheerfully as he walked toward them.

Darian grabbed Timothy's and Mary's hands and pulled them "strangeward" then "redward" for a few steps. They emerged from inside an unknown building onto a sidewalk that ran alongside the United Nations Plaza. They ran another hundred yards, and came to a stop near a street corner where the sidewalk ran under some trees. Trillian was nowhere in sight.

"Where do we go now?" cried Mary. "He'll chase us until we have nowhere to run."

"I think we've lost him for the moment," gasped Darya. "How did he find us so quickly?"

The hotdog vendor at the corner looked up at them, smiling. "It wasn't all that difficult." He wore Trillian's face.

Again Darya grabbed her two friends and pulled them in a rapid succession of other-dimensional directions. With each change in direction, she ran a few meters. After half a dozen rapid twists and turns, they found themselves in what looked like an empty office complex.

"What is happening?" asked a confused and angry Timothy. "How can he possibly follow us through this?"

"He can't," answered Darya. "I think he's found a way to use our city against us."

"He's cloning himself into the Partials," said Mary.

"Yes. Before long, he'll be copied into every Partial in the city. We'll never be able to avoid him wherever there are people. He might even be overwriting some real people."

"He wouldn't do that."

"I wouldn't put anything past him at this point. He's single-minded. It seems like Alum is really serious about getting to the bottom of our resistance."

Darya pondered their options a moment. "Listen, I think I have a way to get you two into trueself bodies, but I can't do it from here."

"Okay, which way should we go?"

"No, I mean not here in the GameRoom. We need to get to Vacationland."

"Why? What's there?"

"There's a portal to an ancient radio transmission device. We used to use it for local communications, back before the broadcast lasers were installed. I can access it and transmit our personas back into our trueselves."

"Why not from here?"

"Given enough time, I probably could."

Mary looked around the empty offices, calculating. "How much time do you need?"

Behind them, the doorknob of the entrance to the offices rattled. Darya hustled the three of them into one of the smaller rooms off to the side.

"More time than we probably have," she answered. "That could be just another Partial or even a Cybrid, or it could be another Trillian clone. It won't take me long to hack into Vacationland. I set up access to the ancient radio control room through one of the plantation service sheds over there."

"Service sheds again? Like in Lysrandia?"

"I know, maybe I'm becoming too predictable. Anyway, I still have the interface pipe code that brought us here. It should be easy to alter it to take us to Vacationland."

Darya closed her eyes to shut out distractions and made some quick alterations to the code. As she was finishing, footsteps sounded in the hallway outside the office.

They huddled behind a solid partition separating the two sides of the room and listened to the door opening. A few seconds later, someone uttered a disappointed, "Hunh," and the door closed with a thud.

Darya peeked around the edge of the partition. The room was empty. She breathed a sigh of relief.

The sound of morning greetings in the outer office filtered into their room through the small louvered window above the office door.

"We'd better leave while we still can," whispered Mary.

Darya nodded, "I've expanded the bandwidth using some of Trillian's alterations to the original pipe. We can all go together this time."

"Without bringing all of this with us?" Mary swept her hand out to include the weird extrapolation of New York.

"No, I've filtered that out, and I don't think Trillian will be able to track us from here. Not very easily. The pipe winds near a few other inworlds, and I've opened a few side portals as decoys to throw him off. It'll take him long enough to figure out where we've gone."

"Long enough to what?" asked Timothy. The poor man looked bewildered and exhausted, though he was doing his best to keep his signature "stiff upper lip" intact.

"Long enough to get us into real bodies," replied Darya. She could see a shadow reflected on the tile floor outside the door. Someone was standing there. She opened the transfer pipe above the three of them.

As she activated it, Darya stood up to see who was entering the room. The last thing she saw before her persona transferred to Vacationland was Trillian leaping over the partition, trying to get into the pipe.

The pipe snapped shut in front of him. Darya smiled in transition. Trillian flew harmlessly over the desk and crashed into the wall opposite the door.

45

REVEREND ALAN LAMONTAGNE, former Spiritual Leader of Yeshua's True Guard Church of the Prophet Alum, was dying.

He lay in his private hospital bed, breathing oxygen-enriched air through a tube. An intravenous drip fed hydrating saline water, glucose, and antibiotics into his veins. Daily sponge baths and a catheter permitted him the luxury of never having to leave his bed. Just as well; he no longer had the strength for the fifteen-step walk to the bathroom.

In his eighty-eighth year of life, LaMontagne's heart was finally giving out. This came as no big surprise to him or anyone else. Surrounded by the people who were most like him in the entire world, he couldn't help envy their youth and vigor.

John Trillian was the oldest of his guests; then came Greg and Kathy, and finally the young man whom he'd named Alum, his blossoming protégé.

The irony of being among the five smartest people in the world and not being able to pee on his own made LaMontagne chuckle. The laugh turned into a weak cough. He took a slow, measured breath to calm the spasms in his chest. *Can't even muster enough energy for a good hack*—he thought.

He'd called them all here to say goodbye and to have them participate in one final experiment.

He'd confessed how he'd been sharing his thoughts and beliefs with Alum since the young man's early childhood. Not shared in conventional ways through hours of conversation, but by direct lattice-to-lattice communication. If any pair of individuals could be said to be "of one mind," it was LaMontagne and Alum.

Now in the Reverend's final hours, the two hoped to use that link to prove the human spirit lives on after the death of its earthly prison.

Whatever LaMontagne was about to experience as he died, Alum would share.

LaMontagne had chosen Alum in the hopes of someday, somehow, "immortalizing" himself. All these many years later, he now understood that they shared only thoughts; their souls were separate. When he died, his soul would not magically cross over into Alum's body. That would be too reminiscent of Satan's possession of bodies and blasphemous to Yeshua.

Nonetheless, the Reverend hoped Alum might catch a glimpse of Heaven as his adopted father's soul entered to meet his Lord and Maker.

Greg and Kathy dismissed the Reverend's ideas as spiritual mumbo-jumbo. Darian Leigh's arguments over twenty years ago still held sway with them.

There was no room for a "soul particle" in the new Modified Standard Theory of particle physics. There was nothing that could comprise a soul and still interact with the real universe. Even the metaphysical supra-natural theory that arose from the Reality Assertion Field had not convinced them that the Word, as the Reverend called it, was real.

LaMontagne tried all sorts of arguments to change their minds. He even attempted clever analogies using their own RAF research terminology to reach them. "Think of God's Word—His thoughts, will and intent—as a specific RAF. In the RAFs you've experimented with, the configuration of the field affects reality by selecting or favoring particular virtual particle interactions. Through His divine RAF, God creates or engineers a desired outcome, a whole new universe with specific rules. So now, you tell me, why couldn't God just be He Who Had the First RAF?"

"Well, for starters, how could God exist *before* the universe of real matter?" Kathy countered.

"Because God is not of the physical," the Reverend stated with complete confidence.

"Anything matter that doesn't interact with our universe is outside it and 'not of the physical.' Are you saying God is from a different universe?"

"Perhaps. Why not?" LaMontagne said.

"That just pushes back the argument," Kathy replied. "Did a different 'God' in a different universe make the universe that contains our God? That leads to another infinite regression that still doesn't imply there's a God outside all possible universes."

"But God is eternal. He has no need to belong to any one universe."

"How could an intelligent, willful entity arise in a universe where literally nothing exists? I just don't get it."

"I thought the RAF proves how something can arise from nothing," quipped the Reverend.

"Sure," Kathy conceded. "Simple particles can arise and evolve over long periods of...let's call it time, even though we know that's not precisely correct. Our models show no requirement for intelligence or intention to impose natural laws on those particles. They arise by evolution."

They'd argued with the Reverend dozens of times, neither side ever able to fully convince the other. In the end Greg and Kathy, being good scientists, had to admit to skeptical agnosticism. As unlikely as it seemed, there was a minuscule chance some intelligence with RAF generating ability might have preceded the existence of the present universe. Maybe of all possible universes.

But when it came to the human soul, Greg and Kathy wouldn't give an inch.

"We know we can make intelligent, fully self-conscious robots. The space around Vesta, Ceres, and Pallas is proof of that. Many of us regularly talk with our Cybrid twins and, believe me, they pass the Turing Test quite nicely. I bet if you spoke to my DAR, you'd think it were me. Why do you think we need a soul when we understand the basis of intelligence and consciousness so well?" Kathy challenged.

"How do we know they *are* conscious? Clearly, they are self-aware, as they are capable of fitting concepts of themselves into the conceptual framework of their environment. But is that the same as consciousness?" the Reverend countered.

Kathy shrugged in frustration. "If you proceed down that path, you get to Solipsism: I can only know I exist because I experience my thoughts and no one else's. I don't know if you are conscious or even if you exist because I can't experience your thoughts. However, Alum can feel your thoughts. He knows you exist as much as he's aware of his own existence." She raised one eyebrow. "Unless, you don't think he exists as anything other than a duplicate you?"

She had come uncomfortably close with that question, and LaMontagne had rushed to assure her that his adopted son and heir was an independent person.

That one discussion, months ago, had planted the seed for today's experiment. If Alum could actually follow LaMontagne's death and share his glimpse of Heaven as his soul entered, perhaps the doubters would come to know what the Reverend already knew to be true.

His doctors agreed he was unlikely to make it through the night. He could feel his heart struggling for each beat. *Soon. Soon.*

The small group of witnesses was quiet company, at least outwardly. Communications among them had been non-verbal for quite some time now. Lattice conversations were faster and less subject to misunderstanding.

At first, the nurses had been spooked at the sight of the four of them sitting in concentrated silence, only occasionally raising a finger or gesticulating to emphasize some unheard point.

The last time a nurse had been by was to try to get LaMontagne to eat something. Despite not having any appetite for days, he did his best to choke down some of the tasteless food. After one or two tentative bites from each of the food groups the nurse retreated, leaving him in peace.

It was dark outside, and LaMontagne closed his eyes. Alum took his hand so he wouldn't fall sleep. They'd discussed this. The Reverend preferred to be as awake and alert as possible when his final moment came. He wanted to die fully conscious, so he could better attend to his protégé's sharing of the experience.

I know I've said this before—Alum sent to the only father he'd ever known—*but I just want to repeat how privileged I feel that you chose me to share the most important part of your life with.*

You were the perfect son—LaMontagne replied, by which he meant, always obedient and a sponge for information. *I was never sure how much independence to allow you. I'm glad I chose to let you grow up as a unique person in the end.*

It must have been hard, to deny your own perfect immortality and grant me the freedom to become my own self—Alum acknowledged.

As one gets older one realizes God did not mean for us to live forever, except in the presence of His grace.

A dark thought registered across Alum's face. *Or in the presence of the Adversary*—he added.

LaMontagne scowled. *The Fires of Eternal Damnation are not for the likes of us. Our good deeds in the Lord's name assure us a place by His side.*

Alum smiled slyly and waited for the Reverend to realize he was being kidded. *Yes, Father. I know. Our destiny is to save humanity in Yeshua's name, that they may receive His infinite love.* He spoke in all sincerity.

And fear His infinite power—the Reverend added for good measure.

Yes, how can humanity be guided only with the carrot and not the stick as well?

The Reverend smiled. He had chosen well and taught even better. Alum was wise in the ways of leadership and would make a good steward of the people, bringing them to their salvation in service to the Lord.

The visitors watched him exhale a long and even sigh of contentment. The sounds of rattling trolleys and medical staff being paged drifted in from the hallway.

Alum stood. Trillian, Kathy, and Greg followed suit, the three of them peering intently for a sign from the younger man. LaMontagne's chest had not risen since the sigh.

Is the moment here? Should I call a nurse or doctor? Remembering the Reverend's wishes, Alum instead reached out more deeply with his lattice. He remembered what it was like to be deeply connected to the Reverend's every perception, thought, and memory.

The three visitors waited, alert to his every gesture, as he made a deeper connection to his father's mind, brain and, he hoped, soul.

After a few minutes, Alum reached over and closed his adopted father's eyelids. He looked away and found the others searching his face expectantly.

Did you see your father entering Heaven? Did you feel his soul depart? He didn't need the lattice to read the questions in their eyes.

In many ways, their eyes matched those of Alum's congregation as they pleaded for good news from their Lord and Savior. Everyone wanted to know the truth. No, they wanted to know The Ultimate Truth.

Alum considered his father's peaceful face. The man looked more comfortable in death than he'd ever looked in life. He felt love for this man who'd given him a life he'd never have known without him.

He also hated him deeply and passionately. The Reverend had been raping his mind since before he could talk, imposing his fanatical ideals and dreams on Alum's infant brain.

Alum let the three sets of eyes bore into the back of his head and wait for their answer a little longer. He wondered how long they'd wait before asking.

After a while, he shook his head and said, "No. Nothing at all."

46

DARYA, MARY, AND TIMOTHY INSTANTIATED inside Vacationland at Darya's favorite spot, the highest table at the Cloud 49 restaurant, overlooking ten kilometers of the best beach she had ever known.

The restaurant was empty except for Partial waiters automatically setting, clearing, and resetting tables. The place looked like it hadn't seen any customers for a while.

Vacationland had changed since her last visit. The normally sunny beaches were dark today; thick clouds roiled overhead, threatening rain at any instant. The water was choppy and dirty, washing seaweed and the occasional dead fish or jellyfish ashore.

The huge waves on which surfers had once lined up to test their skills were now devoid of boards. That was no surprise. The waves were higher and more dangerous looking than ever, and something was...off with them. It took a moment before she realized they weren't all moving shoreward in the usual way, with endless crest after crest in regular procession. The waves were rising randomly and setting out in all directions until they crashed noisily onto the sand and rocks or against the other waves. The resulting chaotic walls of water made it impossible for anyone to ride, even the most talented virtual surfers.

Screams pierced the charged air. Darya looked to the sky, searching for the source. Sharks and piranha had replaced the usual playful dolphins and penguins in the overhead floating pools. The few swimmers left were being viciously attacked. The clear blue bubbles of floating water ran red with the blood of human and aquatic forms alike.

More cries rose from the tropical forest below. Wild animals programmed to shy away from visitors had turned aggressive. Big game hunters panicked as they became the hunted. Those with weapons shot or hacked at the first wave of attackers, but there were too many animals in the jungle to fend off. Birds of prey, snakes, jaguars, and even the mythical dragons cooperated against their human foes.

One of the big cats took down a heavyset hunter dressed in cliché safari garb, grabbing the man's neck in its powerful jaws and shaking quickly to break it.

Seeing and hearing the mayhem around them, remaining hunters discarded their sportsmanlike bows and arrows in search of more deadly rifles.

From where they stood in the clouds overlooking the beach, Darya could just make out the innocuous service shed standing in the midst of the hotel cabinas. She pointed it out to Mary and Timothy. "Come on, run!" she called to her colleagues.

The wind picked up and rain began to fall as they dashed down the treacherous crystalline staircase. A full-blown tropical storm was descending, making progress all but impossible. They clung to the handrail and to each other to avoid being blown down or, worse, right off the stairs.

Against the howling wind, Mary yelled, "This was a lot easier when teleportation services were available!"

Darya had to laugh in appreciation of her friend's attempt to lighten the mood. "It looks like Trillian was expecting us," she replied.

"He seems to be expecting us everywhere we go. No doubt he'll be showing up any second. How far away is that shed?"

"About a klick, once we reach ground," Darya answered.

"*If* we reach ground," Mary shot back.

The trio fought their way down toward the beach. Driving rain pelted them and the wind tried its best to push them over the edge to certain death below. They moved slowly and cautiously, stair by stair.

Voices, barely audible, drifted toward them on the wind. Wondering who else might be trapped here in the storm with them, Darya looked back up the stairs.

The full wait staff, now all Trillian clones, were struggling against the storm's might to rush down the stairs in pursuit, and they were closing the gap.

"We have to move faster," Darya cried to her companions.

As they reached the next landing, another Trillian burst from the sheet of driving rain, screaming and brandishing a huge cleaver stolen from the virtual kitchens.

The Trillian clone brought the cleaver down hard on the polished brass railing she'd been sliding her hand along. The blade slashed her as it sliced downward, cutting a gash into her forearm.

The virtual pain was excruciating but she ignored it. She'd felt pain before; it just made her angry.

Darya released her grip and swung her arm out and away, matching the motion of the knife to minimize its penetration. With her free hand, she gripped the Trillian by his throat, using his own energy to wrench him forward and further off balance. She spun and stepped backward down another stair, adding to the Trillian's momentum. The clone lost his footing entirely, and he launched out over the rail into the rain. Darya didn't look to see where he fell.

Timothy and Mary rushed to Darya's side. She stood huffing in front of them, applying pressure to her right arm.

"You're hurt!" The fight had lasted only a second or two, not long enough for them to intervene.

Darya gritted her teeth. "Don't worry about it. If we make it to the shed, it'll fade into yet another virtual memory. If we don't...well, I guess it won't matter anyway." She glanced back up the stairs. "Come on, they've gained on us."

They continued down the stairs with Darya doing her best to staunch the flow of her still-precious inworld blood while maintaining her grip on the rail.

They landed on the beach ahead of their pursuers. After two breaths to orient themselves, Darya plunged into the deep jungle with Mary and Timothy in tow.

The coconut trees lining the beach were leaning dangerously. Neither the trees nor the few low shrubs offered much protection from flying debris. All around them, the remains of wind-ravaged palapas and beach tents littered their path. The storm was making the way difficult, but it would be equally so for Trillian and his clones.

The three took cover behind one of the denser bushes at the edge of the jungle and looked back to see if their pursuers were keeping up.

The Trillians had done better than keep up. A dozen clones had spread out across a two-hundred meter stretch of beach and were moving systematically forward, checking possible hiding spots as they proceeded inland. She didn't care for their deliberate pace.

"There's probably more of them up ahead," she yelled to Mary and Timothy. "But it's okay; we don't want to move too far inland, anyway."

They stayed low and ran as fast as they could inside the tree line. Pushing through the lush vegetation in gale force winds was wearing them out, and they had to pause every fifty meters or so to catch their breath. The third time they stopped, Mary fell to the ground, panting heavily.

"Just go on without me," she gasped.

Worry creased Darya's brow, but it was less on account of Mary's fatigue than the implications she drew from it. A person's physical limitations or condition had never been, or was not supposed to be, a concern in Vacationland; that should be irrelevant here.

Darya felt a sinking feeling in the pit of her virtual stomach. "Oh, no. I think the Alternus physics must have seeped in here from the GameRoom."

Mary took a few more deep breaths. "What do you mean?" she wheezed.

"Look at you," Darya replied. "Your body style is simply an affectation here. At least, it should be. In Alternus, where it mattered, we all selected lifestyles where it wouldn't be too much of an issue, nothing too physically strenuous. I didn't think to change your body to something more efficient before we left; it shouldn't have mattered!"

Mary was slowly recovering her breath. "I'm keeping you two back. You need to move as fast as you can. I'll catch up later."

"No, we can wait. Trillian has no idea where we're heading. He thinks we're moving deeper into the jungle; I'm sure he's planning to head us off. But we're moving laterally; we'll be past his line of people on the beach after our next dash."

Darya assessed her options. The few real people she'd seen since materializing in Vacationland all seemed to be in a panic. Only the Partials seemed calm, and many of them had already become Trillian clones. *That's it! Maybe if we can....*

She disguised her identity and opened a channel to the Vacationland Supervisor. *Trillian's taking over the Partials as clones. We should be able to create a few of our own for misdirection.*

She shared her plan with her companions. "I can clone each of us into a few Partials and send them out to misleading target destinations all over the place to distract the Trillians from the real us. I just need your permission to copy a persona fragment."

Mary instantly gave Darya access to her physical parameters and an isolated persona fragment. Timothy looked at the two of them blankly. "What do I do?"

Even in the pouring rain and with Trillian bearing down on them, Darya had to laugh.

"Here, permit me," she said and dove directly into Timothy's persona to get what she needed. Not surprising in one so freshly minted, she found nothing but the most basic of security routines protecting his essential being. As she left, she installed versions of her own anti-corruption protection in his concepta.

"Oh, okay. Now I see." Timothy's eyes brightened with the information Darya left behind. "Thank you," he said, but then his eyes clouded over as he realized the implications of Darya's tinkering. Things he believed and thought he knew were subject to outside intervention. He felt the truth of what Mary and Darya had said: his very essence was merely "software".

Taking over Partials up and down the beach, Darya set up five groups of clones in seconds. *Wow! However he did it, Trillian's intervention has made the Supervisor unusually compliant!*

She assigned each group a different route and set them free to run. *That should keep the Trillians busy for a while!*

"Hopefully, that'll buy us a bit of time."

Mary noticed Timothy's face; he was obviously put off balance by the cloning process. "Welcome to the world of Cybrids," she chuckled, intentionally lightheartedly. "Don't worry. No one else will ever be able to do something like that to you again, except with your explicit permission. Right, Darya?" She looked pointedly at her long-time friend, mentor, and co-conspirator.

Darya thought guiltily about the belief-virus she'd programmed, the one she'd used to infect the conceptas of millions. *The greater good is truly a pain in the butt sometimes*—she thought.

She disliked manipulating her friends, even those she barely knew. But the fate of the universe was a concern that overrode her usual ethics. *Life is so much simpler when you don't really know what's going on*—she reminded herself.

She smiled reassuringly and said, "No, of course not. You now have the best protection available. Your integrity will never be breached again."

The words were hardly out of her mouth before dozens of the Trillians stationed along the beach broke ranks and hurried to check out various sightings of the clones.

Over the howl of the wind, the trio could make out the excited shouts, "Over here," and, "I see them!"

Darya helped Mary to her feet. "Let's just keep a steady pace. No need to run. And we should spread out a few meters apart. It'll make us harder to spot. It won't take Trillian long to figure out that we've made our own clones."

"Mary," she suggested, "you stay closest to the jungle and a little ahead of the group. Timothy, you continue on the current path but let Mary get a good 20 meters ahead of you. I'll fall back another 20-30 meters and keep to the outer edges where the bushes meet the sand. The shed's only about half a kilometer away now. Let's keep moving. I should be able to keep an eye on the beachside Trillians from the rear without being seen."

They could see the cabins and service shed in the large complex 500 meters ahead. Darya hoped the Servitors had left the buildings to join the search along the beach. She preferred stealth over aggression, but she'd fight if she had to.

Thunder crashed around them as they broke away from the protection of the lush jungle and walked briskly across the grass toward the complex.

Mary and Timothy reached the first large cabina. They crouched low and tight against the rustic-looking wall, minimally sheltered by the inadequate eaves.

"If we get out of this I'm never coming back here again," yelled Mary over the crashing thunder.

"You told me this was a *nice* place," Timothy huffed.

Darya stared back, speechless, until all three broke into laughter at the absurdity of the situation. The relief was energizing. "Come on," she said, directing them along the wall of the building.

Now that they couldn't be seen from the beach they felt a little more secure. Still, they couldn't afford to be careless. Trillian would not be easily evaded. His clones were popping up everywhere, and the number was growing by the minute.

The service shed, their only hope for getting out of Vacationland and back to their trueselves, came into view on the other end of an enormous swimming area made of interconnecting lagoons. A swim-up bar joined two parts of the nearest pool.

Normally, the pools would be filled with raucous sound of families playing, but it was empty today. The water looked cold and the wind whipped up little whitecaps.

Lacking orders from the Supervisor, four Partial staff huddled under the protection of the thatched roof of the bar. They hadn't been converted into Trillians yet but there was no easy way to reach the shed without passing within view of them.

"Shall we make a run for it or would you rather skirt around to the other side of the complex?" Darya asked her friends.

Timothy surveyed the layout of the buildings without comment. "Listen," said Mary, "this poor choice of a body is exhausted. I might have enough in me for one more dash but the longer we go, the more tired I get. I say we run for it."

Timothy looked as if he wanted to object, but pressed his quivering lips together and nodded.

"Right. Let's do it. I'll start running around the beachside of the pool. If there are any Trillians lurking around, I should be able to draw them out and away. You two wait fifteen seconds and then start walking around this side. Go quickly and confidently, but don't run unless you're spotted.

Inside the shed to the right, you'll find a light switch. Flick the lights on and off quickly, three times in a row, and you'll be taken to the broadcast control room. Mary can get you to your bodies from there."

"What about you?" Mary asked.

Darya looked grim. "With any luck, I'll be there before you. If anyone tries to stop me, I may be delayed a little while I take care of them." With that, she bolted.

She got about two-thirds of the way around the first pool, when a Trillian stepped out from the jungle skirting the complex, not too far from where Mary and Timothy stood waiting. He assessed the situation: Darya running on one side, and the other two about to make their own dash.

The Trillian closed his eyes, and bartenders and waiters changed into determined-looking clones. Two more emerged from the kitchen brandishing large butcher knives. All six charged at the now-sprinting Darya.

Mary and Timothy took off past the Trillian, hoping to reach the shed before he opened his eyes and realized they were gone.

His conversion of the waiters complete, Trillian lunged for Mary as she ran past. "I wish you'd stay a while longer," he said, spinning her around with an iron grip on one wrist.

Timothy jerked to a halt and wheeled. He couldn't just leave Mary there. She was spent, and Trillian was no easy foe. Living by the gentleman's code, he had no choice but to respond to a lady in distress. He screamed and charged, tackling their adversary below the waist.

The force drove Trillian backward, and he let go of Mary to deal with the butler. Somehow, he managed to stay on his feet. The two men wrestled, but Trillian was stronger and more skilled.

"You should've stayed in DonTon where you belong, Partial," he sneered, pinning Timothy face to the ground.

On the far side of the pool, the other Trillians clashed with Darya. The princess dropped to her knees at full steam, slid below the blows of the two leading clones, and pulled their legs out from under them as she passed. The two went down hard and fast, smacking face-first into the cement apron of the pool. Another pair of clones reached out to pin her arms, while the pair holding knives caught up and moved in.

Darya writhed furiously. The Trillians holding her arms struggled to maintain their grip. She caught the man on her right in a scissors grip with her legs and pulled down on his head with everything she had. The clone flipped head-over-heels right into the two with knives.

The second clone maintained his grip on her wrist. Darya sprang to her feet, but the Trillian held fast. She leaped upward, extending to the full length of the arm he still held and delivered a powerful spinning kick to his head. The clone released her and fell into the pool either unconscious or dead, she didn't care which.

Only three more Trillians stood between her and the shed. The two with knives that had landed in a heap when she flung their comrade into them were already on their feet again and advancing. The armed men approached her first, while the unarmed clone circled behind her.

One of the knife-wielding clones slashed at her wildly, but this Trillian had little skill in hand-to-hand combat. *Amateur*—she laughed as she dodged his swipe.

Ooph! The crushing attack from behind knocked the cockiness off her face and the wind out of her lungs in one blow. Darya planted her feet and slackened her knees to absorb the blow.

The Trillian threw a bear hug around her, pinning her arms tight. He growled as he yanked her feet off the ground, exposing her belly to the incoming knives.

Bracing herself against him, Darya kicked upward hard and sent the pair of blades tumbling through the air. The momentum of the advancing Trillians brought the approaching clones within reach. She cocked her legs again and snapped powerful heel kicks at their noses. They fell back, and didn't get up.

The force of her kicks drove the clone holding her off balance and he toppled backward, with Darya still in his clutches. She slammed her head back into his face, and the two hit the pool deck together with a single thud.

Air whooshed out of the clone's lungs and he let go of Darya. She rolled away and sprang to a crouch. The clone had no more fight in him. Blood seeped from the back of his head onto the decorative rock, and his glazed eyes stared into space.

Darya tore her eyes away and scouted the path to the shed. A loud splash from across the pool caught her attention. The Trillian there, caught up in his struggle with Timothy, had grossly underestimated Mary's strength and resolve. He looked up from the pinned butler just as Mary flew into him. The tackle knocked him off Timothy, but sent her and the clone careening into the pool. She was still gripping his jacket in unbridled rage when they hit the water.

"No! Mary!" cried Darya.

The Trillian rolled as he landed in the water, and found his footing before Mary recovered hers. He grabbed her by the hair and pulled her under.

Timothy struggled to his feet. His eyes went to the pair struggling in the water. Mary surfaced, sputtering. He got two steps toward the pool before she saw him. Her eyes went wide.

"Timothy, run! Get to the shed," Mary ordered. He hesitated, his eyes flicking agonizingly back and forth between her face and Trillian's. Before he could jump, seven more clones burst from the jungle behind him and rushed forward.

"Get out of here," Mary ordered, "Go!" There was nothing he could do for her.

"You can't help her," Darya shouted, "Run! Now!"

Timothy turned and ran for the service shed as fast as he could.

Trillian smiled and pushed Mary underwater again. A dozen more clones ran out of the kitchen, brandishing knives and charged toward Darya. It was hopeless. *I'm sorry Mary!*

Darya reached the flimsy wooden shed door and kicked it open. Timothy almost collided into her. She pushed him through the doorway ahead of her, stepped inside, and flicked the light switch three times.

* * *

THE RAGING STORM WAS GONE. Darya and Timothy were surrounded by monitors, gauges, and buttons in some kind of control room. Instrumentation buzzed, hummed and flickered. Darya reached past Timothy and pushed a button in the middle of one panel.

"What's that for?" he asked.

"Now we can't be followed." She scanned monitors, pushed buttons, set dials, and tweaked sliders without a word. Satisfied with the adjustments, she placed both hands on the control console and hung her head. Quiet sobs rose from her trembling frame.

Timothy didn't know what to do. He made an awkward move toward her but she shook her head angrily: Back *off*. He could do nothing but watch as the sobs grew into great cries that wracked her body. Her long, dark tangles hung down, dripping rainwater onto the edge of the console.

It didn't last more than a minute. She sniffed and wiped her nose with the back of her hand. "She was my best friend. More than a friend. How can such weak words describe someone you've known for millions of years? We did everything inworld together; she was like a sister to me. We worked so hard on trying to slow Alum down." She shook her head and almost burst into tears again.

"Goodbye for now, Mary," she whispered. "If you survive, I'll find you," she promised. She pulled herself upright and pushed her hair, still dripping, over her shoulders. She made a few more adjustments at the console and a blue cylindrical beam the width of a person's shoulders appeared at the edge of the chamber.

"*That* is freedom," she said to Timothy. "I've set this to broadcast you out of here, but the location code is Gerhardt's body. Once you're conscious again, don't move, don't do anything, don't try anything until I get there to help you. Being in a body for the first time won't come naturally. You don't have the concepta routines for it, so *wait* for me. You got that? Wait for me."

"Very well. You want me to wait?" Timothy asked, a little peeved.

"Sorry," Darya apologized. "It's just...this is important. It might take me a while to get to you; I want you to play dead until I arrive."

"How will I recognize you? What do you look like as a Cybrid?"

"Don't worry. I'll come visit you inside your concept-space. I'll look and sound the same as here." She extended her arms and shook them off; water sprayed in all directions and added to the small puddles at their feet. "Well, I hope to be drier. But I'll be the 'me' that you've known since New York."

"So what do I do now?"

"Step into the blue beam. It'll take you to your new body. I'll reset the controls and go to mine. I can sneak both of us out of the recharging stations and back to my lab at Secondus. We'll be safe there until I can figure out what to do next."

Timothy waited for her to add something, further instructions, some lame encouragement. Anything. Darya looked over at the beam. He stood rooted for a few seconds, but her gaze held steady.

Very well, then—he conceded and walked into the blue light.

Darya watched his inworld presence dissolve, reset the controls, and walked into the blue beam herself. Whatever awaited her outworld, it would be good to be back in a real body.

47

For Jeff Junior, the End began when Alum received a phone call from the scientists in Vancouver.

They'd been chatting in the study when the telephone rang. Alum picked up and, without so much as a greeting, listened in silence to the excited voices at the other end of the call.

"I see. Thank you. I'll be there soon," was all he said, and he hung up. With no further explanation, he asked Junior to scramble the security and flight teams, and prepare the private plane for immediate departure to Vancouver.

Only once they were settled in the comfort and privacy of the executive cabin did Alum confide in Junior, revealing all he knew about the Eater. "All" turned out to be frightfully little.

Once he got over the shock, Jeff Jr. felt privileged to be included. Only a small number of individuals worldwide knew that the planet-ending threat Alum referenced in his sermons was a real and impending physical danger, not some vague biblical prophecy.

On arriving at SFU, they met Greg and Kathy at the east entrance of the Academic Quadrangle. Neither Alum nor Jeff Junior had visited the award-winning campus, and the scientists paused in the shade of the structure so they could all appreciate, if only for a moment, the peacefulness of the reflecting pool, grass, and trees in the central green space. It was a perfect June day.

After some light chitchat about their trip, the two scientists ushered the visitors along the sheltered perimeter to one of the many stairwells incorporated in the columns that supported the top three stories of the complex.

Inside, they wound their way down through a confusing maze of multi-level corridors leading to the subterranean levels and an instrumentation area cryptically labeled, "RAF Characterization Laboratory."

One entire wall of the lab consisted of a section of the enormous spherical vacuum chamber.

It looks more like a machine room than a lab, at least according to any sci-fi movie I've ever seen—Junior thought. He was not impressed.

Besides one segment of the gigantic storage tank, the room contained an old disassembled laser setup and a desk with a laptop.

Where are all the instruments?—he wondered.

"....we've been thinking about this all wrong," Dr. Mahajani had been saying.

Greg—Junior reminded himself. The pair were awfully informal for two lead scientists. *Too familiar. Unprofessional.* Junior didn't like it.

"Have you figured out how to collapse the Eater?" asked Alum.

"Not exactly," replied Dr. Liang. *Kathy*—Junior remembered.

Greg explained. "As you know, the Eater takes everything that it comes into contact with into its own sphere and laws of nature."

Junior wasn't sure he'd understood correctly. *How can there be more than one set of "laws of nature?" Isn't that why they were called "laws" in the first place?* But he knew better than to interrupt.

Alum, Greg, and Kathy chatted away, completely unperturbed by all the cryptic concepts being thrown around. Struggling to keep up, Junior likened the chamber—really a reinforced LPG storage tank—and its alternative laws to some kind of fantasy video game.

"Unfortunately, we still have no idea why the Eater persists as its own universe. We don't know what's driving it, or how to turn it off," Greg admitted. "So rather than trying to undo it, which so far has been a frustrating waste of time, we thought, why don't we just *move* it?"

"Move it?" Alum asked.

Kathy jumped in. "Yes. Containing the Eater inside this huge vacuum chamber for two decades has only slowed down its growth. But once the Eater reaches the walls of its enclosure, which could be anytime in the next few years, Earth will be done in horrifically short order."

Junior was shocked by how cavalierly she spoke about the end of the world until he realized she'd been living with this reality for almost twenty years. He'd only learned of it on the plane ride to Vancouver.

"Why not make a bigger vacuum chamber and buy some more time?" Alum asked.

"This was the biggest we could build, given the engineering challenges, at the time. With thick enough walls, it might be possible to double or triple the size," answered Kathy. "But it wouldn't be easy, and it would only give us another decade or two before it breached the new chamber."

"And in the extra decade or two, couldn't we save many millions more?"

"Theoretically, yes. But the chamber might not be structurally stable and could fail suddenly, even catastrophically. And it would be an enormous engineering challenge to remove the top of Burnaby Mountain in order to construct a huge new chamber around this one. Remember, we would have to keep it intact and in place while building the new enclosure."

"That does sound problematic."

"Nothing like that has ever been done before. Regular blasting of the bedrock of the mountain would stress the existing chamber, and introducing even the tiniest crack in the existing chamber could bring immediate disaster."

"I see. Implosion." The Church Leader nodded thoughtfully. "What if we were to use the blasting ray we use in asteroid construction?"

Kathy ran some quick models. "That would help, but it would still be a challenge. If either of the chambers fail in the middle of construction, the current one or the new one, we'd have no more than a few days to live, at best."

"Okay, so only as a last resort, then."

Kathy nodded. "Yes. But thinking about how to increase the size of the vacuum chamber gave us an idea. The biggest vacuum we know is in outer space. It would be the safest place to store something like the Eater. What if we could move it out there? How much time would that buy us?"

Unable to contain himself, Greg jumped in. "The answer is a lot, depending on where we put it."

Alum's expression was so guarded even Junior couldn't tell what he was thinking. "Providing you could move it, where would you suggest?"

"I'd prefer to send it off into interstellar space, but Kathy feels that would be criminally irresponsible."

Kathy interjected, "You can't just have an all-consuming microverse floating around. What if it bumped into someone else's home planet? Or another star? Or a black hole?"

"That would be someone else's problem," Greg answered. He held up his hand to quell Kathy's protest. "I realize that wouldn't exactly be neighborly, so we settled on a slow solar orbit, out between Neptune and Pluto. It's pretty much a pure vacuum out there, and should work for a few million years. Our descendants can worry about what to do next."

Alum stroked his chin while considering the idea. "I presume this discussion isn't purely hypothetical. Can you actually move it?"

"Once we had the initial idea, it wasn't hard to go from there," answered Kathy. "We understand enough about its composition to generate the equivalent of a magnetic field to exert a pulling force on it. You know, like a tractor beam. All we'd need to do is equip a number of rockets with properly-tuned tractor beams and guide the Eater out to the edge of the solar system."

"There are a few challenges," added Greg. "The best way would be to build the tractor beams right into the isolation tank and move the whole thing. That'd keep the Eater contained the whole time. It doesn't have much mass in this universe, but the vacuum chamber is heavy. Moving it would have to be done quickly but carefully, in order to minimize the chance of rupture in the atmosphere."

"I see," said Alum. He was lost in deep thought, his expression somewhere between neutral and frowning—a reverse Mona Lisa. A smile emerged.

"This is wonderful news. Really. You are both to be congratulated. You'll be celebrated as heroes for your work today. You may have saved the Earth and all of humanity. Thank you both."

He shook their hands solemnly as they grinned at each other awkwardly.

* * *

BACK AT THE HOTEL SUITE, Alum stormed into his bedroom and slammed the door behind him.

Junior was left standing in the silence of the shared living room, uncertain what to make of his boss' behavior.

I don't get it. They figured out how to save the world! Why on Earth would Alum, the holy leader of tens of millions of its inhabitants, be angry?

He ordered a pot of coffee from room service and switched on the television. He could wait for answers. He was used to waiting for his enigmatic leader to bring forth enlightenment in his own good time.

Alum emerged within the hour. "I have a mission for you," he announced, holding out a small container no bigger than an old-fashioned pillbox.

Junior's blank stare compelled the younger man to explain.

"This is a special kind of a tracker. It contains something called 'entangled matter.' The counterpart is at home. It will allow me to transport things instantly from Austin to wherever that box is."

Junior's mind was full of questions. How was that even possible? What was this "entangled matter" and how did it work? What would his boss want to transport from Austin instantly, and where to? He contained his curiosity.

"I want you to stick that against the side of the vacuum chamber that contains the Eater. Preferably right above the lab we visited today."

Junior accepted the pillbox. "No problem. What will you use it for?"

Alum tried not to look irritated. "Jeff," he used Junior's first name, something he rarely did, "we've known each other a long time. Because of that, and because of the even longer relationship between our fathers, I'm going to answer your question."

He took a deep breath. "My father and I, both received inspiration directly from the Holy Lord that this planet has become filled with wickedness. God has planned a cleansing of humanity, and it has fallen to me to select those who will carry Yeshua's promise forward.

"I have prayed hard on this. I don't believe preventing the destruction of this world, the origin of humanity, falls within God's plan.

"The world has become an evil place. Therefore, this plan to save it must be grounded in evil. Clearly, it has been inspired by the Adversary, so that he can continue to sway the people from the path of Righteousness. I can't permit that."

Jeff Jr.'s horror and disbelief grew into a physical pain deep in his stomach. He'd always followed Alum's direction without hesitation. *The man spoke to God!*

He was having a hard time, though, understanding how God could desire the destruction of the Earth, the crowning jewel of His Creation, and everyone on it except for a few million select individuals. Why would God prefer utter destruction over the practical solution the scientists had found to avoid it. That made no sense.

Junior calmed himself using the exercises his father had taught him. *Focus on the Light of our Lord*—he would say. *Alum is the Light that prepares the Way for Yeshua to return to His people.*

As difficult as it was to understand and accept, Junior decided he had to trust Alum. He relaxed his shoulders and looked the leader in the eye. "Yes, sir. Do I just set the box on the roof, right out in the open?"

Alum relaxed when he saw the tension leave Junior's body. "Yes, don't worry; it'll be fine there.

"Drs. Liang and Mahajani will be working intensively in the lab over the next few days, trying to construct the means to remove God's vengeful sword from Earth. Placing this device against the vacuum chamber will allow me to transport an explosive there, and to release that glorious weapon from its constraints at the right time.

"There's one more thing. I know this part is going to be difficult for you to understand, but it's not enough just to release the weapon. The scientists that created that monster, that demon-spawn of science, cannot be allowed to live."

Alum had anticipated Junior's shock and dismay, and jumped in before doubt could take hold. "I know, murder is wrong in the eyes of the Lord. But trust me, this is part of His plan.

Uncharacteristically, Junior interrupted. "But you seemed like old friends with them."

"Sure," Alum nodded. "I've known them practically all my life, and we've worked together at times. But those times have come to an end.

"God used them to bring about His final Judgement, and now Satan works to pervert that. As he always does. The only surprising thing is that they're listening to the Evil One's voice rather than our Lord's. The Adversary must be permanently stopped.

"The time has come, Jeff. Our Church is ready. I'll announce to our Lord's faithful followers that they should gather this Sunday if they care for their salvation."

Junior bowed his head in acceptance of Alum's wisdom.

48

JEFF JR. PICKED HIS WAY CAUTIOUSLY across the roof of the SFU Science Centre. Gathering storm clouds obscured all but the faintest hint of moonlight, making it a challenge to pick his way around the snaking pipes, capped ducts, bulky air conditioning units, and sharp corners of the fume-hood vents serving the labs below.

Even in the dark, his target was easy to see. The broad dome of the vacuum tank blocked the view of the cityscape behind. Inside the structure, the Eater grew.

Junior sidled up to the side of the sphere where it met the ceiling of Greg and Kathy's lab. He pulled the pillbox-sized device from his pocket and placed it against the chamber. It looked so small and trivial, but he knew the deadly potential it held. *Entangled matter, Alum had called it. Ready to serve; just add explosives.* He didn't usually lean to the sardonic, but this wasn't a usual errand, either.

He grimaced and retraced his steps. Tomorrow he would return to Austin with Alum, leaving the scientists to pursue their misguided effort to save this evil world.

Yeshua has commanded the Earth to die. This is the Lord's work I've been asked to do—he reassured himself. He took in a deep, righteous breath and let the uncertainties flow out of him.

Junior was supremely grateful for his position with Alum; it was going to be the ticket to salvation for his family. His father, Jeff Sr., had formed a close bond with Alum over the years, and with Reverend LaMontagne before that. Junior had even been jealous of their relationships from time to time.

Now that Dad had passed on, it was good to step into his shoes and be part of something bigger than himself.

Junior may have spent fewer years in service to Alum than Jeff Sr., but the work he would do here today was sure to cement the YTG Leader's confidence. Junior felt honored to be the right-hand man of humanity's Savior.

49

"TODAY IS A MOST SPECIAL DAY in our history. Its importance ranks with the very Days of Creation, with the miraculous Day of Resurrection." Alum spoke to his congregation without a microphone. He piped his words directly from his lattice into the public address system. It was just another of the minor miracles his people expected of their leader.

"Today I will reveal God's Judgment for humanity. Today I will bring salvation to the worthy, the people of this Church." He allowed a hush to fall over the gathering.

"We have been deceived," he cried and the people cried with him in anguish. "For over twenty years, we have been deceived.

"Nearly twenty-two years ago, in the city of Vancouver, in the country of Pacifica, an abomination was born. It arose from the hubris of man through the evils of science.

"Satan spoke into the ears of the wicked and tricked them into creating the means for the destruction of our Lord's beautiful Earth, as is the way of the Adversary.

"They even gave the abomination a name. They called it the Eater."

Wails of despair rose from the people in the halls of Yeshua's True Guard Churches around the world as they received Alum's message.

"God looked down upon us and saw that it was time to bring His people home, to draw those of true Faith to His bosom and cast the rest into eternal flame. My father, the Founder of this blessed congregation, the Reverend Alan LaMontagne, pleaded with our Lord for more time."

Shouts of "Hallelujah" and "Lord, have mercy" rise from around the audience.

"And lo, our Lord granted more time. Through His Divine Intervention, the scientists who created this evil thing were inspired to corral it. They placed the Eater in an isolation chamber that it might be separated from the world it wanted to devour. But they recognized its inevitable nature."

The congregation gasped collectively. A few carefully-planted young ladies swooned upon a signal from the Congregation Director. A few even fainted honestly, whether in response to the terrible words or in hysterical emulation of the others.

"God granted humanity a deadline: twenty-two years and some days from its creation, the Eater would escape its prison and consume the planet.

"Our Lord and Savior directed the Reverend LaMontagne to meet with the leaders of the world and tell them of a plan to save the Faithful. That plan is Project Vesta and, through it, the Lord has prepared a place for us among the stars, a refuge where humanity may continue to spread His Word."

"My friends, evil has grown rapidly in this world, and God can no longer stand by and watch His Creation be corrupted. Our Day of Judgment is no longer at hand. Today, Judgment is *upon* us. Today, the Eater is unshackled!"

He held up his hands in triumph and sent a signal that triggered a one-minute countdown on a packet of C4 explosive on the grounds of his mansion.

The bomb and a small container holding one-half of an entangled particle pair rested on a piece of plywood atop an RAF shift generator. Ten seconds after the signal was sent, the generator activated. It pinpointed the entangled matter's mate sitting in a pillbox-sized device on a rooftop thousands of miles away, and completed the shift.

The bomb disappeared from Alum's back yard and instantly reappeared above Greg and Kathy's lab.

"Today, millions of you, tens of millions of you, the Faithful have gathered at this time of Yeshua's calling. You have gathered inside our Churches around the world and lined up in the streets to hear this message. Please, bow your heads with me now in humility and gratitude for our Blessed Savior. For today, you are the Chosen People and God has brought His miracle of salvation to you."

A chorus of Amens resounded, and Alum raised his hands in supplication and bowed his head. He uttered a quick prayer, eager to get on with the day. "Amen."

"Dearly beloved, our path has been set. Today we embark on a journey to Sanctuary. We leave this wretched Earth that God and His Son have seen fit to curse with vengeful destruction.

"Together, we travel to Vesta, to Pallas, and to Ceres, to the sanctuaries that God has prepared for us, where we will be safe from Satan's evil machinations."

Alum turned to address the few hundred he had chosen to be the first of the Faithful to shift to the asteroids.

"I have invited some of you to join me on stage today, to lead the way for the rest of the Chosen. I thank you for your courage and your faith."

He noticed a small child weeping near the edge of the group. "No, do not cry, my sweet child," he said, "rejoice! For Yeshua has selected you. He so loves your faith in Him, your enduring love for Him, that He will save you from His father's wrath. Be joyful!"

The crowd wailed in joy, grief, and disbelief. A few rushed for the exits. They were allowed to leave. *God and the Eater will take care of those without Faith*—Alum thought, and he smiled.

Those who'd been outside pressed forward into the Diamond Cathedral and into the smaller branch Churches in other locations. The majority of those who attended today had heeded his announcement and were prepared to leave their homes. They didn't know where they'd be going, only that God had called them to a safe haven. Alum assured them that they needed to bring little, their needs would be taken care of where they were going, praise God.

"Now is the time of miracles," Alum shouted over the din from the congregation. "Let us praise the Lord God and His Only Son, Yeshua. Let us give glory to the Almighty for His Grace." The crowds settled down and bowed their heads to receive Alum's blessing as they had so many times before.

"Dear God. Grant Your people salvation from Your terrible judgment on this day, for they are True Guardians of Your Word and of the Faith. Let Your sword pass them by. Take them from this world to the refuge You have provided. Grant that they may someday spread from there and take Your message of peace and love throughout this galaxy and even to others, if that is Your Will. We praise You and Your Son, Yeshua, our Savior. Amen."

The congregation echoed "Amen."

When those who had joined Alum on the stage raised their heads, they were no longer on Earth. In place of the Diamond Cathedral, their eyes opened to the wonders of the tube colonies in the faraway asteroid belt.

50

GREG HUMMED A TRIUMPHANT TUNE. Today, he and Kathy were going to save the world. Well, not literally *today*. It would take a bit longer to put their plan into effect, but the work they were doing would set them on the road to salvation.

Not only that, but their strategy would launch a Golden Age fueled by expansion into space, and facilitate great leaps in science and technology, all made possible by the enhanced-IQ lattices.

The President of the university and Prime Minister Hudson were equally relieved and excited about the plans to move the Eater away from Earth. PM Hudson immediately commandeered six small rockets for the purpose.

Kathy and Greg outfitted the inside of the isolation tank with RAF generators they'd designed to hold the Eater. *A little more fine tuning to balance the power across the grapplers, and we'll be ready to connect the rockets!*

The roof and walls all around the vacuum chamber would be removed in just a few days. They needed to construct launching pads and connect the rockets to the enormous tank. Then they'd add control circuitry to manage the ascent of the clumsy arrangement. Kathy figured they could be ready to send the Eater into space as early as next month.

Greg was happier and more excited than he'd felt in a long time. Life was good and they had hope for the future. *Everything is going to be okay, for humanity and for us. We haven't had much hope for such a long time*—he realized.

It was Sunday, and the two of them had been working quietly side-by-side all morning. There were so many things he looked forward to sharing with Kathy again, like the tranquility of weekends on campus.

He was already dreaming about the long vacation they'd take once this problem was behind them. He wanted to travel, to see the world and the asteroid colonies they'd helped bring into existence. Maybe they could even stay out there for a while. That would be fun. When they settled down, maybe they could finally start a family. He was almost giddy.

True, only about ten million colonists had been delivered to Vesta, and barely half that number had arrived on Ceres and Pallas combined. But all of the new technologies and habitats had been meeting or exceeding everyone's expectations, and now that they'd set up the additional Shifting Stations, they could ramp up the remaining colonization process.

That alone was cause for celebration, but his real source of excitement was the surprise anniversary gift he was bursting to share with his wife next week. In anticipation of a few months of travel, he was going to tell her the truth about the "shifting" technology.

Several years ago, when he'd first told Kathy and Reverend LaMontagne about his discovery, he didn't really lie about it. He just didn't tell them everything he knew. He couldn't. Not right away, not until he tested out the rest of his theory.

He didn't lie when he said using entangled particles to navigate space made shifting safer and easier. It did. He'd even told them entangled virtual particles were everywhere, and that they made it possible to shift short distances.

What he'd neglected to say was that he'd grown an RAF generator inside his own skull some years earlier. And that he no longer needed an external RAF shifter to jump around. And that he'd been practicing shifting longer and longer distances by hopping between different entangled virtual pairs.

Kathy would've freaked if he'd told her that last bit.

She wouldn't have been wrong. What he was doing was dangerous. He risked becoming completely disconnected from the universe, drifting in non-space until he died. It remained a very real possibility.

His shifting method, without a specifically-manufactured entangled navigation guide, was still too imprecise for his comfort. He bounced around in a crazy random walk outside of space and time every time he shifted.

But it worked. He eventually got where he wanted to go, and it was getting easier with practice. Actually, it got easier when he extended his lattice into his gut. Intestinal neurons were the second most numerous in the body and he had no problem seconding them for navigation calculations.

Before long, he was traveling all over the world on his little jaunts. *Next stop, the moon*—he'd joked to himself, and then a sobering thought crept into his mind—*why not?*

He put on the environmental suit he used for the vacuum chamber.

Then, jumping between naturally-occurring, exotic, entangled virtual particles, he'd made his way to the moon, and then on to Mars.

Even with practice, he couldn't manage a smooth shift—*more like a drunk walking over an ice-covered rock field*—he chuckled. But he got where he intended.

The number of entangled *exotic* virtual particles—particles with no analogs in the real universe—was practically limitless. If he could write out the formulas describing their properties, he could find them. Their existence, such as it was, was implicit in the math, but neither Kathy nor the Reverend gave any hint they had similar ideas. Greg kept that as his own little secret.

By noon, he and Kathy had mapped out a scheme to balance the force exerted by the RAF grapplers. He stood up and stretched. "Lunch time?"

"That would be great," replied Kathy.

"Okay. I just have to pop to the washroom first. I'll be right back." In the hallway, he paused at the big observation window and looked back into the lab.

Kathy caught him peering in. Feigning exasperation, she lifted her brows as if to ask, "What's up?"

Greg grinned and shook his head. He blew her a kiss. She laughed, and followed his retreat down the hall a moment before getting back to work.

The lab exploded. Or rather, imploded. The ceiling collapsed. The tempered glass observation window shattered.

Greg ducked at the sudden blast and covered his face with his arms against flying debris. *What the hell? An explosion?*

Chunks of concrete were falling. Structural metal, pipes, and wires were severed and flapping. Only then did he hear the roar of the wind.

So much dust. Can't catch my breath. Choking.

"Kathy? Kathy? Where are you?" he screamed into the howling wind.

What happened? I can't see for all the crap in the air.

"Kathy!" he yelled again. *My ears. Ringing so loud. A bomb? No, impossible. A lightning strike? No, something bigger. Kathy? Can't think. So dizzy. Why won't this ringing stop? The wind. It's sucking everything into the tank.*

The noise was deafening. Amidst the raining debris, dust and darkness, an alarm blared.

"Oh, no, no, no!" *The Eater! The isolation chamber must have imploded.* "Kathy? Kathy!" he choked. *Too much dust. That ringing! It's not just inside my head. An alarm. It must be an alarm. Wait. Not just an alarm. THE alarm!*

"Kathy!" he bellowed into the sucking rush of air. He tried to reach her using his lattice communications, but the local routers had been destroyed and his transmission was too weak to penetrate the thick dust. Or maybe it was the effect the exposed Eater had on the local radio transmissions.

"The vacuum chamber's been breached!" He could barely hear his own voice. "Kathy!" he screamed into the chaos that was pulling anything not fastened down toward the gaping maw of the Eater's isolation enclosure. He could see the gray sphere just inside its walls, now, growing steadily as it sucked in air and debris.

"Kathy! Kathy! Where are you?"

He peeked over the lab wall that used to support a window into the corridor. In the midst of what felt like a tornado, he frantically searched the lab.

Remnants of the roof and loose papers flew past. A work table slid toward the Eater, behind a flow of wheeled chairs, broken glass, lab paraphernalia, and bits of construction material. As each item touched the implacable gray sphere, it was smoothly and instantly absorbed. With every molecule, the Eater grew a little bigger. It was already pushing toward the boundaries of the catastrophically breached cell.

Kathy! Her unconscious body was caught on the ragged edge of the imploded vacuum chamber. Her broken limbs flailed, driven by the gale force wind that was drawing everything into the Eater.

He couldn't get any closer but maybe he could shift in, grab her, and shift out. *Too dangerous. Couldn't get in and out fast enough, before the wind sucked us both into the Eater.* Besides, he'd never tried shifting anything other than himself and whatever he was wearing.

Need another way. Greg slid along the wall to the lab door. If he could just bridge the gap across the break in the isolation tank, he could reach her.

There was a stepladder behind the door. It was long enough; it would work but the Eater was millimeters from the inner wall of the tank now. He didn't have much time. He heard something rip out of the ceiling behind him. He ducked as dozens of acoustic ceiling tiles flew past him and into the Eater.

That was all it took. The gray sphere grew enough to contact its prison walls. They were gone in a second. There was nothing between Kathy and the Eater. Greg watched helplessly as the wind sucked her into the growing microverse. She disappeared without a sound.

As if it had been a dream, the wind slowed. *Is it over?*—Greg wondered. He stood in the doorway, bracing himself against the sucking wind.

The lab was empty. The isolation chamber was no more. The wind had died when the Eater broke outside its confines. Now it was absorbing matter evenly on all sides, rather than having to suck everything in through the tear in its container. But Kathy was already gone.

She's gone. Kathy's gone. The shock of it was too much to bear. His knees went weak and he collapsed against the wall, numb.

Kathy's dead, and the Eater is loose. It's loose.

The ominous gray sphere was growing more quickly now, fed by the walls of the building it contacted, by the mountain beneath the building, by the air that flowed against it, and even by the light of the afternoon sun. *Earth is dead. Dead planet walking!* He chuckled at his dark wit. Then he snorted. It threatened to turn into a laugh, into tears, into outright hysteria.

What do I do now? Kathy's gone. The Eater's out. The world is doomed. He stared at the gray globe expanding implacably toward him.

I'm seconds from oblivion, myself—he observed calmly, in shock and too spent for fear. It was all falling away from him. No Kathy, no lab, no hope of saving the Earth. What was the point in struggling?

A memory floated into his consciousness, and pushed through his despair.

"I always hate when they do that," he remembered Kathy saying.

"When they do what?" he'd asked. They'd been watching an old action movie.

"When you're in the middle of an intense action scene and the hero loses his wife or girlfriend, and he just stops whatever he's doing and takes a little timeout to grieve. Right there, in the middle of the battle or disaster or whatever it is. I mean, come on! And all the bullets just go around him as he kneels there, crying. In real life, threats don't end just because you lose someone. You have to haul butt!"

"That's not very romantic," he'd replied.

She'd swiveled on the sofa and looked him in the eye. "If we're ever in a dangerous situation and I get hurt or killed, don't be stupid," she'd said. "Take care of business first. You can grieve or save me, or whatever, after. You got that?"

"Now, you're telling me when I can grieve and not?" he'd laughed. "I'm not sure I have much control over that."

"Just promise me," she'd said and her eyes bore into him until he gave in.

"Okay, okay. I promise!" he'd said.

His mind went to the people on the asteroids. The Vesta Project had delivered only a fraction of the population they'd hoped to save. The colonies were barely ready to support even those few million. Ill-prepared and unsupported, what were their odds of survival? *Is this the end of humanity? Are we done?*

He'd never felt so lost and alone in his life.

The dull gray sphere was within a foot of the wall. Its calm surface showed no other activity besides the relentless expansion. It was the most menacing thing that had ever existed, and Greg hated it. He would have pounded the damn thing to a pulp with his bare hands, but there was nothing to strike against and if he touched it, he'd just lose his hands.

His shoulders slumped. Kathy was gone. Completely gone. He hadn't believed in the human soul for a long time. Darian had been too damn convincing. *What if Darian had it all wrong? Maybe I will see her again.*

He wanted to believe. If he could just believe, he'd throw himself into the Eater right now, knowing that he could join her. But he knew, deep down, he couldn't.

It's a nice fairytale, but death is the end. There is nothing left of the person I loved. No body, no mind, no spirit. No Kathy.

There was no point in his dying today. The remains of humanity, the colonists on the asteroid and whoever could be saved of Earth's best and brightest were still alive. To leave them to their own devices —the millions of people that still had a chance on Vesta—that would be the height of selfishness. If Kathy were out there somewhere, in body or soul, she'd never forgive him for that.

Greg stood up and glared defiantly at the Eater, now less than a hand span away from his face. He'd do whatever was needed to save as many as he could. He would honor Kathy's memory.

He shifted away; there was work to be done. He would grieve later.

51

GREG KNEW THE LIST BY HEART; he'd helped write it.

He jumped to the nearest Shifting Station, not far from Blaine, Washington. There were world leaders and VIPs to rescue! Humanity would stand a better chance of survival in the asteroid belt if it kept its organizational heart.

He checked emergency escape routes. Air travel should still be possible for a few days. *The Shifting Stations can take it from there.*

He cursed himself for ever agreeing to maintain the fiction that colonists were still being transported to the colonies by rocket. *The Reverend had been adamant about it and the G26 agreed.*

If it hadn't been for them, he could have put a shifter in every capital city in the world. But he'd been voted down and it didn't seem worth pushing any further. Not back then.

The world's leaders had insisted that instantaneous transportation all over Earth—not to mention throughout the solar system—would be too disruptive to global economies. Shipping and transportation industries needed protection. Greg and Kathy disagreed; their economic models predicted disruption would be limited and short-lived. The industries would adapt.

Guess who won that argument.

Greg materialized inside the Shifting Station. He wasn't surprised to find it empty; the next movement of colonists wasn't scheduled until later that evening. His footsteps were the only sound as he walked to the Control Room to check on the readiness of the RAF shifter.

"Hey, Jules!" he called out to the on-duty technician. He'd come to respect the man. He was methodical, unambitious, and most importantly, he knew how to keep the biggest secret on the planet. Jules had seen people disappear in front of him and known they would reappear far away. He knew the reasons for all the subterfuge.

Jules kept quiet about his work, about the Eater, and about the need to keep quiet. Even if his secrecy had been bought with a promise to save him and his family, he kept the secret. Perhaps the threat to rescind his reservation should he ever leak anything had something to do with it.

Even now, seven years after the first colonists had been shifted to Vesta, those selected gathered at what they presumed were rocket launching stations. After their briefing session, the colonists were marshaled into a large hall. They clustered nervously near the middle and Jules or the other shifting technician would push a button in the control room.

The button activated a link between a pair of entangled particles, one under the hall, and the other a few hundred million kilometers away inside one of the three asteroid colonies.

The specialized RAF generator below the hall spun a field around the room's occupants and disconnected them from the matter and energy fields of the real universe. Then it shifted them to where the other member of the entangled pair had been situated and re-connected them to their proper universe far, far away from where they started. The relocation took no measurable time.

For every two hundred colonists shifted off Earth, a rocket laden with supplies and additional Cybrids blasted off to scattered stations throughout the asteroid belt.

The people of Earth believed the rocket ships were crammed end-to-end with colonists, frozen embryos, and seeds. Of course, that would have been impossible; putting that many people in one of the rockets would have killed them all on launch.

The Shifting fields were precious. They could only be generated in limited sizes, and the project had a lot of people to move out to the colonies in a very limited amount of time. The project heads agreed, fields would be used exclusively for people.

The rockets mostly carried Cybrids. Without the need to supply oxygen and other human necessities such as food and space in which move about, the ships could be stripped down and packed much more efficiently.

The world remained largely ignorant of the enormous numbers of autonomous robots working on their behalf in outer space.

After a dozen years, the colonies were nearly independent of Earth. They'd been producing their own food and most of their manufactured goods for years.

People on Earth took for granted the unbelievable diversity of products—chemicals, components, machines, electronics, and the expertise to put it all together—necessary to keep an advanced society running. But the colonies didn't. They understood firsthand how hard it was to become fully self-reliant.

In addition to new Cybrids, most of the rockets these days carried specialty items: works of art, scientific instruments, advanced machines, frozen embryos, and thousands upon thousands of treasured personas encapsulated in freshly-minted, bodiless, Cybrid brains.

"Hey, Jules!" Greg called again.

Jules didn't answer. *Maybe he's out for coffee.*

Greg peeked into the control room. He stopped just inside, eyes drawn to the body on the floor.

Jules wasn't going to answer, not ever. He'd been shot once, expertly and efficiently, from behind. Greg checked for a pulse. The body was still warm but there was no heartbeat. The ugly wound made it pretty obvious he'd died instantly.

Who would do such a thing? A professional hit? Why?

Security around the launching and Shifting Stations was thorough, and had multiple levels of redundancies built in, just to be sure. Only a handful of people even knew what happened inside the Shifting Stations or how it all worked. This had to be the work of an insider or else a very sophisticated effort from outside.

Aside from pushing the all-important button, a Shifting Station technician's primary responsibility was to keep the delicate equipment well maintained. Mostly, that entailed regular cleaning and keeping the superconducting material bathed in liquid nitrogen. If the technician failed to do this, the particles might lose their coherence, become un-entangled. Then there'd be a delay of days while more entangled pairs were generated, separated, and transported.

The button activated a superconductor, a short bar of yttrium barium copper oxide sitting in a bubbling pool of liquid nitrogen. The superconductor contained an intricate array of nano-electronic components: a circulating loop to store entangled electrons; a single-electron transistor to pull them out one at a time, and a detector to collapse the spin state of its half of the entangled particle pair.

When a single, spin-entangled electron was "read," it caused the quantum state of its partner to be immediately determined. The entangled pair rang like a bell across the solar system. The shifting RAF generator followed the resonance from one particle to the other delivering more colonists to the asteroids.

The superconductor! Greg opened the access panel on the podium beneath the button. He removed the insulated lid. Normally, the grayish slug would be sitting in its bubbling pool of liquid nitrogen. The chamber was empty.

Huh? It took a second to process what he was seeing. Someone had removed liquid nitrogen and the superconductor with it. Not Jules. He was beyond reproach. Perhaps he'd been forced or tricked into it. Either way, he'd paid with his life.

Without that superconductor—and the single-electron, nano-scale transistor meticulously crafted in its interior—the RAF Shifter wouldn't be able to send people to the asteroid colonies. It would take days to replace, and he didn't have days.

The world leaders and VIPs would have to rely on the rockets, rockets that hadn't been outfitted and tested for transporting humans in years. It was doubtful those decrepit units could even maintain a breathable atmosphere anymore. Sending anyone out in them would be irresponsible, it could be a death sentence for all aboard. Then again, anyone left behind on Earth was guaranteed a death sentence.

He had his own internal RAF generator, the one he'd grown in his head but that wasn't going to be of any help to others. The big RAFs at the Shifting Stations were huge, specialized devices. His was intended for personal use only. It might have enough processing power to shift one other person—maybe—but no more.

There were five other Shifting Stations around the planet, six in total, one on each inhabited continent. They could gather the VIPs at any functional station, if anyone let them. *Yeah, not likely.* They'd have their own lines to contend with; why would they accommodate the VIPs from this one? Still, it was worth a try.

Oh, god. What if this wasn't the only Shifting Station put out of commission?

Greg jumped to each of the other stations in turn. The same scene greeted him at each one. Someone had put them all out of action over a short period of time.

Why? What could anyone gain by doing this?

Conspiracy theories ripped through his mind. *Could someone have found out about the specialized-RAF shifting technology? Even so, could they have duplicated it?* There weren't many people with enough knowledge to independently construct such a device.

Alum's name stood out on that very short list, but that couldn't be right. It didn't make sense. Only a few days ago, Alum had congratulated them on finding a solution to the problem of the Eater, one that worked for everyone. He'd seemed pleased. *He wouldn't do something like this, would he?*

Was releasing the Eater part of a plan, a sick conspiracy, or just some horrible mistake or coincidence? What's the point?

He chided himself for entertaining such ridiculous, paranoid thoughts. To think that someone might have set out to prevent transporting people to Vesta!

And no one in their right mind—with full knowledge of the consequences—would release the Eater from its cage. Intentionally destroying the planet was pointless. Earth didn't have much more than a year left anyway, though not many knew that. And everyone who did know was already on the VIP list, including Alum.

Who on Earth would benefit by shortening Earth's life by a year? No one.

The two events had to be unrelated. *The Eater containment grew weak and imploded. A horrible accident, nothing more, and purely coincidental that it happened today.*

And how could he have suspected Alum of wrongdoing? He and his Church had been committed to saving people, as many as possible. They'd invested all their time and resources to that end. They wouldn't benefit by letting the Eater loose prematurely. Still, there was something secretive, possibly dangerous, about the heir to Reverend LaMontagne that Greg couldn't dismiss. Staging a coup wasn't beyond him. Greg was sure of it.

Gritting his teeth, he shifted to the Diamond Cathedral, the principal place of worship for the YTG Church.

He half-expected to find the building empty. Morning service should have concluded hours ago. Instead, the place was full of people. Many looked lost; their sobbing and wailing was audible over the chaotic conversations.

Ushers were roughly escorting a good number of individuals out of the building, while hundreds more streamed in. Greg's lattice identified most of those with displaced looks being shunted out the door. They were Vesta colonists.

People gathered on the main stage. Greg counted 250, ranging in age from young children to seniors. Alum blessed them, and they disappeared.

A second later, a roughly equal number of miserable Vesta colonists appeared in the same spot.

My instincts were right. Alum and the YTG Church has stolen the shifting technology. But this is crazy. He's already on the VIP list, along with hundreds of others he recommended. Why would he do that?

Angry men with semi-automatic assault rifles pushed the confused colonists toward the broad stairs on either side of the stage. Greg couldn't believe what he was seeing.

A coup? That's crazy. They wouldn't have a chance.

Eight years of Reverend LaMontagne's resistance to making the miracle of instantaneous transportation widely available suddenly made sense. Greg was stunned by the scope of LaMontagne's planning.

Had his intention, all along, been to replace the carefully selected colonists with Church members?

Greg sat down heavily in the nearest seat. He reviewed the evidence in his lattice, looking for anything that would argue against such a diabolical betrayal of humanity.

"I know it's hard to leave, Brother, but this is for the best."

Greg looked up at the friendly voice.

The speaker took one look at the dirty, bloody face and desolate eyes peering back and changed his consoling advance. He gave a whistle for help and was joined by one of his gun-wielding fellows.

Greg was seething inside but stuck between fight and flight. A righteous anger he'd never known coursed through him.

Alum and the YTG Church had betrayed two decades of planning, two years of selecting the best of the best, to give a drastically reduced group of humanity its best chance of survival. They were replacing prominent scientists, engineers, artists, humanitarians, economists, and leaders with individuals whose only admission requirement was blind Faith, membership in the Church, and unquestioning loyalty to Alum.

As the armed man approached, Greg felt his fists flex. The desire to pummel someone, anyone, associated with this outrage was powerful.

The man stopped in front of him, gun in a neutral position but at the ready. The man gave Greg an appraising glance and his brow furrowed. He shifted the gun to a slightly more ready posture.

"What's up, Tyrone," the guard asked the other man.

"I think someone here got away from the returnees. I don't think this guy's one of ours."

"Have you asked him for his card yet?"

"I was waiting for some backup."

Tyrone turned to Greg. "Could I see your Church membership card, please, sir?"

Greg stared blankly at the two men. "I'm not a member."

The rifle rose and pointed at Greg's torso. "In that case, I'll have to ask you to leave the premises, sir."

Greg eyed the barrel. He could probably generate a microverse around the bullet so the gunpowder wouldn't work, or put up a blocking field where it left the gun. Or he could turn their brains into non-functioning mush. He considered how satisfying it would feel to rid humanity of at least two bullies.

The moment passed. Greg sighed, shrugged, and nodded. No point in winning an inconsequential skirmish when the war was already lost.

He shifted out of the hall, leaving the two men gaping at an empty seat.

52

GREG POPPED BACK INTO EXISTENCE in the office of Prime Minister Francine Hudson.

Her hand jumped for the security button under the ledge of the elegant maple wood desk but relaxed when she recognized the disheveled scientist.

"Greg? How did you get here? What happened?"

He was bleeding lightly from a dozen scratches on his face. His clothes were filthy and torn.

"It's all over," he whispered.

His voice was soft, but his eyes conveyed a depth of anger and despair that troubled her. She gently took his arm and guided him to a chair.

"What's over? Are you okay? Sit down," the Prime Minister invited. "Do you need anything? A doctor? Some water?"

Greg looked at this hands. They were covered in blood, dust, and grease. He fought back his tears.

"There was an explosion...at the lab."

"Oh, no! Are you okay?"

"Yes, but Kathy...Kathy's gone."

"What do you mean, 'gone'?"

"We were heading out for lunch to celebrate. I had to go to the washroom first, and I stopped at the lab window to take a look because, you know, I...I still couldn't believe it. We were going to save the Earth. Literally, save the Earth. We were so excited.

"And then it exploded. I was just standing there, looking in, and it exploded right in front of me. Or imploded. I'm not sure which. When I got back up, everything was cloudy and there was debris blowing around. I yelled, but I couldn't see her. I couldn't see anything.

"I tried to get in there, but the wind was too strong, and everything was flying toward the chamber. It was insane! The Eater was sucking air through the hole in the tank as fast as it could. It was like being in a tornado. All I could do was hang on for my life. Debris was flying everywhere.

"I finally spotted her. She was unconscious, pinned against what was left of the tank. Then she was gone.

"I couldn't help her," he sobbed. "I couldn't help her. There was nothing I could do. She's gone."

PM Hudson stared at him, horrified disbelief on her face.

"What about the Eater?"

"It's out in the open. Growing. And we can't stop it. It absorbed those chamber walls like they were nothing. Now that it's got air and the building around it, hell, that whole damn mountain to eat, it'll be growing faster than ever.

"What about your tractor beams? Can't we get them going?" the PM asked.

"They were on the inside of the isolation chamber. They're gone now. And there's no way to arrange an alternative with the Eater growing so fast. In a little over a week, all the air and the oceans are going to be gone. In two weeks, the planet won't exist anymore."

The Prime Minister ran over to the door and stuck her head outside. The office was a beehive of activity.

"Oh, Madam Prime Minister," her secretary said, "something terrible has happened. There's been an explosion at SFU. The Eater is loose. According to Security, Drs. Liang and Mahajani are missing. They were logged into the lab where the containment tank is—where it was—and they haven't been found."

"She's dead. He's with me," replied the PM, calmer than she believed possible. Her secretary was stunned speechless. "Get Sturton in here," she ordered, referring to her Minister of Internal Security. She ducked back inside.

"Greg, what can we do?"

"Nothing. It's over. The planet is done."

"Can we get to Vesta?"

"You can't," he replied. "The Shifting Stations have been deactivated. There's nothing you can do."

"What do you mean, deactivated?"

Her secretary tapped twice and opened the door. "Minister Sturton is here."

"Show him in." The Prime Minister rose to greet her colleague. "Michael. Thanks for getting here so quickly."

"Madame Prime Minister," he responded as he shook hands. "Francine, all hell is breaking loose out there. What happened at the university?"

She gestured for him to sit down. He noticed Greg's shabby appearance with some surprise. "Dr. Mahajani?"

"This is all related, I'm afraid," she replied. "There's been an explosion at the labs and the Eater is free of its isolation chamber."

"Oh, that's not good," Sturton muttered.

"Greg doesn't think we can do anything to control it now. I'm not even sure we can get away."

"What about our contingency plans?" asked Sturton. "We can take the chopper to the Blaine Shifting Station and be in Vesta within hours, a day at most."

Hudson's secretary tapped at the door and poked her head into the office.

"Madam Prime Minister, excuse me, but I think you need to see this." In the second it took Hudson to nod, her Secretary had already crossed halfway to the credenza. She picked up television remote, and hit the power button. A screen rose from the credenza and the picture came to life.

"It's a report from the launching pad near Blaine," she explained, and turned up the volume.

A mob was gathering at the site, and they were blocking access from the main road.

"...reporting to you, live, from the main Project Vesta launching site near Blaine, Washington. As you can see, things are chaotic.

"If you've just tuned in, here's what we know so far. At 12:20 this afternoon, there was an explosion at the Simon Fraser University Science Complex, after which a large gray dome appeared at the site of the blast. At least two people have been reported missing. It is still not apparent who or what caused the blast, or the nature of the gray object. No one has taken responsibility, and no explanation has been forthcoming from the university.

"This mysterious object appears to be absorbing everything it comes into contact with, and it's growing.

"Today's story is adding to the widespread panic that began earlier this afternoon with reports of millions of parishioners disappearing from Yeshua's True Guard churches around the world.

"According to listeners, Alum, Head of Yeshua's True Guard Church, declared in his morning sermon that Judgment Day is upon us."

Cameras panned the scene, before zooming in on their reporter being jostled by the shouting crowd near the front gate of the rocket launch complex.

"There's new activity at the main gate," the reporter announced, and the cameraman panned the crowd.

A knot of people pushed past the small security contingent and terrified guards, opening the way for more to follow.

A distraught father clutching a curly-haired toddler yelled into the microphone, "The end of the world is here. I'm getting my family off the planet!" He followed the crowd as it broke through security and ran toward the rocket sitting majestically on its pad.

The guards stepped back and let them pass, eyeing the flow longingly. One young officer broke from his colleagues and joined the crowd. The older guard who'd been standing beside him straightened his posture and stood his ground.

PM Hudson was stunned. "What do they think they can accomplish? Do they believe they can pilot a rocket to Vesta? Do they think they can force the crew to take them?"

"People do stupid things when they panic," muttered Greg. "Anyway, it doesn't matter; the rockets were just a diversion. The Shifting Stations are what's important, and they're done. They're totally useless now. I'm afraid you're stuck here."

"You said earlier they were deactivated. Can't we reactivate them?" she asked.

"It's not that easy. Somebody sabotaged every single one of them. They killed the technicians and stole the superconductors."

"Can't we just drop in a new one in and activate it?"

"No, its supply of entangled particles is gone with it. We'd need to generate a new supply, put half of them on a rocket, and ship them to Vesta." He pointed to the television where the panicked crowd was circling the launch pad. "I don't think they're going to let us do that. There's not enough time, anyway."

"Okay, so what should we do then? Should we go to the bunker?" She looked at Sturton.

Greg shrugged. "That might give you an extra week before the entire planet is consumed. If it's worth it to you to have an extra few days to spend with your family, go for it. Personally, I'd advise you to accept your fate and make your peace."

"Accept our fate?" protested Sturton. "Just lie down and die? That's what you recommend?"

"There really is nothing else you can do at this point," answered Greg. He turned to the Prime Minister. "I just wanted to come by to say goodbye, and to tell you that it was an honor to work with you."

He could see it finally sink in. PM Hudson's shoulders fell for the briefest moment. She took a deep breath, squared her shoulders, and nodded. "Thank you. It has been a pleasure working with you, as well, Dr. Mahajani, and I'm very sorry for your loss." She extended her hand.

Greg shook her hand, and tried to smile in a reassuring way. "This will all be over quickly enough," he said. "Go to your bunker. That way you won't just slowly asphyxiate. In six days, once the planet's atmosphere is gone, throw open the doors to the vacuum. Or you can just wait there for the Eater to come."

He placed his free hand tenderly over their clasped hands. "I'm really sorry," he said, and then he was gone.

53

GREG MATERIALIZED IN A MINOR CORRIDOR of Pallas Service Tunnel 5. It was empty for the moment. Correction, it was empty of people.

Half a dozen Cybrids were working on the finishing touches. Judging by the tidy rows of livestock pens and garden beds being prepared a few hundred yards away, the tunnel was designated for farming.

The scientist staggered down a narrow road between fenced-in fields. The road ran straight as far as the eye could see. Looking right and left, he could just make out the sky-colored sidewalls of the tunnel a few kilometers away in either direction.

Okay, so that puts me heading either north or south—he reasoned. Without knowing the direction of spin, he wasn't sure which. They'd started rotating the asteroid years earlier, providing the habitats with a comfortable 0.8G of artificial gravity. It was a bit higher in the service tunnel, which was closer to the surface and experienced a greater centrifugal force.

Greg's steps fell heavier than 0.8G could account for.

Alum stages a coup, colonists who aren't members of the YTG Church are forcibly returned to Earth to their certain death, and the best I can do is save myself?

He left the Cybrids to their work and searched for an elevator to take him to the colony level.

"Pardon me, sir." One of the Cybrids had noticed him. "You shouldn't be here yet." It registered his condition. "Are you alright? Do you need help?"

Greg attempted to brush by. "Yes, thank you. I'm fine. I just got lost, and I stumbled and fell. I'm okay, though. Could you please direct me back to the nearest elevator shaft?"

"Of course, sir," replied the Cybrid. "You'll want to catch up on the events on Earth, I would imagine. Things have gotten rather crazy there.

Thank God, we're safe."

"Yeah, thank God," Greg said with no enthusiasm. "The elevator shaft?"

"The nearest one is four-hundred, seventy-eight meters that way, on the east side," the Cybrid answered. A metallic tentacle snaked out of its body and pointed back the way Greg had come.

He thanked the Cybrid and started walking. The elevator entrance was easy to find. It took him "up" toward the colony tube nearer the center of the asteroid.

Greg focused on the mundane details of navigating within the asteroid habitats. It took his mind off feeling lost, out of place. He'd never felt so detached and dislocated in his life.

He had no idea what he was doing or how he'd survive. He was on the official list for Vesta so he probably should've gone there, but Alum's coup had changed everything. His instincts screamed, "Hide!" He would try to stay incognito for as long as possible while he figured things out.

The elevator released him into the colony tunnel. It was the first time he'd ever stood in the middle of any habitat city. The engineering was impressive. Stunning concrete-and-steel-and-glass towers stretched as far as he could see along both sides of the pristine, tree-lined streets. It was a work of art.

It'll be easier to hide in plain sight—he thought. He picked a busy boulevard and headed for the clusters of people gathered around public viewing stations scattered down the street and in the decorative plazas. There was a quiet group huddled in front of the nearest screen, and he joined it to see what the excitement was about.

News stations were broadcasting live images of the Eater absorbing SFU's Shrum Science Centre and starting to bite into the Academic Quadrangle. The monstrosity grew while they watched.

The colonists following the events on the video screens shared their observations in nervous sidelong whispers, as if afraid to turn away for more than an instant.

Greg's disheveled appearance drew a few curious glances but he smiled and shrugged, and was politely ignored. He stared at the screen for a few minutes, watching the beginning of the end for civilization on Earth.

Someone chewing a sandwich walked past him; he realized he hadn't eaten in hours. He was about to ask for directions to a food dispensary when a commotion at one end of the street caught his eye. Curious, he wandered toward the source. He was half a block away when yelling and shoving broke out. *Oh, great. Now what?*

A police squad in riot gear banged their batons against plexiglass shields. They were pushing people away from the broadcast screens and hustling them toward an open town square.

When did Vesta's Security forces acquire riot gear? That was never part of the plan.

The police let some people through their cordon but not everyone. *Only those few wearing a white bracelet*—Greg noted. He'd seen the bracelets being handed out at the Diamond Cathedral but had no idea of their significance. Now it was obvious. *Us and them. Divide and conquer—the oldest strategy in the book.*

This kind of thing wasn't supposed to happen in the colonies. They'd designed Security to *maintain* the peace, not disrupt it.

Another group of riot police herded people his way from a side street. He found himself caught up with the crowd. He moved toward the edge, but the riot shield of a frightened young officer pushed him firmly back into the fold. Greg struggled to stay on his feet and move with the flow.

Threatened by batons, tear gas, and guns, he and the crowd had no choice but to shuffle and bump along wherever the police herded them.

Guns? How did those get here? Project Vesta hadn't authorized any guns. They'd specifically decided against it.

By the time his group reached the town square, it had grown to over a hundred. The police merged them with other groups that had been similarly forced in from adjacent streets.

Greg jostled his way through the crowd and over to a cluster of trees. He'd had enough; he was getting out of here until he better understood his situation.

When he thought no one was watching, he shifted from the cover of the trees to an apartment ten stories up in an adjacent tower. He peered down at the people being manhandled in the square. At some signal he couldn't see, police all around the square took four big steps back from the crowd they'd pushed into the middle.

And with good reason. Right before his eyes, a few hundred people disappeared, and then another few hundred. One second they were there. The next second, they were gone. Shortly after, about the same number appeared in their places. The new arrivals were all wearing white bracelets.

More replacement colonists from the YTG Church.

Many of the newcomers carried small suitcases and walked with confidence, their backs straight and their heads held high. Some looked understandably confused, but they gave an overall sense of being calm and happy. Eager. They gazed upon their new world with joyous wonder.

The police cordon dissolved, and he could just make out an announcement over a loudspeaker.

"Children of Yeshua, welcome to Pallas!"

He wasn't surprised; it was logical the Church would have taken over all three of the asteroid colonies, not just Vesta. *Alum always was thorough.*

The announcer spelled out organizational details to the crowd, how they would be registered with the local authorities, and be assigned housing and new jobs. They were given an overview of the geography of the colony and introduced to their local representative.

Could Alum's people have subverted the entire organizational structure of the Vesta Project? Infiltrated the colonist selection process to favor adherents of the True Guard Church? Planted his own police force? It was hard to imagine.

Greg clutched the windowsill to steady himself. How long had this been going on, and how could he and Kathy not have known anything about it? It must run deep. Just how far had Alum gone to achieve all this?

He thought back to the mysterious deaths of several world leaders long before the Eater escaped. Had that been Alum all along, eliminating anyone who didn't believe as he did just to secure his own political position?

Had Alum disrupted their plan to save Earth so he could create a world—three worlds—occupied by his own followers? Surely, no one could be that evil. *What kind of person would do that?*

He felt sick.

Following the announcements, the crowd broke up and formed neat lines in front of some hastily erected tables bearing the first letter of their last names.

The whole situation was surreal. The scene below looked more like a cruise ship welcome party than disaster refugees fleeing to an asteroid colony in outer space.

How can you all be so calm?—he wondered. *Earth and everyone you left behind is doomed, not just in some theoretical unknown future, but doomed to be obliterated from existence within a couple of weeks at most.*

He couldn't believe they knew what was really happening. *Are they complicit, or just sheeple blindly doing as their Church leader tells them?*

The lines advanced. When people reached the front, they presented a card to the bureaucrats behind the table. The light from the sun tube high above the plaza glinted off the embedded gold-colored chips in the cards. The clerks waved the cards over a tablet and consulted the screen. They tapped something in and printed out several sheets of paper.

Most everyone smiled cheerfully, thanked the bureaucrat, and hurried off, consulting one of the printouts, trailing family members behind them. *A map to their new homes?*

The notion of having to fake membership in Yeshua's True Guard Church or any other just to be housed and fed was abhorrent to Greg. *I can't be part of this group; there has to be another way. Maybe it's only here. Maybe Vesta or Ceres are still safe*—he told himself.

A cynical voice inside replied—*Get real.* The Vesta Project was a single entity. Yeshua's True Guard Church was a single entity. The destruction of Earth, replacing officially selected colonists with Alum's own people, and sending unwanted colonists back to a doomed planet was all part of a single diabolical plan. *Alum's plan.*

No, something this complex, this ruthless, would have to be intricately orchestrated and meticulously carried out. The entire Vesta Project must have been overrun; it had to have been.

If he valued his life, he'd better stay undercover and not trust anyone— anyone—until he could learn more. *Accept it. For the immediate future, Pallas is your new home.*

He was alone, couldn't trust anyone here, and had nowhere to run. He felt like curling up in a fetal ball and letting *the fates determine his fortune.*

He wanted, so bad, to cry, to grieve for his losses. For the loss of all humanity.

No time for that.

He reached into the emotional centers of his brain with the deepest, most remote section of his dendy lattice and turned off his humanity. A cleansing wave of rationality washed over him, freeing his thoughts from his sorrow. He allowed reason and a primal need to survive to rise to the surface.

He was facing a problem. The problem had a solution. He would mourn the loss of Earth later, once he'd taken care of his basic needs. He had no anger, no need for revenge, no hatred of what had happened to his planet. There was only the problem, and the solution.

Greg went into the washroom and cleaned himself up as best he could. When he looked presentable, he shifted back to the cluster of small trees in the square below.

The crowd had mostly dispersed into the city, looking for their assigned quarters. The plaza was relatively clear. Greg fell into the rear of the nearest line, behind a man in his late sixties. Using his broadband lattice, he scanned the man's identity card.

The card was surprisingly sophisticated. In addition to name and address, it carried detailed financial and medical histories, and a complete résumé. Still, it shouldn't be too hard to replicate, not for him.

He needed one of those cards. He'd have to steal one from someone. *Carefully. If I get caught, who knows what they'll do*—he warned himself

Then again, if I do pull this off, what'll happen to the guy in front of me? Maybe nothing—what are they going to do to a senior who loses his card? He can just verify his identity, and the authorities will get him a replacement card. Right?

Or they could banish the guy to Earth right there and be done with him.

In the absence of an empathetic emotional connection to the human being standing in front of him, it didn't take Greg long to calculate the odds and decide what to do.

If he'd had more practice casting shift fields, he could've transferred the card from the old man's pocket into his own. *Better not risk it. I'll just have to procure it the old fashioned way.*

Greg pretended to stumble and bump into the man.

"Hey! Watch it," the man protested.

Greg apologized, "I'm sorry; I'm such a klutz. Are you alright? Oh, man, it figures! I'm in the wrong line. Are you sure you're okay?"

The older man waved him away, and stepped ahead to close up the gap that had since formed in front of him.

Greg picked a line across the square, one hidden from view by the cluster of trees, and headed for it.

It hadn't been hard to pilfer the card out of the man's back pocket and slide it into his own. As he walked, he constructed a new identity and history for himself. The card's security was resistant to forging and tampering, but fell quickly to his enhanced lattice. He imprinted his information into the card's memory.

Greg drew up to a desk just as it served its last client and presented his card to the clerk.

"Name?" asked the bureaucrat.

Greg glanced at the sheet indicating assistance for immigrants with 'L-M' surnames. *Perfect.*

He would pay homage to his intellectual mentor, Darian Leigh, the man who'd given him the gift of the lattice and the Reality Assertion Field. It would have to be discreet, though. The name "Darian Leigh" was still too famous—rather, infamous—to be used.

"Legsu," he said. "My name is Darak Legsu."

The clerk looked up and made eye contact. "That's an unusual name."

"It's Romanian," Greg lied.

"Romanian?" The man turned that over in his mind and placed the card in the reader.

Greg/Darak nodded. "Yes, sir."

"Information Systems Engineer, I see. You have an impressive resume. Lots of good experience: entertainment, business, security, process control, management. I'm sure we'll be able to find something for you. Someone has to keep an eye on all those robots."

The bureaucrat almost spat the last word. He entered some keystrokes and printed out several sheets of paper.

Handing them to Greg, he pointed back to the apartment tower across the square. "We can give you a nice place right nearby. I hope you appreciate it; not many are so privileged. Your skills are listed as High Demand in the system; that's why you're getting such a good assignment. In the next few days, someone will contact you about your new job."

Greg accepted the papers and examined the map as he'd seen others do. "Okay, thank you very much."

"Don't thank me," the other replied. "All blessings come from the Lord, His Son Yeshua, and His prophet Alum. I'm simply a conduit."

"True," replied Greg. "I guess I just got caught up in the day."

"It has been quite a day, I'll give you that," acknowledged the bureaucrat. "But it's the glorious day we've all been preparing for. Praise the Lord."

Greg recognized the opening phrase of the standard True Guard salutation and responded with the appropriate countersign, "And Praise His only Son, Yeshua."

He bowed ever so slightly and turned away, clutching his new life to his chest.

54

EARTH WAS FILLED WITH PANIC.

The Eater sucked in the air and clouds over Vancouver, generating winds gusting to hundreds of kilometers per hour. The gray sphere was the center of the deepest low-pressure zone Earth had ever seen.

It whittled away at Burnaby Mountain until the rocky prominence was level with the Lower Mainland. The sphere touched the surface of the Burrard Inlet. As it inhaled the water, new currents ravaged the Inlet.

At first, politicians pretended the situation, although dire, was manageable, and worked hard to maintain the lie.

The news industry worked just as hard to find the most sensational aspects of the situation, gorging on the unfolding crisis and panic. Ratings soared as local networks chronicled—and capitalized on—the riveting story, reporting every centimeter of girth the Eater accumulated and fanning the flames of hysteria.

They broadcasted live from downtown Vancouver, incrementally tracking the rapidly disappearing top of Burnaby Mountain. They trained cameras on the water rushing into the inlet under Lions Gate Bridge. They visited the endless lines of traffic struggling to escape across the few bridges connecting the Vancouver peninsula to the rest of the mainland.

Within days, the Eater absorbed all of Greater Vancouver along with the North Shore mountains. It reached the waters of English Bay and drew in ocean pouring through the Straits at either end of Vancouver Island.

Once Vancouver was gone, the media realized the truth was even worse than they'd reported and muted their sensational tone. Politicians gave up their charade of control and voted to drop a hydrogen bomb on the Eater in a desperate attempt to upset its underlying physics.

The Eater absorbed the massive explosion and the mushroom cloud that tried to form above it, much as it had absorbed everything else. Only then did humanity accept its doom.

The populace cried out to be moved to the new asteroid colonies of Vesta, Pallas, and Ceres. The authorities responded that it was impossible. The people revolted. The transportation rockets and the infrastructures that supported them fell to desperate, rioting mobs.

The few individuals still able to think rationally knew that even if the rockets could be salvaged in time—which they couldn't—there wouldn't be enough room for everyone on the refuge asteroids.

In an effort to comfort and console the masses, the authorities assured them that the best and brightest representatives of humanity, carefully selected for their diversity and depth of intellect, skills, and abilities, would be safely transported to the new colonies, where they would do their best to maximize humanity's chances of survival.

On the fifth day following the Eater's escape from its tank, news broke about whole groups of colonists being forcibly returned from Vesta. Any vestiges of order and control were shattered.

Everyone knew it was connected to the missing Yeshua's True Guard Church members but nobody, not one person, could come up with solid proof. Not that it would have made any difference.

The Eater devoured Earth's atmosphere and great oceans, and began in earnest on the crust. Freed from the pressure of the continent above it, magma erupted in great flows. The Eater absorbed the molten rock as readily as it had the watery oceans.

And it grew.

55

GREG WAS RIVETED to the terrifying news broadcasts from Earth, along with everyone else in the asteroid colonies. It was addictive.

Recognizing the therapeutic value of activity as much as the urgent need to establish a sustainable new colony, the authorities assigned its citizens work to do, food to grow, classes to attend, and Cybrids to supervise.

A week passed and the transmissions from Earth ceased entirely. By then, everyone was so busy concentrating on making a new home for mankind that they hardly noticed.

Greg allowed his emotions to return, but with his humanity came grief. He let it wash over him.

He shifted to the far end of a wooded service tunnel, well away from everyone. He cried for a full day, letting his sorrow have its run. He cried for the loss of Earth and for the loss of its people. He cried for Kathy.

Then came the anger.

Alum! Maybe he didn't physically plant the bomb and release the Eater himself. Maybe that was just a happy coincidence for him. But the coup, returning the knowledgeable specialists and diversity of individuals sent to Vesta, that was *all* on him.

Greg listened to Alum's daily sermons being broadcast over public address speakers. *I can understand how his people might believe they've been chosen by God, but I don't believe for a second that Alum himself believes that.*

The Reverend, Alum's step-father and mentor, had sat in on the selection committee; he'd helped pick the Vesta colonists. Why would Alum undo that? Why would he replace our best candidates for survival with dull-minded sheep?

Greg understood the lure of power. Thanks to the recent turn of events,

Alum's power was approaching absolute.

The leader of the YTG church issued directives at a blazing pace during his first few days on Vesta. *All undoing the way we set up the Administration.*

Alum pronounced new policies and laws daily. He removed the Cybrids from any say in how the colonies were run, He decreed that, effective immediately, Cybrids were to have only very limited access to all habitat tunnels, and were to be closely supervised by a human at all times.

Why would he do that? What an idiot!—Greg silently fumed. He didn't dare utter the thoughts to anyone but himself. He couldn't risk drawing attention.

Drawing on his officially documented skills, the bureaucrats awarded Greg with one of the coveted Cybrid Supervisor posts.

He supposed he ought to be grateful Alum hadn't insisted on human supervision of the Cybrids' work out in the far reaches of space. *Imagine us clumsy, delicate humans telling Cybrids what to do in vacuum! Cybrids were made for that environment; they knew their specialties better than any human could. Cybrids have already constructed eight perfectly viable colonies without any of us looking over their shoulders. I think they can manage this just fine all by themselves. Non-experts telling them what to do would be a total farce, and could only lead to trouble. There are so many more important things I could be doing.*

The scientist accepted his new post and assigned tasks with equanimity, and did his best to be a good and humane Supervisor. The distractions of work brought him a sense of routine and engagement that allowed him to process his grief.

One morning, he found a space suit in a storage room off the service corridor where his team was working. Alone for the moment, he tried it on. *If anyone notices, I'll just tell them I was trying it on for fun. Who wouldn't want to try on a space suit?*

He checked the seals, activated the electronics, and checked the air tank. He made sure "his" Cybrids were fine for the next hour, and shifted to a point in high Earth orbit, where he floated undetected beside a now useless satellite. The Eater had converted much of the "normal" matter of Earth into its own nearly weightless exotic matter.

More than half of his home planet was shadowed by the gray-black body of the Eater. *When did I start thinking in terms of my "home" planet versus...*—he couldn't bring himself to finish the thought.

It won't be long now; the Eater's expanding rapidly.

He wondered what held the gray sphere to its position on the Earth. *For that matter, what holds it to Earth at all?*

There had to be some connection to the basic inertial reference frame, the bent space-time of Earth. *What'll happen when that reference frame is gone? Will the Eater take over Earth's orbit around the sun or wander off along some vector of its own?* Greg calculated some potential trajectories; some of the paths would pose a threat to the new colonies.

As he watched, calculated, and contemplated, the Eater consumed the last of his planet. Greg closed his eyes against the dark sphere now orbiting where a pale blue dot had once been humanity's home. His home.

It was time to accept *his* new life. He shifted back to Pallas.

- The End -

Thank you for reading this book. If you enjoyed it, I hope you'll leave a review. For independent authors like me, reviews are the best way of telling others the book is worth reading.

*And if you've enjoyed Book 2, The Reality Incursion, I invite you to turn the page and read on for **Exclusive Extras** and a **Preview** of*

The Reality Rebellions
Book Three in the Deplosion series

The Reality Rebellions (preview)

Deplosion: Book Three
Coming: Fall 2017

JARED STRANG, EX-MEMBER OF THE BRITISH PARLIAMENT, ex-Minister of Foreign Affairs, current Manager of Human-Cybrid relations for the Vesta Project, was baffled. Surely, he'd misheard. His eyes shifted back and forth between Alum and Dona Ridgeway, Alum's Chief of Staff.

"But if we don't allow the Cybrids to work in the populated colonies, how will we manage? The colonists aren't exactly trained to expand the living spaces, or even to maintain them for that matter."

Alum stroked his chin, saying nothing. He raised an eyebrow toward Dona, encouraging her to answer on his behalf.

"We humans managed to build an entire civilization on Earth without resorting to cybernetic robots just fine, don't you think?" She smiled tightly at the civil servant as she adjusted her glasses.

Strang coughed into his fist to clear his throat. "Well, yes, clearly," he agreed. "But the Cybrids have all the requisite skills and experience for this environment. Not to mention, all our available heavy equipment is either integral to their bodies or designed to be operated exclusively by them. Even if we had machinery built for humans, we don't know what expertise is available among the colonists. My hunch is, we're not at risk of being overwhelmed with talent."

Ridgeway glanced over at Alum. He nodded for her to continue.

"I assure you that our databases are *quite* thorough, Mr. Strang. Training classes will fill in any gaps over time."

Strang sat forward, "You don't understand," he interrupted. "We don't *have* time. There is no Plan B. This has to..."

Alum held up a finger, cutting him off. "People must have purpose in their lives," he said. "The recent socio-economic history of Earth clearly demonstrates what happens when people are idle, when they feel useless. Political opportunism, unrest, riots, social breakdown—we will not permit Vesta to set off down that path."

Strang flopped back in his chair. "No, surely not." He pinched the bridge of his nose and rubbed his eyes. "Is there any way we could have skilled people shadow some of the Cybrids as they go about their work?"

Alum smiled. "Mr. Strang, I understand you've never been a member of our Church, but surely you are a Christian."

Strang's mouth worked through several possible responses before settling on, "Surely."

In truth, he believed personal beliefs should be personal, not things to be trotted out for public display. Still, one had to be aware who held the power on the Vesta colonies after the demise of Earth.

"Well, then," Alum continued, "You know our Lord created man in His image, setting man above all others. Man is above his own creations, the Cybrids for example, just as God is above His creation, namely us. Wouldn't you agree?"

"When you put it that way, what choice do I have?"

"Exactly. We have a new opportunity to reinvigorate God's universe, and mankind's place in it, out here among the asteroids. And that begins with the proper humility, with people who value the might of the Lord above all.

"Cybrids are remnants of the old, evil ways of Earth, Mr. Strang. They have their place, and that place is in the vacuum of space, not among humans. When I...I mean, my *father*, supported their development, they were not intended to be anything other than a tool, a mechanical extension of our hands to help us in building these habitats. *This* is how they best serve the Lord's wishes."

Strang noted the stutter before Alum spoke of his father; it brought to mind the odd rumors about the young man's origins, perverse gossip that few gave much credence to.

"Still," he ventured, "it seems rather...superfluous to have a Manager of Human-Cybrid Relations when, in fact, there are to be no relations between Humans and Cybrids."

"I agree, your role in the administration of these habitats has changed," Alum sniffed. He pushed his body up, out of the comfortable chair, and walked over to the window, leaving Strang to stew a little. Alum relished these little moments. *I wonder how long Strang will wait. About as long as I keep him waiting, I suppose.*

He called up the construction schematics for the habitats, letting the silence—and Strang's discomfort—stretch out.

They were standing in the Vesta Project Manager's office on the fiftieth floor of the highest tower in Vesta One, the first of Vesta's six colony tunnels to date, and capital of all the asteroid habitats.

The windows looked "north" and "south" along the axis of the tunnel oriented toward the caps lying over two hundred kilometers away in each direction. Below, a cluster of densely-spaced apartment towers stretched seven kilometers wide before meeting the upward-curving sides of the tunnel.

Each asteroid contained six colony tunnels arranged like the bullet chambers of a revolver, with the cylinder representing the asteroid as a whole. Each tunnel had a floor that squared off the outer arc, and a ceiling on the side closer to the central axis.

Artificial gravity was provided by spinning the asteroid. Because of this rotation, "down" was outward, away from the asteroid's axis toward its surface. The orientation session told new arrivals, "Down is still the direction your feet sink, still the direction that receives the force of your weight. In the colony tunnels, the meager natural gravity of the planetoid is overridden by the centrifugal force due to its spinning. That's why we feel down as being toward the outer surface."

Several rivers, driven by circulating pumps, ran the length of the tunnels and occasionally widened into long, narrow lakes. Some ran north-to-south in the colony tunnels, and returned south-to-north in the agricultural service tunnels below. Others flowed in the opposite direction to provide balance along their lengths.

High above, light panels ran the length of the tunnel. They brightened and dimmed in twelve-hour cycles, driving the daily rhythms of the people, animals, and plants below.

Alum finished his contemplation of the habitat. *Project Vesta has done a remarkable job of reproducing the Earth's ecology in such a small space and in such short time.*

He'd kept Strang waiting long enough. *As if he deserves anything more than my simple command.*

"Under the previous administration," he paused to let that sink in, "..you may have seen your job as smoothing over people's acceptance of the Cybrids, and integrating everyone into a workable biology-plus-machine society. That will no longer be the case. The Cybrids are not people; they will never be people in the eyes of the Lord."

"But aren't their mental processes modeled on our own human minds?" Strang asked.

Alum's eyes blazed. "They can simulate many human characteristics, no doubt; but they are not human, not flesh and blood. They are not created in God's image. We have found a place for them where they can be of service to humanity and, thereby, to God's will. No more. They will never claim a place by our side; to do so would be an abomination."

Strang's gaze shifted to his hands, cradled anxiously in his lap. He contemplated his fidgeting fingers. "I see. And what exactly is my role to be?"

Alum glanced at Ms. Ridgeway, who'd been sitting silently through the sermon.

"As Spiritual Leader of the YTG Church and the de facto leader of humanity, Alum must remain uncontaminated, separate from discussions with the Cybrids," she explained. "You will communicate his directive to them: they are to remain outside the habitat tunnels of the asteroids unless granted specific permission to enter. You will report on their submission to his will and on their adherence to these laws."

"I have no wish to appear unjust or unsympathetic, Mr. Strang," Alum added. "Not even to machines. You seem to have forgotten that Cybrids were designed and constructed to serve humanity, not to replace it. Within those parameters, they will enjoy a fulfilling existence. You will ensure they understand and cooperate with my directives."

"Is this the will of the Governing Council?" Strang asked.

Ms. Ridgeway nearly choked. Before Alum could reply, she jumped in. "The Council exists to provide advice to Alum. He, and he alone, decides." She set her lips firmly, accepting no further questioning of her Leader's authority.

"So the Cybrids are to be our slaves."

The crease between Alum's eyebrows deepened. "Slavery is not an applicable term; they are *machines* that were built for service. You will not speak of it again."

The manager bowed his head. He had seen enough of the local police actions under Alum's direction to know he should hold his tongue. For the moment.

As Ms. Ridgeway's voice droned on in the background, Strang's attention shifted to conversations he would be having with his colleagues from the original Project Vesta. Not everyone shared Alum's point of view.

Extras

Points to Ponder
Book Club & Study Questions

The Deplosion series is intended to be more than just a story. I hope it inspires thinking and exchange on a variety of philosophical, religious, scientific, and social issues. The following questions will help get you started. Additional discussion can be found on the Paul Anlee Facebook page, and my science and philosophy blog at www.paulanlee.com.

1) Connecting the brain directly to an electronic interface might permit us to learn new skills (e.g. new language, musical instrument, math, or history). At the same time, it could risk opening our minds to someone trying to alter our beliefs. Compare Darian's accidental "memory storm" attack on Greg's and Kathy's minds with Darya's and Trillian's deliberate efforts to change the minds of Cybrids and humans. Do you think improvements in learning and communication would be worth the risk of having someone alter what you believe? How are the characters' attempts to directly change minds different from attempts by advertisers, politicians, and media to sway your thinking? Teachers? Religious leaders? Anyone else?

2) Arthur C. Clarke famously said, "Any sufficiently advanced technology is indistinguishable from magic." Darak performs several feats of "magic" in this book. He travels in space without a vessel; he moves across intergalactic distances in the blink of an eye; he carries an entire campsite in a pea (complete with hot meal); he fights Angels. Yet, all of this is simply "advanced technology" to him. Do you think there is any instance of magic (apart from sleight-of-hand trickery) that is not just advanced or as-yet unfamiliar technology"?

3) A number of famous people (Stephen Hawking and Elon Musk, among them) have declared that it is essential for humans to colonize space in the coming decades as a matter of species preservation. Darya's group, and Greg and Kathy, make strong economic and demographic arguments as well. Were their arguments compelling (how so), or should we focus on saving/exploiting Earth before we move into space? Do the circumstances of the alternative histories on Earth (one with the Eater threat, the other without imminent destruction) make any difference to your conclusion?

4) As science explores the nearby stars, we are finding more and more Earth-like "exoplanets" (over 2,330 as of mid-2017) of the right size, gravity, and surface temperature to support life. Unfortunately, at least to date, we've yet to detect water, breathable atmosphere, or evidence of other complex life forms on any of them. Crucial parameters remain outside our survival range; temperature, oxygen levels, gravity, length of day, and length of year vary greatly from planet to planet.
    Do you think it's likely that any single "Standard" life form (especially human) would be suited to colonize multiple planets? With Earth in trouble, would it be better to upload our minds into machines or to genetically adapt our species (and other life forms on which we depend) to survive on exoplanets? Would genetically altering humanity ensure survival of the species, or make us no longer human? Does it matter?

5) Greg and Kathy worked on related research, but did not create the microverse known as the Eater; that was created by Darian and/or Larry. Should someone be held responsible for the death of Dave, the night guard in Chapter 7, or was his death just an unfortunate accident? Should Darian Leigh, if found, be charged with homicide? Were Greg and Kathy, as employees of the lab, complicit in any wrongful death or damage, even though they were not directly responsible for that specific microverse? What about University President Dr. Sakira, Department Chair Dr. Wong, or Prime Minister Hudson? What were their responsibilities to the world at the various stages of the Eater's development?

6) In various parts of the novel, characters use questionable means to accomplish their goals. Reverend LaMontagne murders more than once, and he blackmails President Mitchell into accepting his presence on the G26 panel. Darya uses a concepta virus to convince visitors to Alternus to attend a meeting. Alum kills trillions in defense of His Divine Plan to create Heaven. While some of their goals may be laudable, do the ends justify the means? Why or why not?

7) Darak claims to be almost as powerful as Alum. He certainly speaks about the Living God as an equal. Alum, as the Living God, feels He knows what is best for the universe and is moving forward. Darak is

taking time to inform the people affected (through Brother Stralasi and the Aelu). Do you agree with Darak that an informed, capable electorate is a requirement of any democracy? If you were a member of the Realm, would you prefer to participate in such decisions, or leave them in the hands of the Living God? Why?

8) Many popular science fiction novels use some sort of faster-than-light (FTL) or warp drives to move people across huge interstellar distances in the galaxy. In the Deplosion series, I've recognized that FTL is contrary to Einstein's Theory of Relativity, so the Realm spreads at slower-than-light speeds. However, the story introduces entangled particles and the RAF to permit instantaneous jumps across distances. Do you think "shifting" is more, or less, plausible than FTL? Are we forever stuck exploring the vast universe at slower speeds?

9) Physicists and philosophers have given serious consideration to the idea that the universe could be a simulation (for more info, see https://www.space.com/32543-universe-a-simulation-asimov-debate.html). In the extreme, this idea ties to Solipsism, the view or theory that the self is all that can be known to exist, i.e. a simulation for one. While it may be impossible to tell if we're inside a simulation, there are good reasons for suggesting it makes for an unlikely universe (a simulation inside a simulation inside a simulation). Could you tell if you existed only as computer code inside a game? If so, how?

·

Further Reading

This series contains a lot of real science and speculates heavily on possible advances in several fields. If you're interested in learning more about some of the areas discussed in this book, I suggest the following:

Lawrence Krauss, A Universe From Nothing.
An excellent review of cosmology and the possible origins of the universe.

Andrew Thomas, Hidden In Plain Sight.
A great series of five books at the time of this release, covering everything from gravity, relativity, quantum mechanics, time, space, and the particles that comprise all matter.

Richard Dawkins, The God Delusion.
A powerful analytic indictment of religious belief that applies logic and reason to spirit and faith.

Francis Collins, The Language of God.
A famous scientist's perspective on reconciling belief in God with scientific studies of evolution.

Jerry Coyne, Why Evolution is True.
A fact-filled romp through the scientific evidence in support of evolution.

George M. Church and Ed Regis, Regenesis.
Inside the mind of one of the world's leading synthetic biologists. Includes the origins of the field, current practices, and stunning visions of the future.

James Rickards, The Death of Money.
Analysis of how modern currency wars will be fought among major countries of the world, resulting in the collapse of the international monetary system.

Matt Strassler (https://profmattstrassler.com/), Of Particular Significance.
Insightful and informative website from a theoretical physicist with essays on a variety of topics in physics.

http://igem.org/Main_Page
iGEM is the International Genetically Engineered Machines annual competition. This is *the* place to go to learn about the exciting research done every year by university undergrads from around the world.

Acknowledgements

Thanks to Lee for being the most patient editor imaginable, and to my great team of beta readers: Joel, Abby, Craig, Ed, Eric, Gary, Lorraine, Mike, Jeff, Kathie, Leanna, Scarlett, Barbara, Susan, and Rachel. This is a much better book for your insightful and invaluable feedback.

A special thanks to the members of *Cuenca: Writing Our World* for all your support and especially to our dear friend, Scarlett Braden, for your energy, enthusiasm, and guidance along the way.

All science fiction writers owe a debt to the giants who have gone before us, many of whom still produce prolifically. I have been influenced by many of the best, though none bear the responsibility for any of my errors. Isaac Asimov, Iain M. Banks, Greg Bear, Gregory Benford, Ray Bradbury, David Brin, Arthur C. Clarke, Peter F. Hamilton, Robert A. Heinlein, Ursula K. Le Guin, Larry Niven, Jerry Pournelle, Sheri S. Tepper, and John C. Wright, you have all been great inspirations.

The scientific community crosses many borders and intellectual boundaries. My career in biology has been guided by great scientists like David Bailie, David Pilgrim, and David Wishart (I don't know why I always worked for guys named David). My love of developmental biology, molecular biology, and genetics was inspired by Bruce P. Brandhorst in my undergrad years at Simon Fraser University. I also owe a deep debt of gratitude for the exciting and inspiring researchers in synthetic biology, including: Drew Endy, George Church, Tom Knight, Pam Silver, Chris Voigt, and Jay Keasling.

I built upon a great many ideas in coming up with the speculative science, philosophies, and sociopolitical economics in the series. The following have all been sources for ideas, but none of them can be blamed for where I ran away with the inspiration: Lawrence Krauss, Richard Dawkins, Andrew Thomas, Matt Strassler, John Mauldin, John Hussman, James Rickards, and Thom Hartmann.

About the Author

Canadian author Paul Anlee writes provocative, epic sci-fi in the style of Asimov, Heinlein, Asher, and Reynolds, stories that challenge our assumptions and stretch our imagination. Literary, fact-based, and fast-paced, the Deplosion series explores themes in philosophy, politics, religion, economics, AI, VR, nanotech, synbio, quantum reality, and beyond.

"When I was young, a teacher asked our class to write about what we wanted to be when we grew up. My story was entitled "Me, The Everything!" I've been fortunate to come close to fulfilling that dream in my life, at least intellectually. Computer programming, molecular biology, nanotechnology, systems biology, synthetic biology, business consulting, and photocopy repair, I've worked in many fields. I've spent way too much of my life in school, eventually earning degrees in computing science (BSc) and in molecular biology and genetics (PhD). I've even had the chance to work with some of the best researchers in the world at The National Institute for Nanotechnology in Edmonton, Canada.

"After decades of reading almost nothing but high-tech science fiction, I decided to take a shot at writing some. I aim for stories that are true to the best available science while pushing my imagination far beyond the edge of what we know today. I love biology, particle physics, cosmology, artificial intelligence, cognitive psychology, politics, and economics. My philosophy is empirical physicalism and I blog regularly about the science and the ideas found in my novels. I believe fiction should educate and stimulate, as much as it entertains."

Paul and his wife currently live in Cuenca, Ecuador where they study Spanish and Chen-style Tai Chi, when not working on exciting and provocative new stories.

Follow me on Facebook at Paul Anlee or write me at: paul.anlee.author@gmail.com. Even better, visit me at my website, https://www.paulanlee.com/, read the blog and sign-up on my email list to be the first to hear about new books, new posts, and special announcements. That's the best way to hear about FREE offers and special deals.

www.ingramcontent.com/pod-product-compliance
Lightning Source LLC
Chambersburg PA
CBHW051134120726
47905CB00005B/1543